"Treaty of Treason"

BOOK 1
PRELUDE TO WAR

BOOK 2
THE WAR OF INDEPENDENCE

BOOK 3
CIVIL WAR

BOOK 4
INTERNMENT

PREFACE
County Kildare, Ireland, 1919

Joe Keegan and Sean McKeon stood over the soldier's body, staring at it for far longer than was safe. They realised they had to get moving and they knew they had to get out of the area quickly, there was still danger. The rest of the dead man's patrol was out there somewhere in the gloom of the early morning. Joe and Sean were in a district that they weren't familiar with as a result of orders from Headquarters. Two outside men were needed, unknown to the local IRA, to go in, do the job and get out. They had done their work and the soldier now lying before them was collateral damage. Sean was the first to talk,

"Serves him right, the silly bugger, wandering around on his own, should have known better." It was nonsense as Joe knew but Sean was searching for some logic to justify what had happened.

The dead man's uniform was now staining with more blood from the bullet entries in his chest. The almost black jacket and the tan coloured army surplus trousers confirmed he was indeed a "Black and Tan" and a justifiable target for the two IRA men who had killed him. The Black and Tans were ex British Army recruits, an imported force to support the Royal Irish Constabulary (RIC). They had a policy to shoot first and question later and had a very low opinion of the IRA and the Irish generally. Their commanders had given them license to do whatever they needed to maintain order. Now here was one of the twelve thousand brought into Ireland by the British. He would have been no older than either of them, early twenties, a good-looking young man with a shock of blond hair and a small scar above his left eye.

"Looks like we both hit him." Said Joe, indicating two wounds with his revolver, it wasn't said with any pride, just a matter of fact attitude he found helped in times of danger.

Sean grunted and reached down to search the dead soldier's pockets, looking for maps or written orders, anything that the Intelligence people might find useful. There wasn't much but Sean pulled a set of Rosary beads from one pocket and exhaled as though he hadn't breathed in an hour,

"Jesus" he muttered as he showed Joe who just shook his head unwilling to comment on the find. But the dead man was a Catholic just like them. Joe wiped his brow then said,

"We better get going, this place will be crawling with Tans soon enough". Sean didn't answer just finished his search. They took off in the opposite direction they had come from. Joe followed, ignoring any paths as they pushed through the bracken and shrubs in the field glancing over their shoulders regularly to check for danger.

"This way," said Sean, as usual issuing orders without being aware that he was, Joe didn't question, they were on the run and self preservation had taken over. A safe place to hide was all that counted now. They had done their work and now they had to go back underground, and disappear from normal society.

BOOK 1

PRELUDE TO WAR

CHAPTER 1
1911, County Westmeath, Ireland

The two twelve year olds lads Joe and Sean were walking through the field towards their favourite makeshift hurling field and they each carried a Hurley. Their two week summer holiday starting that day was a welcome break from school in Drumraney, County Westmeath. They were going to join six of their friends for a game of hurling on His Lordship's land.

Joe Keegan had a bruised set of fingers on his right hand. He copped a set of four for back answering the teacher who was a big man and had a reputation for a short temper and a readiness to deal out punishment.

"Damn Sean my hand still hurts he let me have it alright." It had been two days ago and Joe's hand still smarted.

"Did you cry Joe? You know he likes to make the kids cry, don't you?" Sean asked tongue in cheek.

"Did I what? Cry! Come on Sean what do you think I am a baby?" Joe was set back by the question but Sean was just goading him as usual. He saw Sean grinning and thrust his Hurley at him narrowly missing.

"I'll be making you cry in a minute." It could end up in another makeshift sword fight between them but Sean easily ran off out of Joe's reach,

"We've no time for that the others will be waiting, let's get the game going." Sean was at full pace now and Joe set off in pursuit, his hurling stick trying to catch Sean's ankles. They found the others in the field that had recently been harvested and shouted greetings as if they hadn't seen them for weeks. The field was part of the Moydrum Castle Estate of Baron Castlemaine a member of the House of Lords and a much-resented landlord to local small farming holdings.

"Okay Joe you're first pick, then in turns, okay." It was Sean trying to set the rules as usual. Their friends were ready for either elation or humiliation in the time-honored tradition of being chosen for a side. Size didn't matter to the game it was all speed and all of the boys had that. Joe had already picked his side he wasn't being tricked by Sean,

"Seamus, Ned and Alex as usual with me, we won't be changed."

"Okay" said Sean admitting defeat, "let's get started." He often tried to change Joe's sides but Joe wouldn't go along with it, he knew who he needed. It would be a hardscrabble four a side game that had few rules and no referees. There was no doubt that blood would be drawn and new bruises would be earned and later shown off with pride.

The hurling started with much shouting, a man's fist sized rock-hard cork and leather bound sliotar served as a ball and flew around the field with frightening speed. Belying the idea that young boys could generate very much power with a Hurley which was basically a wooden stick that was shaped like a large, shallow spoon at one end. This enabled the players to snap up the sliotar from the ground without stopping, the rules didn't allow them to use their hands to pick it up.

Having been recently cut by his Lordship's labourers, the field allowed the game to flow and propel each team to their opponents' goal to score some points. They weren't supposed to use the field but they were far enough from the Castle to get a couple of hours in before they were chased off. Both Sean and Joe had ability with the Hurley stick and though Sean would never admit it Joe was faster and more skilful. They threw themselves into the game with all the ferocity twelve-year olds could muster. The game had been underway just ten minutes when Joe retrieved the sliotar within ten yards of the makeshift opposition goal posts. He snapped it up with his stick and flicked it into the air lining it up to slam home the goal between the makeshift posts. Sean saw the move and wanted to stop him at all costs. He reached his Hurley across the expected path of Joe's shot, but overstepped and his unprotected head became the only defence against the likely goal.

Joe and the others watched in horror certain their friend had been killed as he hit the ground. He fell like a potato and his eyes were closed as he lay on the ground. The boys rushed to his side Joe stricken with concern. They tried to revive him and make him comfortable none of them had ever seen someone made unconscious like that.

Joe quickly dispatched someone to get Sean's father. The other boys gathered around Joe who tended to Sean not knowing what to do but hoped whatever he did would bring comfort. After a few minutes Sean started to come around but was very groggy and unaware of where he was. The boys made sure he stayed in place and rested. After about thirty minutes Sean's father Seamus arrived and took control. He worked on his semi conscious son without really knowing what he was doing either. Splashing cold water on the face was usual practice but there wasn't any nearby, so it was a few slaps on the cheeks to see if that worked. No ambulances, no emergency services, you either survived accidents like this or became a statistic.

After a few minutes Sean eventually sat up and shook his head, now fully conscious, an egg-shaped lump was sitting on the side of his head behind his left ear, he looked at Joe,

"Ye didn't miss did ye." Joe smiled with relief at Sean's words, he was awake and seemed alright. They would have to wait some days until it became certain there was no permanent damage. Joe would remind Sean for many years that the sliotar had at least knocked some sense into him. Sean recalled seeing the sliotar coming at him but it was all he remembered from the day apart from his father's face slapping treatment. Sean went home with his father and Joe and their friends went their separate ways after the game which they didn't finish due to Sean's injury. They all had to be back at their homes to do their afternoon chores.

Later that night, Sean's mother put a hot poultice of her own recipe on the swelling and the family said the Rosary which she reported the next morning had made the swelling go down. Sean could go back to work with his father that afternoon, he had a blacksmith's forge in his village, Sean had just two younger brothers and they spent their spare time helping him . At a young age Sean could wield a reasonably heavy hammer and learned to bend steel to his will. It was a pastime Sean enjoyed, the physical work appealed to him and he felt his strength growing, even at a young age. He was never beaten at school in wrestling or any feat of strength with boys his own age or even a few years older. Joe was his closest competitor and it was the one area he overshadowed Joe making up for the lack of hurling skills. Sean's two younger brothers usually resisted Sean's challenges for some contest of strength.

By contrast Joe's family now stood at nine children. Their home was cramped to say the least but since no one in the family had much to compare it to they accepted it without complaint. There was plenty of work to go around on a small tenant farm of six acres and everyone was expected to take up their load including the youngest children.

Joe's mother was born Mary McCormack, to a family which farmed about thirty acres over near Tang, thirty minutes walk away. Mary had previously married at sixteen years of age to John Murtagh and they had a good marriage and one child, a boy, named Hugh. But John met with a horrific accident on his land, falling from his horse which broke its right foreleg stepping into a foxhole at full gallop. John tumbled off at speed, broke his neck in three places and never survived the journey to the doctors. He was just twenty seven and had left a wife and small child.

Mary Murtagh through social and church connections eventually met Joe's father Peter Keegan who fell in love with her and had no misgivings about taking on her and her son as his own.

Joe was the first born of Peter and Mary's marriage so at birth Joe had a step brother, four years older than himself. Hugh became one of Joe's best friends and it was with him, that Joe and Sean would share many experiences over the next many years. As his new family grew, Hugh helped by being the custodian of the younger Keegans keeping them focused on their tasks and mindful of the work that had to be done, particularly when Peter and Mary were preoccupied with their own tasks.

Peter Keegan was around six feet tall with a lean and fit body kept that way by constant work seven days a week. Perhaps because he was always physically tired, he never showed his temper to his family, more likely though because that was his natural temperament. He was always loving and solicitous of Mary and a good provider for the family of nine children now, including Hugh.

At supper time, usually around six, they sat on makeshift chairs at a long table that Peter had built himself. Peter said "Grace" and they all responded "Amen". He gave them the nod to start helping themselves to a plate of fresh baked bread on some days, but usually mashed potatoes, turnips, carrots and boiled cabbage but no meat. That might come with the monthly Sunday trip for the markets and Mass in Drumraney if the budget allowed. Then a small portion of mutton might be available for the boiling pot. If they were very lucky some hambones for a delicious pea and ham soup that Mary would make when possible, though often with barley instead of peas, depending on the season.

There wasn't usually much conversation early in the meal as everyone was hungry despite the lean choices, then Joe spoke to his father,

"I nearly killed Sean today Da, he forgot to duck under one of my goal shots and the sliotar cracked him and knocked him out." Joe wasn't exactly smiling but the memory of the event did amuse him a little despite Sean's discomfort.

"He's alright though, he was able to go home okay?" his father responded.

"Yes Da,' said Joe, "we made sure he was okay and his Da came and got him, he's a tough little......" Joe was about to say bugger but knew that would draw his mother's ire and a stern glance from Peter. "...fella." he concluded.

"Well I'm glad he's alright, hurling is a dangerous game at times and if you're not aware of what's happening that's what can happen." Peter held more than a few scars himself from the games in his youth. He finished his dinner and started on his cup of tea and round of bread as did most of the children, when he finished his tea he pushed himself out from the table: "Rosary now," he simply said and all the family knew to take their places and kneel beside their chairs or found somewhere else close to kneel. The babies were excused of course but as soon as they could talk they would be expected to take part. For the moment they played and kept themselves content while Mary watched them closely.

"Hugh, start us off will you." Peter said to his adopted son as he crossed himself and the other children followed suit. Hugh dutifully said the first Our Father to get the Rosary underway in a nightly ritual. The Rosary was said, each of the children offering the first part of ten Hail Marys and the rest responding in unison. Mary finished each of the five Decades with her quiet but heartfelt,

"Glory be to the Father, the Son and the Holy Ghost." The prayers took less than fifteen minutes; it was still light outside so the children were allowed some more play time before bed. Peter resumed his chair at the table and started to roll a cigarette, a ritual almost as certain as the Rosary, he turned to Hugh,

"You and Joe check the pigs and the horse and make sure they're fed and have water. Off you go then and fill the buckets at the well for your Mammy."

Hugh and Joe went off without a murmur they knew their duty and knew they had to do the work. Slacking wasn't tolerated and any complaints would be met with a sight of the back of Peter's hand. He never used it though, for which the boys were grateful, it was the size of the loaf of bread their mother made some days.

The chores continued through the week, on the Friday the brothers finished their work and went to find their mother. They both wanted to visit Reehallen the farm her brother, and their uncle, John McCormack lived on with his own family. It was getting late but the light would hold until 10:30 or so by which time they would be home. Though they certainly could find their way from Uncle John's farm in the dark, they had done so many times previously. Mary said,

"It's alright to go but don't stay too late," Joe took off on his own to fetch Sean from his home. Hugh ambled off into the fading light towards Reehallen and John McCormack a man with a reputation as someone not to be fooled with. A fierce temper but when it suited him a gentle nature that charmed all he met.

CHAPTER 2

John McCormack

It was a ritual now and had been for the last few months. Mary's brother John McCormack was a renowned story teller and held the boys spellbound, sometimes to his brother in law Peter's annoyance,

"He shouldn't be filling their heads with too much of that stuff, "he complained to Mary, "it won't do them any good in the long run." He was referring to John's so-called history lessons which were mainly stories of Irish rebels and revolutions over the years. But John characterised his talks as a continuation of the 'hedge schools' of the previous century. Then Catholic children weren't included in formal education and had to take schooling wherever they could, particularly in rural areas.

"You would be surprised' said Mary, "the boys enjoy it and it gives them a good picture of what's happened in the past." Peter sniffed at the answer he'd rather see the boys concentrating on their chores. He wasn't particularly political himself though enjoyed the odd discussion about what should be happening in the country as much as anyone. He was too busy to get involved in the day to day secrecy that seemed to afflict more and more of his neighbours. Nine children and a working farm that yielded little except hard work overwhelmed most other interests.

'That stuff', which Peter complained about, was John McCormack's view of Irish history and his vast knowledge of its characters. Mostly Irish politicians, priests and laymen, all with a disposition to the politics of Irish nationalism and often revolution.

Varying points of view covered deep and complex issues such as Home Rule for Ireland. Plus the vexed question of the reluctance of the Ulster Protestants to share the Catholic desire for an independent Republic.

Joe and Sean were at John's farm when Hugh arrived, they liked to tell him they had run all the way but in reality, Sean knew a short cut from the village which Hugh wasn't aware of. The Keegan boys and Sean, who was recovering from his hurling injury, still sported a sizable lump behind his ear. They lapped up the stories and listened enthralled as John McCormack laid bare the history of their country over the past one hundred and fifty years and sometimes more. It seemed that every time they met up John had another story about a rebel which they hadn't heard before. Sometimes it was the same character but with new twists and turns.

John McCormack was the almost unimaginable age, for Sean and Joe, of nearly fifty, an eternity of years to twelve years olds. A short stocky man, John was all muscle and sinew determined by the physical work demanded of him. Farm life offered very few labour saving devices apart from horses and a plough and they required a man's strength to guide them through soil that had to be constantly turned and tilled.

He sat now in a comfortable old chair outside his front door. His clay pipe newly stuffed with tobacco was resisting his attempts to keep it alight. His beard was resplendent though ungroomed and his eyebrows had taken on a life of their own reaching out from his face like antennas. His hair had the hacked look from his wife Rose's attempt to keep it under some control. Grey soiled trousers and a charcoal coloured shirt that had seen more years than the younger boys age, sat comfortably on his muscular frame, his hands always scarred though thoroughly scrubbed, sat in his lap.

His facial expression was often benign, reflecting a weariness that said he'd seen or heard it all. But John McCormack was one of the 'hard men' and his attitude to the politics of the day was granite hard and immovable. The hard men weren't for turning and their ideal of an independent Ireland was not negotiable.

"The Brotherhood was where it began," he said quietly. The Irish Republican Brotherhood was the secret society that had captured McCormack's imagination and loyalty in his youth, along with many more rural and city based Irish men and women who believed passionately in its goals and aspirations. McCormack spoke in reverent tones to the young men about the Brotherhood. "It is going through a resurgence at present," he divulged. "A new leader, Thomas Clarke has managed to purge the old leadership which he and others had found unwilling to take the risks that Clarke and his cohorts knew must be taken."

Because it was a secret society one had to be invited to join as McCormack had been. Like him you must hold an undying belief in the independence of Ireland, no partition between the North and the South and the end of English rule on the island.

McCormack continued, he knew he was lecturing them but they had to learn.

"The Brotherhood had started in 1858 in Dublin, so it had history on its side and a list of heroes and defeats which were important in developing revolutionary mindsets. The Great Famine of 1845 to 1849 loomed large at the time of the Brotherhood's birth when hundreds of thousands of Irish tenant farmers were either starved to death or immigrated to America to live in New York and Boston tenements. Those members that stayed in Ireland committed themselves to the use of force if needed, to attain the Brotherhood's goals of Irish Independence."

John McCormack looked at his young audience to see if they were taking in the gravity of his story. He need not have worried they were full of questions, picking up on snippets of information and names of early heroes they had vaguely heard of. Sean was the first to speak, his curiosity always spurred him to ask questions and though not academic in the way of high marks at school he was bright and anxious to learn. Sean was feeling a strong attachment to what he was being told, something was stirring within him that he didn't understand. B

But he did know that he wanted more information and knowledge about the past.

"What happened in 1867, why did they fail Mr McCormack?" He had heard stories from others including his own grandfather and father about the attempted uprising of that year but could never put together the reasons for its failure. Yet another in a series over one hundred years that appeared to end in the same ignominious loss. McCormack could see they wanted to hear this story and it was an important one for them to hear it. He drew on his pipe one more time and exhaled the acrid smoke and leaned forward in his chair, his conspiratorial tone drew his listeners nearer.

"The Great Famine of the 1847 left many people damaged, many died as you no doubt know, many left for the new world as many of them had been evicted and had no home. It would be fair to say that pestilence was on the face of the earth as the Bible says, certainly in this country at that time. The message had passed around the farms that there was to be a gathering, a meeting of tenant farmers, it was to be in Tallaght, a village just south of Dublin. The roads were thick with horse and carts carrying many thousands of men, many others were walking to get there, they came from all directions. The Brotherhood had arranged the assembly. The leaders were fed up with the injustice and poverty that had been inflicted on so many people who were destitute through no fault of their own. They had grand goals; no less than the expulsion of the British and the establishment of an Irish Republic. And it wasn't just to Tallaght that they were headed; in Cork, Drogheda, Dundrum and other places the Brotherhood members and their followers gathered and in many cases police barracks were attacked and put to the torch. The Tallaght numbers were large enough to make the British think that it was to be the centre of action. But the leaders of the Brotherhood had designed the protest to draw the troops out of Dublin so they could more easily start the main attack there. But unfortunately, it all came to very little. There had been a spy in the Liverpool group of the Brotherhood and he had alerted the Irish Constabulary and they were ready with many weapons.

"Without local commanders and a proper chain of command the marchers lost their way and dispersed when the gunfire started, they had no fall back plan and hundreds were arrested in the countryside. Others just went back to their homes and hid whatever weapons they had. The Brotherhood had realised that they now knew they could make something revolutionary happen and it also made the British aware of the strength of the people's anger. It was the birth of the true Fenians, which is what the British called Brotherhood members and the Brotherhood now had a base to work with. James Stephens, James Devoy and O'Donovan Rossa became names that echoed throughout Ireland and contacts with our brothers in America became more important than ever before. After all that's where the money was." he added with an ironic smile.

At the mention of O'Donovan Rossa's name Sean's eyes lit up because of the stories he had already read and heard. Sean had decided that Rossa was his hero and his dedication to the cause grew with the stories about him. Sean had memories of his grandfather telling stories of O'Donovan Rossa and had even hinted of meeting him so he was always keen to hear more of him.

"Tell us more about Rossa," Sean pleaded nudging Joe who was also curious about the legend, McCormack continued,

"Rossa was unable to take part in the 1867 insurrection because he was in an English prison for high treason against the British where he had been sentenced to life in prison. His name and reputation had grown powerfully and his forced exile to America after a Fenian Amnesty was a move the British would often later regret. He campaigned over the long distance to disrupt British rule through bombing campaigns and raised large amounts of money to fund Fenian activity in Ireland." Sean looked at Joe and Hugh, they were enthralled by the stories of the Fenians that McCormack shared. They could stay there all night and listen, but it was getting very late.

"We best be going Uncle John." said Hugh who was responsible for getting the younger boys home. "I'll tell Mammy that you're well then?" McCormack muttered something in Irish that the boys could not quite understand but they would take it as a positive message to take back home.

The three boys walked in silence for a while tracking through the farmlands of the local 'bigwig' as he was known, Baron Castlemaine lived in Moydrum Castle on hundreds of acres of land that the boys now traversed. A titled Irish Protestant who had inherited his land through his father which had been in that family for three hundred years. A symbol of what John McCormack called "the toffs", with more than a hint of disdain. But the boys weren't thinking about him too much this night. Sean was the first too speak,

"Do you think the IRB will stir things up again like they did in '67 and '98?' he asked Hugh, hoping perhaps being older he had some insights he lacked himself. Sean felt more familiar with the organization that he had decided to use the initials to identify them. Hugh was silent for a while and then said,

"From what Uncle John says they'll more than stir things up, I don't know what will happen but the Brotherhood is being very active in a number of parishes and districts, particularly in Dublin." Sean seemed pleased with the answer he was trying to imagine what the IRB would stir up and when.

Joe wasn't so sure, he wasn't looking forward to any trouble and his thoughts always came back to his Mammy and Da and his siblings, he just wanted a quiet life for them and safety above all else. They had already come once very close to being evicted and homeless and it had been very unsettling for them all. The so-called Land Wars that had lasted for thirty years till the 1890s reached into parts of Westmeath which because of its geography loaned its pasture to cattle grazing as much to tillage style farming found in many Counties. After the Great Famine in the late 1840s the absentee landlords were resisting the pressure from the British government for land reform that would enable small tenant farmers to at last buy their land and work it for themselves. This resistance, as often the case, flared into local rioting and skirmishes, throughout the country, reviving the battles which had always been fought over the principles of land ownership.

In 1881 the Second Land Act was passed. The work in Westminster of Charles Parnell, the Irish MP, forced the absentee landlords to sell. They were often broke anyway because of the losses from the Great Famine. Then in 1907 the Wyndham Act enabled Peter Keegan at long last to buy his own land albeit with a loan from the Dublin Government. The big land holdings were breaking down at long last. But Lord Castlemaine still held sway and a large swath of land in Westmeath.

Sean soon became bored with the walk home and grabbed Joe around the neck and they started to wrestle, it was as natural as breathing to them, each trying to assert dominance and each never admitting defeat. It was all over in two minutes with Hugh grabbing each by the scruff of the neck and pulling them apart,

"Stop it will ye, it'll be dark soon, we need to get home before then." Sean was secretly glad, in his enthusiasm to bait Joe he had forgotten about the lump behind his ear caused by the Hurling game and which now started aching again. The three boys walked on in silence, John McCormack's stories still fresh in their mind. Their blood was up with Irish pride and their thoughts were stirred by a new passion they didn't understand. They were unaware that the next ten years would change their lives in ways they couldn't even begin to imagine.

"Do you think we'll ever have to fight the Brits, Hugh?" Sean asked suddenly. Hugh just shrugged and continued walking he didn't know the answer to that question.

For now they had work to do on the farm and the forge and more growing up to do. At their age there wouldn't be much more schooling, their education would come from their families and their work. The politics of Europe which were always on the boil didn't intrude much into lives in rural Ireland. But a burgeoning trade union movement mainly in Belfast and Dublin was starting to shape new thinking in the politics of the country as Hugh would soon discover.

CHAPTER 3
August 1913. A visit to Dublin by Hugh and Peter

Since Hugh was the eldest of the brothers, he was going to Dublin for a few days with Peter to buy a few necessary supplies that weren't available in Drumraney or Athlone. The train journey was slow and made frequent stops. They found out soon enough that a general strike had started in Dublin just the day before Peter and Hugh arrived.

Hugh and Peter Keegan stayed overnight in Dublin with Patrick McCormack and his family, another cousin of John and Mary McCormack.

Peter and Hugh were tired but wanted information, Peter asked Patrick,

"What was the problem with the trains Pat? We didn't see many trams or trolleys at all. There were crowds everywhere and the people didn't seem too happy. They were crying out about the need for revolution, some had pick and axe handles and looked ready to use them. The police and soldiers we saw were all carrying guns. It was a bit frightening I'd never seen so many angry people."

Patrick explained what was happening in the city:

"The strike has thrown the railways, tramways and the whole city into turmoil. The dock workers and the tram drivers had joined forces and thousands were locked out of their place of work, strikers and the police were roaming the streets and fighting started all over. By Sunday the big march was on by the strikers, they just wanted to form their own unions, but hundreds of police baton charged them, two were killed and hundreds injured, it was total chaos."

"Did you go yourself?" Hugh asked.

It was obvious Patrick was upset by the events and he had his family's security to worry about. He nodded at Hugh's question.

"We were there alright and as your Da says, never seen so many angry people."

Now Hugh wanted to go and see for himself if there would be more marching and rioting, his father insisted they stay indoors and be safe. The small tenement house was in a poor part of the city but was comfortable though crowded with two visitors and Patrick's wife and two young boys who were kept away from school and the streets while the unrest was continuing.

Patrick McCormack, like his cousin John, was an avid Irish Republican Brotherhood supporter as was his wife Therese. Peter was curious about the Brotherhood but still unsure of what it actually offered and wanted to keep a distance for himself and his family. Hugh though was intent on hearing what was going on in what was basically a secret society and Patrick was happy to share whatever he knew of the Brotherhood with him. They walked to the small backyard out of Peter's hearing to talk, though Hugh greatly respected his Da he knew he wasn't as excited on the brewing situation in all of Ireland as were himself and Joe and Sean. Peter would let his politics be known when the time suited him.

"So what is happening with the Brotherhood here in Dublin Patrick? There's so much to take in." Hugh asked.

"There are chapters forming all over the country" Patrick confided to Hugh in a quiet tone, "from Sligo to Belfast and down to Cork and Kerry, there's plenty of interest and this trouble here with the unions and the bosses will kick it along. Sure, there are plenty that have had enough of the British and feel the time is getting close to do something." Hugh's eyes widened.

"What do you think will happen?"

"There's talk of the IRB training an army to do something, but that's all I know, there's always plenty of talk and talk's always cheap. But this time the feeling is stronger and everyone you speak to has an anger that won't be easily satisfied, particularly in this city. We understand that the Brotherhood or those who headed it up have made a decision. They will do whatever is necessary to finally throw off the yolk of colonisation and become a self-governing entity and a Republic. If force was what was necessary then so be it. The Brotherhood has secretly started recruiting able bodied and reliable men for the Volunteers, and secret training was underway in various locations." He wasn't sure how Hugh would react to his next comment but he had to know, "One obstacle is the Church. It frowns on any secret society which makes it difficult for many men to sign the IRB pledge fearful of bringing down the wrath of the bishops or the parish priest." Hugh took that in without comment he didn't realize the politics it implied.

Patrick enjoyed proceeded to tell Hugh about John McCormack's involvement in the Brotherhood.

"The old man is in the movement in a bigger way than he has let on. He is responsible for a lot of meetings and recruitment around the Drumraney and Athlone areas. He is feeling out who could be trusted and who would sign up to the Brotherhood's belief that freedom from the British Empire could only eventually be gained by force of arms." Patrick went on intent on hoping Hugh was committed. "John knows the history. The negotiations to deliver a Home Rule Act had started in the 1890's. But they were continually stymied by the Protestants in Belfast and the absentee landlords in England who controlled the voting in the House of Lords. They had already once rejected the Bill even though it had passed the Commons with a decent majority and they were expected to keep on doing so." Patrick stopped talking for a moment and went into his laundry and came out with a folded newspaper,

"Here take this, some good reading for you and your friends." It was the latest edition of 'Irish Freedom' a newspaper recently started by Bulmer Hobson who had returned from the United States and rejoined the Brotherhood and rose through its ranks. As John McCormack had explained earlier to Hugh and the others, the older, more conservative leaders of the Brotherhood were being replaced by the newer, younger ones like Hobson. The newspaper carried articles promoting the Brotherhood's ideals with stories from men who would later make a major impact on the Irish march to freedom. Hugh briefly looked over the paper and folded it into his coat, no need yet to trouble his Da about such an unusual gift.

They spent the night in with the McCormack family and as they packed there roll the next morning Hugh wondered what his father would think of John McCormack's politics and asked him.

"Patrick said Uncle John was well into the Brotherhood, might even be an office holder, do you think Da?" Peter was silent for a few seconds before giving an answer, he realised that Hugh now at sixteen was growing into manhood and couldn't be denied the truth of anything if he asked. He was measured in his response to him:

"John's his own man, always was, and the McCormack's have always been political, even my own mother in law ...." he trailed off not sure of what to say, his step son's enquiry was genuine and fair but he didn't want to mislead him. "........my own mother in law being a McCormack was always talking about revolution and getting something done, but as always nothing was ever done, not without someone ending up in prison at any rate. John's brothers were and are respected men in the county and that comes with some kind of influence that's never fully understood. But if you say they are into the Brotherhood, that would explain it, but it's a long path and one I've chosen to stay off, I'm never sure where it will end up. You and your brothers should do the same." He finished without any menace in his voice but a soft warning looking at Hugh and putting his arm on his shoulder, "you have plenty to do on the farm, and we have a big family to look after, that'll keep us all busy without anything else."

It was Peter's way of saying he didn't want any part of the Brotherhood, not because he disagreed with its aim and objectives but he was a tenant farmer with nine children and he couldn't afford the luxury of politics. Hugh nodded as if in agreement but he couldn't wait to get back and tell Joe and Sean what he had learned of their Uncle John and also tell them about Patrick. They would share the contents of 'Irish Freedom' which was filled with inspirational yarns and anti British propaganda and promotion of Labour Unions and their place in society.

For now, they had to figure out how to get back home with their limited supplies they had purchased, trains were usually regular to Athlone and stations nearby but the strike had put paid to that option. So, they started walking towards the outskirts of the city to get on the main road and hope their thumbs would deliver a ride to somewhere that got them closer to home. Hugh was wide eyed as he walked through the streets of the inner city and along the walkways beside the River Liffey, he hadn't been to Dublin before, the only city he had visited was Athlone but it was much smaller and less populated. The tenement housing and streets crowded with all those now out of work and on strike and their wives and children, gave off a dangerous air. Although they didn't know what a slum was compared to a crowded street, father and son exchanged glances occasionally that shared an unspoken thought that they were glad they lived in the country and not in the city.

 They had decided to take leave of Patrick's hospitality. He had enough to worry about with his own family. Hugh and Peter could feel the tension and see the anger and frustration on the faces of the locked out workers as they walked along. Occasionally someone was on a street corner calling for revolution and waving crude signs and attracting an angry crowd.

They had to strike out on their own with limited instructions on how to find the main road back to Athlone. Peter didn't show his concern to Hugh but it was far from clear as to how they were going to get back home.

CHAPTER 4
Hugh and Peter return from Dublin

Mary Keegan as usual was working as hard as ever in what passed as a kitchen in the small home of the Keegan family. Caring for nine children from a one year old to the eldest at seventeen was a burden that no women trained for. But a strong belief in the Catholic religion insisted that no form of birth control, apart from abstinence, was allowed, and it was not considered 'proper' for a wife to deny her husband what the church considered his conjugal rights. So, eight children in eleven years were not unusual in rural Ireland, and of course there was Eugene or Hugh as he was always known from her first marriage. It was Mary's lot to be exceedingly fertile and Peter's ability to complement her fecundity was equally consistent, but she accepted that it must have been God's will because the children just kept coming.

After her first husband's death, Mary needed to fend for herself and Hugh with her family's help. A family which she was proud to say had gone to the trouble of educating their daughter at least to year eight of school so that she had learned to read and write and develop a sense of some understanding about the world she grew up in. There was also the political education from the endless discussions at the dinner table.

It was three years after her husband John's death that she met Peter through the church and their friendship grew into a love affair such as one could have in those troubled times. Then as they say, one thing led to another and eventually her brother John quietly suggested that she and Peter needed to make it official which they did at a quiet church wedding with family and a few friends in

Drumraney's St Mary's Catholic Church. Three months later Joe was born.

In other times and places there could have been a scandal and certainly there was no shortages of village gossips putting forward their own opinions and raising their eyebrows when Mary was seen in the village. But Peter was deeply in love with her and she with him and the addition of further children soon stopped the gossip and they settled down into being a family well accepted in the community of Drumraney. Mary and Peter obtained absolution for their 'sin' by the simple expedient of a timely confession with the parish priest who knew of Mary's condition.

It was the few years that Mary spent without a husband that had made her more independent and curious than many women who lived the rural life. She took a keen interest when time and funds allowed in the publications of The Irish Homestead, a newspaper put out by the Irish Agricultural Organisation Society and the Irish Country Association's pamphlets. Later she would join Cumman na mBan a women's organisation attached to the new political party Sinn Fein and actively support its activities when she could. Peter didn't always share Mary's enthusiasm for politics or whatever was going on in Dublin as he put it, but it was Mary's escape from the hard work and drudgery of the rural life. Peter's lack of enthusiasm for current events and politics was coloured by the fact that he, unlike Mary, could neither read nor write and was only able to add his mark of X to each of his children's birth certificates.

The information about the '1913 Great Strike' in Dublin became known to Mary through talk around the village and the church. Though she was concerned about Peter's and Hugh's safety she looked forward to their return so she could receive firsthand accounts of what had happened and what they saw in Dublin. She was relieved when they walked in late afternoon three days after they had left Dublin.

Peter gave her a brief report of their trip home,

"Using our thumb and pleading for a lift mostly, there were no buses or trains. It took six different lifts and a lot of walking and two nights sleeping and trying to keep warm in the fields." He said his fatigue evident.

Hugh also didn't feel up to handling a long discussion with his mother about Dublin, pleading with her that the next morning would have to suffice. Her eyes lit up though when Hugh produced the Republican newspaper that Patrick had given him, any new reading matter was welcomed. After a brief meal both Hugh and Peter took their tired bodies to bed, Mary lit a new candle and settled down with the latest political news from the IRB.

At breakfast the next morning Mary detected a change in Hugh so she challenged him,

" Your Da says that Dublin was big and busy and you met some new cousins. Did you enjoy the trip?" Hugh still deep in thought about the trip answered as best he could,

"It was sad to see so many people struggling and living like they did, life in the city's not for me," then added after some more thought, "the strikers are in a bad way, no work, no money, it shouldn't be like that, they didn't do anything wrong, they just wanted a union to look after them." The only boss Hugh had ever known was Peter and though he drove his sons hard, he was at worst a benevolent dictator but someone who understood his sons' work load and helped out with it.

Mary wondered if Hugh had become more curious about politics. She knew her cousin in Dublin was a typical McCormack who'd sooner have an argument about politics than a hot meal.

"And did Patrick talk to you about what was going on with the Brotherhood?" Hugh was a bit surprised by the question but knew his mother had insights he could only guess at.

"Aye, and he told me about what was going on and what was likely to go on. It seems there's trouble of kinds down the road apiece, he thinks the Brotherhood will be in the thick of it." The discussions with Patrick had hardened Hugh's attitude about the struggle with the English landowners and brought the vision of an Irish Republic into Hugh's thinking more sharply than he had ever considered. The slow trip back from Dublin and the scenes of the countryside and villages as they rode on yet another cart had given Hugh plenty to think about. He tried to picture a new Ireland somewhat like the one John and Patrick McCormack envisioned and which men like O'Donovan Rossa and Charles Parnell had imagined; a people free from colonial overlords and able to determine their own future.

"I'm worried Ma, it's hard to see what the future holds for all of us." Hugh's view of the world was narrow due to his rural upbringing. The farm had been the only thing he had known and seeing Dublin with its slums which many had described as the worst in Europe with their heaving masses of people had turned his head. By comparison he could see the mansions and wealth of the Dublin elite, the difference was astonishing and stark. The idea of Unions and worker's rights were new ideas that appealed to him greatly and the thought of joining the new army of Irish Volunteers which Patrick had talked about had great appeal for him. But for now, he wouldn't mention that to his Ma. "I suppose the good

Lord will sort it out one way or the other soon enough." He knew the reference to religion would satisfy his mother.

"We'll say the Rosary with that in mind," she said and continued with her work. The next morning Hugh managed to get his treasured copy of the "Irish Freedom" newspaper from his mother but she said she still wanted to read more of it. Hugh agreed but it was his intention as soon as he could to share its contents with Joe and Sean and their Uncle John whom they were due to visit that afternoon when time allowed, for more stories and history lessons which they had been hearing now for some months.

The boys were never disappointed, John McCormack looked over the newspaper Hugh had brought and skimmed through the dense typewritten pages. The boys didn't even know that he could read but it was obvious he could as he consumed the headlines and took in the stories.

"I haven't seen a copy of this for months.' He finally said, "Patrick had sent a few but not regularly." The content was about the activities of past agitators for the Irish cause.

The 'Irish Freedom' article about Wolfe Tone and the Society of United Irishmen captured Uncle John's attention and he embellished it for the three boys. His knowledge of history had the boys enthralled.

"Here's a story you should know. The United Irishmen over one hundred years ago in 1798 and inspired by the French and American revolutions, emboldened the Irish, both Protestant and Catholic, to rebel against the English rule which was oppressive and heavily taxing. They were even supported by the intervention of French troops who had been organised chiefly by Wolfe Tone who arrived at Ireland's shores with a force of fourteen thousand French soldiers. But due to bad weather the troops were unable to land and returned to France. Eventually one thousand French troops did land and joined with local Irish rebels mainly around Wexford and fought a number of battles which continued on for many months. Sadly, Wolfe Tone was captured and sentenced to be hung but he cheated the hangman by slitting his own throat thus becoming a martyr for the cause of Irish freedom and a hero to generations of like-minded Irishmen down to this day. The news of the battles travelled around the world."

"Was he at Vinegar Hill Uncle John?" Hugh this time recalling fragments of earlier tales.

John was impressed by the question, and saw that the boys were taken in by it,

"The Battle of Vinegar Hill in Wexford in 1798 was a huge battle with thirteen thousand British troops attacking the United Irishmen, but Wolfe Tone wasn't there. In 1810 the battle would be the inspiration in far off New South Wales in Australia when a number of our transported Irish rebels staged their own ill fated battle of the same name. Sadly, another defeat but also another blow against the establishment and reminded them that the Irish never forget their duty to their country." That would be their lesson for the day thought John, he had seen the response in their eyes and the concern for the old times, he had done his job. And his job, though he would never admit it to himself was to engage the youth of today with the fire of yesteryear to carry the torch or independence forward.

"It was their struggle that made the difference then and will now,' said Sean aware that the others nodded their heads in agreement with him, "we need to make sure their efforts are never forgotten."

John McCormack smiled and handed the newspaper back to Hugh.

"Time to let Sean have a good look at this, it will help his thinking." Sean was the most smitten with the fervour of the old times, Joe and Hugh were too but not as deeply as Sean.

"Should I join the Volunteers Uncle John.' asked Hugh, anxious to get some confirmation or direction and keen to do something. John wasn't going to walk into that one.

'That's more a question for your Da and Mammy my boy. Give it a few weeks or months and see what comes up around hereabouts. There's sure to be some local groups looking for young men your age."

John could see Sean almost smart at the comment realising that he was still too young to be considered for such a venture. He was looking into the future hoping against hope that he wouldn't be left behind in this new struggle. The subject of revolutionary politics was dominating much of Sean's thinking despite his young age.

Finally, John gave them the news that had that week devastated most of the politicians in Dublin and forged a new determination in the leadership of the Brotherhood,

"The House of Lords in their usual way has ignored what most of Ireland wanted and expected this year." They could see he was angry and struggled to contain his anger, "They have used the excuse of a possible war now in Europe and have put off voting on the new Home Rule for Ireland Bill." The three lads were shocked as they had been expecting the Home Rule Bill as had most of the country, and now it had been snatched from them as if by an angry parent.

The Lords' decision would have enormous consequences for England and Ireland as it threw explosive fuel onto an Irish fire that had started with the General Strike in Dublin. Sean took the decision almost personally and he burned inside for a way to make a difference.

CHAPTER 5
1914 Drumraney

The regular visits to John McCormack's farm continued over the following months whenever Joe and Sean had time. Hugh often joined them but as the eldest in his family he had more responsibility and his time was less his own.

McCormack in his unofficial capacity as an IRB recruiter covering a large area of the midlands stretching from Athlone to Mullingar and across to Roscommon had lately developed a more structured approach to his task. This day he had gathered a group of about twenty young men all keen for news. Whilst he enjoyed talking to all the young men as a matter of course he realised that he had to educate them as well about the history, it was important they understood the sacrifices of those who had gone before them. He was lecturing them but he felt that was necessary. They looked up to him for guidance through the complicated political situation they saw developing but for which they lacked a good understanding. McCormack gave them the official IRB line and history this would be their political education. They wouldn't find these truths in English history books.

"We have to accept that the British will never give us our independence and Home Rule willingly. Sure, they make soothing sounds and promises that will never be met but in the finality of it all we can only trust ourselves to deliver a goal that we have been seeking for hundreds of years."

He then gave the group the story about Wolfe Tone and the United Irishmen again causing Joe to wink at Sean as they had already heard it. But as usual McCormack had further details, they hadn't heard before.

"Tone went to America and then Paris and even met Napoleon Bonaparte to seek his help in sending an invasion force to Ireland to help the Irish Revolution of 1798."

The young men in the audience looked at each other quizzically. They had heard all their lives of struggles for independence but never with the passion and power that McCormack presented and certainly not with so much detail, "...and what had they wanted?" asked McCormack, "simply to be given the same rights as Englishman and not be treated like serfs." McCormack was under full sail by this time and everyone was captured by the passion of his speech as he told them of the help from the French and the bloody defeat told earlier to Sean, Hugh and Joe.

McCormack continued, "Though defeated in '98 the spirit lived on with the likes of Daniel O'Connell who continued the fight through the halls of power in the Parliament of Westminster. He had been scarred by the 1798 Rebellion seeing young men hacked to death for their beliefs. But O'Connell's weapons were his words and his wit which he used in courts and Parliament and fought for the Emancipation of the Catholics, which meant my young friends that Catholics could finally sit in Parliament, a birthright that had been denied them for hundreds of years."

This was again history that the boys had heard rumoured but not taught in their schools but delivered informally by their elders. The passion shown by McCormack was lighting a fire under their desire for independence and inspiring them with stories of the bravery and audacity of men like O'Donovan Rossa.

Then he went into the more recent story of Charles Stuart Parnell who had fought the English in their own Parliament for Irish Home

Rule. McCormack greatly admired the Irish born Parliamentarian and spoke of Parnell's work and the effort he put into Irish Land Reform,

"Charles Stewart Parnell was a giant in the story of our struggle and he was born in County Wicklow to a well off family in 1846. He grew up in a period that made him see the fear and terror that many people had on the land. Why? Because they were being exploited by the gentry and had no rights and had not long came out of the Great Famine. But he was up against powerful forces who had much to lose and by championing Home Rule he made them enemies of himself and Ireland. He was a Member of Parliament and considered to be one of the great Parliamentarians of the modern era. His Irish Parliamentary Party held the balance of power at Westminster in 1885 and that is when he pushed very strongly for Home Rule which Prime Minster Gladstone incorporated into the Liberal Party's platform."

John could see the boys were intrigued by this story of Westminster intrigue and party politics. Parnell was not a soldier or a fighter in the familiar military way but his bravery was of a different kind, one that the lads would grow to understand. His world was a long way from their world and McCormack continued,

"Because of his position he was close to the edges of the struggles and he made many enemies with his pursuit of Home Rule and his desire for Land Reform to help the rural poor. But his fight was not an easy one, his enemies could tell that he was very much against the English and his Irish nationalism was seen as a betrayal to his class. His leadership of the Land League that strove to give peasants more rights was seen to be stirring up the Irish rural tenants and couldn't be allowed to continue. The more his fame grew, as it did after his visit to America where he got many audiences with powerful people, the more he was resented. That's when the Tories decided he had to be destroyed.

"First they imprisoned him on charges that he had sabotaged the Land Act, this was under a newly proclaimed law, The Coercion Act. Then Parnell pushed more strongly for Home Rule in 1885 which upset the Northern Protestants and they actively opposed the Land League and Parnell's party in particular. It was British politics at its fiercest and finally the Conservatives got back into Government.

"The scene was set for a disgraceful attack on Charles Parnell. They went so far as to accuse him of murder or at least being involved with the Brotherhood in the murder of the Chief Secretary of Ireland and his Under Secretary! The Times newspaper published the lies which Parnell successfully challenged and discredited. The letters accusing Parnell of the crimes were proved to be forgeries and the Parliament had no option but to ignore them. But since Parnell had rubbed shoulders with members of the Brotherhood he was tainted as far as the House of Lords was concerned. They had to retract those charges of course, he was not involved in the murders of course but they wouldn't let up.

"Eventually, he was found to have been …" and here John McCormack had to choose his words carefully, talking as he was to boys who had no knowledge of such things, "let me just say, he had a friendship with a lady who was married to someone else. Well the scandal that followed was too much for his colleagues in the Parliament and his life was made a misery though he kept up his good work for the Irish Land Reforms. But lads it shows the extent to which the powers of Westminster would go to discredit anyone like Parnell who had the effrontery to demand rights for all Irish men and women. It's not inaccurate to say that he was hounded to his death at the early age of forty five. His body lies in Glasnevin Cemetry in Dublin."

As usual McCormack left his charges wondering and needing more information. They were immensely curious about the history and they wanted to expand their knowledge about the men and times McCormack had told them about. But time was always an issue and he dismissed them before he could answer all their questions. His suggestion was to find out for themselves by reading the literature the IRB had available and visiting their local library if they were lucky enough to have one. "Education is everything." McCormack insisted to his charges, but it came out as "edication' in his brogue and the boys made a joke of his pronunciation but the message stayed with them for the rest of their lives.

The three friends and their compatriots in training were now becoming more aware of the challenges that Independence for Ireland and membership of the Irish Volunteers would demand of them as young men over the coming years. Independence no longer seemed a distant ideal but one that was within this generation's reach and in the struggle to come many lives in their country would be changed forever.

CHAPTER 6
1916 Two years on, an historical Easter beckons

Sean and Joe were now seventeen and their friendship and their competiveness grew stronger. Joe unkindly goaded Sean about his lack of interest in improving his sporting skills,

"You need to train more. The County selectors won't be picking you if you don't show more enthusiasm for the game." Sean wasn't so sure he wanted to train harder. His head and heart were taking him away from the interest in sport and he was spending more of his spare time reading up on the history of revolutionary activity in Ireland for the past one hundred years.

Joe continued to develop his skills as a Hurling player, the local Parish Priest and hurling team coach Father Slattery certainly felt Joe had the skill and temperament to go further in the sport. He had been earmarked for County selection and he took as much time as his father Peter would allow for training and away matches. It wasn't easy with a farm to run and there were many chores to be shared amongst the older boys in the family. There was Hugh, Joe's elder by four years and Thomas, James and Patrick all a couple of years younger than Joe but able to pitch in with the heavy work and take the load off Peter. It was not for nothing that rural families grew larger as the years went on. Someone had to do the heavy work.

Father Slattery wasn't that much older than the players he worked with, energetic and good looking with a shock of red hair and a ready smile. He worked with the Gaelic Athletic Association or as it was more widely known the GAA, to organise as many Hurling games as possible for the young men and Camogie for the girls in his parish. But always with the blessing of the GAA, as he said on many occasions to his players,

"If the GAA doesn't want you in, you won't be in." It was the main officiating sports body for the whole country. It controlled Hurling for the boys and Camogie for the girls as well as Gaelic Football, Handball and athletics. "Without the GAA's nod your skills could be wasted and if you were a Protestant or if because of your job you had taken the Oath to the British Crown, don't even bother to apply. But such was their love of the game some Protestants joined the teams despite the ban."

Joe's dedication to his chosen game continued unabated despite the distractions of other important matters. When he could Joe went on cross country runs for more than an hour to build up his strength and endurance. Fitness was important if he was to make a career in hurling which was his cherished goal.

The Irish Volunteers had stepped up their activities and were recruiting and training and Joe and Sean were keen to take part and were shortly sworn in. Hugh made an announcement to the two friends in early 1916 when the winter was finally starting to wind down, but he said his news was shrouded in secrecy and not to shared by the friends,

"Now that the Volunteers are recruiting more young men into the ranks, you have to be fit and willing and dedicated to the cause. The training will be in secret, often at night or early morning and at least three nights a week. All I can tell you is that the Volunteers want you all to be prepared and well trained." The two friends knew instinctively that Hugh's information was coming from the IRB, no doubt through his Uncle John McCormack whom he had taken to visiting more frequently.

"Who are the Citizen's Army, Hugh? " Asked Sean who had heard the name but knew nothing of the organisation. He looked quizzically at Joe as well who shrugged his shoulders and looked blank.

"They're a group that formed in Dublin after the General Strike in '13, the Union leaders could see how the police were treating the strikers and they needed to be protected. There are a few hundred of them but you have to be in a union to join." This was news for Sean and didn't mean a great deal but Hugh's comment about needing to be in a union put an end to his questions.

Hugh's task was to organise the local lads around Drumraney and other areas of Westmeath generally. He was under the eye of John McCormack and his associates, all IRB members, the men who had sworn to the IRB that they would carry the fight no matter the consequences.

Peter Keegan had allowed Hugh and Joe to join in but insisted it would be only after their farm work had been done. Peter was not taken up by the romance of revolution. Mary Keegan took a more rounded view and had worked on Peter to let the young men join she was keen to hear of any political news as soon as Hugh could share it.

Sean's father took a different view entirely to Peter Keegan and told Sean:

"Get involved as much as possible, this may finally be the time when the movement can make things happen. God knows when another opportunity will present itself." He was referring of course to the fact that the British Empire was embroiled in the European war and perhaps not able to focus on the Irish "problem" for the present.

Sean was grateful for the support and with Joe attended all training and meetings. Hearing from the men who sometimes travelled from Dublin or Athlone to talk to them about tactics and what would be expected of them. This particular night was cold and frost had already started to appear, a warm turf fire was much more appealing than the cold barn at the McCormack farm, but Sean was intent.

"Keep your religion close to you," the first speaker said, which Sean found strange as he had never imagined losing such a thing. "There will be temptations to take your activities into areas that God would not approve of, always be aware that we are dealing with other human beings and man-made laws." It wasn't till many years later that the man's words came back to Sean when he found himself in situations and he had to make split second decisions about whether his enemy would live or die. It seemed incongruous that a man who was effectively there to lecture about how to make war would sound such a warning but the IRB was leaving nothing to chance and this approach kept the Catholic Church onside.

John McCormack followed up by explaining the situation as clearly as possible to the Volunteer recruits:

"We don't have tanks or artillery or large trucks to move people and equipment around the country side. Our job will be to hit quickly, hit hard and get out. So, we can fight another day. We will be mainly on foot so we'll need the support of local people and shelter to be made available when we need it." The Irish Volunteers handbook was to be the example of the Boers in South

Africa who had earlier in the century fought just such a campaign against the British. "Our enemy won't be as mobile as us they will need to rely on transport to move their people and equipment around, our favoured terrain will be the mountains and fields where it will be difficult for them to bring heavy equipment."

Sean was fascinated by the concept and his mind wandered off to consider a variety of scenarios and he imagined himself dodging bullets in windblown fields. Unlike Joe whose world was revolving around his hurling, Sean was now thinking like a soldier and he embraced the Volunteer's training with enthusiasm. McCormack continued, "You will be trained in the use of dangerous explosives and all kinds of weaponry particularly small arms and some devices which haven't been invented yet. You will hit and you will run, but make sure you have somewhere to run to." John McCormack was getting ahead of his contemporaries. This indeed was the plan for how any conflict would play out but for the present there was no conflict. Indeed, the powers that be in the IRB in Dublin had not formulated detailed plans but only talked in general terms. But it was obvious to many of the old hands that what McCormack had described was the way the conflict would play out when it started.

Due that year in late April, Easter 1916 was drawing nearer. This Easter was destined to become iconic in Irish history. That revered and holy period held in awe by the Irish Catholics would be a time that would forever separate the British past from the Irish future and it would all unfold over the next few weeks.

McCormack and his friends from Dublin wanted their audience to understand what they would be up against when any fighting would inevitable start.

"No less than the might of the British Empire." Said Tom Burney from the Dublin IRB. "We will struggle for weapons so it is important that anything that can be a weapon is used that way. In the North it will be much tougher for our people, we know for a fact that the Ulster Volunteers have been supplied arms from England and though the Parliament won't admit it, they have gone out of their way to strengthen the Protestants in the North. The Prods want their own government there and their leaders have made it clear they won't be part of a southern Ireland dominated leadership"

The politics of Protestant versus Catholic wasn't new to the young men listening but they rarely gave it much thought and considered it to be Ulster's problem, not theirs. But it was always an intriguing and inexorable element of their country's history.

"The reality is that any fight we get into will be as much about religion as politics," Burney added, "and even though the British have knocked Conscription for Ireland on the head, for the time being, we are sure they'll bring it back when they need it." Then his face reddened and his voice rose dramatically. "The last thing we want is Irish blood spilt for the British Empire!"

This point was heavily emphasised and the audience knew that volunteering for the war in Europe by joining the British Army was not and never would be IRB policy and though they couldn't stop all Irishmen enlisting they would not support those who did.

Joe and Sean had no trouble obeying the edict as they were both under eighteen but Hugh had pressure put on him from the local Constabulary to go and join the fight but he ignored it and went on with his work on the farm.

Despite the warning from the IRB, Sean was tempted. He was keen to see action and learn more about the military however he could;

"Should I go Joe?" he asked his best friend one Sunday after mass "I'd like to get amongst it and learn how things are done. I can lie about my age, they won't care."

Joe was more reserved and had respected and understood Hugh's reluctance to sign up.:

"They'd have you as an Irishman certainly but purely as cannon fodder boy. Don't you read the papers? They're going down like flies over in France and Belgium. No. Stay here, Hugh says there'll be plenty to get involved with for the Volunteers soon enough." Joe's comment was tongue in cheek. He knew Sean followed the events in Europe more closely than he did and he himself rarely read the newspapers and preferred the sports section when he did.

"Sure, and he won't tell anyone anything, it's all whispers and rumours, as usual," Sean complained, impatient and critical of the IRB leadership and their secretive ways. Joe responded sharply,

"If Hugh says there's something going on, there is, we just have to wait and see and be ready." That's all there was to it for Joe. Sean would have to be patient and not throw his life away on a British battlefield in another country just to satisfy his curiosity.

The two young men continued their clandestine training with the Volunteers in and around Drumraney with many hours spent in the fields. They learned how to pull apart and put back together Lee Enfield rifles and various makes of revolvers and developed an understanding of how explosives worked and what damage they could do. Hours spent learning how to camouflage and walk through woods without making any noise were followed up by hand to hand combat lessons much more sophisticated than their boyish wrestling. John McCormack was heavily involved in all aspects of the Volunteers activities and fed the recruits a diet of propaganda and rebel stories and when he could information from the meetings of the Brotherhood. Though Sean and Joe weren't invited to the meetings Hugh was and he kept them informed as much as he felt he could. But all he could say as Easter approached was that,

"Something is in the wind."

There was no shortage of rumours, whispered stories in pubs, churches and sporting events and anywhere else people met, the talk conveyed what Hugh had said, "Something is in the wind." But no one around Drumraney knew exactly what, except perhaps John McCormack, and he wasn't saying anything more than was necessary.

It was not only the locals who were kept in the dark as Hugh explained many months later. Some of the IRB leadership had set up a Military Council which liaised with the Volunteers and the Citizens Army. The Council deliberately kept many of their own membership and even some of their own leaders uninformed about what was going to happen at Easter. They were terrified of any leaks to the British Army or the Dublin government. Eoin MacNeill who was nominally the leader of the IRB was heavily involved in trying to land a shipment of rifles and ammunition from Germany. But he was inexplicably kept out of the decision-making process and indeed was unaware of how far plans had progressed for action in Dublin for Easter week. The decision to keep him uninformed about the Rising would have disastrous consequences for the IRB plotters.

CHAPTER 7
EASTER 1916

On Sunday 16th April, the week before Easter Sunday, Hugh, Joe and Sean responded to orders from John McCormack with nearly a hundred other young men from around the district with whom they had been training. They assembled at three farmhouses in the area. They were told they were going to take part in special training in the countryside around Drumraney. There were not enough rifles for each man, just the few that they had used to practice how to dismantle and reassemble, plus a number of shotguns and non military rifles often kept on farms. At least Joe felt comfortable with the 'weapon' he had; it was a Hurling stick. Sean wasn't concerned assuming the Volunteers would supply the weapons when they were needed,

"This must be it Joe," he said, his excitement mounting as they joined in the day learning more about weapons and explosives. Joe was more relaxed but enjoyed the activity as well,

"We'll see what happens, for now we're just running around in circles." He would have preferred to be at Hurling training. They stayed at the McCormack farm all day training and returned to their own homes after dark.

Then four days later on the following Thursday Hugh informed them,

"We all need to be at McCormack farm on Easter Sunday morning at 3:00 am that means the whole Company. We'll get our orders then." Peter Keegan took the news from Hugh with some trepidation, he had seen how his sons had become more involved in the training and he wouldn't stand in their way.

"Mind how you go then." Was all he said when told where the boys had to be on Sunday. In the next village, Sean's father just encouraged his son to be careful and follow orders, at last things were beginning to happen. John McCormack had received his orders from Joe McGuiness from Longford the county next to Westmeath, they were signed by Patrick Pearse a man known by McCormack as very senior in the IRB. At 3:30 am, McCormack assembled the men in the early morning darkness. He was clearly ready for action, looking determined and resplendent in his new Volunteer uniform. He read from the papers in his hand.

"Company A and Company B will proceed to Athlone and attack the military barracks there; the goal will be to capture as many weapons as possible and make the area unusable for the RIC. This Company, Company C will be given the location of four road bridges which they will destroy with explosives. This will delay any British troop reinforcements to the area. Four groups of eight men will each attack one bridge." He looked out on the group in front of him nearly all in civilian clothes, a few in Volunteer uniforms, they were mostly young and all less than twenty-five years old he guessed.

He now spoke with great passion "I can inform you finally that our great struggle has now started. This is the beginning of the campaign to rid Ireland of the British overlords and achieve our long sought-after goal of an Independent Irish Republic. There will be armed activity by the Irish Volunteers all over the country and we will do our part as we have been ordered. The Brotherhood will not rest until this is accomplished. Long live the Republic!" He shouted and raised his right fist. All the men cheered in support.

Sean looked at Joe, his eyes blazing with excitement. He knew this was what he was born for, to fight for Ireland, he had no doubts and he knew no fear. Joe and Hugh were excited as well but more circumspect about what was expected of them, unlike Sean they did not expect it to be all easy going. There were various murmurs and discussion amongst all of the men waiting. Now it was war and they were going to soon find out what that actually meant. They waited in the gloom of the early morning before the sun came up.

However, all the sunrise delivered was a bitter pill of disappointment and they received it in a shocked state that brought home to them what being a soldier and having to follow orders meant.

Because the IRB leadership had made a mess of their own plans, there would be no fighting the British Imperialists that day in Westmeath or most of the other counties of Ireland. No liberation of the Irish people that day and no national uprising. Because of reasons difficult to comprehend, Dublin that Easter weekend would become the only battle standard for the whole country.

John McCormack couldn't believe his own eyes or ears when handed the second order that fateful morning signed this time by Eoin MacNeill the President of the Irish Republican Brotherhood based in Dublin.

"Stand down all men. All Previous orders are now cancelled and you are to await further instructions.

Signed

Eoin MacNeill   April 22nd 1916"

"Jesus, Mary and Joseph I was so confused," he would confess a couple of days later to his brother Tom, "there we were, all two hundred or so of us ready to march off to do damage to the targets we were set, a bunch to attack the Athlone Barracks and the rest to blow up four bridges. The men were on edge and ready to go, then this," he slapped the piece of paper in his hand and shook his head.

"You weren't the only ones" Tom replied, "I have spoken to the men from Dublin and it seems the same thing happened all over the country. Men ready to go and fight then stood down at the last minute without explanation." Tom lowered his voice to whisper level though no one was around to hear, "It seems the guns they were expecting from Germany never landed, ten thousand of them. How they expected to get them delivered all over the country is a mystery anyway, and Roger Casement who had arranged the shipment was rolled up by the Constabulary in Kerry near where the guns were supposed to be landed, seems they had been waiting for him for a week. He was dropped from a German submarine and they picked him up within twenty four hours. The whole thing was a shambles and that's why O'Neill sent the order. Not only that," he added with a tone of disgust, "O'Neill himself hadn't been told of the plan for the uprising by the Military Committee, and he's the President of the whole Brotherhood! Then he decided that he wanted to show them who was the boss and sent the order to stand down."

"Sweet Jesus," said John McCormack "we could have all been slaughtered." McCormack was emotionally shattered, was he seeing the start of another great Irish defeat?

But the order was either ignored or not received in Dublin. The Volunteers and the Citizens Army were too committed to stand down and hundreds of them marched onto the streets of Dublin targeting four important government buildings and other targets in the centre of the city. Dublin would soon be ablaze!

The Easter adventure came to an abrupt end for the volunteers of Westmeath.

But Sean wasn't prepared to be sidelined that easily.

CHAPTER 8
Easter 1916 Dublin City

When Hugh and his father, three years earlier had returned from their Dublin trip, Sean had pestered Hugh for news of the events there, the strike, the police attacks and the Citizens arming themselves for protection. Sean couldn't get enough information. He wanted to know the lie of the land, what parts of the city had been affected, and most importantly where did Patrick McCormack live and what were his politics? Hugh was happy enough to share whatever information he had, after all none of them were in Dublin, and Sean kept revisiting the topic with Hugh seemingly wanting to check every detail. He had also pestered John McCormack for information about his cousin Patrick and whatever he knew about the Citizen's Army and the developments in the capital city.

When the order was received in Drumraney early on Easter Sunday to stand down, Sean quickly came up with an alternate plan he wanted to put into action. He only told Joe and no one else,

"I'll go to Dublin if there's no fighting here." He said after the Easter stand down order was given, such was his enthusiasm for military action of some sort, "There will be something happening there and I want to be part of it." In fact, no one knew exactly what was going to happen in Dublin except a few senior men in the IRB and even they weren't sure how the action would proceed.

Early on the morning of Easter Sunday Sean walked back with Joe to their home, he could no longer contain himself,

"I'm going Joe, I'll get to Dublin and see what's happening. You should come with me, will you?" Joe wasn't convinced, and he was sure it was against some orders but he wasn't keen as Sean to see things happen, best to wait till they had more direction from the bosses.

"Don't be in such a hurry there will be plenty for all of us once it starts." They were still only seventeen years of age and Joe knew his Da wouldn't welcome his wandering off to Dublin, whatever the reason. They argued on for some time and Joe was concerned about what Sean might decide. Sean saw he wasn't going to convince Joe to go with him but his mood as he left Joe was all determination.

It took Sean seven hours to travel the fifty odd miles to Dublin, and he doubted many times if he would make it before dark which would make his task of finding Patrick McCormack's home more difficult. But make it he did via trains and buses and the occasional horse and cart ride; he had thought Athlone a big city but Dublin was much busier and more intimidating. He got off the train in the main city station and fought not to be overwhelmed by the sights of crowds of people and big buildings. He was surprised to see armed British troops wandering the streets not something he had seen around his home district so much, instinctively he gave them a wide berth not realising that the next day he would be even keener to keep out of their way.

He took Patrick's address from his pocket and tried to get his bearings, John McCormack had given him some directions but they were vague, he had given them willingly but never expected the lad would ever need them. Sean used his initiative as always and by pestering passersby got the general direction of where to go. He set off on foot not wanting to trust the city transport system. It was another hour before he stood at Patrick's door nervous and unsure if he would be welcomed. He wasn't a relative, just a friend of John McCormack and Hugh and Peter Keegan. He hoped those names would ensure Patrick's acceptance.

Patrick McCormack opened the door to Sean's knock, as an IRB member he didn't like to see strangers at his door but it was obvious the young man wasn't from Dublin Castle and he waited while Sean gave him his story and why he was there.

"Sure, and what good would you do without a weapon if there is trouble?" Patrick asked, not giving anything away. Sean had insisted he was there to do what he could for the revolution which Patrick himself wasn't even certain was going to happen.

"I could run supplies and deliver whatever needed to be delivered, I'm young and fit and ready to be of use."

"And you say you're with John McCormack's company in Drumraney, is that right?"

"Yes Mr McCormack" Sean replied enthusiastically, "We've been training for months and we were ready to move this morning on new targets but were all stood down just before dawn. None of us knew why. But I wanted to come to Dublin to see what was going on, that's why I'm here." This last piece of news from Sean troubled Patrick, he hadn't heard of any stand down orders, on the contrary he was waiting on the order to move into the city but he was still unsure of Sean. He was a last-minute complication he didn't need. At the same time, he didn't want to send him away if his story was true and he tended to believe the youngster with his enthusiasm and youth.

"Alright, you better come in and stay here, I'll have to take you at your word but I'm telling you that if you aren't what you say you are there will be dreadful consequences for you lad."

Patrick was trying to frighten his visitor but Sean had to realise that the hard men of the IRB wouldn't take chances if they decided they couldn't trust him. He would find out soon enough, volunteers were generally welcome but they came with a risk.

Patrick's wife served a starving Sean some bread and cheese and milk and watched as he took to their little ones. He had a natural liking for kids, they never annoyed him and they reminded him of his visits to the Keegan household with its brood.

Patrick was warming to Sean and he asked him questions about Hugh and Peter and what was happening in their county with the Volunteers and his answers were pretty well what he expected. He also described the McCormack farm and house to Patrick's satisfaction so he finally felt confident about his origins.

Another knock came on Patrick McCormack's front door at 3:00 am Easter Monday morning. He answered at once he had not been in bed but dozing in his downstairs front room.

"Patrick, it's time. The unit is getting together now behind St Stephen's Green." He knew the caller, Seamus Sullivan a neighbor, close friend and trusted member of the Brotherhood. He collected his Lee Enfield rifle, went up the stairs of his home and told his wife he was going. She feared the outcome of the day, she had no new words but as a strong supporter of him and the Brotherhood and its ideals she accepted that he must go. Patrick tried to ignore the tears in her eyes and the tremor in her voice:

"Go with God and bring us home a Republic." Was all she could say, Patrick nodded in the affirmative not trusting himself to say much, he kissed her then whispered, "Look after the boyos." nodding to the children asleep in the next room. With that he was gone, she heard the door close downstairs and said a prayer to accompany him.

Patrick collected Sean downstairs and introduced him to a surprised Seamus as he explained his presence,

"He'll be of good use to us, he's well trained and from good stock." He had invested in Sean and hoped he wasn't going to be disappointed.

Patrick and Seamus were joining over fifteen hundred other men and women in the streets of Dublin to carry out their duty. They had all been to meetings for the past six weeks when they were told of their units' orders and then told to go home, keep their wits about them, train themselves in handling their weapons and wait for their orders.

The city was still quiet in the early predawn but the three men and many others were scrambling around the city to meet up with their units. They hadn't been told of what was going to happen elsewhere or what the other targets were in the city. Sufficient that they knew what their orders were, which was to find their unit and join it in securing St Stephen's Green.

The three men scrambled through the tight inner-city streets which were filled with tenement housing, small shops, the odd factory or warehouse and carts waiting for the horses or donkeys to drag them around the city during the day.

"Do you know the way?" asked Seamus, he felt he did but wanted to be sure that Patrick who would nominally soon be his commanding officer also knew.

"Yes, follow me it will only take ten minutes." Both men were unaccustomed to carrying rifles around but they managed and were comforted by the ten rounds of ammunition they had been given the week before. "Down here," added Patrick as he turned another corner into a wider street. They had been told there wouldn't be many police around as the authorities had no expectation of what the day would bring. Then they saw another group of men with rifles heading in the same direction as themselves. "We must be going in the right direction or they're lost. It's only three blocks now." He was right, they came upon the Green quickly itself surrounded by buildings and streets with the hospital on one side and the Gaiety Theatre on the other. Men had already marched there from Liberty Hall and others like Patrick and Seamus joined them from various parts of the city. Major Mallin of the Irish Citizen's Army was in command and he set about having the men create barricades from whatever they could find. They had to make the open Green as secure as possible as the British soldiers would be on them soon enough. The Green was strategic to the city, eleven streets came into the area and it controlled access to many intersections that could be used by heavy vehicles.

"Sweet Jesus look at that would ye," said Patrick to the men around him, "it's Countess Markievicz," and there she was, as involved as any man in the group and they were told she was second in command. Her holstered revolver on her hip and her army uniform with jodhpurs and leggings were crowned by a slouch hat sporting a large ostrich feather. The enigmatic Countess whose title came from her Polish husband was to be a commanding presence in the fighting over the next few days. She was a senior officer in the Citizen's Army and loomed large in the politics of the times, an active suffragette and supporter of the poor and homeless in Dublin. She later created problems for the British Army who didn't know how to treat a woman in the front line and nor did her own troops.

The Citizen's Army made up the majority of the rebels who took over St Stephen's Green and a smaller amount of men including Patrick McCormack and Seamus were from the Irish Volunteers which made up the bulk of those who occupied the General Post Office and other Government buildings around Dublin. Patrick's IRB group had been seconded to the Citizen's Army to spread the numbers and balance the forces. He wasn't sure why they were with the Citizens army but he rationalized that they were all on the same side anyway. Who knew what went on when the leaders were issuing orders?

But that mattered little now that the hot war had started, as Patrick often said to his colleagues,

"There's no more talking now, we have taken on the British Empire and there'll be a reckoning. But that's what we want, we won't be taken for granted any longer, doffing our caps to the toffs. We'll be our own masters sooner or later." Patrick was pushing the IRB's point of view; the leaders knew there would be death and consequences for whoever went into the front line but it was a price that had to be paid.

The Countess met with Patrick and saw that he was a leader of a group of about fifteen men and they were Irish Volunteers and there to follow orders. Patrick explained the youthful Sean to her but she dismissed him with a shrug,

"He's your look out, now take your men and guard the park entrance over at Fusilier's Arch, there'll be another group along to join you, don't let anyone enter, send any civilians to their homes and of course keep an eye out for British troops, they'll be along in numbers soon enough." With that she turned on her heel and found another group that needed to be positioned, Patrick watched her while she organised the troops in formations around the Green. She was an impressive officer who obviously knew what she had to do and gave confidence to all the men she spoke to.

Patrick took his group to the Fusilier's Arch a memorial which had been put in place about ten years earlier, and located his men in a half circle around the entrance. Shortly after they were joined by another group of rebels from the Citizen's Army led by a young man of about twenty who Patrick recognised from his neighbourhood. He was a union organiser and had his men in place in no time. Between the two groups, they would be able to hold the entrance to the park until heavy equipment arrived with the enemy but that would be some time away and a worry for another hour. Civilians started coming to the entrance asking why their usual short cut through the Green was denied them, they had no idea they were watching the start of a revolution that would change the country forever. Sean watched as Patrick went about his duties, his eyes wide with wonder and admiration as to how he handled his responsibilities.

Patrick tried to calm the onlookers, groups grew larger and it was like there was a new tourist attraction in the Green and they had all come to see it,

"Go to your homes and stay there, but you must leave the streets for your own safety." The Dublin residents looked at him quizzically and at others in the Green who tried to move them on. A few wanted to argue, there was confusion and not a little hostility to this change to their daily routine. Many questioned why the men were there, some in uniform and some in civilian clothes but most with rifles and bandoliers around their chest. Many of the Dublin people had relatives fighting in France with the British Army and at the time without the benefit of any political news or warning they saw the rebels as traitors not immediately understanding what was happening or why.

The scenes were similar all around the city centre, rebels taking government buildings, all armed and dangerous and fewer police or soldiers around as it was a public holiday. Confusion reigned all over not least among the British soldiers and the Constabulary in Dublin who had no prior warning about the insurrection but were starting to worry about what was going on. It took many hours on that Monday for the army and government to realise what was happening.

A one sheet declaration by a Provisional Government to the People of Ireland heralding the Proclamation of the Republic of Ireland, which henceforth would be independent of the United Kingdom, was read aloud outside the General Post Office and posted prominently around the city by the armed rebels who had occupied that building.

News travelled by word of mouth and Patrick McCormack and his men were informed of the Proclamation by early afternoon. They looked at each other more seriously now, the future had arrived and now they must defend it. Major Mallin of the Citizen's Army and Countess Markiewicz and other officers were organising men and barricades with delivery carts and any motor vehicles commandeered and turned into protection walls for the rebels. The men took their positions and waited for the inevitable retaliation from the British Army.

By early afternoon the British finally realised that something major was going on as their Intelligence reports confirmed their worst fears and they started to organize themselves. Unbeknown to the rebels in the Green the British soldiers had now occupied buildings around the Green and soon after heavy gunfire started coming from the higher floors above the tree tops. Sean made himself useful by helping to build the barricades and running messages to the officers for Patrick, he also helped to distribute food and water to the men who couldn't leave their posts. He was so busy and involved he didn't have time for fear or to consider the dangers of what might happen to them all.

The men watched Major Mallin and the Countess for orders which came quickly,

"Defend your post and don't shoot any civilians, we're not at war with them, just the army." Patrick and Seamus and their mates sharpened their wits and took aim at the buildings and firing. They were grateful when it started to get darker making them lesser targets and brought some respite from the fusillades.

Patrick and his group were firing volleys into the void created by the increasing haze from gunpowder smoke, not sure what they were firing at but keen not to hit any civilians.

There was screaming and explosions and smoke and even fire, the British troops were seasoned veterans whereas the rebels had not experienced anything like this before. Certainly, the training they had done had not prepared them for the mayhem. Sean was staying right beside Patrick ready to follow any orders. There were men all along a barricade firing rifles and trying to ensure they weren't targets themselves. Suddenly the man beside Patrick slumped forward over his protected rampart, no scream, no noise, Patrick pulled at his tunic,

"Kevin what's the matter, are you good man?" Patrick and Sean had never seen a man killed before and the swiftness and suddenness of the action had taken their breath away. They rolled Kevin onto his back seeing a hole as big as a coin in the middle of his forehead and blood trickling down his face, "Sweet Jesus." Patrick muttered and crossed himself not knowing whether to scream for help or keep firing. Then a voice behind him, stern and sharp, brought him to his senses. It was Major Mallin,

"Keep your wits about you lads or you'll be next, they'll collect your friend in a minute." Patrick's eyes widened and he turned his head to speak to the Major but he had moved on. He knew the advice was correct as he heard more firing and volleys coming from the British troops. Patrick took Kevin's rifle and handed it to Sean,

"You better get used to using this lad, get some ammunition from Kevin's tunic, they'll hand out more soon enough." He looked at Sean's surprised expression, "you do know how to use it don't you?" his voice sharpening.

"Aye " said Sean and took the rifle and moved the bolt checking for a bullet in the chamber, he had been a fast and keen learner at his training and felt confident now he had a weapon to use. Sean had been struck by the presence of Major Mallin and his calmness in the face of the danger and Kevin's death he had been cool and in control despite the mayhem around him. The lesson on leadership would not be lost on Sean.

"Don't waste any bullets, we don't have many." Patrick barked at Sean as he took one last look at Kevin who was being taken away by the stretcher bearers with red crosses on their arm bands. Sean had cleared his pockets of any ammunition.

There was so much noise and shouting that Sean and Patrick believed the whole British army had arrived. Motorised vehicles, shouting officers and noncoms were ordering their men into place around the Green. The excessive noise meant the army wanted the rebels to know the army had arrived in numbers and meant business. Through the bushes and barricades Sean and the men inside could see glimpses of men running and sand bags being placed and barricades built on the other side of the hedges and fences. Patrick also noticed that the Shelbourne Hotel across the street had been taken over and sand bags built high to create a defensive position. No one inside the Green knew what the rebels' plan was, Patrick suspected that they would just try and hold out for a couple of days and hopefully join up with other units around the city. The IRB leadership wasn't expecting a capitulation by the British but they also weren't sure what to expect. With such foresight many uprisings are stillborn as this one would prove to be.

Major Mallin and Countess Markiewicz and other officers of the Citizen's army were busy making the rounds of stations talking to the men to keep their spirits high. The evening dragged on.

From time to time they heard rumours of what was happening elsewhere, despite the Army's best efforts to isolate the Green, couriers from other units managed to get messages through. Sean and Patrick heard the whispers among the one hundred and fifty plus men held up in the Green and rejoiced as much they could with the news that the General Post Office in the main street was being held by a group of rebels. They were withstanding the British onslaught that grew by the hour until eventually there were over ten thousand British troops grappling with the Irish Volunteers and the Citizen's Army occupying various parts of Dublin.

The rebels would later reflect on the last dispatch of James Connolly one of the leaders in the GPO, when he wrote: 'Courage boys, we are winning…never had a man or woman a grander cause, never was a cause more grandly served.'

Countess Markiewicz spoke to various groups during the night including Patrick and Sean and confirmed what was happening at the Post Office. She didn't have a comprehensive view of all actions for the day or who was winning, or what even winning would look like. But she insisted that the men at the Green would play their part bravely.

Patrick was bold enough to ask:

"How many men do we have in the city?" the Countess shrugged her shoulders and answered,

"We hope we have enough. But the British will have more. We will hold this position until we are told to do otherwise. Be prepared for the worst, there will be more troops and more action." With that she went off to another group away from the Fusilier's Arch. Patrick turned to Sean,

"Well you can see what you have invited yourself into now, sure and you weren't aware of that before you left your little village. From what she's saying it's going to get busier tomorrow. So, keep your head down." Patrick felt responsible for Sean who was only a few years younger but he recognised that Sean had taken on the full meaning of the revolution and would see it all out. Sean just nodded in agreement he was taking in as much as he could. But Patrick was right he hadn't known what fighting with guns against those who wanted to kill you was going to be like. But too late for that now, he would do what he could and not disgrace himself.

By nightfall, the rebels realised that their cover in the Green was totally inadequate and they needed to find more shelter. The orders came and they all were to leave the Green and take up positions somewhere safer that could accommodate them. It was the Royal College of Surgeons in Ireland (RCSI) office building across the street that was chosen and the rebels took it over at five thirty on the Tuesday morning after a harrowing and cold night in the Green, they would spend the next five to six days there. Gradually, all the men had left the Green and took up positions in the office block. The men could hear heavy artillery rounds exploding and knew they had to be coming from the British side as the rebels had no big guns. Sean wondered what it would be like to be on the receiving end of those blasts.

As it was, he was soon to find out. He had seen Patrick talking to Major Mallin in their new headquarters in the Surgeons' building. Patrick kept glancing at Sean and nodding, eventually he summonsed Sean to join them.

"Major Mallin is looking for a volunteer to go into the city and try to find out what is happening and get back here quickly." Sean just looked at him waiting for the next lot of words. "He thinks someone young like yourself will have more chance of getting through any checkpoints, but of course you must avoid them if possible. You have some identification that says you're from Westmeath I hope?" Sean again just nodded and produced a student card from his old school with his home address, he thought he should take it with him when he first decided to come to Dublin in case anything happened and his parents had to be informed. He hadn't thought it might be this dramatic though. Patrick continued "Good, if you are stopped just make out you had come to Dublin to visit some friends, you have my address but you got lost and caught up in the mayhem. Play on your youth and act scared, they shouldn't want to hold you, of course you can't have a gun on you." Patrick was adamant about that it would be enough reason to be shot if caught with one. Then, Major Mallin spoke,

"You may be safer out on the streets than here lad, at least for a few hours, make your way to the Post Office and keep your eyes open, keep out of sight and don't speak to anyone. Find out what you can and make your way back here, use the back entrance, we'll be looking out for you." Sean managed a yes sir in reply. He wondered why they had chosen him but as Patrick said, he was young, an older man would be more suspicious. Sean soon realised that combat situations didn't give a lot of options you went with what you had and took your chance. Patrick had recommended Sean to the Major as a reliable messenger, plus it would get him out of the shooting for a few hours.

"God go with you" said Patrick as Sean gave him his rifle and left the building as quickly as he could.

Just keep heading north towards the river Patrick had said, but Sean didn't have a map and had to rely on instinct. Watching carefully for any military patrols or RIC officers, Sean kept to the side streets and somehow found the River Liffey and turned right to where he could see fires in the distance. He came to the Ha'penny Bridge and as there was no one around hurried across it careful not to break into a run and attract attention. The Government hadn't had time to impose a curfew as yet that would happen the next day when Martial Law would be imposed on the whole country. Some people were still walking around like tourists as though nothing was going on. As Sean approached Sackville Street (later O'Connell Street) which housed the GPO, the area became busier and more troops than he had ever seen were sitting in trucks and along the sidewalks. He stayed within the crowds who were being contained by the police and he kept away from the danger areas. Despite the dangers people were attracted like a moth to a flame by the activity. Sean saw an alleyway and went down it hoping it would take him closer to the main street which it did. He poked his head around the corner and was taken aback by the destruction he saw, a number of buildings were ablaze and looked ready to fall down. He could just make out the tower on the GPO and saw the field artillery on the street and British soldiers attending it. He was just about to walk into the street when a bullet flew past his head missing him by inches, he threw himself back into the alley and ran to the other end, clearly

Sackville Street was not welcoming pedestrians this day. He wasn't sure what he would report to Major Mallin but he felt that what he had seen didn't bode well for the revolution. He stopped running when he reached the crowd still in the back streets hoping he was out of sights of any trigger-happy soldiers. He could hear the talk of the people around him and tried to make out what they were saying, but they knew little, it was all speculation, hearsay and gossip but it would have to do as intelligence for the Major. The best gossip he could take back was that Mount Street Bridge was being held by the rebels further down the river and the Army was suffering substantial loss of men trying to take it.

Sean made it to the back entrance of the College of Surgeons building near the Green and it became obvious that he was not the only scout sent out into the city. Not that it mattered, in war you are only told what you need to know not what everyone else was doing. He found Patrick and was taken to Major Mallin and passed on what he had seen though he had little good news. His sighting of the artillery was confirmed by others who also reported a British gun boat on the river firing into the city towards the post office. The British had come out in full force once they knew what was happening which was that the whole country might be in revolt and would have been if not for the incompetence of the IRB and Volunteers leadership.

For the next four days, the rebels in the building survived on bread, cheese and water if they could get any and took positions firing at wherever they thought British troops might be. It was a forlorn time and the disconsolate expression on Major Mallin's face was consistent with the unusual lack of confidence shown by Countess Markiewicz.

At midday on the Sunday after Easter the rebels in the College of Surgeons surrendered joining the other groups in various parts of the city who, though wanting to hold out accepted that their position was hopeless. Sean and Patrick along with many others were spirited out of the building before the surrender, their orders were to keep the fire of revolution burning however they could. The battle may have been over but the war had not been lost, thundered Countess Markiewicz.

     #   #

The remaining one hundred and twenty rebels who had taken the Green originally surrendered to the British army around midday and were among the three and a half thousand, mostly men but some women, arrested that day and the following days. Nearly five hundred people including many civilians lost their lives that week in the bloodiest expression of Irish nationalism in many years and hundreds more were wounded and thousands left homeless. The British Empire had faced its first major challenge from those it had colonised over the past three hundred years and everyone's world would change beyond imagining.

The next morning Sean bid goodbye to Patrick who hadn't been able to bring home a Republic to his wife and thanked him for his trust. He made his way back to Athlone then Drumraney by train along with many others deserting the devastated city, he was leaving the carnage of Dublin behind for the time being. He was anxious but excited to tell Joe and Hugh what he had experienced and if he could, how much it had changed him. At the very least, he now knew what a fight they all had before them to gain independence for their beloved Ireland.

     #   #

During May, shortly after he had arrived home, Sean was with Joe and Hugh when the news came through of the executions of the leaders of the rebellion. Hugh read the newspaper reports to them,

"The seven signatories of the proclamation of the Irish Republic had all been put in front of a firing squad at Kilmainham Jail and eight other leaders of the revolution shortly after had joined them in their macabre end. James Connolly had been tied to a chair, unable to stand because of his wounds to face his executioners." In August Roger Casement whom the British could never forgive for approaching Germany for weapons joined his fellow revolutionaries by being hanged in Pentonville Prison.

The executions were an astonishing act of arrogance by the British and were a major factor in turning the tide of Irish passion and opinion against them and behind a now revitalised national mood of rebellion.

Hundreds of rebels were transported to English prisons, eventually to Frongoch in Wales which eventually became known as The Republican University as Irish prisoners were tutored fully with rebel stories and how to next fight the English. Eight hundred and sixty of the prisoners were released in July and many of the balance in a general amnesty in December 1916. 'As a present to the Irish people.' the British Prime Minister Lloyd George proclaimed apparently on a mission to win back Irish hearts and minds. But it was more of a gesture to an America sympathetic to the Irish cause to try and lure them into the still raging European war.

Hugh read another press statement he knew Sean would want to hear:

"Countess Markiewicz had been sentenced to death, not by a Court but by the British Governor, the sentence was commuted to life imprisonment due to her gender. Eamonn de Valera's death sentence was also commuted because of his American parentage."

The Countess was ultimately released in June 1917 with many of the other leaders.

Sean and Joe were now totally committed to the cause of Irish Nationalism and a Republic. The Irish Volunteers would later become the Irish Republican Army a military organisation dedicated to the mortal struggle for Ireland's future. The two friends' ambitions were in lockstep with those of the IRA. Their paths had been laid out and would take them on a journey that would require great sacrifices.

CHAPTER 9
1917 – 1919

The two years between the end of the Easter uprising in 1916 and the start of the War of Independence brought turmoil to the country while a ferocious war raged in Europe. Hundreds of thousands of young lives had been lost on the fields of Belgium and Northern France. Names like the Somme and Flanders Field and Villers Brettoneux would live in history as a testament to the futility of war and its waste of human life.

In Ireland the people led by the firebrands of the IRA and Sinn Fein continued to protest against rule by Britain. Many of the political and military elite of the Easter events had been released from Frongoch prison in Wales and were back in Ireland still agitating for new actions. The main leaders had been executed after the uprising. It had been an event which galvanised the resistance and gave it a national spirit and momentum it had previously lacked. The sixteen who had been executed for their part in the uprising became household names and heroes to virtually every Catholic Irishman and Irishwoman. Prayers and masses were held throughout the country in their honour vast processions accompanied their funerals. Their memories would never die.

Sean and Joe joined with a local Westmeath leader named Sean Hurley who had organised a small Company around Drumraney which would later join other groups and grow into the Athlone Brigade. Now young men in their late teenage years, Sean and Joe enthusiastically joined in the parades of the newly formed Company. Hugh was required on the farm to work with his father and for the present had less time to spend on military training.

Joe was also pursuing his love of Hurling and trained and played as much as time and commitment allowed. It was obvious he was a natural athlete and had a gift for the game which was physically demanding and dangerous. Joe now in his late teen years was a handsome young man with a farmer's tan and black hair and brown eyes. This separated him from the more traditional fair skinned and auburn haired people found in much of Ireland. His colouring was thought to have come from earlier Spanish influence and was shared by his brothers. It was not uncommon in the west of Ireland. It also gave Joe an impressive presence and his wiry six feet tall frame confirmed his athleticism.

Sean was more of the traditional Irish look with auburn hair turning to red or ginger with curls to match. His skin was fair but his frame like Joe's had been shaped by hard physical work and his pursuit of sport. About the same height as Joe, Sean was also handsome and they could have been seen as brothers except for their different colouring. Sean shared Joe's interest in Hurley and also Gaelic football but did not pursue them to the same intensity as Joe. Sean preferred to immerse himself in the administration of the IRA Drumraney Company and worked with the older hands to grow enlistment and train new men. He also read as much as he could about the history of Ireland both ancient and modern. He also loved the mythology of the country which had its own magic. Tales of the "little people" or leprechauns abounded. They were part of every village and district each with their own distinctive flavor.

Sean and Joe met regularly and discussed and argued the political situation. Their reading was confined to the Westmeath Examiner and the occasional Dublin papers like the Irish Independent if they could get hold of them. Virtually every county had its own newspaper or two and most were independent and outspoken on the events of the day both home and overseas. The young men had plenty of news about politics. The IRA and numerous political parties pumped out significant amounts of news and propaganda for searching minds. The challenge was not to believe everything you read! It was almost as good as a university education which these young men could never contemplate. Apart from the cost the places were reserved for the privileged few, mostly Anglo Irish families in Dublin. Often the only recourse for young Catholic men in Ireland was to join the priesthood and receive a wider education in the Maynooth Seminary. But that option never appealed to Joe or Sean, they took their learning from their talks with the likes of John McCormack and his generation and immersed themselves in revolutionary politics.

Like everyone else they were appalled by the treatment of men who were still in prison and continued to be arrested for being part of an underground movement. Men like Thomas Ashe who had fought valiantly in Easter 1916 and who had to disengage and surrender after a battle with a large unit of British soldiers. After spending time in an English prison and then being dispatched back to Ireland in a general amnesty. Ashe was rearrested in County Longford and sent to Mountjoy prison in Dublin. There he and his friends went on a hunger strike and demanded prisoner of war status but they were initially refused any concessions. Ashe's death changed the equation and to pacify the city the authorities granted Prisoner of War status to the remaining rebels in prison. For weeks stories of Ashe had filled the newspapers and he quickly became a new and revered hero for Joe and Sean.

"Jesus Joe would ye look at this," said Sean as they sat at Sean's home reading the Dublin newspaper. "Thomas Ashe has been force fed and now he has died. The Brits had refused him any assistance except shoving a tube down his throat and it killed him." Sean was beside himself with rage and continued reading, "It only took eight days and they killed him." Sean shook his head in confusion unable to console himself. Joe took up the newspaper and kept reading. His anger was manifest as well and he ached to do something meaningful rather than just sit there and complain about Ashe's treatment. Then he had an idea and new Sean would support him.

"The funeral is in Dublin and the mass is at the Cathedral." He looked up at Sean "The least we should do is honour him there."

"Good idea Joe, we need to be there." Sean was fired up as much as Joe burning with frustration at the idea of their hero's death so the next day they gathered the few things they needed and told their families they would be back in a couple of days. Despite the inconvenience their families understood their need to go to the funeral and honour the man who had been killed so callously.

They travelled to Dublin by train, Sean's second visit and Joe's first and despite the solemn nature of their visit, Sean walked Joe around the city and showed him the sites where so much had taken place just over a year earlier. Many buildings were still in ruins and Joe couldn't believe the amount of destruction that had taken place. Sean was keen for Joe to see St Stephen's Green where he had spent those dangerous days in 1916.

"It was fierce Joe, they came at us like devils with everything they had, cannons, thousands of soldiers, tanks and armoured cars. We were outnumbered and out gunned a hundred to one." Seeing it all for himself it now made sense to Joe. Being told about it from afar didn't work, you had to see the damage to understand the dangers everyone must have felt.

Sean and Joe made their way to the Cathedral for the mass for Ashe but couldn't get inside. It was packed and hundreds more stood outside. The body was then moved to City Hall and Sean and Joe lined up with thousands of others to pass by the coffin of the man they never knew but felt immense respect for. Joe was amazed at the outpouring of grief by those around him at the City Hall and in the city generally. Many thousands more lined the streets as the coffin holding Thomas Ashe was transported to Glasnevin Cemetery for its final resting place. By this time Joe was in tears and struggling to understand his own feelings, Sean put an arm around his shoulder as always the calm one, and comforted him. The whole experience had affected them strongly and as they made their way back to Athlone and their homes they talked about what Ashe had achieved, one man with huge courage had forced the British Government to grant political status to the Irish Republican prisoners who had been imprisoned as a result of the Easter Uprising. It was an immense achievement and his ultimate sacrifice burnt into the hearts of Sean and Joe and their countrymen.

The next month the men proudly joined the Drumraney Company in a national activity that the Irish Volunteers Executive organised. All members of every active unit in the country, in defiance of British restrictions, were to parade in uniform, if they had one, in their local areas. It was an action that did little more than organise the many Volunteers members to join a parade and show national defiance and symbolically it sent a very strong message to the British Government and their representatives at Dublin Castle. Sean and Joe marched proudly beside each other, Sean with a rifle shouldered and Joe the same though, like many others, with a Hurling stick as they marched through a village near Athlone.

It was not the only show of patriotism in the country that year.

In 1918 the whole of Ireland was part of the United Kingdom, the same as Scotland, England and Wales, and as such had elected representatives in the British Parliament at Westminster. However due to the conflict of World War 1, the returning soldiers and the change in population plus a wider voting franchise granted for both men and women there was a new demographic in Ireland which was to change the political landscape. Traditionally the Irish Parliamentary Party sent representatives to London voted in by a more conservative and older electorate. But in this year the ultra Nationalism of the new Irish party Sinn Fein created a new wave of voting preferences and Sinn Fein gained seventy three of one hundred and five seats available to Ireland. It was the biggest change the country had ever seen and the sentiment for change and Irish Independence and Republicanism gained a momentum that would not be easily stopped.

Shortly after, the National Executive of Sinn Fein at their Convention at Mansion House in Dublin named Eamonn De Valera as President of the Irish Republic. At a separate meeting at the Gaelic Athletic Association owned Croke Park, Cathal Brugha was named as Chief of Staff of the IRA by the IRA Army Council. These elected Office Bearers were just two of the seventy-three Sinn Fein politicians that then refused to take their seats at Westminster after the 1918 election.

This would be a government for Ireland not Westminster.

But the Irish Republic, the IRA and de Valera's election to President was not recognised by the British Government. As far as Britain was concerned Ireland was still a subservient colony of the British Empire.

Sean and Joe heard the news of the appointments and revelled in their significance, they knew this was a major step in the direction of a Republic of Ireland. No one could pretend anymore that major events would not now unfold.

And the next major event would be unfolded by the Irish not the British.

CHAPTER 10
GAELIC SUNDAY

Up to this time Joe hadn't been overly involved in the actual politics of the movement they had both joined leaving it to others to determine its goals and navigate the way through. Instead he had focused on his Hurling and was nearing County selection. It seemed though that the politics within the Gaelic Athletic Association had been having an impact on his political views. They were after all a major influence on the national viewpoint and used their weight to move matters along politically when they could, using sport as their chosen vehicle. Politics was impossible to escape in the day to day life of most Irish people. Joe had come to some conclusions which he insisted were his own and explained them during yet another political discussion with Sean. Joe said it simply but forcibly,

"There will be a Republic and it will be all thirty two counties, it will be one Ireland on one island." He was sincere and dogmatic and Sean was in no doubt he was passionate in his belief. Joe had arrived at a personal point of view that he was comfortable with. Sean was sure he had been indoctrinated via his sports interest but he was impressed with his friend's words and congratulated him on his stance. Joe said again, "It has to be a Republic Sean. We can't allow the British to push us around any longer." As was his habit, Joe was emphasising his point by the use of his Hurling stick, pointing and shaking it at nothing in particular but mindful that it held menace. Sean had no doubt about his own commitment to the issue but as was his habit he tended to take a more pragmatic and practical view of what it would all mean to themselves personally and to the country. He was looking past independence at what the country would be like after it happened. There would be a need for strong government, a strong army and dedicated servants of the people and he knew he wanted to be an important part of that future.

For the present those dreams would have to wait, there were many issues to be dealt with long before the ideal Ireland arrived.

To bait Joe and lighten the mood, Sean tried to wrestle his Hurling stick from him and for the next five minutes they were at each other as they had been continually since they were kids. Always in good heart, wrestling of a kind, no punches, just holds that could be painful but never malicious. It was a test of strength of sorts but usually neither one would come out on top, that wasn't the objective. Finally, they stopped and settled on a draw,

"I'll let you off this time Joe but don't be shaking that stick at me again." It was typical Sean trying to sound tough and in charge but Joe knew where he was coming from and replied in kind,

"Try and take it again you cute hoor and I'll brain you with it." They both had a chuckle at each other's comments till Joe turned serious, "You're hearing about what the GAA has had to put up with?" he asked. Sean had heard some stories but knew Joe would be closer to the issue that had been brewing behind the scenes for some time.

Conscription to the British army had been in the public space in Ireland since 1914 and wouldn't go away. The British appointed administration in Dublin was sympathetic to their master's needs in London and so kept the idea on the boil, much to the consternation of most people in Ireland. The administration was well aware that the GAA was a potent force in the land and a strong opponent of conscription and they sought to curtail its opposition fearful that it would become a vehicle for insurrection. Joe told Sean the background:

"You know the government a year ago told the GAA that there would be an entertainment tax which was going to include all sporting events? Well the GAA resisted and refused to pay the tax and barred their member organisations from doing so as well. Of course, the coppers couldn't keep out of it and started harassing the GAA's sporting events to enforce the tax laws, causing more bad blood. A proclamation no less, was issued by the Lieutenant General, which banned" and here he searched his memory and quoted, "The holding or taking part in any meetings, assemblies or processions within the whole of Ireland. The GAA was informed this included sporting events and they were required to obtain permits if they wanted to hold any matches." Sean now understood that Joe had been talking politics with people in the GAA as he was never that close to specifics of what the government was doing day to day. He listened as Joe went on: "The GAA calls this a spear into the heart of Irish social life. It was obvious that the government wanted to stop any public assembly for any reason. Scared shitless they were that the conscription issue would blow up and cause riots or worse. Well the GAA isn't going to stand still for that rubbish and we have big plans coming."

The use of 'we' struck Sean it was becoming clearer to him that Joe's thinking had been shaped by his involvement with the sports organisation but in a positive way. Seeing Joe in this new light also informed Sean that the whole tenor of thinking was taking place throughout the country. To Sean, seeing Joe's immersion into the politics was in a small way confirmation that a sea change was possible. He hoped the rest of the population felt the same way.

"So, what's afoot then and when?" Sean asked.

"The GAA is planning for Sunday, August 8th. What will happen is that this will be Gaelic Sunday. Gaelic games all across the country, in every village and town and city. Hurling, football, camogie, handball, athletics, whatever the locals can arrange on the fields they have available, whether they're proper fields or paddocks. At three o'clock that afternoon there will be thousands of events and it doesn't matter who wins or loses, as long as they are played." Joe was smiling, obviously pleased with himself and his involvement in what was planned. "I've been working with Father Slattery and a few of the local teachers, anyone who volunteers in sports. In Drumraney alone we should have over six games, more if we can find the space to hold them. This will come in handy." He said as he shook his Hurling stick once more in Sean's direction.

Sean was impressed, he had been so immersed in his work with the Brigade that he had not realised what was going on elsewhere but it was obvious the GAA had decided it wasn't going to be pushed around by the government. Nationally it had a lot of influence in the sporting clubs right around the country and it was going to send a strong message to the people of Ireland who knew that without regular competition and organisation any sport would be useless.

"You can count us all in for sure. We'll be playing, I'd love to get the stick around your shins and show you how the game is played." Sean said with a wicked smile, but Joe responded in kind, and replied,

"You should be so lucky you'll be on your back before you know it, crying for your Ma and looking for a way home."

Came the great day and Drumraney played its part and people came from great distances to take part as players or spectators. It was a day that many would remember with fondness. It was that spirit of competitiveness and good nature that sport generated that made the day a success, **'A National Day of Defiance'** the press called it, and as Joe would say, what else would you call it. The next day Joe read from a newspaper to Sean;

"Fifty thousand participants in over fifteen hundred games at venues all over the country, all starting at three o'clock in the afternoon, rain or shine. Plus, many thousands more as spectators, who took up every vantage point to cheer on their team. Every town and district had its own venue whether it was on the banks of rivers or on village greens, wherever posts could be stuck up and spaces cleared, the games took place and the occasion provided a unique display of the popularity of Gaelic Games. In one never to be forgotten tournament we crossed our Hurleys with the lion's claw and emerged victorious." Joe was beaming with pride and grateful he had been able to be part of such a day's organisation. He ignored the bruise on his shins that he was sure Sean had delivered in a long outstanding payback for a lump Joe had left on his head when they were much younger.

For now, there was more military training for the two friends to prepare for who knew what?

CHAPTER 11
1918 THREAT OF CONSCRIPTION

Still locked in a seemingly unwinnable war in Europe, Britain needed more troops. Ireland seemed a fertile patch for more fighting men even though many thousands of young men had already joined the British Army and had been sent to Europe to fight in the trenches. But on March 25, 1918 the British Parliament passed a law extending the Conscription Act to include Ireland. The young men targeted went in the other direction and flocked to join the Irish Volunteers even though such a move would not exempt them from conscription.

Sean was on hand to see the growth of volunteers as he was helping in the administration of what would later become the IRA's Athlone brigade. Many young men who until then had resisted the romance of the revolutionary activities of the IRB decided that if they were going to be in an Army, they'd prefer to be in one they could call their own. Sean was delighted to tell Joe and others that he had read soon after the March 25 announcement that the US President Woodrow Wilson had told Lloyd George that he foresaw political trouble in America if the conscription of the Irish went ahead. The unspoken message was that it wasn't an idea that America could support politically. Nevertheless, the British government pushed through its Military Services Bill clearing the way for Irish conscription. But events overtook the need for it. And the issue of Conscription in Ireland was resolved with the signing of the Armistice on November 11th.

Finally, the war in Europe was over but for the Irish the issue of Home Rule was now definitely back on the agenda and passions were rising. The younger and more restless leaders of the IRB and the IRA and Sinn Fein had a louder and stronger voice and were intent on being heard. The time had arrived to demand Home Rule and a Republic and if it wasn't granted, they would take it. Sean found himself in conversation one day with John McCormack who had been put forward as a candidate for Sinn Fein in the upcoming elections for Irish members of the British Parliament, due on December 14.

"So, John, what will you do in the Parliament, are you looking forward to going to Westminster?" asked Sean who had little understanding of the political processes that drove such matters. John smiled at the younger man,

"Well we'll do nothing of the sort it's not our intention to go to Westminster and argue the toss with the gentry over there and get nowhere. They'll just ignore us, pat us on the head and tell us to go and sit down and wait our turn. Well we've done enough of that over the years and we won't be doing any more of it." Sean was a little surprised and didn't understand.

"But surely you will have to go and argue for Home Rule and start the process, isn't that what elections are for?"

"Usually, and if you were an Englishman you would enjoy going to Westminster for that purpose. But we are definitely not Englishman, we are Irishmen and by not going we will be making the point that our Parliament will be in this country, not someone else's, our capital will be Dublin, not London. They'll be forced to see our point of view. The days of pretending that we are honorary Englishmen are over, and pretending that we are British subjects is well past time. We will be Irish citizens with our own Parliament and our own Constitution and our own Republic." They were the words of a true revolutionary who believed that what was seen as a pipedream by some was a realistic and achievable goal. In

November 1918 the Armistice in Europe set the scene for momentous Irish Parliamentary elections in December.

A few days after the election Sean was visiting the Keegan farm and listened in on a conversation Hugh started with his father and mother,

"Did Uncle John win his seat Da?" Hugh asked his father. John McCormack had run on the Sinn Fein ticket for the seat that straddled Westmeath and Longford.

"He did my boy, so there'll be politics aplenty in the McCormack household." Hugh knew his father had a limited interest in politics so he looked to his mother for more information.

"Yes, he won and so did another 72 Sinn Fein representatives, so Sinn Fein have 73 out of 115 Irish seats in Westminster." She then added with a laugh, "Not that it matters none of them will go to London anyway. That's all part of the plan." Through her contacts with Cumann na mBan, Mary had heard the news soon after it was posted.

"What is it going to mean Ma?" Hugh asked not quite understanding the politics of the situation. Obviously, it was good news that Sinn Fein had been successful, but where to from here?

"We'll just have to wait and see but I'm sure the IRB leaders have plenty in mind." It was all Mary could add. Certainly the whole country was in waiting for the next political move and what it would mean. Hugh went to discuss the matter with Joe and Sean. Politics had become the favourite topic in many Irish households throughout the country and now the younger lads were keen to know what the future held. Seventy three Sinn Feiners not going to be in London, no one knew what would come of it! Sean mentioned his earlier talk with John McCormack when he had indicated then that Sinn Fein would boycott Westminster. Now it would come to pass.

Christmas 1918 came and the Keegan family celebrated with their cousins the McCormacks at their farm. After the Christmas mass on Christmas morning there was a gathering at the McCormack farm and as was the custom a lamb and several chickens were prepared for the big lunch. The women of the families, as also was the custom, prepared the meal. The men had saved a few bottles of stout and some homemade brews of beer and poteen and Irish whisky also flowed, loosening tongues and making for a lively Irish Catholic Christmas day.

Sean and his family joined in the afternoon, every one trying to keep warm around a big open fire in the yard. They wouldn't stay late as the days were short and there was a need to get home before dark. At this time, many lived in fear of the Spanish Flu epidemic which had ravaged many countries around the world and everyone knew someone's family who had suffered loss of life because of the epidemic.

In spite of the dangers, politics needed to be discussed and Sean, Joe and Hugh huddled together and talked of the future and all congratulated John McCormack on his victory. Even Patrick and his family had come up from Dublin to share in the festivities. Sean was proud to introduce him at last to Joe and talked about the events of Easter week 1916 which they had shared.

Inevitably a game of Gaelic football was called for and despite the snow on the ground all the men, young and old took part in a game that appeared to have few rules apart from a constant battle for the round ball. It was one of the few days of rest the farmers and their families had during the year and the Keegan family eventually had to pile onto their skip and head home. More farm work beckoned the next day even though the winter had truly set in.

#   #

January brought the year of 1919 which would become significant in Irish history. In Dublin on January 21st the first Dail Eireann was established by the newly elected Sinn Fein members who had refused to go to Westminster. Those who could went to Dublin instead to make their very own Irish Parliament at the Mansion House but many elected members were still in British prisons! This action sent an unmistakable message to Westminster which refused to recognise the new institution and labeled it outlaw. But the new Dail officially proclaimed the Republic of Ireland and took over the responsibility for the Irish Volunteers who later that year became the Irish Republican Army. Michael Collins and other Cabinet members were deep in deciding tactics for armed conflict if the British denied them what they wanted.

On the same day, a few miles north of a Tipperary town near a quarry named Soloheadbeg, two RIC policemen were killed by an IRA ambush that sought the gelignite that the policemen were guarding on a patrol.

It was the first action of what would become the War of Independence for Ireland.

BOOK 2

THE WAR OF INDEPENDENCE

CHAPTER 12
1919 – 1922
County Kildare

Joe Keegan and Sean McKeon hadn't targeted the young Black and Tan they had just killed, he had made himself a target. He just happened to cross their path at a bad time. They couldn't allow themselves to dwell on the soldier's fate, that wouldn't help their situation, it would hinder it. Their responsibility now was to escape and reach their safe area. Taking out GHQ appointed targets when they found them, then disappearing was what they were told to do. They were following orders and the 'Tan got in the way. That's war, Sean said to Joe with no further explanation.

As young men they couldn't fully process what they were doing. Taking a life when necessary is surely a soldier's job, but thinking like that never made it easier. Sean and Joe often talked about the speed at which their lives had changed and why. They were caught up in the IRA movement and you had to make a decision, if that decision was to get involved, then this is what involvement meant. Sean couldn't make any more of it than that, he had his strong beliefs in what they were doing, what was happening in the country but that was it. They were in it and they would see it through, you blocked out everything else.

What was now called the Irish War of Independence had been underway for a number of months. The two young men were beginning to feel the impact the life of a guerrilla soldier was having on them. Sometimes their target was a Black and Tan officer, other times it was a suspected traitor, an Irishman who had committed the unforgivable sin of giving information to the enemy. It was never pleasant work and they discussed it between themselves but accepted it as part of their duty, the results didn't bear thinking about.

This day they had been running for some time since the shooting without sighting any pursuers, though they heard some shouts at one point but couldn't see anyone. They found a small group of trees that offered some cover. Sean spoke quietly,

"Let's take a break here for a while and see if anything is happening." Joe didn't need a second invitation. They each slid down beside a big tree to catch their breath both looking from where they had come, aware that the danger they couldn't see or hear was more of a threat than one they could see.

They reloaded their revolvers, they had used three bullets each, and they waited in silence not wanting to make any noise to draw attention to their hiding spot. It was going to be a long day, they were worn out and needed to wash, eat and sleep. They hadn't slept in their own homes for over three weeks. Joe started to say something but Sean shut him down with a stare and a wave knowing what was on Joe's mind. Killing the soldier was unplanned and wasn't their original task but GHQ would call the killing a bonus. Talking about it now wouldn't help.

After a break they started walking again keeping to the hills and woods for cover. They had been going for four hours when they stopped, Sean took his bearings refreshing the information he had been given to find their temporary hideout. They were in the hills of County Kildare and he knew they were close his sense of direction hadn't let him down.

They saw the shelter after some more searching. It appeared abandoned and was well hidden away among trees and shrubs, two miles from the nearest village. It was a decrepit hut for shepherds who needed shelter from the cold winters of central Ireland. The winds that came off the west coast Atlantic Ocean had a ferocity about them that all of Ireland felt in one way or another.

The temperature had dropped steadily during the day and the men were more than grateful for the shelter. They had been walking and often running and skirting villages and main roads for the past four hours to ensure they weren't seen, getting as far away from their last encounter as they could. Patrols of Black and Tans were always a possibility and though they wanted to trust all their fellow countrymen there was the constant fear that someone would report their movements to the authorities. It had all been part of their training, don't trust anyone you don't know and even then, be very careful.

It was late afternoon and getting dark and cold,

"I'd kill for a Guinness and a lamb roast." said Joe quietly, only half serious.

Sean smiled,

"More likely some dried bread and water if we're lucky." They walked within fifty yards of the shelter, it would have been generous to call it a cottage and approached it slowly and kept out of sight to ensure it was deserted. There were no lights or movement. Sean signalled to Joe with a finger to his lips keep quiet, and pointed to his eye with one finger, and made a circling motion with his hand; let's look around first. They drew their revolvers from out of their coat pockets and circled the cottage which promised shelter. It would have in the recent past housed a permanent resident, probably a shepherd. It was built of stone with one window and one door and the stone fences in the field seemed to go on forever. They got within eyesight of each other after circling and Joe saw Sean's eyes bulge as he targeted his revolver at the front door. He was within a moment of letting off a shot when he stopped,

"Bloody fox," he said and let the gun down as a red fox scampered into the shrubs frightened by the movement of the two men. Their nerves were on edge and they looked forward to some kind of rest for the rest of the night. "Joe, we'll have to risk a peat fire but we need to keep the smoke to a minimum, my clothes are soaked and I bet yours are too. My shoes could grow turnips they're that wet." Joe nodded in agreement but what they could actually do would need to be decided when they saw inside. Joe pushed the door open confident enough that they were safe, at least from foxes. Sean stood beside him revolver at the ready and aimed directly at the middle of the door opening, there wasn't much to see, the inside was black as pitch. Sean edged to the door and let his eyes grown accustomed to the darkness if there had been enemy inside they would have been dead by now.

Joe shrugged which Sean took to mean we may as well go in and be done with it. They pushed through the door revolvers at the ready, no one was there. An old wooden table with two chairs sat in the middle of the floor, a fireplace and something that resembled a bed on the far side, bits and pieces of crockery and cutlery were in a metal bucket, there was no tap, no kitchen of course. They looked at each other and Sean closed the door and said,

"Well it's not the Connaught, but it will do." It was a reference to the top hotel in Dublin, now housing Black and Tan officers and no one else. "No steak Joe" said Sean. But as they had been promised the local IRA people had left dried bread and cheese wrapped in a gingham cloth in what looked like a picnic basket, and thankfully some dry matches and half a candle to see them through the night. Sean with a big grin on his face lifted a bottle of the black stuff; a bottle of Guinness stout to be drunk with the bread and cheese.

"Sweet mother of God" said Joe, "they can keep the Connaught this will do me."

"I'll take first watch" said Sean, "but let's try and get this fire going and dry these clothes." It took them the best part of half an hour to arrange the fire and spread the wettest of their clothes to try and get them dried. They wrapped themselves in some smelly blankets always keeping their revolvers in close reach. The peat fire lit the room and they had agreed that if the smoke attracted attention Joe would pretend to be a shepherd seeking shelter. Sean would stand behind the door ready to start shooting with both revolvers if needed, they wouldn't be taken alive. But it was pitch black now outside with a lot of cloud cover so they were feeling more comfortable than they deserved but they had done a good days work and covered a lot of territory and the local IRA had done well in preparing the hut. They never knew who would come or who had been but it was always ready for those who needed it.

As promised Sean took the first watch of two hours, he was dog tired but determined not to doze off. But the half bottle of Guinness and the peat fire offered too much comfort as he watched Joe nod off as soon as his head touched a makeshift pillow. After an hour Sean's head dropped to his chest, it was a dangerous time if anyone was watching the hut. Sean's head suddenly shot up, what was that sound, another fox, a stoat, badger, Black and Tan? He listened intently, nothing further, just his damned imagination. He gripped his pistol tighter; another hour and Joe could take over. He cursed his own initiative to take the first watch, always wanting to be in charge. Joe didn't care he was laid back about most things thinking more about his Hurling matches and training than Black and Tans or the war. Sean wished he could be like that but he was driven by something he didn't understand. Now their War had started in earnest the adrenaline of the times controlled his every thought and drove him harder to what end he didn't know. He and Joe had done the job they had been sent out to do. An informer had been identified in County Clare and the practice often was to bring in outsiders to deal with the problem rather than put it on locals who might be intimidated at the thought of 'taking care' of one of their own. Sean and Joe had been satisfied that the man was guilty, the local IRA court had found him so but that never made it any easier. Execution was always an unpleasant business.

The next morning at first light they would go their separate ways. Joe back to Drumraney to his home and his work as a company quartermaster in the Athlone Brigade and himself to Dublin and General Headquarters or GHQ as it was better known. He wondered if the 'Big Fellow' would be there and if he'd meet him. The legendary Michael Collins, whose official title was Director of Intelligence but who, most accepted, ran the whole clandestine war against the English. Sean wasn't sure why he had been summoned to Dublin but it had been hinted that a promotion was in the wind. Good leaders were hard to find and GHQ needed them now more than ever.

The night time silence was absolute, but at least he was awake again, and they were still alive. He looked at his wristwatch a battered timepiece that had seen better days from when his parents gave it to him two years earlier. He'd give Joe a nudge shortly and take a well-earned sleep, God knows he needed it. For now, he had to keep awake at all costs, no more dozing off, the next time could be fatal. After a short while, Sean woke Joe from his slumber and gratefully took his long fought off sleep. When he woke it was still dark but they had each managed to grab at least four hours sleep during the night by changing shifts,

"What's for breakfast?" Joe asked in jest knowing their supply of food had been used up.

"A swig of water if you're lucky," answered Sean with no hint of humour. They had dressed and though the clothes were still a bit damp, they were better than they were when they arrived. The shoes had dried as well, the peat fire had served its purpose and the cloud cover and bad weather had reduced the chances of anyone seeing any smoke. Sean pulled a map from his coat pocket,

"Look at this,' he said as he spread it out on the old table. He pointed at a spot on the map, "This is where we are, I'd guess we're about ten miles from Dublin which is due east and Drumraney is due north west. We need to separate so I can get to GHQ and you can head back home, needless to say we both have to be very careful. We can't afford to be baled up, if we're caught carrying guns you know what will happen." Joe knew alright, straight to Dublin Castle for an interrogation and a kicking from the detectives there then straight to Kilmainham or Mountjoy prisons, no trial, no magistrate and God knew what fate. Depending on the mood of the officers it could even be summary execution, 'shot while trying to escape' was the often used epitaph or if you were lucky, transportation to and five years in an English prison.

"We'll need some luck then especially as we get closer to the towns" said Joe, they were both aware that any young men were viewed with suspicion. The best place to hide was in plain sight preferably in a crowd of people and not on your own walking down a country lane. Buses and trams were useful but likely to be raided by Tans or police as the mood suited them. That was what Martial Law was like. Though it wasn't officially proclaimed until December that year the population knew the British authorities didn't worry about official approval; the Tans basically did what they liked.

The two young men made sure the fire was totally out and tidied up what they could, dawn was starting to break. They needed to make a move before it became too light. Sean thrust out his hand to Joe,

"I don't think I could have done all this with anyone else, you're a good man Joe and I wouldn't want anyone else watching my back." For Sean that was a speech he was not comfortable making, it sounded too formal, too desperate, but it was heartfelt. Joe took Sean's hand and they briefly hugged each other the way men do when they're not sure what else to do.

"Good luck boy and we'll see you back at Drumraney in a week or so.' Joe said more in hope than belief. They pulled on their oversized cloth caps and long overcoats, had one last look around and went out the cabin door. Sean as usual took the initiative,

"You go first, head to the town I showed you on the map, there'll be some lads there who will look after you, stay cross country and keep off the roads you should make it before dark.' It was obvious stuff but Sean needed to say it, he wanted his friend above all else to be safe and get home to his family. Joe grinned the impish grin of a cheeky kid,

"Don't be giving me orders ye little bugger or I'll have to take ye down," he made a mock show of a punch to the midriff of Sean, then said, "and don't be talkin' to too many strangers yeself, ye know there's some bad people out there." They shook hands again briefly and Joe went without looking back. He was focussed on his task of finding the University and Seminary town of Maynooth where he remembered, they churned out priests like sausages and the population there preferred to remain as neutral as possible. Of course, there was an IRA chapter there as in most villages and towns. Joe hoped he wouldn't have to bail up and shoot any priests and put his mortal soul in danger, better he thought to just focus on self preservation. Maynooth would take the best part of a day and though he would prefer to travel at night he would rely on the gloomy weather and seldom used trails to get him there albeit without a map and only his sense of direction to guide him. Sean had given him a sketchy map and a number of landmarks to look for and work out how far he was from his target at any time, still it would take all his navigation skills to make it. He didn't fancy spending any more nights outdoors without food or shelter. He had only one name in Maynooth and he had to remember it. If he was caught with any written instructions or maps it would be deadly for him and the man he had to contact. He understood that the IRA weren't trusted everywhere. The War had made them as desperate and demanding as much as the enemy they were fighting which was why he had to be careful to whom he spoke and trusted.

After walking through countryside for five hours and following his instincts and his limited map which he would now have to destroy, Joe found Maynooth in the late afternoon. Unfortunately, the first thing he saw was a truckload of Black and Tans about one hundred yards away, and they appeared to be celebrating. He had to become invisible very quickly which he did by stepping into a side street whose name he recognised from his map and walked another four blocks away from the Tans. There was a warehouse building, one of three along the street. From the directions Sean had given him he was sure one of the two buildings was the one he needed. After a few minutes Joe couldn't risk being outside any longer so he took the first door and drew a deep breath as he entered the building, hoping he had picked the right one.

# # #
#

Sean's task was no easier than Joe's though he had less distance to travel and he set out five minutes after Joe left in the direction towards Dublin and his meeting with GHQ. He had been walking for more than two hours through fields when he stopped abruptly, hearing voices beyond a hedge which probably meant they were on a road. The voices were clear and not trying to be quiet they were obviously confident in their position. Sean instinctively drew his revolver and as slowly and quietly as he could, sheltered behind one of the many shrubs in the field. He could not see any houses; a stone fence was about fifteen yards away and could offer shelter if any bullets started flying. For the moment Sean would have to stay put and hope no one had seen or heard him. He could hear the voices now that he was concentrating and they were definitely not Irish:

"How long does the sergeant want us to stay here, godforsaken hole that it is, barely had time to get me breakfast when he grabbed me and told me to get out here with you." The man was seriously grumbling and like all 'other ranks' could never see the sense in orders from higher up especially when they weren't explained. Another voice responded, more serious and probably senior to the other man,

"We shouldn't be here long you can see it's an intersection, that's why we're here, to question anyone who comes along."

"Dumb fookin' Paddies, better not try anything if we do stop them. I won't take any shite from them, they'd be sorry." His was a younger voice and he tried to make it sound menacing. False bravado if he'd ever heard it Sean thought. He assumed there was only two of them and wondered whether he shouldn't just poke his head out of the hedge and shoot the both of them. He was tempted but common sense gave him pause, any gunshots would bring reinforcements and he would have more trouble than he needed. He chastised himself for being so bloodthirsty. Is this what the war was doing to him? If you see an enemy uniform just shoot it and damn the consequences? He decided that yes, that is what the war was doing to him but he couldn't allow himself to become fool hardy just to prove a point and become a dead hero. He put his revolver back in his coat pocket and quietly crawled away from the voices. He waited till he had gone at least one hundred yards before standing. Walking over a small hill and out of any sight of the road he took out his map and searched for the crossroads one of the voices had mentioned. He found it on the map and could see where he was in relation to it, so not too far from the outskirts of Dublin. Soon he would run out of trees and bushes to hide in and would need to expose himself to the urban environment, buildings and footpaths and roads would need to become his friends. He walked up the next hill away from the road and as expected there was the outline of buildings and houses a few hundred yards ahead of him. He took a deep breath and headed for what he thought would be the nearest road hoping that once he reached it, he could blend into the cityscape and avoid attention. It was then he heard another voice,

"You, what are you doing there?" it was male and loud, Sean froze and moved his hand to his revolver before slowly turning towards the speaker. He was obviously a sheep farmer he had a large crook in one hand and was holding a sheep by the scruff of its neck with the other, it had apparently gotten itself stuck in some blackberry bushes. Sean was happy to see he didn't have a shotgun which many farmers had taken to carrying with them at all times.

"Found a shortcut, just saving my legs, didn't think anyone would mind." Sean was trying to sound as casual as possible he didn't want an incident now particularly with an unarmed shepherd. The man nodded and let go of the sheep. Then to Sean's surprise he picked up a shotgun which had been lying against the stone fence where the sheep had taken refuge. Sean froze, his next action would be critical but the man obviously didn't want to get involved any more than Sean did.

"Mind how you go then, there are Tans all over the city." With that he turned and walked away, the sheep freed from the entanglement it had encountered. Sean let out his breath and relaxed for the moment but knowing this was his lot on the run. Any incident could turn ugly but he had to continually control his reactions. He congratulated himself for not making a mess of the encounter. It was getting dark so he was starting to feel safer and he left the field and entered the open road. Another five minutes walking would see him amongst some buildings, somewhere, anywhere to be out of sight.

Sean recalled that he hadn't been in Dublin since his last visit with Joe when they went to Thomas Ashe's funeral. As he walked into the built-up areas a few landmarks started to look familiar. He had memorised the address he was looking for, it wouldn't do to get searched and have information like that on him it would mean grief to too many people. Dublin was more the centre of the undeclared war between Ireland and England than was rural Drumraney. He could feel the tension in the city, the expressions of ordinary citizens as they rushed about were strained and the constant police and military presence kept everyone on edge. The tension was greater for the military men, their enemies weren't in uniform, they could be and often were, anyone of the civilians they passed by. That's why there were so many stop and searches. Any man or women could be stopped and searched and their identity demanded and if they refused, they were dealt with summarily and could be dragged off to the nearest police station. Sean's plan was to hide in plain sight, stay amongst large crowds if he could. Try not to walk on your own for too long, you were an obvious target that way if you came across any patrols.

Sean finally found the address he had been searching for: Vaughan's Hotel, tucked away in a side street in a city area. It was one of the unofficial headquarters of the IRA leadership who were known to come and go frequently. It was beside a newsagent, tobacconist store and a couple of other small shops and there were rooftop connections on both sides to allow for quick escape if required. There was a busy bar downstairs, full of smoke and talk and many of the patrons would not have realised what meetings were going on upstairs.

As a stranger, Sean attracted attention and he ordered a stout though he wasn't much of a drinker himself. He suddenly found himself standing with a man on either side of him, and leaning in closer than Sean thought necessary.

"What would you be wanting as well as the stout?" one of them asked. Now Sean hoped the information he had been given to make his contact would be correct otherwise he would have a lot of explaining to do.

"Cathal Brugha." Was all he was told to say, the men on either side looked at each other, it was a name they knew and it held significance. Brugha was the Minister for Defence in the underground Irish government.

"Leave the drink." One of them said, "Come with me" he led Sean up the stairs beside the bar area, it was guarded by two other men who Sean had no doubt were armed, they stood aside and let the group pass. Sean was led into a bare room that held two chairs and a small table. "Sit there and wait." He did as they said, still nervous and unsure in this strange surrounding where he knew no one and understood less. He had been sitting on his own in the room for five minutes when the door opened and a new man came in. He was tall and good looking with a friendly face and a ready smile which he didn't use much with Sean, he didn't give his name. He asked for Sean's and where he came from and who he knew in the Athlone Brigade. Where they did their training and had their meetings and where he had been for the past two weeks. It was obvious the man knew the answers to the questions he asked as he nodded knowingly with each of Sean's replies.

"General Brugha's not here at present but we've been expecting you and I have your orders." There was no informality, it was all military business even though no one was in uniform. "You are to head back to your home but move and live in Athlone for a few days, the local men will find you rooms. They'll be on the edge of the city away from the Army Barracks so you'll be able to move around easily. You are to have the rank of Captain and work with the other commanders. You will from time to time be contacted by John McCormack or his men who you know, with special instructions from the Brotherhood. GHQ has been happy enough with the activity in the midlands but it has to be stepped up now as it does all over the country, and we do mean in a big way. More active units, more attacks on RIC Barracks and make life as difficult as possible for the RIC, and the Tans. Your brother officers have been given the same orders, we may have to set the countryside alight and we will if need be. We know that will bring harsher measures against the civilians but they all have to understand this is war and we mean total war. We're determined to win what we started out to do and it is men like you and your comrades that will make it happen." He stopped talking but held out his hand, "Michael Collins. Good to meet you son, you come highly recommended and we know you'll deliver what we need." Now he had a broad smile on his face and Sean couldn't help but smile back even though he was overwhelmed by the moment and the sight of a man who had become an IRA legend in such a short time.

"Thank you, sir, I'm honoured and I won't let you down."

Collins was always quick with a reply and took the formality out of the meeting with his rejoinder,

"Enough of the sir, we'll leave that to the Brits." He smiled again shook Sean's hand and left the room and one of the other men came in,

"Congratulations Captain McKeon, we'll get you something to eat and a place to sleep for the night and you can head back on the first train in the morning for Athlone. Come with me."

And that was that, Sean now knew why he had been ordered to Dublin. He was now a captain and had new orders to step up the pace of the rural war and make life miserable for the enemy. All he had to do now was to determine how to do that.

# # # #

As Sean had made his way to Dublin and reacquainted himself with that city, Joe had taken refuge in a building in Maynooth soon after he had seen the truckload of Tans. He was pretty certain they hadn't seen him but he could take nothing for granted. The building he reached was an old warehouse and the day was coming to an end for the few workers there and they were preparing to go home. Joe would have to risk making his presence known. He couldn't afford to be locked in the building all night; he would prefer to be travelling towards home.

There was a young man on his own Joe had to chance it,

"Would you be telling me how to find the Shamrock Hotel, I think I took a wrong turn somewhere and I'm lost." He tried to look as innocent and earnest as possible unsure if he was succeeding. The youth who was probably only sixteen looked at Joe with some suspicion unsure and taken by surprise, but he took the question in his stride.

"There's a Hotel down MacNiece Street about five minutes walk, would that be the one?"

"Aye I'm going to meet my cousin but his directions were wrong." Joe answered, "I was walking past and noticed you fellows here and thought someone could help me. So, I'll go out here to the left and follow the road?" Here the youth went to the door and looked out both ways,

"Best wait a few minutes there's Tans down that way and they'll give you a kicking if they find you on your own." Joe felt a surge of release that he had found a fellow traveller.

"Good advice, they're not the friendliest fellows are they."

"What's your cousin's name." asked the boy finding more confidence. Joe only knew one name in the town and he had to risk it,

"Tim Coogan." He said with authority, "Do you know him?" hoping to God that he did.

"No" was the quick answer, "but my Da might." Before Joe could stop him, the boy had walked over to a bench where a much older man was finishing up. Joe now had to decide whether to make a run for it or continue to brazen it out, he reasoned that at least while he was in here, he wasn't on the street or in sight of the Tans. The boy's father wandered over to Joe, Tim Coogan was a code name that he had been told to use. If anyone knew what it meant they could help him if not he would plead ignorance.

"Tim Coogan is it?" there was something about the half smile on his face that gave Joe some comfort as he gave the answer he was told to expect in the right circumstances. "I think I can find him for you." Joe had gambled as he would have in a Hurling game, which way to run, who to trust. In his situation he felt that most but not all the Irish civilian population would come down on the side of the IRA, his luck held, the man was obviously someone who could help him.

"My name's Tim." He said holding out his hand. The man grinned: "we had been told to expect someone. Welcome to Maynooth." Joe had picked the right building and soon found himself shelter and food for the night and safe transport back to Drumraney followed by a major change to his life which he never even imagined.

CHAPTER 13
ATHLONE

By the time he got back to Athlone, Sean had given a lot of thought to the War he was fighting. It was obvious that the war was not the conventional type that some of his comrades who had returned from France in 1918 had described. There were no front lines, no trenches but plenty of targets and the ultimate goal was well defined but the national tactics were opaque to most people at his level. The GHQ people he had spoken to in Dublin talked about getting rid of the English and getting self government but few of them seemed to have a road map of how to do that and what it would look like when it was achieved. The politics were difficult to understand and follow, there were few rules and few places to get answers, it was up to individuals to work out a way out of the maze for themselves.

It was a war that hadn't been declared, as if there was no starting line and no finish line and it was all but impossible to tell who, if anyone, was winning. Stories were constant about the terror that was affecting the population around the country. The Black and Tans were supposed to be there reinforcing the RIC but they were an undisciplined lot, a rabble, many had called them. They were terrorising the people who suffered in silence because they had no weapons to fight back with. The Tans and the RIC had the British Administration on their side and the people were left to their own devices. Their only resource was the IRA who they turned to by supporting them however they could, offering food and shelter whenever it was asked for. But the IRA response was not always effective or as quick as people would have liked, it was more a series of reprisals. If the Tans terrorised a village or a group of farm houses on the pretext they were looking for IRA members they usually left houses burned out or hay feed lots destroyed. Then the IRA groups would burn down a barracks that sheltered the RIC and the Tans who in turn would do more searches and take out more reprisals. It was tit for tat and the IRA tried to retaliate first, striking when and how they could, wherever they could, with few arms and ammunitions and tried not to lose any men.

Sean learned that Joe had gotten back to his home safely and briefly met him and told him of his promotion. Joe was happy for him, there was no envy, promotion was the last thing Joe sought, all he wanted was to spend more time playing Hurling and training with his village team. There was a County wide meet coming up and Joe had his eyes set on County selection.

But Joe remembered something and commented to Sean just to tease him'

"I ran into Fianna O'Farrell at church last Sunday," he said with a look of mischief, "she was asking after you and was keen to know how you were." Joe was sure Sean's face flushed but he swatted the comment aside.

"I thought she was still in school and pigtails." He said giving little away to his friend. "I've got more to do than worry about girls Joe and what they might talk about." Joe thought he was being overly defensive but left it there. Friends always weren't totally open with each other when it came to the opposite sex.

Sean later met with his Commanding Officer who knew of his promotion and congratulated him and tried to clarify the situation and answer Sean's questions. Sean would be now back in a static role commanding a company with no more roaming around other counties.

"We're fighting what the Spanish call a guerrilla war Captain, that's why we don't always have everyone in uniform. In many cases, as you know, most of our people don't have a uniform, just their day to day clothes. It's not so the Tans can't recognise us it's because that's how we have to operate. We don't have our own barracks; the ones we seize we have to burn down and leave because we don't have the field arms to fight off large scale attacks." Dick Bertles was stating the obvious as was his habit. He was an experienced guerrilla fighter and was in charge of one of the three battalions of the Athlone Brigade but he had no real headquarters. He worked out of spare rooms in public houses or even church halls if he found a sympathetic priest. Sean had met him during their training and admired his zeal and courage but now needed to know what was expected of him in his new capacity of captain. Having not long returned from a three-week operation with Joe, he didn't know the current state of affairs in Athlone and around the nearby counties of Westmeath, Roscommon and Longford.

"What do we do next? I've mainly been involved with one off operations and the last few months I've been living off the land and travelling at night and now I've been made a Captain but I don't have a company and I don't know who most of men are." Sean was genuinely bewildered, it had been easier before, just getting orders and going off to do whatever was asked of him. Now it would be different. Bertles didn't make it any easier but did explain what he and the command expected of him.

"You'll have a company alright; it will be 'B" company of the battalion and made up of about one hundred and twenty volunteers from around your district and you will be spending much more time on operations. GHQ wants us to move into a new stage of activity and they mean heightened activity! We need to stir the pot and do it violently. Most of our men have been leaving their homes and farms and spending a few days on a mission, attacking the RIC Barracks and making life difficult for them. Then dealing with the reprisals from the Black and Tans and then going back home and trying to avoid being arrested. The men can't spend too much time in their homes anyway because they are constantly being raided by the Tans and being chased for arrest. So, your barracks will be the fields of the counties and the odd home or barn of IRA supporters. Not a lot unlike what you have been doing recently except there will be more of you and you will be in charge. How does that make you feel?"

Bertles wanted to know that Sean had the self confidence to take on the responsibilities of his new rank and Sean appreciated the direction and clarity of his duties.

"I'm more than willing to get done whatever is asked of me." Then hesitated, "but we are going to need more resources if we're going to be effective." This was nothing new for Bertles the lack of resources was the element that was holding back the whole IRA war effort. Not even enough rifles for each volunteer.

"The Big Fellow has promised me personally he will get us as much as he can, and I do mean mines and bombs and Lewis guns when possible, we have to fight fire with fire." Sean knew the 'Big fellow' was Michael Collins the man who had given him his promotion. He was effectively running the war for the IRA from Dublin and directing the army despite not being Chief of Staff. He was running a clandestine Intelligence Department and his own new kind of urban warfare, the rules of which he was writing as he went along. "But we also have to help ourselves and that means bigger and more daring raids wherever we suspect there are things we need, that means attacking fortified barracks closer to the big towns and coming face to face often and violently with the Tans and the RIC. We will have to take from them as many arms as we can carry away. It's not going to be easy or pretty but it's got to be done, not just here but all over the country. The war is being stepped up son, we are raising the stakes and we will get a lot of resistance. Not only from the enemy but from our own people because we will make it unpleasant for the Brits and they will make it much more unpleasant for our people who aren't going to like it."

Very soon Sean would find out exactly what Bertles meant about raising the stakes.

#   #
     #

For Joe this would be the most important Hurling game of his playing career. He had played all over the county of Westmeath and against other teams in Roscommon and Louth. The priest at Drumraney had put together what he considered a 'special' group of young men and melded them into a team of confident Hurling players despite the ongoing 'War'. The breaks in training came when some of the team were not available as they had to go and do special training or even operations and Joe had missed several weeks while on missions with Sean. Father Slattery knew nothing of what or where they had been, and he didn't ask he only knew that Joe wasn't available for a few weeks at a time.

Sean had given up reluctantly on the playing and training his mind turned completely to his new role of Captain in the Brigade, and his own Company. Joe was also in the same Company but wouldn't give up on the Hurling, it meant too much to him and he enjoyed it immensely. The thrill of making things happen on the playing field fitted into Joe's approach to the game, constant movement and tactics to overcome the other side and working with teammates to produce goals and ultimate victory. As a left corner-forward playing in his favoured number fifteen jumper, Joe's personal goal was to score as many goals as possible for the team and he excelled at it. Part of his responsibility though was not to be selfish; it was a team sport after all as Father Slattery continually reminded him.

Joe had been playing competitive Hurling now for seven years starting in younger grades and making his way to the senior team three years ago as a seventeen-year-old. He held his position due to his aggression and ability on the field and his continuing tally of goals for the team. Now what was coming up was his ultimate test and as the priest told him, on the quiet, if he performed well, County selection for Westmeath was assured. County had been a dream of Joe's for the past few years ever since Father Slattery motivated him by suggesting he was a chance and now suddenly it was a possibility!

The match was to be held in Athlone, always a danger for a number of reasons. Any young fit man was considered by the British army as a potential recruit for the IRA and many of them were. The problem was that at this time the Brits had to catch them at it before they could arrest them. The team arrived by lorry in Athlone and the Tans were out in force. They watched the team very closely even searching their bags for weapons or any documents that might incriminate them.

"Sure, and you don't think we've come here to fight a war?" Father Slattery said to the officer who had sent his men to search the Drumraney dressing room. The other dressing room was considered safe by the Army as the team had come from County Down in the North. They had a cohort of Protestant players who were there because of their love of the game and the competition and weren't interested in the religious politics. Many also sympathized with their opponents and their struggle for independence.

"You never know what we might find when we go through a bunch of Fenians." Answered the officer, "you just make sure you boys behave yourselves and don't cause any trouble."

"God bless you and your men." Father Slattery said as much in jest as anger, the two-edged comment was sure to rile the officer but Father Slattery had to keep his temper under control. If he lost it the match would end in a brawl before it even started. His team had filed into the dressing room and their annoyance at being singled out for a search gave vent to plenty of comment to the soldiers searching.

'Go and see what the Prods have got in their bags, I'm sure I saw a machine gun and three grenades in someone's bag.' Said one boy,

'Make sure the Union jack is flying or we won't play.' Another added sarcastically. The officer glared at them deciding whether he would just start laying into them to teach a lesson but seeing how young and fit they were stayed his hand.

"That will be enough." Father Slattery said aloud, "Get your gear on and get ready for the game, you can save what you feel for out there." The sledging of the team from the north was reactive they were after all mostly Catholic with just a couple of Protestants players. That fact should have been acknowledged positively instead of with name calling, as Father Slattery would tell them later.

The young men settled down and got into the playing gear. Blaise Phelan, one of Joe's friends and a gun midfielder for the team commented to Joe about an incident as they got off their truck before the game.

"So, Joe it seemed that you took a bit of a liking to my cousin Maggie when I introduced you outside." Joe was taken aback; he didn't think anyone had noticed the prolonged look he bestowed on Blaise's cousin. He had indeed been smitten and confused with feelings he had never had before. As a young man, working on his father's farm and being tied up with IRA training, he had never had the opportunity to meet many young ladies and certainly none as pretty as Maggie. She was just seventeen and Blaise had never mentioned her before. He didn't even know she was going to be at the match and she was a hit amongst his team mates in the short time he had for introductions. Maggie and her younger sister Rose, who was just fifteen, and two younger brothers John and Ned, had been brought to the game by their father John because Blaise was visiting Athlone and was playing in the game. He was a cousin to them all and they only occasionally caught up. Joe for the moment was lost for words, he knew he had to reply but he couldn't think of what to say. His unrestrained grin told Blaise all he needed to know he hoped it wouldn't put Joe off his game and extended an invitation.

"We'll have a chance to catch up after the match before we head home, I need to speak to my Uncle John, you can come with me if you like." Joe liked the idea, smiled again, but didn't say anything further and focussed on getting into his game clothes.

Despite his thinking occasionally taking him back to the young lady he had met earlier, Joe's performance during the game matched Father Slattery's expectations. He had given the team simple instructions:

"It's just an opposing team a bunch of players and you need to beat them to stay at the top and win the county trophy for Westmeath." They knew what tactics were needed and Father Slattery was a man of few words.

Joe scored two goals and was dominant in the attack generally helping to bring victory to the Drumraney team. It was a physical game as most of them were with plenty of swinging Hurleys finding their mark and causing bruising or worse. The speed of the opposition surprised Joe who had a habit of underestimating any opponents and he smarted as he was brushed aside by their star player who found a goal for himself. Joe quickly sprang back into action and raised his game finding the speed and determination that Father Slattery wanted to see. A crack from a Hurley stick too high and near his mouth stunned Joe and he came off for a few minutes but stopped any bleeding and he was back into it. By half time they had gotten on top of the visitors who ran out of steam, victory was confirmed with Joe's second goal and he was cheered off the ground as the final whistle blew.

After a brief cold shower and a change of clothes, Joe sought out Blaise and made sure he would be with him when he met his cousins. John Egan was a dour man with a somewhat theatrical moustache that reminded Joe of an advertisement he had once seen in a newspaper for moustache wax. He didn't want to appear disrespectful and of course didn't make any comment but found Mr Egan's attitude a bit intimidating as it was related to protecting his young and attractive daughter from handsome young Hurling heroes. It was new ground for all of them but at least Joe had an excuse for the introduction being a playing mate of Maggie's cousin. They all made some small talk and Joe could see that Maggie was responsive to his few questions about her schooling and if she was working. They were dumb questions he realised later but asked for the sake of making some contact. It was unlikely Maggie would be working. Athlone was under the heel of the Black and Tans and her father and mother would be watching her and her sister closely to ensure their safety.

After a short while, Blaise had to pry Joe away from the meeting. They had to make their way home and it was a long walk if they missed their transport. Joe did his best to leave a positive last impression and even managed to shake Maggie's hand to the dismay of her father,

"I hope we can meet again sometime." Joe said as Blaise literally dragged him away. Joe kept looking back as he went to his transport and was certain he saw Maggie respond with a smile.

"Sorry to be the one to give bad news Joe." Blaise said trying to get Joe's attention, "but I've heard Uncle John tell my mother that he's thinking of sending his two daughters to Australia to stay with an aunt of his in Sydney. They think it's far too dangerous for their girls to stay on in Athlone with the present troubles." Joe was thunderstruck and stared at Blaise,

"You can't mean it, sweet Jesus I felt I just met an angel and you're saying that!" Joe didn't say anything else on the way home his mind was now focussed on how he could arrange another meeting with the young lady who had stolen his heart so quickly.

CHAPTER 14
1920 The Year of Terror

There was a strong Republican sentiment in the county of Westmeath and the IRA had recruited well since the 1916 Uprising, with Brigade strength numbers in the Athlone area, including three battalions broken into companies in the various geographical districts. After sustained barracks attacks by the IRA in the latter half of 1919 the GHQ sponsored raids on two hundred and fifty eight barracks countrywide at Easter 1920. The RIC then mostly retreated to the safety of the bigger towns such as Athlone and Mullingar in Westmeath.

This left the countryside largely unpoliced and the IRA stepped into the void and effectively became the government for the county and indeed most of the rural countryside. Authorised by the newly elected, though still unrecognised by the British, Dail in Dublin, District Courts around the country were also set up and senior and respected members of the community acted as Judges. They dealt with disagreements between farmers and trades people and anyone else who had a grievance that needed a hearing. It proved to the population that the new Dail and the IRA could be trusted to do the right thing and bring law and order with more fairness than that experienced under the British rulers.

In March 1920 General Macready was appointed Commander in Chief of the British forces in Ireland. The British realised that the RIC was losing control of law and order and were losing the respect of the people generally and resignations were increasing. The newly recruited Black and Tans kept arriving in larger numbers and enforced law and order throughout the country with devastating consequences for the Irish population generally.

Though Sean had been proud of the trust put in him by GHQ, he now realised he had a bigger job than what had been initially described by Commander Bertles. Westmeath was home to two large British barracks, one in Athlone and the other in Mullingar. The two towns were about thirty five miles apart as the crow flies. Now with the increased presence of the Black and Tans, the IRA companies were unable to move around with the freedom that a guerrilla army needed and enjoyed in some other parts of the country. Also, much of the countryside was unlike the counties down south, it was flat plain county and used for cattle and sheep grazing. Due to the relative scarcity of hills and valleys there were fewer places to hide and not many mountains to offer shelter.

As always there was never enough arms to do the damage that GHQ wanted the locals to do. Sean had raised the situation again with Dick Bertles who had been very positive and hadn't wanted to criticise his Brigade leaders, whom some felt had let the local companies down.

"Well, "said Bertles "don't forget the effort we made on Easter Sunday last. We did as well as any group in the country with the number of RIC barracks put out of action. I know you're looking for the knockout blow, and so are we all but that's not going to happen in a war like this, particularly against an enemy with the resources the Brits have." Sean knew Bertles was right but he was young and ambitious and wanted to make a difference to the war effort,

"Can't GHQ send more arms? We have around five hundred men we can call on but they all need rifles and ammunition."

"Well the five hundred could quickly shrink to two hundred if the heat got too strong, don't forget the argument in the pub with a Guinness is easier to make than a victory in the field." Bertles was right of course, the IRA numbers had swelled as they had all over the country especially during the Conscription crisis of 1918. But men were necessarily and continually dragged back to the mundane work of their farms and feeding their families, not many had the freedom of Sean whose family supported him. Now that the RIC was reinforced by the Black and Tans, they and the Tans were following a ruthless doctrine of suppression. Bertles thought Sean needed to know exactly what they were now up against and shared a document he had with him.

In June 1920 Michael Collins was delivered a one-page document by a sympathetic RIC officer who had been present at its presentation. It was a copy of the speech given to RIC and new installed Black and Tan soldiers in County Kerry by Colonel Gerald Bryce Ferguson Smyth, it said in part: *"Martial law, applying to all Ireland is to come into operation immediately....I am promised as many troops from England as I require, thousands are coming daily.....we are to strengthen your comrades in the country stations..........if a police barracks is burned or is not suitable, then the best house in the locality is to be commandeered, the occupants thrown into the gutter. Let them die there, the more the merrier..............when civilians are seen approaching shout "Hands Up!" should the order not be obeyed immediately, shoot and shoot with effect. If the persons approaching a patrol carry their hands in their pockets........shoot them down. The more you shoot the better I will like you and I assure you no policeman will get into any trouble for shooting any man........General Tudor and myself, want your assistance in carrying out this scheme and wiping out Sinn Fein."*

There it was in plain English, the undeclared war had been declared as far as the IRA was concerned and GHQ in response had upped the stakes to this provocative, and under the rules of war, obviously illegal order. The British walked around this particular technicality by referring to their activity in Ireland as a 'Police Action'. Sean looked at Bertles, tears brought on by his anger were in his eyes. The reality of what they were all now facing was apparent and terrifying.

Many of the soldiers now fighting on both sides in Ireland had witnessed carnage in Europe and had been exposed to the violence of armed confrontation. The War for the Independence of Ireland was a different kind of war to Europe, there were very few pitched battles and those that took place were between relatively small numbers. The IRA never had the armed capacity to take on the might of the British Empire head on. Indeed, there were not even enough rifles to give to every man who joined the struggle. The war became one of attrition in virtually all of the twenty six counties in the south and the six in the North. The IRA would use tactics including ambushes, sabotage, raids, petty warfare and hit and run with mobility to make their point. The targets were selected by local commanders working on a plan from GHQ in Dublin whose goal was to make the country unworkable and ungovernable for the British Administration. The primary target for the IRA was to be those that enforced British rule, mainly the Royal Irish Constabulary (RIC) and the Black and Tans who supported them. Their workplaces, and even where they lived, would be considered fair game

The Dail, made up of elected Sinn Fein members who refused to take their place in London now met in secret in Dublin, and declared that the RIC were no longer to be recognised as the legitimate source of law and order in the country.

The country effectively had two governments now and the struggle for control would escalate dramatically during 1920 while the British poured in more forces. Fifteen hundred Police Auxiliary

Cadets, the brainchild of Winston Churchill, were mainly ex-officers of the British Armed Forces who arrived and were given police powers to assist the increasingly demoralised RIC. The "Auxies" as the came to be known were supposed to police the undisciplined activities of the Black and Tans but usually just joined them in creating more mayhem.

Thousands of small actions took place throughout the country, in the southern counties, the activities were numerous, supported by the local population and the growing strength of the IRA. In the North, and in the Midlands, insurgents were all active with a variety of guerrilla tactics designed to make British rule untenable.

Dublin Castle in the city of Dublin was the head quarters of British government agencies and police forces and continually clashed with the clandestine forces under Michael Collins and the leadership of the IRA.

It was in Dublin that Hugh Murtagh had found himself in mid 1920 having been sent there by his local IRA commanders in Westmeath to liaise with GHQ and get more arms. Hugh was now Quartermaster of the Athlone Brigade. He met up again with Patrick McCormack with whom he had first come across in 1913 when he visited the city with his father Peter. Hugh stayed with Patrick's wife and now three children in what could only be termed the poorer part of the city. They were hard working and proud citizens who had been repressed for most of their lives, and so joined the IRB and the IRA proudly determined to make their country their own. Mary McCormack was an active member of Cumann na nBan the women's paramilitary party that assisted in all IRA activities. Patrick had already been tested under fire with Sean when their group had taken control for a week of St Stephen's Green in the middle of the city during the Easter

Uprising of 1916. Now he continued his activities with the Dublin Brigade.

"Hugh you've come to the right place to deal with GHQ, I'll introduce you to some people whose names will go down in Irish history because of their dedication and work." Hugh never doubted Patrick's word he had heard plenty from Sean over the past few years about his cousin. Patrick had been arrested after the Uprising and he had to spend a few months in Mountjoy Prison. Now he was back in the thick of the insurrection just like his comrades in Westmeath.

"The Brigade wants me to get more rifles and ammunition, we're held up in what impact we can make against the Brits without them. We would like about five hundred." Hugh said, trying to convey the urgency of his Brigade's needs. Patrick smiled but didn't let on that the number was impossible. He believed the war was about spirit not just the number of weapons one could get hold of.

"We'll see boyo, we'll see. We'll do what we can and do what we can with what we've got! Tomorrow we'll go to GHQ and talk to some people."

CHAPTER 15
Drumraney Activity

Sean had determined early on which men he wanted with him to achieve what Dick Bertles had told him what was expected of him, and Joe Keegan was first on the list. He was joined by a group of volunteers mostly from farms in the area and they were men who had already taken part in other operations. The company's activities were relatively small scale and concerned with the acquisition of arms and the disruption of regulated services. And there was always the RIC Barracks which had to be dealt with.

Attacks were nearly always at night. There were not enough arms for daylight confrontations. The barracks at Glasson near Athlone were a particular target and the first larger scale ambush activity Sean and Joe had taken part in.

On the planned night of the attack at Glasson, Sean had assembled perhaps thirty men who had all volunteered for the operation. However half of them were only armed with pitchforks, improvised pikes or even hurling sticks such was the shortage of rifles. It was a Saturday night and some men had been reluctant to give up the only night off they had from farm work during the week.

"Perhaps this time Joe we might be able to liberate some rifles for the lads and keep them interested." Joe agreed by nodding, he didn't know what he could contribute and knew little of how it would pan out, but he finally added, more out of bravado than knowledge,

"We'll have them on the run in no time Captain." He had taken to calling Sean by his title but Sean wasn't sure if it was a mark of respect or an old friend taking the piss. He suspected the latter.

They met with two other men who had had some experience of stalking local barracks and discussed Sean's plan. Sean took command and took a drawing of the geography of the area out of his coat pocket. If arrested, having such a drawing on his person would have had him taken to Athlone barracks and charged, then court martialled. But he avoided any likely meeting with RIC or Tans by staying away from main roads and the villages, visiting his parent's home only occasionally at night. The rest of his time, like Joe's and a number of others was spent sleeping in friendly barns and doing drills to hone their military skills.

"There are no other buildings around the barracks for three hundred yards. The windows have metal shutters and the door is solid steel, the weak spot is the roof and that will be our secondary target, the first target will be the front door." Joe looked askance and said,

"And how do think that will work, just walk up and ask for a jug of milk?"

"Of course not" replied Sean a little testily, now he had to tell them that he had changed the plans and that the attack wouldn't be at night but early the next morning. "This is how it will go. It will be early Sunday morning and we know that two of their lads go to the local church early. We will grab them as soon as they are out of sight of the barracks and take their uniforms from them." He looked around to make sure the men were still with him, though they all looked at him with pained expressions unsure of where he was going with the idea. "Myself and Jimmy

Connaughton will put on the uniforms and go to the front door of the barracks, the uniforms should be enough to get them to open up and when that happens, we all move in." Sean seemed pleased with himself, like all plans it appeared simple enough and he saw no reason why it wouldn't work. "Questions?"

"Won't the men inside realise that you're not the same men as soon as they look at your face?" it was Joe who thought he saw the weakness of the plan.

"We're going to say we're from another barracks with some orders from headquarters. That will make them open the door." Joe and the others nodded in agreement not able to think of anything else. Sean was pleased with himself certain that he had covered all the elements of the operation.

He hadn't.

His men with rifles arrived late that night at a point not far from the barracks and assembled, the others joined them and they made for a rag tag bunch, no uniforms and little resemblance of an army unit. They weren't happy to learn that they would have to wait till morning for something to happen. Equally Sean wasn't happy that a few of them had diverted to the local pub on the way to the assembly point, he could smell alcohol on a couple of them. He decided that perhaps some of them needed a drink not knowing what danger they faced so didn't make a big deal apart from a quite word on the side to the offenders.

They settled well away from the barracks and kept themselves occupied for a few hours. Before first light Sean picked five of the men to go with him to give cover if needed and he and Jimmy Connaughton left their rifles behind but carried revolvers, the rest of the men took up positions around the bushes for cover still two hundred yards from the barracks. Sean had binoculars and watched the front door. Within minutes the door opened and two officers came out in full uniform and headed for the village. Sean and Jimmy and the three other men including Joe followed them out of sight of the barracks and bailed them up, Joe and Sean holding revolvers and the others rifles.

"Where are you off to gentlemen?" Asked Joe, "bit early for a Guinness I suppose." The officers knew their game was up and didn't look too happy, one of them responded,

"I suppose the IRA don't respect men going to church being such heathens themselves." Joe was about to give him a backhander before Sean stepped in.

"Take off your uniforms and hand us your weapons and be quick about it." Sean was holding a revolver and the men knew better than to argue. They followed the unexpected command and stood there in their underclothes and Sean motioned for the other three led by Joe to take them away, "Keep them safe." Was all he said as the group walked away. Sean and Jimmy quickly put on the uniforms which fitted reasonably well and headed back to the barracks building. He had ordered Joe and the other armed men to take up positions within range of the barracks so they could see what was going on and move in on Sean's signal. Sean waited fifteen minutes before he made himself visible to the front door of the barracks. He had seen that his men were all in place and knew the time had come to act. He marched to the door and thumped it heavily four times, half expecting it to open like any residence. But it didn't. A voice from inside shouted,

"Who is it?" Sean's cover story was ready,

"We're from Littleton barracks with new orders for you."

"What's your name?" came the gruff reply.

"Scanlon." Said Sean knowing that was the name of one of the officers from the out station.

"First name." Came another gruff question. Sean panicked a little, he didn't know that officers first name. So, he guessed.

"Nicholas." He shouted. Then there was about three minutes silence until Jimmy saw the slit in the door open and two barrels come out. Jimmy didn't have to tell Sean to move.

"Jesus!" Sean shouted and they bolted for the nearest cover which was twenty yards away. Just then shots started coming from the slit in the door and from some upper windows covered with sheets of metal. The rest of the IRA men didn't hesitate, they could see the plan had failed and started shooting at the building to give Sean and Jimmy cover. Jimmy was a keen Hurler and had plenty of speed and ran towards his comrades with bullets hitting the ground around him. Sean decided to return fire and as he ran, he turned and let off three rounds at the door, then turned and tripped, he was ten yards from safety and Joe and the others watched in horror as he tried to get up but was obviously had an injured leg. Without thinking, Joe tore from the cover behind the rocks and grabbed Sean's police uniform jacket and literally hauled him to his feet,

"Come here you clumsy oaf." Forgetting he was talking to a senior officer not just a friend, together they stumbled to safety hearing bullets from the barracks flying through the air. They crashed to the ground.

"What happened" asked Joe. Sean just ignored him,

"Keep the men firing we'll keep them down for a while then take off. Has anyone been hit?" Joe shook his head realising Sean was embarrassed that his ruse at the barrack's door hadn't worked. "I've done my ankle I think." He pulled up his right trouser leg to see what he'd done, but there was blood all over it, he had been hit in the lower leg by fire from the RIC. Joe called Ned Irwin over who acted as a First Aid tender and he pulled out a bandage to cover the wound.

Sean gave the order for the men to move away in groups of three every two minutes, he and Joe and Ned Irwin would be the second last group to move.

"Keep firing a few shots at the building but don't waste ammunition." Bullets were too precious to use unless they were going to do some damage, "there'll be reinforcements here for them before too much longer my guess is that we have ten minutes." The men started to drift off till there was just six of them left. Joe and Ned Irwin picked up Sean between them and he hopped on his good foot holding onto their shoulders his foot hurt like the bejesus but they got him away from the area. Just as they moved into a wooded area where they could have a break, Joe noticed the truck of Black and Tans coming into view on the road about four hundred yards away,

"Hope the lads had time to move out," he was referring to the last group of three who had fired the last shots to give everyone else time to escape.

"They'll be fine," said Sean confidently, he knew if nothing else the men he was with were experts of getting out of situations like this. The countryside was their ally and they knew it well.

"We have a doctor who can look at this foot," said Ned Irwin, "it might be okay but he'll have a better idea than me." Clandestine medical help was on offer from many doctors but it was a matter of knowing which ones could be trusted.

"On your feet captain, or perhaps I mean, on your foot." Joe was making jokes again, anything to bring lightness into the situation as they lifted Sean and the three of them shuffled through the woods to the man Ned knew who would help. They had left the RIC men tied to a tree shivering in their underpants and vests, he knew their comrades would find them soon enough.

Sean was annoyed with himself as Joe had suspected. The mission had failed, they weren't able to steal any more rifles or ammunition and Sean felt like a fool. He knew he would have to lift his game dramatically if the next action, planned for a week from now, was to work. The new orders to increase hostile activity had come from GHQ and were part of a country wide action that would have a significant impact on the war and the enemy.

CHAPTER 16
Athlone Brigade Quartermaster Hugh Murtagh visits Dublin 1920

On his second visit to the city Hugh Murtagh was in thrall to the busyness and mayhem of Dublin. He was still a country lad at heart and his rural naivete was evident even though the war had knocked some of that out of him. He was wide eyed at the pace and action of Dublin, so different to his much slower home county where the only time he saw crowds was on the occasional visit to Athlone or Mullingar.

This Sunday morning, Patrick took his family and Hugh to Mass at a local church after which Hugh and Patrick ventured closer into the city. They were not armed, carrying a weapon in Dublin was dangerous because of the constant likelihood of being stopped and searched. The Black and Tans used such searches as a tactic to keep the population cowed and young men in particular were a regular target.

They had only walked two hundred yards in the direction of Sackville Street before they were pulled up by four Tans, each carrying a rifle with bayonets fixed and ready to use them.

"Where you off to Paddy?" one of them asked using the name that they treated as generic and which they knew annoyed most Irishmen. "Sure, the pubs not open yet on a Church day?" he obviously thought the comment funny as he grinned at his three mates. Patrick had warned Hugh not to respond in anyway except by complying. The soldiers pushed both men against the nearest wall and proceeded to search them reaching into pockets and taking out anything they found and dropped it on the ground after they lost interest in it.

"Where are you from Paddy?" said one of them to Hugh, a big man who looked as though he would have enjoyed any resistance. Hugh was surprised to be spoken to and didn't answer immediately.

"Come on Paddy, I asked you a question." The soldier started to raise his rifle butt and would have used it if Patrick hadn't intervened. Then he decided to prod Hugh with his bayonet instead, a new experience for Hugh.

"He's my cousin and he's visiting from Athlone. We've just been to Mass and I'm showing him around the city." The answer was the right one but Patrick had learned with the Black and Tans in Dublin there was no such thing as a right answer, he waited for the inevitable challenge.

"Don't take that tone with me Paddy or I'll knock your block off" said the soldier who had raised his rifle butt on Hugh, he was looking for any excuse to dish out a hiding and he knew he wouldn't be disciplined for it. Patrick's tone had not been disrespectful but whatever answer was given wouldn't have been acceptable, so he said nothing more just accepting that they were helpless and outnumbered. Patrick was annoyed with himself for not taking the smaller side streets and keeping off the main road, he should have realised there would be patrols of Tans. All the while Hugh stood mute, at least now Patrick thought he would know what city living would be like. Just then a truck load of Tans pulled up, this could be a disaster thought Patrick, they'd both be given a good kicking just for the fun of it or maybe taken down to the police station and held for hours, again for no reason. But their luck held, a soldier shouted from the truck,

"Come on we're heading back to barracks, new orders. Get on board." Patrick let out a breath as the men started to respond but one of them had to make a point which he did with his bayonet by poking it a bit too savagely into Patrick's mid drift.

"You're lucky this time Paddy, but we know where to find you if we need, so watch it!" Patrick knew it was the usual warning from the Tans trying to convince everyone they could pick you up at any time, they jumped into their truck and Patrick allowed himself a wink to Hugh to try and calm him. Hugh had turned a much paler shade and though he had seen men baled up in Athlone for just walking around it had never happened to him personally and he was shaken by the experience.

"You look like you could use a Guinness" said Patrick "but I think we'll wait till later for that. Let's head down this way now." With that Patrick headed for the nearest laneway to get off the main street and Hugh followed, grateful to be away from their encounter with the Black and Tans. And more than grateful it hadn't turned out more dangerous.

The picture of the busy main street environment would stay with Hugh for some time: Police and Black and Tans all over, what looked like plain clothes policemen, military lorries full of armed troops. Even an armoured vehicle with a mean looking machine gun mounted on top. A couple of streets were blocked with barbed wire barricades patrolled by more soldiers and Hugh admitted to himself that he wouldn't be sorry to see the back of the city.

But he needed to remember there was a war on and he still had a job to do, he now realised why he wasn't given an introductory letter to the Dublin Brigade Quartermaster which he had asked for thinking it would make his job easier. If the Tans had found something like that it on him, it would have been almost a death sentence on its own.

Personal introductions were the only safe way to proceed with the business he had to carry out. Patrick was walking more quickly now he obviously had a destination in mind and Hugh hoped he wouldn't lose him; he had no idea where he was. As they walked, Patrick was showing off his knowledge of the area and stopped at the crossing of a busy road.

"A hundred yards down there is cafe you should never go into, because if you do you may not come out. It's the Cairo cafe and its home to the most murderous gang of thugs you'd ever see or hear of. All government men of course and they have approval to knock off whoever they think they should. They're called the Cairo Gang." Again, Hugh had never heard of such a thing. "And up there is the castle, Dublin Castle a real hornet's nest of the worst the British have sent over here." Hugh had heard of it as had most Irish people, but he didn't need any warning, it was the last place on earth he would want to go.

They had reached Parnell Square and Patrick had picked up the pace.

"There it is, Devlin's Pub. The people we need to see are in there. Keep close to me now." Hugh didn't need any encouragement after their encounter with the Tans he had been looking over his shoulder expecting at any time to be bailed up again.

"Who are we seeing Patrick, can you give me a name so I can address them properly?" Hugh said, "I'm here on behalf of my Brigade and I want to impress them, not think I'm a culchie."

"You will be meeting Tim Conway, I'm told he's the Dublin Brigade Quartermaster and knows where everything is but don't expect him to tell you anything or promise you anything. He'll have to get permission from Mulcahy the Chief of Staff anyway and he's as tight as they come, he's been known to deny his own mother a Christmas present." Hugh didn't know whether Patrick was telling the truth or exaggerating, he only knew of these people by name or reputation. "All you can do is ask and plead your case and see what comes out of it, but I say again, don't expect too much. There's not much to go around."

Patrick stood with Hugh across the road from Devlin's pub and his voice took on an exceptionally serious tone.

"When we go inside," he said nodding to Devlin's across the busy road, "you'll be as welcome as a summer shamrock. Mrs Devlin will give you a great meal and a bed for the night and someone will arrange your train back to Athlone. You need to know that Devlin's is one of the Big Fellow's unofficial headquarters and he comes and goes as it suits him. But that's a state secret." He added with extra seriousness tapping the side of his nose but with a bit of a smile. "You may see some bigwigs from GHQ as well, they all come and go as they need to and there would be some interesting decisions made at the bar I'm told." Like many things in the country at the time, Patrick's information was all secret but everyone knew about everything because of the rumour mill that worked overtime in the absence of official bulletins. "You will also see some tough looking characters there. You've heard of the hard men; well these are the hardest of hard men let me tell you. Just look the other way if they look at you." Patrick was referring to members of The Squad, the casual assassins that Collins used when necessary.

It amazed Hugh that the most wanted man in the country, the Big Fellow, Michael Collins, was so often seen in public, the problem the British Secret Police had was that they weren't sure what he looked like! That plus his personal approach to his own safety seemed to surround him with an air of invincibility, 'so far, so good' he was often heard to comment in his offhand way.

Patrick looked at a large clock on a building near Devlin's and said happily,

"It's past noon, let's have a pint" and with that marched Hugh across the road into the pub. The pint was taken slowly then Patrick took a wide-eyed Hugh upstairs and found a room and knocked on the door. It was clear Patrick was known to the men in the pub.

"Come in" answered a low voice and they went in to find a man about forty years of age sitting at a desk. He held out his hand to Patrick who introduced Hugh as the Quartermaster from Athlone.

"Tim" said the man to Hugh, offering his hand, no surname, Tim knew who Hugh was and what he wanted he wouldn't have gotten this far if he hadn't been vetted. "Before you start, I can tell you it's no point in asking for five hundred rifles, we haven't got them and we can't get them. There's a waiting list a mile long for that number." Hugh expected as much but he had to put his Brigade's case.

"We have a Brigade, three battalions made up of six companies, about six hundred signed up volunteers but only about forty rifles and some shotguns and a few revolvers. We'd like to do a lot more but the RIC have pulled everything back to the towns and there's nothing left in the countryside, so there's nothing to raid, nothing to find. We're keen to take the fight further but pitchforks and Hurling sticks aren't much help." Hugh was worried he had gone too far and the expression on Tim's face wasn't at all encouraging but he had a job to do and couldn't go back to Brigade without the full story. Conway's expression darkened further before he replied.

"I know the problem son and you have our sympathy and support. We know the danger you all work with and respect the Brigade's efforts. The Midlands is tough because of the Tan barracks in Athlone and Mullingar and we know they're thick on the ground there and that's why we need to be able to use what rifles we do have in other areas where there are less soldiers. It might sound strange but we don't want pitched battles with the Tans. We want you to annoy the shit out of them and we know you'll continue to do that." Tim sat back and folded his thick arms. That was the end of the discussion thought Hugh feeling downhearted, but then he continued, "We're planning a shipment to Longford and Donegal and since we hadn't heard from Athlone, we didn't know what you wanted, so it's good that you came at the right time. We can let you have fifty rifles and five thousand rounds and one hundred grenades, they'll be there within a week. Tell your bosses not to piss them up against the wall, and the ammo is too precious for practice as well." This time Tim had finished, he nodded to Patrick who affected something akin to a salute which Hugh copied and they stood up to leave the room.

"Thank you, I'll pass on the good news at Brigade." Hugh said glad to be dismissed and somewhat overwhelmed by the GHQ atmosphere. He looked forward to getting home, he wasn't sure he would last too long in the intensity that was Dublin. Hugh was happiest working on the farm particularly making leather ropes and thongs, or repairing almost anything that could be used around the farm. As he waited on instructions as to how to get home he reflected on his visit and recalled Sean's story about visiting GHQ which was very similar. Sean didn't seem as intimidated as much as Hugh had been. Probably, Hugh thought, because of the changes in Sean, he enjoyed the heavy atmosphere, the intrigue, the secrecy and the drama of it all. The war for Hugh never offered simple solutions but Sean apparently had bought into the complexity of it all.

CHAPTER 17
The Big Houses

Hugh returned from Dublin and shared the news of arms supplies with his fellow officers who were grateful for any contribution from GHQ. The struggle against the British continued unabated and the relentless and brutal crackdown by the Tans and the Auxiliaries accelerated. Supposedly the "Auxies" as they became known were supporting the RIC but it appeared that they had taken over the running of the war and all police action. The RIC who were mostly Irishmen were usually sidelined and made subordinate but they were still the recognised force for oppression in the country. So much so that local IRA Brigades actively opposed their activity by coercing the local traders. Documents were served in towns across the country like this one in Roscommon town in August 1920:

"Notice is hereby given that all intercourse of any kind whatsoever is strictly forbidden between citizens of the Irish Republic and that portion of the Army of Occupation known as the RIC, that a general boycott of said force is ordered, and that you will cease to transact any business whatsoever with said force. Any person infringing this order will be included in said boycott."

The IRA widened their activity by targeting not only RIC barracks for destruction but also any civil administration building that housed British authority. Court houses also became targets and were attacked and burnt to the ground.

In retaliation, the Tans often terrorised villages or towns using the excuse that they had information that IRA men were hiding there. The Tans knew they wouldn't get much opposition from frightened women and children if their men were away. Often their raids were fuelled with alcohol, as happened when they commandeered a local pub and helped themselves to the contents in Limerick. Two truckloads of Tans had shot up the town hall clock and terrorised the locals for hours.

So, it continued, reprisals were met with reprisals, terror with terror, cold blooded murder with cold blooded murder. Attacks and ambushes were the orders of the day and isolated incidents flared into more serious but limited confrontations as the IRA continued to hit and run. It went on all over the country and in Northern Ireland the Ulster Volunteer Force carried out pogroms on Catholics killing innocent people and causing retaliation by the IRA. Thousands of Catholics there had also been forced out of their work on the Belfast Docks by Militias.

In the south, the RIC numbers had been reduced by resignations of hundreds of officers who could no longer deal with or control the terror. Local Judges resigned in fear. Flying Columns of IRA men had been formed and created havoc whenever they found suitable targets. Attacks were answered by more reprisals by the Tans and the Auxiliaries.

To up the ante the order had come from GHQ that the 'Big Houses' were to be a new target for the men in the field. 'Big Houses' were large often stately homes that had been in the countryside for many, perhaps hundreds of years. They were the homes of the landed gentry, mostly Protestant and absentee landlords who had inherited the properties. Westmeath due to its grazing land for cattle and sheep had its fair share of 'Big Houses'. Sean enthusiastically accepted the orders, now he would be able to contribute his efforts and put behind him the debacle of the recent failed attempt at securing the police barracks at Glasson. Sean knew the men didn't blame him for the failure, putting it down to the fortunes of war that are always going to occur in any raid, but it affected him and he was keen to make amends to himself if no one else.

"So, what are they having us do now Sean?" asked Joe with a grin as they sat in a barn in a friendly farmhouse near Moate. He had seen Sean receive the orders from a dispatch rider that morning and he suspected it was something new. Joe's attitude concerned Sean and he wondered if Joe and some of the others understood the seriousness of what was constantly being asked of them.

"Well what is it?" Joe asked again becoming a bit annoyed at what he felt was Sean's tendency to keep the men in the dark until the last minute. Joe wondered what had happened to the young friend he had grown up with, certainly the war had affected them all but Joe worried that Sean was drifting off into a world of his own. It may be Joe thought that that's what being the officer in charge does to you.

"Get the men gathered together and we'll go over what has to be done." Sean answered leaving Joe somewhat annoyed. A few months ago Sean would have treated Joe to the news confidentially. Now it seemed Joe was just one of a group, not Sean's close and trusted friend. Joe shrugged his shoulders and went to round up the rest of the men. There were still ten of them holed up at the farm and it was good that finally they were going to be active, boredom was not a good ally in any war but it was a constant. Their activities had been confined to cutting trees down to block roads or digging trenches for the same reason or cutting telegraph wires to affect communications of the RIC and the Tans. They were all the mundane but necessary things that had to be done between the dangerous face to face confrontations.

Sean looked at the men in their ragged clothes, mismatched jackets and dirty linen shirts and shoes or boots that were in great need of repair, they were looking like anything other than an army. But as Sean knew their hearts were in the right place and after all they had been forced on the run by their enemy. He unfolded the sheet of paper he was holding and spoke to them.

"You would have heard that the Tans and the Auxies burnt down six houses and terrified the people in Coosan and two of our men were killed after searches. Then they burnt some more houses in Mount Temple. There was no need it was just sheer bloody brutality. In West Clare the Tans shot up the village of Lahinch and killed two of our men. In Cork they have devastated the town with the Town Hall destroyed and churches burned and fifty good men arrested. It goes on and on and GHQ has determined it's time to make a bigger statement." Here Sean paused and made sure he had everyone's attention, "Moydrum Castle." Sean couldn't miss the reaction from Joe, whose head shot up, they knew the place well as boys and had often used its field, without permission, for their Hurling games. Sean went on, "You know where it is and it has been put on the list by GHQ as a target. We've been selected to carry out the work and we will meet up with another group of lads from Mullingar. It will be burnt to the ground along with a number of other big houses around the country side. The big houses can't be left as refuges for the Army and RIC the bigwigs who live there will now know that they aren't safe anymore. We're taking the fight to them to show that nowhere is safe for anyone who wants British rule on our island."

Some of the men were a little surprised to hear Sean's fiercer than usual words, he tended to lead by example rather than inspire with words. It was obvious he was animated by the order and keen to make a statement.

Moydrum Castle was the home of Lord and Lady Castlemaine, the former was a member of the British House of Lords and consequently no fan of Irish Republican aspirations. He had sacked any Irish staff who refused to join the British war effort in Europe. Castle was a grand name but in fact the house was more in the style of a large Manor with some castellated towers.

Sean took two days to work out a detailed plan and he visited the area with Joe. They walked around the outer grounds of the property as if they were thinking of buying the place, but they weren't challenged. Sean was also made aware that Tan officers from Athlone barracks often stayed there and so they should be prepared for resistance.

Finally Sean was ready to carry out the order, he gathered his men on the third day and they waited till dark.

His Lordship was away from the castle at the time and had left his family in the care of eight servants, some of whom would be armed. The building was approached carefully by the IRA men unsure of who may be in residence, their intelligence wasn't always one hundred percent correct. This time it was and there was to be no resistance, no Tan officers were staying there. But the men took defensive positions anyway as Sean bashed on the huge wooden front door with his rifle and demanded entry. From inside the lady of the house asked him what he wanted. Sean was direct:

"We've been ordered to burn the house down and you will have to leave at once." It was no less than what Lady Castlemaine had been expecting for some time and after she got over the initial shock she prevailed on Sean's good manners and humour to let her save some of the family treasures. The mostly Irish servants didn't offer any resistance. Sean was somewhat taken by surprise by the Lady's response but agreed to the request. Even letting some of his men help the servants with moving items out of the house. "You have fifteen minutes, that's all." He had no way of knowing who might turn up but it was not a good idea to delay any action against the enemy once you started. Joe appointed four men and they worked with Lady Castlemaine to save what they could. They took out a huge armchair which was used as a front row seat by the Lady to watch her house burn down. The men proceeded to douse the inside with petrol they had with them and Sean gave the order to set fire. It only took minutes for the house to take alight and two hundred years of family history went up in flames, or as Sean would tell it later, "two hundred years of British imperialism was destroyed in fifteen minutes." The men were pleased with the efforts and grateful there were no casualties on either side. They next moved on to nearby Creggan House and torched that as well with no casualties or resistance.

Lady Castlemaine was no doubt bitter for her loss but reportedly refused to criticise the men who carried out the attack saying they acted like gentlemen at all times, much to the frustration of her husband. The 'Big House' burning in Westmeath and others around the country had the desired effect. It made headlines in England bringing home to the English people that there was a real war going on in Ireland. GHQ had made the point that Michael Collins and the IRA leadership had intended, which was to make clear to the Brits that the Irish weren't going to be pushed around anymore. The destruction of the 'big houses' was a dramatic statement.

All over the country the Irish leadership had increased the pressure dramatically and was pushing the British as never before. Now they were hitting the British homes away from home, Irish 'Big Houses' had helped and housed generations of so called gentry from England to resettle in Ireland. Indeed, many of them considered themselves as Irish or at least Anglo Irish, a concept that the House of Lords was never able to accept. The big estates had stayed and the Land Reforms of the early part of the century never satisfied everyone, only the bankrupt estates had been broken up. It was a British solution to an Irish problem and many measures were stillborn simply adding more fuel to the ongoing resentment most rural Irish felt.

John McCormack was heard to make the point on many occasions,

> *"The Brits just don't get it, they never had and they never will, this is our country, our land and we want our own government and determinations without interference from the British Parliament. They just have to accept it, we want them out of the country and if they don't go, we'll throw them out."* It wasn't exactly how the IRB had worded their policy and it was a message that all Irish understood.

The neighbouring County to Westmeath was Longford. The IRA had a very active Battalion there led by Commander Sean MacEoin, a close friend and confidant of Michael Collins. MacEoin was making a reputation for himself and his unit was a major problem for the British.

Sean and Joe and five of their company were sent to join MacEoin's column in defence of his home village Ballinalee. It was in danger because MacEoin and fifty of his men had earlier that week found their way to Granard a town in the north of Longford which the British Army had targeted to be burned to the ground. MacEoin's men surprised a group of the attackers and his thirty five rifles caused their retreat and they moved onto their next target in Longford. There they boasted they would next attack and destroy Ballinalee because the Longford Brigade led by MacEoin needed to be taught a lesson.

MacEoin's men quickly returned to Ballinalee. As expected, a large contingent of soldiers in eleven lorries descended on the village the next night to sack it. It was nearing midnight and the IRA men were ready and in place and surprised the soldiers and a gun battle proceeded for the next five hours. It caused the soldiers to evacuate the village in a hurry leaving behind some of the loot from their foray into Granard and welcome supplies of ammunition and revolvers and even food for the IRA men. Sean and Joe took part in the fighting escaping without injury.

Activities were also taking place nearby. Volunteers from Boher, Tang and Drumraney positioned themselves outside of Athlone and attacked two lorries which were coming from Longford. Despite the paucity of arms and ammunition, the IRA contingent led by Hugh disabled the lorries and the following skirmish caused two RIC deaths and the death of a young IRA volunteer.

The reprisals continued and Ballinalee was attacked again a week later by several hundred soldiers who burnt down many homes and the blacksmith forge of Sean MacEoin's family. It had been a typical Tan overreaction to their humiliation a week earlier. Rather than seek swift revenge, MacEoin thought it best to send a strong message, the intent of which would not be missed. Sean accompanied MacEoin and a group of men to the county home of James Wilson, Currygranne House, another 'big house', but currently untouched. Wilson was the brother of Field Marshal Sir Henry Wilson who was the commander of the British forces in Ireland. MacEoin took James Wilson to see the destruction that had taken place at Ballinalee and simply warned him that if one other house or farm was damaged by British forces in County Longford then James Wilson's home would be destroyed with him in it! It had the desired affect and no further homes were attacked in that county. The lesson was not lost on Sean who learned that threats of terror and reprisals can be as much as a deterrent as an actual event.

Sean's life was changed by this officer who bore a similar sounding name to his own. Joe and Hugh thought Sean was not only changed but had hardened into a military mindset that they felt was contrary to good sense.

But such were the times, and fighting men subscribed to whatever doctrine would get them through and if that meant having to change who or what they were then that was a price they had to pay. Sean met MacEoin again shortly after in Ballinalee, ordered by his Brigade officers to join the Longford Flying Column for more experience.

"We'll be off tomorrow first light, you can sleep in the barn and mother will bring you some food, but be ready when you hear my orders." MacEoin said to Sean, It was a no nonsense approach which Sean admired. The Commander hadn't even asked Sean about his orders just summed him up by looking him up and down, "we've a few truckloads of Tans we have to welcome, are you ready for it?", MacEoin was confident Sean was capable as he had been briefed about his involvement so far and had seen him help out weeks earlier when Ballinalee was attacked. He needed reliable men who could handle the stress of fighting and the unstructured endurance of survival in the hostile countryside.

"Yes sir," said Sean "I hope I'll be able to help." It sounded inadequate but Sean hadn't decided how to handle his new CO who was only a few years older than himself.

"You will or you'll go back home." was all MacEoin said. "Be ready at first light, the others will be here in good time." The CO wandered off to the cottage as Sean noticed two other men coming down the road towards it, their rifles slung over their shoulders and looking as if they were heading for a night out. They were the first of fifteen others who came in the same way over the next four hours. It was still very cold at night and the men met in the barn and tried to keep warm as "mother", as the CO had called her, brought in some hot soup for their sustenance. Sean introduced himself to each man as they arrived, similar to his own company they were from all over the local area and their mission was to destabilise the enemy however the commanders saw fit. Small and deadly actions taken often. Get in, kill and get out.

Up till that time Sean's activities with his group had mainly been attacks on RIC barracks and engagements with perhaps a few Black and Tans with quick short actions and a retreat to the woods. Now there were twenty men with the CO and they moved swiftly into position once they reached their target area. The plan was to ambush two lorries of Auxiliaries and capture their weapons, they wouldn't take prisoners because they couldn't house them, nor would they kill them all, that wasn't the purpose of the attack. Whatever casualties eventuated would be as a result of what happened when the action started. Firstly, they planted a land mine on the road near a bridge and as the lorries approached the CO had the men perfectly positioned. The explosion killed the driver of the first lorry and the Flying Column opened fire pinning down the remaining soldiers. They fought back and exchanged fire for two hours which for Sean was the longest sequence of action he had taken part in except for Ballinalee. Unbeknown to the Rebels, one of the soldiers escaped to try and reach some reinforcements. Eventually the Auxies surrendered when their commanding officer was killed, another four had been killed and eight wounded. Sean watched as his CO treated the prisoners with respect and insisted his men not abuse them physically but gave them water and saw to their wounds. It was not usual to stay around after such an incident and MacEoin's men were getting restless. They collected whatever weapons they could, taking a handy haul of a Lewis gun, eighteen rifles, twenty revolvers and eight hundred rounds of ammunition. They couldn't delay their retreat any longer as a lookout had seen a convoy of lorries with reinforcements heading their way. MacEoin gave the order and the men melted into the woods each making their own way to their designated hiding areas. Sean was impressed with the military precision and demeanour of MacEoin and vowed to himself to follow his example when leading his own men. He reflected sadly that he had not seen such professionalism in his own Brigade command.

The aftermath for the civilian population of the area was dramatic and costly and one farmer was killed for no apparent reason. Six villages were also raided searching for IRA men and a number of farm houses and fields were destroyed by fire. The raids the Auxies carried out were to ram home the message that such attacks by the IRA and civilian protection of any IRA men would be met with more indiscriminate terror.

Soon after, Sean returned to his home area and carried on with his orders as they arrived from the Athlone Brigade command. He had been blooded in a new way and saw through MacEoin's action what being a soldier really meant and he fashioned his own thinking to make sure he would succeed the same way. Ireland was going to need men like that when the new order was established and they had their own Republic.

CHAPTER 18
Bloody Sunday November 1920

1920 continued to deliver mayhem and terror all over the country. The Black and Tans goal was to instil fear into the Irish and let them know who was in charge and their viciousness grew as the war progressed.

The IRA command in Dublin led by Michael Collins decided it was time to bring matters to a head. What was needed was a decisive action that would change the course of the war. The British Intelligence forces operating out of Dublin Castle were constantly lifting IRA men off the streets of Dublin. Taking them into the Castle and beating information out of them, holding them sometimes for weeks without trial or any legal representation. The Intelligence operatives were known simply as the Cairo Gang after a café they used for meetings. They watched each other's backs and hunted in packs for IRA operatives, supported by the state apparatus. Collin's plan was simple but desperate. He had his own band of men, known as The Squad, who were prepared to be just as ruthless. A minor player in the Collin's group was Patrick McCormack, Joe and Hugh's cousin who lived in Dublin and had been a member of the IRA and IRB since he was sixteen. But Patrick was not to be a shooter who would put himself in the firing line, Collins saw to that personally knowing that Patrick had a wife and children. Patrick was a driver who delivered men when requested to special operations and waited outside ready at the wheel for speedy getaways.

On Sunday November 21st Patrick was contacted very early in the morning and given his instructions, he was to collect his vehicle at the usual place then pick up two men at the Hotel he knew was used by The Squad. He knew the two men by sight but they never exchanged names only brief greetings. Then he drove them to an address which they gave him. It was one of ten addresses that would be attacked that morning by The Squad.

Patrick parked the car one hundred yards down the road from his target address and kept the engine running, his two passengers got out and strode down the street, Patrick edged the vehicle closer to the entrance, he needed to be outside the front door at the moment they emerged. He heard six gunshots and his hand gripped the wheel harder, his foot on the clutch and accelerator and his heart beating so hard he felt it through his jacket. The two assailants came quietly out of the front door entrance and climbed into the car,

"Go" was all one of them said, then added "Not too fast", now was not the time to attract attention. Patrick drove the men away from the city to a prearranged drop off point then continued on to a private garage and left the vehicle out of sight. Patrick took a deep breath and walked home to his Dublin tenement looking forward to a late breakfast with his wife and children.

That morning nineteen British secret service agents were victims of shootings and fourteen of them died that day and one other a few days later. The Intelligence Service was decimated and Collins had made a dramatic statement and his reputation for cold blooded tactics was confirmed. It would prove to be a turning point in the war.

It did not take long for the British Administration to take revenge, whether officially sanctioned or not was never confirmed, but revenge it would be. That afternoon a Gaelic Football match between Dublin and Tipperary was scheduled at Croke Park and the crowd was expected to be around fifteen thousand. As the game was underway an armoured car mounted with a machine gun plus two lorry loads of soldiers entered the Park and drove onto the playing field in the middle of play. Without warning the soldiers opened fire on the crowd and the players. Fourteen people were killed including one of the players and another eighty were wounded including women and children, many whilst trying to escape the carnage.

'Bloody Sunday' as the day became known was the most visible manifestation of the violence that bedevilled the country so far in the war and it was traumatic for both sides. When violence is unleashed it is difficult to reign in and when the young men in Westmeath heard of the events they were horrified as most of the country was. Joe was visibly upset,

"Jaysus Sean what have we made. Sure, it was going to be a battle we thought for independence but now we have women and kiddies being shot down for going to a football match. God save us from the hell it's become." Joe crossed himself in the manner of Catholics who are seeking closeness to their creator, and then buried his head in his hands. Such was his alarm he was unable to speak further.

Sean looked at Joe and tried to assess his own feeling at the news of both massacres. Thirty lives wiped out in the name of war in one day and many others ruined by the violence. What had become of their little country and what to make of the North? The Catholics in Belfast and Derry were virtually in a state of siege, victims of a pogrom, and their government was run by Protestants who wouldn't assist them and indeed persecuted them.

Finally, Sean said what he felt,

"It's war Joe, it's war and it's ugly when we have it in our own backyard but we have to push through it. Our future needs us and we have to be strong." All he could do was put a hand on Joe's shoulder as some kind of comfort.

Joe heard the words but they were not what he expected, Sean didn't feel the same way as he did and Joe wondered why his friend had changed so much. Violence had the effect of controlling your very being and as they were so close to it, they each had to deal with it in their own way. Sean continued,

" Violence is needed and it will happen and we have to accept it." He was looking at Joe and met his gaze with a steely determination, a coldness that would not consider anything less than what was necessary for victory. Joe was confused by Sean's response, he had simply thought about the football match and had never ever imagined violence against children could be possible in the way it had happened. For now he decided to ignore Sean and took his own counsel and his thoughts turned to Maggie, she was the balm that would help his confusion about the day's events. He knew he had to see her one more time before she was lost to him perhaps for all time when she would have to leave Ireland.

CHAPTER 19
A Visit to Athlone for Joe

The opportunity for Joe to go to Athlone came unexpectedly and though he could hardly hide his excitement he indeed had to as the visit would entail a funeral. His father had told him that he had to accompany his mother to Athlone. A cousin of hers had recently died and she wanted to go to the funeral. Also, it was a chance to stock up on some necessary supplies for the winter that was approaching. The trip would be about ten miles over rough country tracks until they got closer to Athlone, their pony trap offered a bumpy ride but Joe couldn't have cared less about that. This was his first chance for some time to see Maggie who lived with her family in Irishtown a suburb of Athlone. It had been a couple of months since he had last seen her at his Hurley match in the town. He had been unable to stop thinking of her and hoped that what her cousin had told him about her being sent to Australia had not yet come to pass.

Joe had been busy with his farm work, his IRA involvement and his Hurling. He had been to Dublin a year ago when he represented Westmeath in Dublin against Dublin in the qualifications for the All Ireland Hurling finals. Joe remembered fondly his visit to the capital with his team, the only time he had been there since with Sean, when he had attended the funeral of Thomas Ashe the hunger striker who had died from mistreatment and whose funeral drew thousands. Again, he saw the devastation from the Uprising in Easter 1916, buildings still unrepaired and roads still torn up. The urban warfare had cost many lives but had lit the flame of revolution for the whole country and had a profound impact on Joe and his teammates. The match though was less memorable, Dublin had been All Ireland Champions two years earlier and had a champion team mostly made up of students from the University College Dublin and they beat Westmeath easily.

The trip to Athlone took about four hours with an early start and many rests to make sure the horse could handle the trip. The approach roads to Athlone saw many British Army troops with trucks constantly honking to get past slow moving pony traps. Joe had been told not to have anything on him that could indicate his IRA connections. He made sure he was able to be free of any trouble to ensure he could look after his mother. Mary Keegan was less circumspect and carried Cumman na mBan literature confident that the Tans wouldn't be game enough to search a woman. Joe was mercifully ignorant of his mother's belongings.

They were able to leave their horse and trap on the edge of the town in the stable of an old friend, giving the horse a chance to rest for the journey back to Drumraney the next day. They then made their way to Mary's cousin's house and the usual family greetings were made. The funeral would be the next morning and Joe would be sleeping on the couch downstairs. He watched as his mother renewed her friendships with memories from her childhood and enjoyed some of the small talk for a while. As usual, his mother couldn't leave out the politics and little understood the reluctance of city dwellers like her cousins not to want to discuss the current war. Mary was indifferent to the city ways not understanding that the people were more guarded in their conversation.

Joe found a reason to excuse himself, he wanted to find Maggie's house before it got dark and he needed to be off the streets by then anyway to avoid being picked up by a Tan patrol. The address given to him by his teammate Blaise who was Maggie's cousin was correct but the directions weren't exact. Finally, he found the street and took a deep breath as he stood in front of the house he needed. He knocked on the door and it quickly opened and there she was, Maggie as pretty as he had remembered, perhaps even prettier! He hoped she knew him after all this time. He searched for the right words but couldn't find them and whatever came out, came out.

"Maggie, it's Joe, Joe Keegan, we met at a Hurling match some time ago your cousin Blaise Phelan introduced us." He waited for a response, his heart thumping away and his mouth drying then she disarmed him with the friendliest of smiles,

"Joe of course, how nice to see you again, you better come in." She was anxious to get him off the street. Irishtown was full of British Army war widows who had lost their husbands in the Great War and had no truck with the IRA or its work. Any strange young man in the neighbourhood was likely to be considered suspicious, such were the times. "I'll tell mammy that your here." This surprised Joe and he was about to tell her it was her he came to see, not her mammy, then he realised she was simply following protocol. She was only seventeen after all and she needed a good reason to have a strange young man in the house. Mrs Egan promptly came into the front room with Maggie to see the visitor, she was polite but a little distant unsure of what this young fellow wanted. Joe again scrambled for the right thing to say but finally decided to be just honest and not make up any story.

"Excuse me Mrs. Egan for calling unexpected, I have brought my Mammy to Athlone for a funeral and……..well, I haven't been here for a few months and ……….." he baulked at what he knew was coming but he had come too far to back off. "I wanted to see your daughter one more time, Blaise told me she might be going away and ….I just wanted to see her before she went." There he had said it; it was out in the open now and he was glad but his heart jumped every time he stole a glance at Maggie.

Maggie's mother said nothing for a few seconds but looked at the young man and considered her position then she smiled as well,

"Well I suppose I had better organise a cup of tea for your visitor Maggie, I'll have Rose help me." With that she returned to the kitchen and Joe let out an inaudible sigh and started to relax.

It was Maggie's turn now to find the right words, she had thought about what had happened, the unexpected visit from the handsome young Hurling player she had met and still remembered fondly,

"Joe please sit down you must be tired."

Joe took a seat and looked around the small tenement house which was neat and tidy but not ostentatious, not that he would have expected that, they were after all working-class folk in Athlone. He found his tongue again:

"So, Blaise tells me you're going to go to Australia, is that still happening? It's such a long way to go."

"Yes, my Da wants to get us out of Ireland for a while and his aunt in Sydney has agreed to pay the passage for myself and Rose, we'll be going within a few months as soon as the money arrives." While Joe was upset at the confirmation of the news but he could understand Maggie's father's concern. Athlone and Ireland generally weren't exactly the place for young ladies as attractive as Maggie. Not in a garrison town and not with Black and Tans roaming the streets virtually a law unto themselves. Surprisingly he felt somewhat relieved to think Maggie would be in a safer place than Ireland. But Maggie continued,

"All we know is she'll be expecting us to be domestics for her but Da insists it's a good idea for us to go. Rose is only fifteen and she'll miss home a lot." Maggie was looking pensive and even sad, this wasn't what Joe had wanted but realised she must have given her trip a lot of thought,

"It will be an adventure no doubt," was all he could think to reply. Maggie looked into his eyes and he could see that there was a kindred feeling to what he felt for her.

"Perhaps you could even find your way there one day." She said.

Joe was sure his heart skipped a beat on hearing those words but he didn't know how to respond to them directly,

"I hear it's a grand country full of strange creatures and deserts and oceans and hot weather." Which just about exhausted Joe's knowledge of Australia but he didn't want to finish there, "My Uncle John told me that many Irish had been sent there, to Sydney town in New South Wales as prisoners after the revolutions last century. So you may find some Irish friends quickly, not everyone went to America." Joe could feel his face flushing red and hoped he hadn't come across as a know-all but Maggie was interested in what he had to say.

"Sydney is a much bigger town than Athlone and though we're worried we're also excited, it is a big adventure after all."

"How long will the sailing take?"

"About six to eight weeks we're told, that will be strange we've never been on a ship before and we have to go to London to catch it." It all sounded so exotic to Joe, as it was to Maggie and he found he was a little envious of her.

"I'm sure it will be very exciting. Do you know when you will be going Maggie, has the date been decided yet?" She'd already told him a few months but he'd forgotten already.

Before Maggie could answer Mrs. Egan returned with a cup of tea for them each with Maggie's sister Rose offering newly baked biscuits and trying to stop herself giggling at the strange turn of events. Joe was grateful that Mr Egan wasn't home, he doubted if he would have had the courage to say anything if he had answered the door. He would have preferred to come across a truck load of Tans than explain his presence to Maggie's father.

Joe didn't really want to hear the answer but he needed to. He was gulping his tea to stop his mouth going dry again and wondered if he would see Maggie again before she left.

"Perhaps December, if everything goes as Da plans."

"And when will you come home?" that is what Joe wanted to know more than anything.

"That depends on Da's aunty, I think, she's paying for the tickets and we may be there for a year or so at least until everything settles down here. Da wants us away from here as soon as we can."

Joe understood, no final details, he would just have to make do with what he knew. Now he felt it was time he made his return to his own mammy so she wouldn't be worried.

Joe stood and excused himself,

"I need to be going it will be dark soon and the restrictions will be in place." He was also thinking that if the Tans caught him he'd get a kicking but he left that unsaid.

Joe was delighted at having seen Maggie again and he had not been rejected, he marvelled at his own bravado, it was such an unexpected thing for him to do. But he had done it and he would never regret it.

"It was nice to see you again Joe, I hope we can meet again before we leave." Maggie said, it was all Joe wanted to hear "I'll tell Mammy you're leaving." With that she summoned her mother and they all politely wished each other farewell.

Joe took his leave and felt he was floating above the ground but quickly realised he needed his wits about him and headed for the nearest back lane. He needed to find his way out of Irishtown and back to where his mother was staying. He had an hours walk ahead of him and it was now completely dark, he pulled his collar up and his cap down trying to look like anyone else out and about when they shouldn't be.

CHAPTER 20
Political Intrigue and Talk of a Truce

Joe and his mother made it back to Drumraney without incident. Mary Keegan was happy as she had collected more literature regarding Cumann na mBan from some contacts which she would spread around her own community. In its own way, propaganda was helpful to everyone. No-one knew exactly what was happening as they only had newspapers to keep them informed and they were often formal and lacking in emotion. The propaganda Mary had picked up on the other hand gave glowing reports and information on IRA activities around the country. It usually only spoke of victories and failed to mention the roundups and arrests of fighting units. But still the fighting went on, and the winter of 1920 – 21 dragged on, and spring of the new year brought new hope to the IRA men in the field. It had been the best part of two years now since early civil disobedience turned into deadly action with deaths on both sides. The people of Ireland generally felt absolutely war weary. But their message of a desire for independence was getting through to the British establishment which was facing growing social unrest on their own island. New voting rights for men and women there were forcing the political parties to be more responsive and trade unions were using their industrial power in new ways.

Sean had plenty of opinion on the politics of the day for Ireland and what should happen. He often spoke with John McCormack who was a member of the Dail which still met in secret. John had his own views which he picked up and embellished in his personal contact with men who were close to the decision makers. Sean was happy to hear this information from John and share it with his friends over an occasional pint of Guinness when they had the funds. As spring moved to summer, talk of a Truce was everywhere, whispered in pubs and markets but no one knew what was likely to happen.

"Sure, and you know DeValera's been invited to London for talks with Lloyd George, they're saying he may go in July and put the case before the Cabinet." Sean delayed a moment before offering his next thought, "But I'm not sure if Dev's the right man, even John thinks he's too dogmatic and the British will play him for a fool." Joe wasn't taking any of that, he had seen Dev speak at rallies and believed in him as a strong advocate of all things Irish.

"Dev will tell them what they need to hear, we want a Republic and we won't settle for anything less. That's what Dev will tell them." Joe was a bit heated about the point he was making but he felt it strongly and thought everyone else felt the same he was surprised at Sean's answer:

"Well a Republic would be grand and that's what we all want but they don't think that's what the Brits will offer. They'll still want to keep us under their thumb. It's all politics and they are masters at it. Don't forget it's not that long ago they did the Versailles Treaty and left Germany gasping for air." Sean was pleased with his own knowledge, he spent a lot of time trying to keep himself informed of current affairs, but Joe wanted more information.

"So, who is 'they' Sean, who is saying Dev won't get want we all want?"

"Just some members of the Dail and the government and some senior IRA men, John is just repeating what he hears and that's what's coming through."

"Well", Joe responded, "it's not like it's all going to be sorted in one meeting the talks will go on for months."

"Aye and we have to remember that the people in some areas have had enough of the war and the terror from the Tans, there's a need to bring that under control."

"And we do that by surrendering the Republic?" Joe almost shouted and a couple of the others around him including his brothers Hugh and a newly recruited brother James watched to see where the argument was going. Sean drew a deep breath; he had his own ideas but thought now wasn't the time to air them. Based on what he'd heard and he agreed with the thought that the Republic might not be as easily gained as everyone wished. Compromise was a possibility but Dev was not the one who might offer that to the British.

"We'll just have to wait and see what the big men decide." That was as far as Sean wanted to go at this point.

Arguments like this were going on all around the country. The IRA had slowed down their activity and the men in the field worried if a political settlement was likely. If hostilities ceased, they could be expected to lay down their arms and maybe even come out into the open, making themselves visible to the British Secret Service and their army. It was a huge risk and senior IRA men were skeptical and apprehensive about the exposure.

The complicated internal politics could hardly be comprehended by young men in pubs in the countryside. The 'Big fellow', Collins and the 'Long Fellow' de Valera were the main players and they towered intellectually over their followers and they were listened to fervently. They offered leadership when it was mostly needed. They had the same vision for the future but they did not always agree on how that vision would be achieved.

Eamonn de Valera had recently returned from the USA reasserting his authority and showing confidence in victory. He was the erstwhile President of an unlawful Republic and head of Sinn Fein. The IRB on the other hand was less confident about victory. The leadership headed by Michael Collins knew the precarious state of the IRA and its finances and the problems they were having keeping themselves armed and enough men in the field to continue fighting. They after all were the ones actually fighting the war, not Dev. There was also the growing tension amongst the Dail members and de Valera was backed by his clique, among them Cathal Brugha who hated Collins and sundry others who had their hats in the ring and always plenty to say. The politics inside the movement was never easy.

As Sean had said, the people generally were losing their appetite for war. Victories when they came were usually small scale. Not everyone understood the tactics of guerrilla style attacks and killing even if it meant the deaths of the hated Black and Tans. The British reprisals on the people were having their intended effect. The tension of waiting to hear if a son, father, husband or close friend had been killed in action or taken prisoner, not to be seen again for months, was demoralising.

By mid 1921 King George V understood his own people in England were tiring of the continued fighting in Ireland so soon after the Great War and they just wanted some peace. But the Irish problem just wouldn't go away. The government of Lloyd George had in 1920 passed The Partition of Ireland Act which he believed would solve all the problems. The Protestants in Northern Ireland, led by James Craig, got what they wanted which was their own parliament and partition from the south but the Act was rejected by the South of Ireland.

The politics became the main arena and the fighting was mostly put on hold. Eamon de Valera as nominal President of the declared but unrecognized Republic and leader of Sinn Fein went to London in July 1921 to tell the British government what the Irish wanted. An independent Republic no strings attached and a loose association with the British Empire and to finally live their own way without British interference.

But this was a long way from how the British saw things, after all they had an empire to consider and weren't about to accept the Irish point of view, they had too much to lose. Ireland would be offered Dominion status similar to Canada and South Africa with full allegiance to the Sovereign and a Governor General appointed by London with considerable powers. But you will remain part of the British Empire. You can have your own parliament as will the North but members will have to swear an oath of allegiance to the Crown!

This was a red rag to a bull and in their talks de Valera was outfoxed by Lloyd George who had all the power he needed and the backing of his government and parliament.

Dev rejected the offer and returned to Ireland for further discussions with the Dail and the Executive of the Government. This included Michael Collins, simply the two Irishmen did not see the same solution to the age old problem. Dev had been in the USA for most of the previous eighteen months and many felt that he had lost touch with the reality of what had been going on in his own country. The war had been fought under the leadership of Michael Collins who had the IRB behind him and Dev was out of touch.

There would be no Republic! Lloyd George and his Cabinet were definite about that.

As Collins told Dev, we can fight on but we don't have any money or resources and not much chance of getting any. There'll be no help from Europe or America except what money we can smuggle in. We can't match the power of the British Empire and if they chose to, they would crush the country. There was no doubt that Collins wanted the same outcome as de Valera, their Nationalist instincts had driven them both for their entire lives and Collins had continually risked his life over the past two years with his leadership. Republicanism and independence was in the blood of both men and those of their countrymen and women, they wanted independence so bad they could taste it. Collins also wanted to take the fight to Northern Ireland and make the Protestant government pay for their dreadful treatment of the Catholics, there it was a religious divide and the politics was built on that. A pogrom had been underway and many Catholics were seeking shelter in the south, which did not make too many Northern Protestants unhappy.

CHAPTER 21
An Uneasy Peace and a Belfast Visit

While the politics played out in Dublin and London, the Irish people had to deal with their own reality. Their lives had been turned upside down by the insurrection and the effective military occupation of their country. That occupation had been met with a level of violence of which the men and women of Ireland never believed they were capable. Now as a Truce was declared and the talks went on, the violence had reduced but not totally stopped. GHQ had ordered the IRA to stand down and to wait and see what the political talks would deliver.

That was easier said than done. The Volunteers had been running on adrenaline and fear for some time and their enemy didn't just disappear, the soldiers of the British Empire were still in their midst and were still threatening. It didn't take much to start an incident and many people were arrested on flimsy excuses with no due process available to them.

The Truce had an impact on the activities of the IRA which didn't want to lose momentum and increased their training regime. As a staff officer, Sean was directed to a training camp at Glenasmole, County Wicklow run by GHQ. There was an increasing availability of weaponry as the Truce had let the import of arms go unchecked and Sean was introduced to new arms and new methods of warfare.

Sean MacEoin, whom Sean hoped to meet up with again was not at the training camp but in Mountjoy prison having been charged with the murder of an RIC Inspector who led a raid on his home. He was also a member of the Dail, having been elected at the last election. In spite of that, on June 14 MacEoin was brought before a Military Court Martial and sentenced to death by hanging. He was ultimately spared that fate by intense political pressure from his good friend Michael Collins.

The training camp had a major impact on Sean and he took to the training keenly confirming his preference for an Army career in the new Republic when it became available. Many others from the Brigade were also sent to training camps and this was happening all over the country. GHQ was anxious that the men did not just accept that the fighting would be over because of the talks in London. No one knew what that outcome would be. Sean met with Joe briefly before he left for his training camp and shared with Joe his desire to join a national army as soon as the Republic was formed. Joe was surprised,

"You mean you'll like taking and giving orders and running around a parade ground dressed like an Auxie?" This was contrary to the way they bad both lived for the past two years, essentially living off the land and sleeping in whatever bed they could find then moving on to the next skirmish.

"We've got to get some order into the process. Whatever comes out of the truce talks we'll have to make the best of, start building a new country, a new government, a new army. We can't go on like this forever." It was obvious Sean had decided whatever way events went after the war he was going with them.

Joe wasn't so sure, he didn't aspire to an army life, he wanted to get back to playing Hurley as soon as possible. He enjoyed it so much and it was his future, perhaps the national championships one day. And there was Maggie, who he desperately wanted to see again before she left the country. He decided to change the subject.

"You know Hugh and Patrick McCormack and myself will be going up north with the Kildare boys? We're meeting up in Donegal and hundreds of us are planning to go into the Protestant northern counties. There'll be a right old to do, the 'Big Fellow' is organizing them but he doesn't want the world to know. But he'll be damned if he'll let Sir James Craig and his bunch of cutthroats have their own way up there." Joe and the others had decided to take advantage of the truce while things were still quiet and help out up North.

Sean wasn't surprised by the news; he had heard that the situation up there was dire for the Catholics and for anyone who expressed nationalist sympathies and he'd heard rumours that an unofficial invasion was planned, by the South! The centuries old segregation and tensions between Catholic and Protestants in the northern counties, always simmering below the surface, had grown into a new and dangerous threat to all the people there and it wouldn't be resolved by talks.

"Collins will upset the English if they know he's behind it, they think he's wanting peace."

"Hugh told me that Craig's policy is to kill as many Catholics as they can as quickly as possible. They have armed the so-called Police recruits, 'B' Specials they call them but all they are is Protestant killer gangs. Hundreds of Catholics have been driven from their homes and the government there won't help them. The English have sent over soldiers to quiet things down but Hugh says they have just made things worse."

Sean had seen and heard the reports about what was happening in the northern counties and Belfast in particular. A recent riot had seen sixteen civilians killed and one hundred and sixty houses destroyed. No one knew when the rioting would stop and Michael

Collins had acted on his own authority to help the Catholic minority.

"When are you going?" he asked Joe.

"We'll be in Donegal in a few days and so will Patrick and a couple of hundred others, they're ready to go over the border. We had a God almighty row with our Da who had forbidden us to go. God knows he's had it hard for the past eighteen months with Hugh and me running around with the IRA and my other brothers going missing for weeks on end for the same reason."

# # # #

The visitors to the northern counties were to be confounded by the horrors they would see.

Hugh, Joe and Patrick McCormack joined the group of Volunteers from Kildare and Cork to help out however they could. Their base was in the nearby border county of Donegal from where it was easier to slip over into enemy territory and do whatever had to be done and get out. They received more than they bargained for when they stayed in Belfast with IRA contacts for a couple of days.

The Royal Ulster Constabulary (RUC) police force made up exclusively of Protestants was joined by their deputies in the "B" Specials, more Protestant civilian men deputized to help keep the peace. Sadly, the RUC were ill disciplined to say the least and were party to indiscriminate killings of Catholic and IRA suspects. Joe, Hugh and Patrick and others had been sent in to Belfast to shore up numbers but they were in as much danger as everyone else in the area. They did not witness but heard of the atrocities in which six men were tortured and killed by the RUC in the Crumlin

Road area. When a riot is taking place, it is difficult to know who is who, and defending the Catholic population was difficult as they were severely outnumbered and outgunned. The urban terror was something that Joe and Hugh, who had been brought up on a farm, could not handle well, Patrick having lived in the slums of Dublin was more able to handle the chaos.

One particular night was filled with terror as an armoured car drove into the street where they had been billeted and soldiers were bashing on doors of homes and indiscriminately firing into the houses to terrorise the inhabitants. Patrick, Hugh and Joe and others who were armed replied with their own indiscriminate firing of pistols and rifles. Many gunshot wound victims turned up at local hospitals for treatment overwhelming the hospital service that eventually had to turn some away. The three Southerners only stayed a few days more and had to retreat to the hills of Donegal when they heard that their presence had been betrayed. The RUC saw imported IRA men as a worthy trophy to put on display, preferably with their severed heads on a pike.

The violence would worsen for the Catholics in Belfast. As the Truce talks were imminent the northern Protestants were fearful of being betrayed by the British government and decided to make their point with more pogroms and rioting in Catholic areas. They were adamant that they would never be governed by a Catholic majority in the South.

CHAPTER 22
Return to the South

Joe and Hugh returned to Drumraney and Patrick found his way back to Dublin and his family. In the south it was much quieter. Joe at this time took advantage of the relaxed atmosphere during the Truce and decided to try for a meeting with Maggie again before she was lost to him. This time though he would use more guile and try to meet her on her own. His family always needed something in Athlone and though there was not much money available, some traders did extend credit. Joe liked to bargain so he was sent to the town for some provisions accompanied by Hugh who caught up with some old friends while Joe went on his own mission.

Now that he knew where Maggie lived, he decided not to just knock on the door but arrived early in the day hoping that she would need to leave the house for some reason. He took up a position close by trying not to look suspicious which was difficult in an Army town but he had only to wait thirty minutes and the house door opened. Maggie and her sister Rose emerged on their own clearly off to a local market to shop. Joe would give them a small start and then happen to bump into them, total coincidence of course.

"Top of the morning to you ladies." Joe said doffing his cap and trying to sound light hearted and not show his nerves, "Nice to see you again."

Both Maggie and Rose showed genuine surprise, it had been a couple of weeks since Joe had been around to visit and they knew he lived about ten miles out of town. Maggie spoke first:

"Joe, so nice to see you, are you going to market?" Rose looked embarrassed and didn't say anything and just smiled.

"Sure, and I need to get some things for my Mammy and Da and Athlone's the place to come to for market." He knew it was time wasting small talk but it was all he had. Again, he was struck by how pretty Maggie looked and his nerves were giving up on him, he was running out of things to say till Rose came to the rescue.

"There's Fianna, please Maggie can I go and talk to her?" she was respectful of her older sister as was expected and she quickly ran off on Maggie's nod to see her friend. Joe couldn't believe his luck, talking to Maggie would be much easier without Rose around. Still he scuffed his feet and stuck his hands in his pocket.

"So, have you the date for when you'll go to Australia?" he managed.

"My Da says it will be early December, he received the money to pay for the fares and so it's settled." She said this as though she was unhappy with the arrangement but knew better than to show disrespect for her father's decision. Joe again was saddened by the news; he hadn't known what to expect perhaps something had changed and she wouldn't be going after all. But that wasn't to be the case. He was now genuinely lost for words.

They walked towards the local market keeping an eye on Rose who was chatting and giggling with her friend.

"It's such a long way away Australia." Joe said finally finding his tongue.

"Aye, seven weeks on a boat, we're not sure how we'll go with that, never been on a ship before, not even the ferry." Indicating England and Wales with a slight nod of her head "Have you done that Joe?"

"No, never set foot outside Ireland, had no need and no money either. My Da went once a long time ago but he never spoke about it much." The silence set in again and Joe just knew he wanted to sit with Maggie and hold her hand but didn't know how to even start something like that. Finally, they found a bench and sat beside each other keeping a respectful distance as you did with respectable ladies. Joe found the courage to look into Maggie's eyes and uttered some words which he couldn't explain.

"I'll miss you Maggie, I'll miss you a lot." It was a bit silly really, they had only met a couple of times but Joe had once heard of something called 'Love at first sight', maybe that was it. Maggie smiled.

"Thanks Joe, I'll miss you as well." With that she smiled and tears welled in her eyes. They sat there frozen for many minutes neither of them wanting to end the spell they had somehow cast on each other. At last Joe found the courage and took Maggie's hand in his own, it was warm and he congratulated himself for the effort. Maggie didn't retract and indeed placed her other hand over Joe's. It was at that moment their souls were joined as well.

"Somehow I'll manage to see you again Maggie, it will be all I live for." He squeezed her hand gently and a tear rolled down her cheek which Joe gently brushed aside for her. They sat there in silence for another few minutes till her sister Rose came back noticing their hands joined but didn't know what to say. Maggie disengaged from Joe and stood up.

"We need to be on our way and do the market I know my Mam worries so these days when we are out."

"Of course, I'll walk part of the way with you, I have to head back to Drumraney as well."

"Go safely Joe, it's a long walk."

"I'm hoping a kind farmer will let me ride with him." Joe smiled and they started towards the market area. He took Maggie's hand again briefly and held her gaze for a few moments when they parted company. He knew it could be the last time he would see her and he wanted the memory of her to stay as long as possible.

CHAPTER 23
The Truce Holds and Treaty Talks Begin

"Do you realize that this means war, Mr. de Valera?" Lloyd George, the British Prime Minister had said to Eamon de Valera at their July 1921 talks, confronting him with the threat of renewed war if the peace was not settled by the Irish. "I could put a British soldier in Ireland for every man, woman and child in the country."

Mr. de Valera's response was swift and he wanted to highlight the obvious.

"Ah yes, but the problem is you would have to keep them there." He was implying of course that the costs of an ongoing war with Ireland would have tremendous human and monetary costs for the British. So, de Valera after days of talks and arguments, sloganeering and posturing on both sides and putting forward his preferences and demands for Ireland had rejected the British terms. They were too far from what he wanted for his country, in reality not even close.

Thus, the Truce talks floundered. The British were the most powerful empire on earth despite the cost of the recently ended World War and it still saw itself as a major world power. Ireland was a nuisance, a stone in their shoe but it was causing considerable pain for such a small country. The British view was if Ireland gets its way, India and other non-Anglo territories would want independence as well. There would be no retreat by this Government on this matter.

Lloyd George had presented de Valera with a long document listing what the British wanted and insisted on: Essentially Ireland was to remain part of the British Commonwealth of Nations similar to Canada, Australia and South Africa and it could have Dominion status and its own government. The British Sovereign would be Ireland's sovereign as well and its parliament would pledge allegiance to that Sovereign plus Britain would maintain three sea ports there.

Mr. de Valera totally rejected these terms, took his leave and returned to Dublin to consult with his Cabinet. His rejection of the terms started a tumultuous five months in Ireland's political history. He believed and knew in his heart that all Irish people, certainly those in the southern twenty six counties wanted an independent Republic: Their own government without restrictions and to be rid of the British yoke forever and no allegiance to the Sovereign of England.

The struggle within Ireland and with the British would now revolve around what was wanted by the Irish and what would be allowed by the British and that struggle would eventually tear the country asunder. Eamon de Valera was a very complicated man and he had been well self tutored in the guile of negotiations or so he thought until he had to do battle with a much more powerful opponent.

Most Irish people would never had heard of or even knew of the existence of an Italian writer named Niccolo Machiavelli and his book "The Prince". It was well out of their orbit of interests but his philosophy of politics as outlined in the book would have an immense impact on virtually all Irish people. Machiavelli's message for politicians was essentially that 'the end justifies the means.' Certainly, moral considerations had to be made but they could and would be compromised when necessary.

de Valera was an ardent disciple of the Italian writer's political principles and took his roadmap as his own map for his political life. Men didn't get to be leaders of political organizations by accident and if they didn't develop a level of ruthlessness in their character, they didn't last long. Dev as he was known had over the past few years since 1916 developed his politics. His day to day approach to the issue of Ireland would be described by many as single minded ruthlessness. His political doctrine many came to see as extremism. His need to be obeyed would ultimately clash with his comrades and peers, most specifically and heatedly with the more relaxed and easy-going Michael Collins.

Both men had the same goal in life, and they had shared prisons together to prove it and they longed to see their beloved country as a free and independent Republic of Ireland. They would be forced by circumstance to go about achieving that goal by very different methods.

The second half of 1921 was taken up in endless discussion within the Irish Dail as they tried to agree on a set of demands that the Irish would present at a second set of talks to begin in London on October 10th. For the people's sake some kind of result had to be delivered from the talks.

De Valera had been deeply involved in the preparation of the discussions. Indeed as President and the leader of Sinn Fein he was the driving force, he saw his vision as the one that would succeed and the British would have to take it or leave it.

 But his Machiavellian instincts were taking him in new directions. He totally blindsided his colleagues by deciding not to take part in the talks personally. He would send a reluctant Michael Collins and Arthur Griffith and seven others to make the case and win what was wanted by their side. It was a calculated, and as many said a Machiavellian decision for Dev not to go. History would judge that he excused himself because he knew ultimately that the talks would not succeed. The British government would not agree to their demands and that if he went, he would have to return home humiliated. It was believed he needed scapegoats for the task.

Whatever the reason and despite his protests, the men he sent had to deal with what they had which was the authority of the Dail to negotiate an outcome with the British. Collins and Griffith protested strongly that de Valera must go and lead the Delegation. The men chosen by de Valera were inexperienced and lacked the capacity to deal with Statesmen like Lloyd George and Winston Churchill. They had been running the British Empire with all its power, majesty and prestige for a number of years and indeed had seen off the German nation so recently.

But de Valera would not be swayed and did not go to London this time but he still wanted to retain the final decision-making authority. He insisted that the delegation must get the Dail's and his, approval before any agreement could be signed. He tended to ignore the fact that once you give a delegation Plenipotentiary power that is what they have: the power to make a decision themselves.

Lloyd George, Winston Churchill and other British Cabinet members in their delegation however would not finish the talks which went from 11th October to 6th December, until an agreement in writing was reached. They insisted on and had the power to enforce their clauses of the Truce. Their intrinsic terms ultimately were not negotiable. Ireland would become an independent Dominion, have its own parliament but still be part of the British Commonwealth and swear obedience to the Crown. It would not be a Republic.

Michael Collins and Arthur Griffith were under immense pressure as the main negotiators. They were forced into making a decision and signing the Treaty without the option of returning to Ireland for further discussion. "Take it or leave it" was the British position. So, they took it, for their own logical reasons. They knew that it would after all have to be ratified or rejected by the Irish Parliament. They signed the Treaty and went back to Ireland with a Treaty but not a Republic. The intricate and detailed options that de Valera had hoped would achieve his goal of a Republic and the reunion of the North and South were still not acceptable to the British Government. They had made that clear to de Valera earlier in the year. Dev did not take the rebuff lightly. Collins and his followers basically argued for what they believed had to be accepted at the time.

"We'll take what we can get and fight for the rest later because we've now run out of resources. For now we have the freedom to achieve freedom as we want it." Dev and many in the IRA had the opposing viewpoint,

"We will not accept anything other than what we said, a Republic and unification with the North and no subservience to a foreign monarch." On 16th December both British Houses of Parliament ratified the terms of the Treaty and a major debate started in the Dail in Ireland. On 7th January 1922 the Treaty as agreed by Collins and Griffiths and the others was then ratified by the Dail by a vote of 64 to 57. De Valera could not accept the defeat and he and most of his supporters walked out of the Irish Parliament. His parting comment on his humiliating defeat was: "the majority has no right to do wrong!"

The Irish Civil War would be the result. Now everyone had to pick a side.

BOOK 3
CIVIL WAR

CHAPTER 24
Treaty or Treason?

As of January 7th 1922, the good news for the people of Ireland was that the peace would hold between Ireland and the British Forces. A Provisional Government made up from the Irish Dail would be in place to handle the transition from British rule to Irish home rule. The War of Independence for all intents and purposes, to the relief of many Irish people, was over.

But the opposition and passionate speeches of de Valera and the senior IRA men had stirred up a lot of emotion and ill feeling towards the proposed Provisional Government. They simmered in the minds of many people while the transition got under way.

The tension was felt right around the country and it was palpable, you either accepted the Treaty as agreed to by the Dail or you rejected it. From January to April 1922 the country divided into Pro Treaty and Anti Treaty sides. The IRA was still strong but largely disorganised and it was determined on rejecting the Treaty and fighting on. The Provisional Government was formed with Michael Collins as its Chairman and it had the backing of the British and a new Irish national army was created.

The British insisted that the Treaty would be honoured by both sides.

The Treaty decision affected every man and woman who had fought in the War of Independence and the argument was joined in every home and church and pub and public place in the country. New and vicious enmities would be born where before there had been harmony.

It was at Sean's father's home that Joe came in late June many months after the Dail had ratified the Treaty. He had wanted to talk to John McCormack who had guided them in their early years of the struggle, but he was still in Dublin. Joe and Sean had seen each other only briefly over the past couple of months but the Treaty was the topic Joe wanted to discuss now. He knew Sean had signed up to the new army but had not talked to him in any depth about what he felt or intended to. He assumed wrongly that Sean's political leanings were the same as his own.

Joe had been meeting regularly with his IRA comrades and continued his training and involvement with the organization. His belief in what needed to be done was confirmed by the talk he heard and the meetings he attended. Men like Eamon de Valera on the political side and Liam lynch on the IRA side were holding fast to their Oath to the Republic and insisted the rank and file do the same. The meetings were well attended and Joe incorrectly assumed that all his former comrades felt the same as he did. But he had heard rumours and he had suspicions about Sean's sympathies. He hadn't seen attending any of the IRA meetings and Joe wanted to know where he stood.

"Well Sean what will it be for you then?" he suspected he knew the answer but wanted to hear it from Sean so there could be no misunderstanding. Sean had indeed gone in a different direction to Joe. For the life of him he couldn't see the point in continuing the fight against the British, they ran the risk of simply being overwhelmed by their power. Sean had totally accepted the arguments to the Dail put by Collins and Griffith. Take what we can now, build up our country and then strike out for the Republic down the road away. It made perfect sense to Sean who was influenced by Collin's intellect and drive. He had joined the new national army a few months earlier and was stationed in Athlone Barracks under the command of Major General Sean MacEoin. He thought Joe knew all this and was surprised by his challenging words.

"You know where I am Joe, we accept the Treaty as the Dail says and we push on from there. We can now start to build our own country."

Joe fell silent, the anger in him was building but he knew he had to contain himself. They had both wanted a Republic since they were ten years old, it was part of them, they knew nothing else, they had fought for it, killed men and nearly been killed themselves, saw their friends die for that goal.

Finally, Joe had to have his say, if it ended the friendship so be it:

"You're ready to throw away what we have been fighting since 1916 on the promise of a lot of Englishmen who have done nothing but lie to us for the last however many hundred years. Who have exploited us, treated us like scum and stole our land and our heritage, killed and maimed when it suited them. You're going to take an oath of loyalty to a king who wouldn't piss on you if you were on fire and join a Commonwealth of Nations and kiss British arse for as long as it suits them? Jaysus Sean, I'm amazed that you can't see through the fog they created. Dev and the IRA want us to fight on and not take this rotten compromise."

"And Collins says we should take it, he's just as committed as Dev and he's got more sense, he's being practical, he knows the

English will grind us down if we don't go along with the Treaty." Sean's passion was just as aroused on the issue as Joe's.

"But it's not a Republic man. We're only part of the way towards what we wanted. Collins, as much as I love the man, has sold us down the river. He was the IRB and the IRA and what is he now? An Englishman with an Irish accent." That was too much for Sean.

"Take that back and apologise, no one has done more for this country than Michael Collins, if it wasn't for him, we would have all been killed by the Black and Tans and be fully occupied by the British Army. He has shown that Ireland won't be cowed any further. He did all that while your precious Dev was skulking around in America with his cap in hand and begging for money. We wanted independence and that's what we're going to get. We'll have our own government and our own army; the British will leave with their tail between their legs and we will run things ourselves."

"Yes, and I guess it will be officers like you that will be putting Republicans like me in jail. You'll have your army alright but it won't be strong enough to hold off the IRA. Already we hold the majority of counties and we won't give them to any Provisional Government."

"Then they'll be taken from you," Sean responded, "the people and the Dail have said that what has been agreed with the British will stay. We have no choice other than to accept and work with the Treaty." They were both aware of the situation in Dublin where IRA men had been occupying the Four Courts buildings since April 14th. The pro and anti Treaty sides had created an ever-widening gulf but each side held off unwilling to shed Irish blood. The temperature was rising and options for the Provisional

Government were running out. They were under constant British pressure to end the standoff at the Four Courts. Joe had already made up his mind and sought out the Drumraney Flying Column. He intended to continue the fight with like minded friends and comrades. He put his final point to Sean:

"So, the lives of the sixteen martyrs who were killed after the Easter Uprising by the British mean nothing to you? James Connolly, Padraig Pearse, Tom Clarke, who were executed in '16. The lives of men like Kevin Barry and Terence MacSwiney and Thomas Ashe whose funeral we went to in Dublin, have been given up in vain. Is that what you are saying? Is that what you believe now?" Joe's response was the passion of the time and it was heartfelt, he could not understand how men like Sean whom he had known most of his life could just disregard his commitment and indeed his Oath to fight for a Republic.

Sean was standing now; his fists were clenched and his blood truly up. He looked at Joe as fiercely as he felt and he tried to hold himself together. He knew whatever he said wouldn't get through to Joe who felt cheated out of his Republic and all it meant to him.

"Don't talk to me about disrespect Joe, it's done, I've made my decision and I'm staying with the new army and I'll continue to fight for what I believe in. I understand it is different to what you believe but that is how it goes for me." Just then the door to the room opened and Sean's father came in, his face reflecting his turmoil.

"We've just heard that the Four Courts have been fired on by artillery and much of one building destroyed, there have been casualties." He knew what it meant without saying it. The Civil War had unofficially been declared.

Ireland was at war with itself. And now so were Sean and Joe.

Joe's anger was reflected in his expression but there was also much disappointment and sadness, tears welled in his eyes but he could think of no more to say as they walked out of the house. He took one last look at Sean and then spat on the ground and walked away from the best friend of his life. Joe's and Sean's destiny was determined as were many others in their beloved country by events that day.

CHAPTER 25
The Civil War Erupts

On the night of April 14, 1922, the IRA leaders including Rory O'Connor, Liam Mellowes, Ernie O'Malley and two hundred others occupied the Four Courts in Dublin a precinct in the city centre containing Ireland's main Justice Courts and civilian records going back hundreds of years. It was the first and most provocative act of the Civil War by the IRA. The initial response by the Provisional Government led by Michael Collins was to virtually ignore the action seeing it as a stunt rather than something more sinister. However, as the weeks wore on and the occupiers showed no signs of leaving, pressure started to mount from the British Government on the Irish Government to resolve the issue. It made them both look weak and indecisive as Winston Churchill said and it was contrary to the spirit of the recently signed Treaty and its ratification by the Dail. Who was actually running the country was the question implicit in Churchill's correspondence to Collins? Something had to be done. Consequently, on June 22nd, over four weeks since the buildings had been occupied, using artillery supplied by the British Army, the Four Courts were attacked. Combined with sabotage from inside the buildings a great deal of damage was caused. The men inside held out till June 30th when they were ordered to surrender as reinforcements could not get through but fighting continued throughout Dublin city till July 5th. One of the gun battles resulted in the lingering death of Cathal Brugha a senior IRA officer and perhaps the most resolute of the Anti-Treaty leaders.

Matters moved swiftly after the Four Courts surrender by the IRA, they had been seriously outgunned and could not withstand the military power thrown at them. Several senior IRA men were arrested and gaoled. The first of many thousands who would suffer the same fate over the next twelve months, though some of the senior men managed to escape later to continue fighting.

It was early July 1922 and Sean had rejoined his new army unit and given the rank of Captain at the age of twenty three. He would be responsible to Major-General Sean MacEoin the man he had admired so much during the War of Independence and with whom he had fought at times against the British. MacEoin had decided very early on which way the wind was blowing and there was no doubt in his mind that the IRA had to be brought under control. His mindset, like the younger Sean's, had changed from that of guerrilla fighter to the regimentation of a standing army with all of the discipline and rigour that was demanded.

No more lying in bushes and sleeping in barns, no more relying on the kindness of farmers to feed them, they were an army at war and they would take what they needed. The Irish Army very quickly started to recruit young men many of whom had been too young to take part in the War against the Black and Tans. They were trained and then given a rifle and the authority to arrest men who were still IRA and had fought in the War of Independence.

The new Irish Army had personnel of around eight thousand at the time of the Four Courts surrender and over the next twelve months they recruited rapidly and often without sufficient care, with arms and uniforms being supplied by the British. By the end of 1923 they had fifty thousand soldiers under arms

The Athlone Barracks became the Headquarters of the Midland Command whose Commanding Officer Major-General Sean MacEoin set out to secure the counties around Athlone for the Provisional Government. In July MacEoin led a troop of up to three hundred soldiers to Collooney in County Sligo to clear the area of Republican or, as they now called them Irregulars, who held many of the villages in the area. Sean McKeon was put in charge of some of the operations and led his men with bravery and daring earning the respect of his senior officer. By good fortune and with British Army help, Sean's troop had access to an artillery piece and it gave them substantial advantage. Sean turned the artillery onto the tower of a Protestant Church that was housing the Irregulars and after a five-hour battle and much house to house fighting forced the men to surrender. Seventy men were arrested and eventually found themselves imprisoned in Athlone and later in the vast prison camps of the Curragh.

General MacEoin then turned his attention to the counties nearer to Athlone, of Roscommon, Longford and Westmeath. It was in Westmeath that the younger Sean would come up against his boyhood and War of Independence comrades. He was not alone, a number of other IRA men from his former Brigade had also enlisted in the new army. There were to be many spiteful confrontations.

MacEoin was explicit in his orders to his near namesake Sean McKeon,

> "Take your men and go out into the villages and farms and arrest any man who won't declare for the Treaty. That's the only option they have. If they don't accept the Treaty and refuse to acknowledge the new Government in Dublin then arrest them. If they don't agree it means they are IRA sympathisers and we can't afford to let them roam the countryside making mischief."

MacEoin had made this clear when he had met with IRA leaders in Sligo and Athlone and left them with no illusion that he was prepared to use all his authority and that of the government to get matters under control. There would be no court of appeal and no warrants.

There had also been no formal Declaration as such of a Civil War, and the IRA certainly wasn't in a position to formalise a Declaration. The Four Courts debacle and the pressure from the British government had forced the hand of the new Irish Government and its new army. There was no going back once the Four Courts had been fired on. No one could sit on the fence any longer.

Sean McKeon as a new Captain went about his task with what many described as enthusiasm and almost revived the activities of the Black and Tans. Many men were arrested in the dead of night as they slept in their homes. The farms and villages of the three counties delivered up over one hundred and twenty IRA men on one sweep alone, men who when asked refused to endorse the Treaty. This included twenty of his former colleagues in an around Drumraney, Moate and Tang, men who had been in the same Company as Sean during the struggle with the Black and Tans. Many of the men arrested recognised Sean and left him in no doubt of their opinion of him.

Many hundreds more were arrested from the neighbouring counties of Mayo, Galway and Sligo in the following months. Most were sent to Athlone gaol and later to Mountjoy prison in Dublin then later distributed to the prison camps of the Curragh. Not many IRA men responded to General MacEoin's call to endorse the Treaty and the new Government. The wounds were still too raw and the lure of the IRA's call to fight on for a Republic, too strong.

Though Sean's company raided many farms and villages and scoured the public houses, he missed by minutes the man he had sought most. Joe Keegan escaped from a friend's farm where he was staying when their eleven-year-old daughter saw the army vehicles coming. She had woken during the early hours and had been clever enough to raise the alarm. Joe escaped on a motor cycle he had in the barn.

Joe's capture became personal for Sean he had never forgiven Joe for the insult he felt in front of Sean's father when he last saw Joe. It was his strong belief and MacEoin's that men like Joe had to be brought under control. The Civil War or insurrection as MacEoin preferred to call it had to be stopped before it ruined the country. Joe's passion about the Treaty was not his alone, there were already many hundreds of prisoners clogging up Mountjoy, Cork and Athlone prisons and many others in the larger cities. There would be many more to join them as the Army pursued the IRA throughout the country.

Joe and a number of former comrades had formed the Drumraney Flying Column led by Thomas McGiff. It was a small but active group who were constantly on the run relying on local farmers and householders to supply them with food and shelter. But as Joe and his comrades noted, when the Black and Tans were on the rampage the people were much more supportive. Nowadays they were in two minds since there was an Irish government in Dublin, as far as many of them considered, the war was over, everyone should just return to their own homes.

The IRA command felt different of course, there was still a war to fight to get the Republic that was rightly theirs. Local commanders like McGiff made their own decisions in consultation with other local IRA leaders about which targets to attack and what to do to achieve their goals. There were small scale skirmishes with Free State Army groups from time to time or when an Army barracks was seen as fair game. And there was always a train to try and derail or train tracks to destroy, usually between Athlone and Mullingar which would affect the transport to and from Dublin.

Joe was welcomed into the Column as his experience and record were well known to the other men who had fought with him and his brothers before. The nearby County of Roscommon was awash with IRA activity and the Flying Column would join with them when able. They had held the town of Castlerea for a short time but were overwhelmed by the Army numbers. This would become a familiar theme as time went on. The IRA or the Irregulars, as the Government and the press preferred to call them, could put up a fight but then would have to melt away as their resources couldn't match their enemies. Their tactics were always hit and run.

When they could, they would do as much damage as possible such as when they focused on the Big Houses which became targets as they had in the War of Independence. They were usually set alight by the men who attacked them after they had evacuated the occupants. These were often absentee landlords' staff or titled gentry from England who were usually made to stand by and watch their homes destroyed. Joe had been involved in raids two years earlier and felt no remorse then and he felt none now. He and his comrades were living off the land often marching twenty miles cross country overnight to avoid Free State patrols to find a new target. Always trying to keep the enemy guessing about where they would strike next. They had no grand 'Big Houses' to rest in and they followed the orders of the IRA head quarters to attack these obvious remnants of British rule.

But there were other matters to consider as well and collecting arms was often top of the list. Tom McGiff's brother Dan had joined the Column and Joe joined him and three others for a raid. They had been on a march for nearly three days resting when and where they could. The idea was to steal some rifles from a small

Free State post near Tang they knew about. Joe had fallen behind to fix a boot that had served him well but was now getting beyond repair making it difficult to walk in. He stopped to make repairs while the others went on and then he heard gun fire. He ran to catch the others but saw them being overwhelmed by probably thirty Free State troopers. The Columns intelligence advice had let them down badly they were seriously outnumbered. Joe found his way out of the area and had to break the news to Thomas McGiff about his brother and his three men being arrested. Joe found Tom in an abandoned barn beside a house that had been burned to the ground, there were fifteen left in the Flying Column and Joe found Tom smoking outside the barn.

"Joe, where are the others?" Tom asked as Joe walked into the yard, the five of them had left four hours earlier for Tang. Joe took out his tobacco pouch and started to roll his own cigarette he would tell Tom straight off what had happened and he thought he would let the leader know what he felt was wrong with their operation.

"You know Tom, they walked into an ambush, there were thirty Staters in the barracks, not five as we had been told and they made short work of our lads. Dan tried to make a fight of it but they didn't have a chance they had to surrender, they wouldn't have even had thirty bullets between them. You know our so-called intelligence apparatus as they call it is next to feckin' useless, don't you?" Tom looked at Joe not wanting to give anything away but he knew he was right, the people in the villages could no longer be relied on for information as they had against the Black and Tans when they all believed they had a common enemy.

"How did you get away?" Tom's question wasn't accusing but he needed to know what had happened. Joe lifted his right foot to show Tom his boot which was barely clinging to his foot, he had just walked five miles back from Tang to this farm and the boot was in tatters.

"This bugger here was falling off, I needed to stop and fix it and Dan told me to make sure it was safe otherwise I'd trip on it and probably shoot someone. By the time I was ready to catch up I heard some firing, I could just see over a rise I was hiding behind and saw what was happening. They had walked into a trap, there was nothing I could do, they were outnumbered ten to one so I turned around and came back here. My foot feels like a lump of rotting pork." He sat down and pulled off his boot and sock showing a mass of blisters, some whole, some broken. Tom wasn't disbelieving, he knew what they were all putting up with but it wasn't as though he could send Joe off to the quartermaster for a new pair of boots, there weren't any.

"You did the right thing Joe, no point in getting yourself picked up." Tom dropped his head he was very close to his brother Dan and they had fought many a battle together. Somehow, he would have to find the wherewithal to go on. He stayed silent for a full minute his head still slumped forward and Joe wondered whether he should leave for now. But Joe felt there was something else bothering him apart from the bad news of his brother Dan being arrested.

"What is it Tom? What's wrong?" Joe asked. Tom stayed silent a while longer then answered.

"I don't know what it means, it mightn't mean a damn thing but we just heard that Arthur Griffiths had died. He had a stroke and it happened a few days ago in Dublin." Griffiths was virtually Collin's second in command, a conservative presence to Collin's dramatic personality and a respected leader in the new government.

"Jaysus," said Joe not sure of what to think, "he was a good man, no doubt, just took the wrong side." In death, as in life everything in Ireland was political. Griffith had given his life to the cause having gone through the purgatory of the Treaty negotiations with Michael Collins. He had been abused and ridiculed by the anti Treaty IRA and by his old comrade de Valera and others he had called friends. An unselfish man, he gave too much of himself and finally the tension of the days had beaten him down. Together he and Collins were trying to hold the new government together and pull Ireland out of its past instead they were fighting a vicious Civil War in which he believed there could be no winner.

"I don't think it will make any difference Tom. The government and Collins will find someone to replace him and the war will go on until…….it stops." Joe didn't know he was going to say that but it was how he felt, the war just went on and on. Tom looked at him and nodded.

"Yes, Joe I think the same thing. Not much will change for us. But you're right, he was a good man. Honest and hardworking and he believed in what he believed in, the same as the rest of us, Ireland independent and free. God rest his soul." Tom wouldn't allow a tear but he wiped his hand across his face as if to finish a chapter of history they had just witnessed.

"Amen." Said Joe, and crossed himself as had Tom, it was all he could think of to offer.

Tom hadn't finished, he looked at Joe,

"You know we get messengers from the villages, good lads who disobey their Mams and bring us information." Joe nodded; he knew of the silent network that sometimes, but not always, worked to their advantage. "I'm sorry Joe," Tom continued, "it seems we've both may have lost something we held close today. There's a rumour that your brother Hugh and a dozen others had been picked up around Drumraney they say Tom McCormack was with him." Joe sank onto a hale bay near Tom,

"Jesus, Mary and Joseph." He uttered, not in prayer but in anguish, he dropped his head into his hands it was a bitter blow for Joe who had hoped he could link up with Hugh again so they could fight on together.

"That's not all Joe, we heard it was a company of Staters led by your old friend Sean McKeon. He arrested all of them."

Joe kept his head down, his heart full of anger, hating the war and hating Sean for his part in it and for his treachery, and most of all for not being part of what Joe was part of.

CHAPTER 26
Sean in Command

Sean McKeon and his company of mostly newly minted soldiers were being kept busy around the counties. There always seemed to be more IRA people to track down and arrest. The Government in Dublin had become increasingly aggressive in its activities with the IRA. In early July, the Government decided that from that time on, captured Anti-Treaty IRA men would be charged with a criminal offence and not be treated as prisoners of war. They would lose the label of freedom fighters that the IRA men carried with pride.

Michael Collins meanwhile was trying to keep things on an even keel between many of his old comrades in the IRA and the hardliners in his own government. They were spurred on by British politicians who insisted the IRA question be settled and quickly. It was proving difficult for Collins, who as many agreed was a fair-minded man and wanted what everyone else wanted for his country, peace, prosperity and freedom from British interference. The IRA leadership angered him as he felt that holding an ideological position on the Republic was self defeating. He kept coming up against a brick wall with the Republican adherents who steadfastly refused to give him any leeway despite the fact this it was his leadership that got them any freedom at all. Didn't they know that he personally had carried the fight into Ulster and armed the IRA there? He wanted the northern counties as part of the Free State and the way to do that was to cause the Protestant government to become disengaged and lose heart. Make those counties ungovernable. It was a misplaced reading of affairs, the more the IRA pushed in the North, the more the Protestant government pushed back with British backing causing more mayhem and misery.

To prove he was a listener and also to prove his sincerity, he chose against much advice to take an inspection trip into the 'badlands' of his native County Cork. Here were the ultimate 'Hardmen' of the IRA, men who held unchangeable positions on the Republic. But Collins thought he could sit down and talk to them and bring 'an end to this damned thing' as he called the Civil War, refusing to give it a proper name. Eamon de Valera was reportedly in the area, though his clout with the military leaders was not as great as it once was. He was respected as a politician and for what he had done for the cause. But the IRA leaders felt he had spent too much time out of the country to fully understand the situation. Now Collins wanted to talk to de Valera and the men who held sway in the county, men like Tom Barry, Tom Malone and Tom Hales all former comrades and friends. Collins belief was always that jaw boning was preferable to fighting.

But he was stopped in his tracks when the news of the death of Arthur Griffith reached him, a man with whom he had gone through the torment of the talks with the British Cabinet. He was a man with whom he joked he had signed his own death warrant when he signed the Treaty. He was a great and respected ally of Collins'.

He rushed back to Dublin for the funeral service and despite his own physical ill health brought on by relentless pressure and politics. He led the huge funeral procession from the Cathedral to Glasnevin Cemetery where the man he admired so much was laid to rest with other heroes of Ireland. Collins was now more determined to make Ireland's peace work for everyone on both sides of the growing divide. He went back to Cork after the Griffith funeral to come face to face with the nemesis there.

#

In many ways Michael Collins was Ireland. Born in 1890 he was in his mid twenties when he joined the Easter Rebellion in Dublin in 1916. Described by many as a "larrikin" he embodied many of the character traits that became popular Irish identity. Always quick with a smiling greeting and often a practical joke. He was admired by the many who chose to follow him. Charisma is an often overused word but nothing is more appropriate to describe the personality of this man. People are drawn to those with charisma. It is something felt, transferred from one soul to another often without words. People just knew they wanted to be in his company and the IRA men who followed his orders did do without question. Those who opposed him weren't met with disdain or contempt but respect for their point of view no matter how at odds with his own he found it. He would argue till the cows literally came home but that was just his way. He knew that men and women, if they believed in what they sought then they should argue and fight for it and tear out any injustice they encountered.

That's what Michael Collins did for Ireland, he felt its intrinsic values in his very being. Values that couldn't and shouldn't be traded away for short term gain but needed to become the fabric of the country he sought to create. Religious and political differences were important but couldn't be allowed to separate people. They needed to find what was common to them each and make that part of the fabric that the country would need to make its way in a challenging world.

"The Big Fellow" as he was called was just that, big in body and soul, he endured prison and

hardship and danger every day of his short life for his country. The Civil War broke his heart, as it tore apart his country for which he had bled and seen so many of his countrymen do the same.

He had been sacrificed by others when sent to negotiate the Treaty that caused the current

fighting and what he demanded of them for Ireland was: **"Give us the future..we've had**

enough of your past..give us back our country to live in – to grow in – to love."

Sadly, for Ireland he was to be violently denied the chance to do what he dreamed of for Ireland.

On August 22nd, Collin's convoy near the end of its tour of Cork was ambushed by a party of IRA men and he was cut down by a bullet to the head and died almost instantly. He had been cavalier about his own safety and stood with his revolver blazing away at an unseen enemy. It was probably the way, some thought, he was destined to die.

His death took a toll on both sides as he was admired widely even by those who wanted him dead. General Sean MacEoin had been a friend and ally of Michael Collins and mourned his death deeply, despairing that such a strong and popular figure like him could be taken out of the picture so cheaply.

Michael Collin's funeral procession in Dublin drew many tens of thousands of mourners and took hours to pass through the city after the Requiem Mass.

#

Sean sensed his CO's frustrations and without waiting for new orders increased his activity against the IRA Irregulars determined to hunt them all down. He set off a new round of raids and arrests around the counties and Westmeath gave up another fifteen men to the jails of Athlone. He knew who he needed to arrest and wouldn't stop till he had all Anti-Treaty men in custody.

He requested a meeting with his Commanding officer.

"General, we have intelligence that the Irregulars are planning an attack in the Glasson area. It's near Athlone and the story is that some of the leaders want to make a big statement and bring down the army with a show of force."

"How good's the intelligence?" asked MacEoin who knew that information like that was easily over cooked and badly delivered. "Are they a reliable source?"

Sources of intelligence were necessarily always kept secret, men and women who risked their lives either for money, favours or just to spite the IRA for some perceived atrocity. If they were caught, they could end up in a roadside ditch. Usually with a sign around their neck warning others that here was a reason not to risk what they had done, that justice had been meted out by the IRA. Retribution was swift and merciless even if the wrong person was sometimes executed.

Sean knew he couldn't tell his CO the identity of his informant and MacEoin wouldn't want to have known. As much as they needed the intelligence, his memory of being betrayed in a similar way during the War of Independence was still fresh in his mind and he detested those who gave the information whatever their motive. Sean responded by saying,

"Well we understand there will be about thirty Irregulars and they seem intent on an ambush for no other reason than to kill whatever Free State soldiers they come across." Sean was confident that Joe Keegan and Tom McGiff would be amongst the raiders.

"Well take fifty of your men and get over there and ambush them! We have to show them who is running this county and the country. This nonsense has to stop so we'll do whatever we can to take them out of action." MacEoin was keen for the younger officer to make a statement with this attack. Thirty IRA men would be a good haul for any action and if a few of them were killed along the way, well, that's what happens in war.

"General." Said Sean and dismissed himself and went to round up the men and resources he would need. Sadly, it turned out his CO's advice and misgivings about intelligence was prescient. The information about an ambush was correct but they had given Sean the wrong day.

As he was preparing his men to move across the county there had already been a small group of National army soldiers who had gone to Glasson led by Commandant Sean McCormack, a name Sean knew well. The McCormack family like many others in Ireland had split over the Treaty and some of the men of that name Sean knew had stayed IRA, others like Sean joined the army. John McCormack who Sean remembered from his boyhood and his stories of the Irish Rebels of yesteryear was the father of Sean McCormack and still a member of the Dail. But others in the clan saw them as traitors reflecting the ugliness in society that the Civil War had wrought. It was as many predicted, brother against brother.

Tom McGiff's and Joe's group of thirty attacked the car carrying Commandant McCormack as it drove into the small town. They were there to inspect the burnt-out RIC barracks which had been destroyed a couple of years earlier by the IRA. The Army was now determined to reoccupy it. Tom McGiff said that they wouldn't have the barracks for long if he had anything to do with it and put his plan in place. Military intelligence goes both ways, and Tom knew that Sean McKeon would be arriving with a larger troop the next day. By then Tom's group would be gone. The idea was to engage whoever was there and then melt away into the forest again. Hit and run!

Tom and his men waited till Sean McCormack's military vehicle arrived in the main street accompanied by a lorry load of troopers. The group opened fire on them both, but they sped up, obviously they had missed the drivers who were a usual first target. But eventually they came to a halt with the IRA men surrounded it still firing, McCormack was killed in the shooting.

Later reports were that Sean McCormack was shot while attending a wounded man, a fact denied by the IRA but the story took its own momentum and spread around the county promoted by a censored press. Although there were plenty of shots fired, the idea as Tom McGiff explained to his men was not to kill for the sake of killing but to show their strength and capability in military terms. Tom had flirted with the idea of occupying the barracks themselves but called it off knowing Sean's company would be there in numbers the next day. He took his men away from Glasson into the shelter of the countryside.

Sean McKeon's anguish was all the greater when he heard that Joe Keegan and Tom McGiff were amongst the group of thirty who laid the ambush. These two men were at the top of Sean's list of those he keenly wanted to get into custody.

CHAPTER 27
The Bad News Reaches the Column

Getting away at the last minute and surviving by the skin of your teeth was part of the job description for guerrilla fighters and Joe felt the tension every day. It was the same at Glasson get in hit hard and get out before you were overwhelmed by superior numbers. Tom McGiff had told him that he made sure the attack on Glasson was told in advance to the Staters, that the IRA was going to hit the town! Joe was taken aback,

"Why in God's name would you do that?" Tom just smiled,

"Don't worry Joe, we've seen to it that they have been given the wrong day. We were long gone before the Staters got there in numbers. They knew we were in the area so I thought we would tell them where, just not when." Joe accepted the message but was apprehensive, his trust in McGiff was total. But he couldn't help but be concerned about such a tactic as telling your enemy where you were going to strike next, even if the message was wrong. But that was the essence of the war they were fighting and there were no guarantees. The rebels took huge risks all the time to gain any advantage.

Days later they were at their redoubt in the hills when a scout brought in the newspaper the *Freeman's Journal* which had an account of their action. Tom said it was full of lies but enjoyed the story anyway. The newspaper also brought news that they had heard as gossip but hadn't been able to confirm, Michael Collins had been killed in an ambush somewhere in Cork!

Joe personally was devastated; he had admired Collins as their leader during the Tan War and always looked up to him but like so many others couldn't accept the Treaty Collins had signed with Arthur Griffith to end the conflict with Britain. But he was gutted nonetheless.

"God Tom, what a man the country has lost. I know we've been fighting against what he did but I always thought it would work out eventually and we'd all get along together. Good Christ, what a mess. God knows what will happen now without him to guide that government."

Tom looked at Joe and identified with his anguish, lost for words momentarily he eventually found something to say.

"I think you're right Joe. I thought he would have sorted it all out as well with the IRA but who knows now? There's no one to take his place. God love old Cosgrave, who'll probably take over, but he's no Michael Collins."

Joe was becoming more and more despondent despite his strong feeling of national pride and belief in what he was fighting for. But he had to admit that he was missing three things in his life, his family who he was only occasionally able to visit. His Hurling which he had had to give up because circumstances didn't allow. And of course his heart ached for Maggie and the question of whether he would ever see her again. Perhaps because he had no choice, he struggled on in spite of it all.

The sentiment the men held over the death of Michael Collins could be seen as strange and out of character for their position, their arch enemy had been killed and here they were lamenting his loss. 'The Big Fellow' had been loved all over the country especially when the Treaty negotiations were going on and it seemed that the war against the hated British had finally been won.

But not all wars are won the way people would like them to be and Collins' Treaty earned him new and powerful enemies. Former friends and allies, just months before, had been hailing him as the conquering hero and now with his death it seems they had prevailed.

Without the restraining hand of Collins and Griffiths, new forces would emerge in the Dail and in the Provisional Government and the National Army. Already summary justice was rife throughout the land and used by both sides. It didn't take much evidence to find someone guilty and then executed. No courts and no defence accepted, just the Martial law of the day and that law usually wasn't seeking fairness just revenge for imagined or real slights. People throughout the country could be subject to random violence from either side without recourse to justice.

The men who now came to power did not have the outlook or compassion of Griffiths and Collins. They soon lost patience with the IRA anti-Treaty forces and determined a different way of how to win the Civil War and how to get the country back fully under proper government. At the same time, they had to deter any British temptation to come back and take over.

It was a way that would be bloodier and it would be more brutal than what had come before and indeed more brutal than the Tan War.

CHAPTER 28
The Civil War Intensifies

In October 1922 the Provisional Government decided to push the issue with the IRA. They intended to take full control of the country and do it by force with their vastly expanded numbers of recruits. The IRA had refused to accept the legitimacy of the Government and their ratification of the Treaty with the British. On 12th October the Army (Emergency Powers) Act was announced. Taking effect on the 15th of that month the new law authorised execution of anyone arrested carrying arms or ammunition. At virtually the same time the Catholic Church issued a Pastoral Letter announcing the excommunication of anyone bearing arms against the National Government.

The gloves were off and many members of the IRA, who were loyal and devoted Catholics were devastated by the Church's edict of which they had hear rumours but never expected the Church to go so far. They viewed the pastoral letter with great bitterness saying that the bishops had given their opponents a licence to murder. Particularly hard was the fact that in the prisons around the country priests were not allowed to administer the Sacraments to any IRA member. For many IRA members however, their faith would continue without the priests and the church. They labelled the Pastoral Letter as pointless because it was based on the premise that the Staters were the legitimate Government. It was a premise which many had never accepted or recognised and the Irish Bishops never had the approval of Rome to make such a proclamation

In that same month the IRA reacted against the new Government edicts. They were determined to drive the country into chaos to push their ideals and a large number of incidents took place all over Ireland from blowing up bridges to destroying trains by taking up tracks and forcing derailments. A further General Order was announced a few months later on January 8th, 1923 extending the Emergency Powers Act which would punish any Republican found in possession of any plan, document, or note "for a purpose prejudicial to the State of the National Forces".

This cast a very wide net and left no one in the population in doubt that any involvement with the IRA would be a perilous pursuit.

Kevin O'Higgins was a member for the new Dail who was elevated to the Cabinet as Minister for Justice and External Affairs and proceeded to stamp the government's authority on what had become a chaotic social environment. Like many on the pro Treaty side, he had changed his mind from demanding a Republic. His moderate stance was expressed in his speech seeking election: *'I have not abandoned any political aspirations to which I have given expression in the past, but in the existing circumstances I advise the people to trust to evolution rather than revolution for their attainment.'* It was splitting hairs but it was O'Higgin's justification.

O'Higgin's die was cast like many others, for the present they had abandoned the ideal of a Republic of Ireland and settled for self government and Dominion status within the British Commonwealth. O'Higgins drove home his advantage as a Government Minister with ruthless determination. He considered the IRA members not as revolutionaries but as criminals and proceeded to treat them as such in prisons around the country. His government's great fear was that the British would dismiss the Treaty and return and take over Ireland again because of the civil unrest. It was never likely, but men like O'Higgins and William Cosgrave who was President of the Executive Council having taken on the role after the deaths of Michael Collins and Arthur Griffith, used it as justification for their severe laws. Indeed Cosgrave, who although he insisted, he was not in favour of executions went on record saying: *'I am not going to hesitate if the country is to live, and if we have to exterminate ten thousand Republicans, the three million of our people is greater than this ten thousand.'*

The new laws and crackdowns made moving around the countryside more and more difficult for Joe Keegan, Tom McGiff and their small group and many others throughout the counties. By the very nature of their activities they raised suspicion wherever they sheltered and had to be extremely careful about whom they could trust for that shelter. The new laws had made many people apprehensive about helping the IRA men who were living fugitive lives. The true believers, as Tom called those who supported them, were still able to be relied upon.

The column found some safe shelter near Drumraney on a farm as the men wanted to see their families for the first time in six months and most of them came from the area. Tom gave the men two days leave to go home and return to this farm after their visit. Joe was keen to see his younger brothers and sisters and of course his parents whom he hadn't seen for nearly six months. He wondered what the welcome would be like especially from Peter, his father. He knew his mother supported the IRA and believed in the Republic. Peter was less political and saw the new war as an impost on Ireland and an unnecessary burden on a country already struggling economically.

Joe ventured into a village near to his home late in the afternoon with a weather eye out for any State troops or Garda. He found the general store and purchased a shilling's worth of sweets as a gift for his young siblings. Then he slipped into the local pub quietly hoping that no one would recognize him. He wanted to buy a small bottle of whiskey to share with his father and brothers and his Mammy if she chose to. His hopes for anonymity didn't last long, the owner of the pub Paddy Murtagh had been there since forever and was Hugh's uncle, he recognized Joe straight away.

"You're a stranger around here now Joe, not seen you or Hugh for a long time." Joe ignored the greeting and asked for a small bottle of Jamesons pretending he didn't know what the man was talking about. But he wasn't in any danger Paddy was a believer as well. The barman looked at the clock on the wall, it was near four in the afternoon and whispered, "Have a quick one on me out the back Joe, but you better be on your way before five, the Staters come in and have a couple then. They'll recognize you sure enough."

Joe nodded his agreement and paid for the whiskey and slipped behind the counter and into a back room mainly used for storage by the publican. He was happy to sit on his own and relax, it had been a hard day, crossing fields and moving through any village he couldn't avoid with two others he had travelled with. The tension of avoiding arrest was telling and being a fugitive more demanding as time went on. He sank into a chair out of sight of the rest of the patrons. Paddy came in with a pint of Guinness and Joe's eyes lit up,

"Haven't had one of these for months," he said as he took a long draft. "How do they do it for the price?" He smiled as he wiped the foam from his lips. Paddy's voice was now more serious than before.

"You know they lifted Hugh and James a few weeks ago and McCormack and three others who had been troubling them." Joe knew and acknowledged with a nod. "The Staters and your old friend Sean have been moving around the whole county and MacEoin has the place locked down tighter than a drum. Do you have a piece on you?" Paddy was referring to a revolver which he was certain Joe would be carrying. Joe looked at him, he had few people he could trust outside his family and had convinced himself that Paddy was one of them, he just nodded slightly again as he took another draft of Guinness.

"Best leave it here with me I suppose you're here to visit your family?" Joe nodded again without speaking, "Well the last thing they need is for them to raid the place and find you and a gun, they'd lift them all, even the kiddies." Joe thought Paddy was joking about that but Paddy wasn't smiling, "It's that tough here Joe, I kid you not. You can pick up the piece on your way out, I'll leave it hidden behind the wood pile out back, if the Staters find it I'll just say someone must have stashed it, they can't blame me for it." Joe finally spoke,

"You're a good man Paddy, always have been, I'll do that, I don't want to take a gun into the house. My Da wouldn't like it I know, best not to complicate matters." Paddy spoke again, he was an uncle after all of Joe's step brother Hugh and a man he could trust.

"Families need to look after each other when they can Joe, God knows it's a difficult time and many of us admire what you're doing but a lot of others think you're an idiot, it's likely that you'll end up like Hugh in Athlone prison before too much longer. It's sad, but you know you're losing the war with the Staters don't you?" Joe didn't commit an answer just looked at Paddy and drained his glass,

"Thanks for the Guinness Paddy it's done me the world of good and thanks for your help."

"Go out the back-way Joe and God go with you," Paddy shook Joe's hand and looked him directly in the eyes, "Give my regards to your mother, we don't see her too often, she's one of the best." Joe nodded his agreement, he didn't need any confirmation of that, his mother was the rock on which the family rested, Peter did the work but Mary supplied the kindness, the support and tender love that mothers somehow have in abundance. He left his gun with Paddy and slipped out the back door looking forward to seeing again the only woman in the world he could love apart from Maggie.

It was still light and would be for a few hours but Joe didn't want to approach the family home until it was dark, you never knew who might be watching and the last thing Joe wanted was to put them in danger. The village he left behind was small and it didn't take him long to find a wooded area off the track and he was less than half a mile from the Keegan farm. He made sure he was out of sight and would allow himself the luxury of a sleep without having the usual guards posted. He was tired and the Guinness had relaxed him sufficiently. Within minutes he was dead to the world but not before he said his usual prayer before he went to sleep, "Thanks be to God and his Holy Mother", it was a habit he had formed since a child, having heard his father say it every night. He knew he had to thank something that he was still alive and able to be where he was.

He must have slept for two hours or more and he woke with that suddenness that living with fear brings. He was now fully awake but he still lay perfectly still listening for any sound that signaled danger. The chill of the ground had entered his body but he still chose not to move, his hearing strained and any noise was amplified by his concern. After a few minutes he knew he had to risk making a move and slowly sat up surveying the area. It was starting to get dark making everything look more suspicious, a light breeze pushed through the trees. Joe reached for solace of his revolver then remembered he had left it with Paddy He now felt vulnerable, as soldiers do, without a weapon.

Finally, he was convinced he was still alone and rose to his feet stretching the sleep out of his system. He was hungry and thirsty as he walked off towards the farm knowing he would have another hour to wait before the darkness had set in.

Joe sat on a tree stump just within the trees and looked out at the farm house where he had grown up. The night had arrived and he watched the smoke from the chimney in the kitchen, the light from the paraffin lamps inside the house made the windows glow with a yellow haze. It must be like this every night he thought but now without himself, Hugh and James and perhaps Patrick another younger brother. God how time flew he thought, Patrick was just a boy when all this started.

Joe walked a perimeter of the house well away from it, looking to see if there were any sentries posted. He knew he was a wanted man and the Staters had a price on him and Sean would reward any man who brought in Joe Keegan. Every now and then someone left the house for some reason and quickly returned. Joe decided it was time, he would go to the back door, he looked in through the window beside it, his siblings lounged around reading or talking, his father smoking his pipe and his beloved mother standing as always by the wood stove preparing some kind of food for the small tribe.

He tried the door and it was open, he pushed it slightly and stole in, the lamps giving just the right amount of light to make everyone out. Suddenly, he realised he didn't know what to say but he stood there with a huge smile on his face and finally,

> "Da, Mammy I've come home."

#   #

Tom McGiff also managed to visit his family farm not a great distance from the Keegan farm. There would be less people there as Tom's brother Dan had been arrested a few weeks earlier and was now in prison which just left his grandmother and three sisters to make do for themselves. Their father had died before the first world war in 1914. Tom at great risk to himself, had earlier raided a farm belonging to a former RIC Inspector who lived closer to Dublin. He liberated two chickens as quietly as possible as he didn't want to go home empty handed, he rung their necks in the dead of night and made his way to his grandmother's farmhouse. He surprised them all as he had not been home for nearly a year. He helped them prepare one of the chickens which were fully grown and joined them for a tastier meal than he had for many a month.

#   #

There were unexpected tears in Joe's eyes after he entered the farmhouse, just the sight of his mother standing at the wood stove, her apron on and her hair tied back in a bun and the inevitable wooden stirrer in her right hand was as if he'd never left the house. She looked around at the voice and her own tears started,

"Oh, Joe thank God you're safe, we never know how you are, but you're here at last." She went and took him in her arms and gave him the biggest hug he could remember and the tears flowed more freely. Joe looked out to his father Peter who he knew would be less demonstrative but Peter was overwhelmed as well and joined the hugging. His eyes were wet with tears but he held himself back. Then his siblings came to hug him, Thomas and Patrick, the oldest boys at home, hands and face washed after a day in the field, helping run the farm. Joe's younger sisters, Teresa,

Frances and Mary Ellen, now little girls who seemed to have grown so much in the months since he had seen them. Joe realised what home and family meant to him and in a strange way, what he felt he was fighting for. This was Ireland and this was his family and no one could take that from him.

He unloaded his pocket of the sweets he had brought for the young ones and they took them, counted and shared them as children do. To his mother he said he hadn't been able to do any shopping for presents and laughed, then took out his Rosary Beads and gave them to her,

"Look after these for me and you can give them back when we meet again." Mary was still wiping her eyes and Peter was steering him to the family dinner table. Joe took out the small whiskey and said to his father, "Da the pub was open and I spoke to Paddy Murtagh, he wanted you to have this." Peter was not a big drinker but he enjoyed a quiet whiskey when he had the chance. He took the bottle and placed it on the table.

"A toast to your visit would be best." He said and collected three mugs from the kitchen cupboard.

Joe still wasn't sure how Peter felt about the Civil War and his part in it, he wasn't sure how to word his questions but Peter would know what he was asking anyway.

"Da, have you been able to see Hugh or James? They're in Athlone you know since they were arrested." Peter shook his head.

"No, they won't let anyone near them, the Staters are afraid of anyone knowing what is going on. We tried and Patrick tried but no good."

"And what is going on Da, do you think?" asked Joe probing for Peter's thinking.

Joe's father looked at him his eyes looking like tears forming again, but he held back, it was more an explanation than the answer Joe had been looking for.

"Joe, your Mammy and me know that you and your brothers and even Thomas yearn for the Republic. It's right that young men demand the best, demand what they think is rightfully theirs, and we don't disagree but we are older and that makes us less able to take on what needs to be fought for. At least for me it does. Your Mammy is stronger than me and wants to argue with the authorities about the politics of it all. But I have other things to think about," he motioned to the young ones playing on the floor still sharing their sweets, "it takes a certain amount of fight out of me, I'd like to do more, but I'm so tired of it all, it's been going on for seven years now on and off. We need a rest we all do, even you boys who have decided to carry it on. I'm sorry Joe I think Michael Collins had the right idea when he agreed to the Treaty. It gave us a chance to take a break and reestablish ourselves as a people, as a nation. I know it's not what you want to hear Joe but that's the way we see it, I see it," he looked at his wife who didn't offer any agreement or disagreement. He continued, "This argument has gone on in houses all over the country for a number of months now, it doesn't mean we are pro Treaty Joe, it just means we want the fighting to stop and everyone to be safe, for there to be peace. There isn't any now but the country needs it."

It had been the most political words Joe had ever heard his father utter, he wasn't angry with him. It was expressed so well he could totally understand what he meant and what he wanted. His was a different generation with different responsibilities. The fire for the republic was still there but it had been put on a back burner. Joe spoke not to hurt his parents, but wanting them to understand his feelings.

"Thanks Da, I know it's a tough time for everyone and we in the army feel the pain, but…" he delayed now, "but we have decided to go on, we think there's a chance that the Provisional Government will come round to our thinking." Normally it would be the start of an ideological argument, pro and anti, both sides putting their strongly believed points of view forward and challenging the other to respond. But Joe didn't want to argue with his parents, not now, not tonight. His mother was gracious and Joe knew she spoke for her husband also,

"We respect what you believe Joe and your brothers, all we want is for you all to be safe and have a good life."

"I'll drink to that," said Peter and motioned to the two boys and his wife to share a toast to Joe.

"And to Ireland," added Joe, "and a Republic!"

They sat and had a small supper and talked about where Joe had been and the boys were curious about what he had seen and in what actions. Like most soldiers Joe didn't like to talk about these things except in general terms, but they passed the time and Joe warmed to the good feeling being with his family had brought him.

Peter looked at the clock on the mantle above the fireplace. As usual he was the practical one, life had to go on and things had to be done.

"Time for sleep boys, can you stay Joe, will you stay around tomorrow?" his mother looked expectantly hoping for a positive answer,

"I can, but I'll have to go tomorrow night when it's dark, and stay out of sight here in case there are any visitors." Everyone hugged Joe again and went for their beds. Joe would sleep on the floor with some blankets and a pillow his mother supplied. Feeling safer than usual Joe was asleep minutes after closing his eyes.

It seemed like only minutes to Joe since he had dropped off but the whole families sleep was broken four hours later with a loud rap on the door, they all woke swiftly. Joe knew it wouldn't be Staters, they wouldn't have bothered to knock, not at the Keegan's, a family with known IRA members. It was a young man named Eddy, looking harassed,

"Sorry to awake you Mr. Keegan" he said to Peter "but Paddy Murtagh asked me to come round," at the pub last night a few of the Staters were getting rowdy and Paddy heard them talking about their plans to raid a number of houses in the Drumraney area this morning, they'll be bright and early and Paddy wanted you to know, as he knew you had a visitor." Peter and Mary looked at Joe. Their plans for a quiet day ruined, Peter just nodded to Eddy and thanked him,

"God go with you lad and thanks for the message."

It was the way bad news travelled in the countryside nowadays, furtive visits in the dead of night and whispered messages. Joe knew what it meant he gathered his things and bid goodbye to his siblings and his parents. His eyes met his mothers. He knew what she wanted to say but hoped she wouldn't, but she must,

"Look after yourself Joe, we want to see you again safe and well." They hugged and Joe took Peter's hand,

"Goodbye Da." there were no more words to match how he felt, he hugged his father and went out the door into the pitch-black morning.

It was as well that he knew the area as he was able to find Paddy's pub and retrieve the revolver where Paddy had said it would be. He hoped that his friends had received the same message he had and that they would find their own way to safety. The plan was to rendezvous back at the shelter and retrieve their rifles and move on to their next safe location. Joe was on the move again, in the dark and alone, scared but not scared, hearing all the sounds that he hoped would warn him of danger. He gripped his revolver, thankful to have it back in his possession.

All of the Flying Column men managed to get home and see their families and leave the area again after their short visit.

CHAPTER 29
The Keegan Farm Has Another Visitor

The army lorry came to an abrupt halt on the dirt road outside the Keegan farm at 6:30 am the next morning. Then a further lorry with more soldiers on board did the same. A total of sixteen armed soldiers from the Free State army now surrounded Peter and Mary Keegan's small house, their firearms ready and primed for action. The officer in charge rapped on the door of the farmhouse, it was opened straight away.

"We're here to search your property under the Emergency Powers Act, we have reason to believe that you are sheltering IRA men." Peter Keegan had opened the door and looked down on Sean McKeon who was perhaps four inches shorter than the farmer.

"Sean, it's good to see you again after so much time, how are you son?" but the officer was no longer the friendly youth who had been a friend of his eldest sons, he was all spit and polish. His green uniform neat and tidy and his leggings polished to a bright sheen, his pistol holster high on his waist but no longer holding a pistol, that was in Sean's hand. Peter's voice disguised the contempt he felt for the young man who had sold his soul to the new state army. It was one thing to take sides thought Peter another to become a standard bearer for your chosen side. Sean would have none of the goodwill. He had a job to do and had to show his professionalism to his men, he was a Captain in the Free State Army and not a man to be trifled with. Didn't these people understand there was a war on?

"Mr. Keegan, we're here to search your home." And with that brushed past Peter Keegan and confronted Mary Keegan who found it more difficult to hide her contempt, so Sean ignored her, simply touched his cap and waved four men into the small house.

"Look everywhere, upstairs and down the back and in that barn." Sean knew the place well as a youngster he had played Hurling and football with the Keegan boys in the yard and the fields nearby. More men rushed into the house pushing the Keegan's aside, the young girls hid behind their mother. The eldest Teresa stood wide eyed, at eighteen years of age she was no longer a little girl that Sean remembered but an attractive young woman with flowing dark hair and dark eyes to match.

"Hello Sean," she said, Sean came to a halt not sure who she was but quickly taken in by her looks. He was about to utter her name but decided to ignore her and move further into the house, shouting at his men. Teresa was younger than Sean and remembered fondly the days he had visited their home with her brothers. She had decided then he was handsome and took a shine to him. Now she was shocked at how he had spoken to her parents.

After a couple of minutes, two soldiers came down the stairs dragging Thomas who was an age that raised suspicion, over twenty he could have been IRA and probably was knowing the Keegans, but it wasn't who Sean was looking for, he knew who he wanted. He shook his head at the men who then threw Thomas aside. Another two brought in Patrick and again Sean shook his head and Patrick was discarded the same way.

"We heard you had a visitor Mr. Keegan, has Joe been here today?" Sean asked, Mary was first to speak,

"We haven't seen Joe for months and you know it and if we had seen him do you think we'd tell you?" there was venom in her voice now and she cared little. Worrying more if her lies would be forgiven at her next confession or if would she be condemned under the new Pastoral Letter of the Catholic Church telling believers to deny the IRA any help?

Sean was in a quandary now. He had been sure his information had been correct perhaps he had left the raid too late. If his men hadn't carried on at Murtagh's pub till late last night he could have been there earlier. He ignored Mary but picked up some papers from the kitchen table, Mary never bothered to hide her connection to Cumann na mBan the women's auxiliary that helped the IRA so much. The papers were hers, newsletters which she read and enjoyed.

"You know Mrs. Keegan these are banned publications; the Government doesn't allow them free distribution." His arrogance was showing more now and his power was on display but Mary was not to be cowed.

"Well that's their bad luck because I want to read them and I will." She had thrown his power back in his face and Sean flushed with anger and embarrassment, he couldn't leave empty handed, he nodded to two of the soldiers,

"Take him away." And Thomas was dragged out the door.

"Will you not stop till you have all our sons in prison Captain, your friends from boyhood, your Hurling friends, your good friends." It was Peter now challenging the young officer. His fists were taut with rage holding himself in check at this outrageous affront to their home and their dignity by someone who had once shared it all with them.

"He'll be back tomorrow; we have some questions we have to ask him." Was all Sean said. He knew he had the authority to do whatever he needed to and taking men of a certain age away from their homes was a regular occurrence. He needed to show some results from the raid. "Give Joe my regards if you happen to see him, good day to you." Sean walked out of the now disheveled house, his men who had made the mess followed him, the others had searched the barn and nearby fields in vain. Joe had been given the warning in time and was well away from his home by the time Sean's men arrived. Peter and Mary hoped Thomas wouldn't be given too hard a time but it was another cross to bear. Thomas hadn't any connection to the IRA and they hoped that would keep him safe.

CHAPTER 30
On The Run Again

Joe found Tom McGiff and the rest of the column at their agreed meeting point. At least the Staters hadn't found this spot or still didn't suspect the farmer who owned the land.

"Well Tom did you see your gran and is she well?" Joe asked.

"Aye, she's grand and she's as tough as anyone I've ever seen, raising my three sisters at her age and providing everything for them, even giving them schooling at home. I was sorry to leave but I had no choice. I suppose you got the same message from Paddy Murtagh as we all did?"

"Aye," said Joe "he's a good man and he won't be cowed by the Staters, they don't know how to take him or what to do with him. They'd put him in prison but they'd have nowhere to get their Guinness." Joe smiled at the thought and Tom agreed.

"He's what our side needs alright, and plenty more of them." With that Tom changed his mood to a more serious one, "Have you seen much of Dublin Joe?" Joe was surprised by the question,

"I went there once to a funeral a few years ago, with my old friend Sean," he said smiling at the thought of when the two men were friends. "Why?"

"I want you to go there again and see a good man name of Ernie O'Malley, not just a friend but a big man, senior officer and he is running his Division out of Dublin."

"I've heard the name, but I thought he was down Cork way with Dan Breen's mob."

"He was but Head Quarters wanted him in Dublin, where he could do more damage, he's a hard man and had some interesting times in the Tan war. He's not the Quartermaster General but he'll know who is and will put you in touch. We need some serious explosives and a few Thompson machine guns and more ammunition. I'm sure they know we can't buy them at the local store and our supply line has just about dried up. It's getting harder and harder to fight this war as you know." It was the first time that Joe had heard anything negative from Tom who was truly at his wit's end. When you're running a column in the midlands as Tom was it was becoming impossible to raid barracks and steal some weapons as they had done before the Civil War started. Not many friends could be relied on and Tom knew his column was barely tolerated in some areas. Tom went on, "and we need a radio to communicate with the others, anyone, our HQ, Dublin, Cork, we don't know what the hell is going on in the country most of the time until we pick up a Dublin paper. And they're censored and just put the other side's case. We're working in the dark and I know that's what we have to do but we need more support more information." Joe could see Tom was quite frustrated, he wondered how he kept going, it seemed as if you were fighting a war on your own. Being an effective fighting column was one thing but you needed to know what was going on elsewhere.

"I could be in Dublin by dark tomorrow and I'll leave soon. I'd rather travel at night than by day." Joe was looking forward to a change and wanted to contribute more to the fight, it would be good to meet some senior men and pick their brains.

"I'll send Dan Crowley with you Joe; you'll both be on the same mission. You can travel together but try and keep separate when you can so if one of you gets lifted the other might get through. No notes, no maps, no plans and no weapons, you have to remember where I'm sending you and find your own way. But we need to get through to HQ in Dublin, our men in Athlone are getting thin on the ground and with the Army stationed there it's becoming very dangerous. We need to be out in the country, hit the towns and get out again. But…" and here he showed his real exasperation, "……. we need something to hit them with hard!"

Tom couldn't have been aware but many field commanders like him were in the same boat. There was a lack of communications, lack of weapons, lack of resources. Most importantly there was a lack of a sound plan to take the whole country and defeat the Government. There were minor skirmishes everywhere but no big confrontations, no big battles that could grab the headlines and the population's attention. Tom couldn't say it to his men but he was starting to lose heart wondering if the men in charge of the IRA had what it would take to win this war. And all the time their ranks were being reduced by continual arrests of any suspected soldier or sympathiser.

Joe and Dan Crowley met with Tom again within an hour. He gave them the details of where they could find Ernie O'Malley using another safe address in Dublin. They committed both to memory and the message that Tom needed specific supplies and fast and where they could be dropped. Dan and Joe decided it was safe enough to pick up a train for Dublin. They couldn't take the risk of being armed as they knew they would almost be certain to be searched at some stage of their journey. They'd walk three miles to Tullamore and get the train, they could make it for a six o'clock departure. The weather was getting cold and the night was coming early. Tom asked them if they had their identity papers. In their cases they were forged passes from the police station in Athlone, with a signature no one could recognize. The vaguer the paper the less likely they'd be picked up. Tom briefed them further:

"Remember you're two labourers heading for a building job in Dublin promised you by the Mayor of Athlone. His name's Frank Buchanan, the Dublin Staters wouldn't know him from Adam anyway but he's a friend of your uncle's and there's work to be done clearing wreckage in the city. And if they ask tell them you've signed the pledge just say yes. You won't have guns so they'll let you through I'm sure." The Pledge was the agreement men were asked to sign to prove they were pro Treaty and if you didn't, you'd end up in prison.

They managed to catch the train on time and as expected there were plenty of soldiers around who kept eyeing the two men with suspicion. But they remained unchallenged until they were about thirty minutes out of Dublin. The train was stopped by an army patrol and six soldiers led by two officers entered their carriage,

"Where are you going lads?" the lead officer asked as he stood over them, he had ignored the families on the train and zeroed in on the two men. Joe had their story ready, they felt safer being together despite Tom's warning.

"We've got some laboring work lined up in Dublin Colonel, we've been sent by the Mayor of Athlone to meet his friend whose house has been blown up." The officer was not amused or taken in it seemed.

"Enough of the blarney with the colonel stuff you cheeky bastard, you know damn well I'm not a colonel. But we don't know who you are do we?" the implication was always that they were IRA. Any men above a certain age were always treated with suspicion. Joe and Dan pulled their papers from their coat pockets and passed them over and an address in Dublin where they were headed for the work, a fake one that they hoped had been bombed out. The officer nodded to one of his men to take the papers offered he looked at them but didn't make any comment. The officer didn't bother looking at them himself, "So you're going back to work are you lads, sick of the IRA are you, getting too many beatings." Now was the time for Joe to eat humble pie,

"No sir, we're not IRA, we've signed the pledge, never were members, never."

"You're lying son, every one of you were into something and you don't look like a Black and Tan to me so you must have been on the rebels' side." It was an obvious statement and true in most cases but Joe had to continue the subterfuge,

"No sir, me and my friend here had to work the farms with our Da's. There was no time for any fighting." It wasn't very convincing but it was the best Joe could do .He wished he'd still had his revolver with him, he'd take the grin off this monkey's face. The officer looked at his wrist watch. It must have been close to closing time and he wanted to be away, he'd done his job, terrified a couple of travelers and questioned some likely IRA. He signaled for his men to frisk Joe and Dan to make sure there were no weapons. They both stood up and were searched. The soldier nodded the all clear to his officer

He took the papers from the soldier and asked Joe,

"And these are your real names or ones made up for you?" he smiled at his own joke pretty sure he was right, it hardly mattered what their names were, if they weren't in Free State Army uniform as far as he was concerned, they must be IRA. "Keep your nose clean boys we'll be looking out for you in Dublin." With that he turned and walked away after returning the papers to Joe. They got off the train after they'd swaggered through two more carriages and found a few more people to terrify. The train started off and only then did Joe dare to look at Dan both their faces drained of colour. It didn't take much to end up on the wrong side of the law these days and if you were a young man you were fair game. Joe was first to speak,

"When we stop in Dublin we go in opposite directions, no point in being together, there's a pub near the safe house address Tom gave us, we'll meet up there in say two hours. Good luck Dan."

"And you Joe", they shook hands as the train pulled into the station and went their respective ways. It was nine thirty and the dark streets of Dublin beckoned and offered the men hope, some measure of protection. There were plenty of friends of the IRA in Dublin but the challenge was to find them.

For over an hour Joe stalked the side streets and laneways of Dublin on his walk from the railway station. On two occasions he narrowly missed army patrols, his heightened sense of danger keeping him on full alert. The first time he almost walked into a group of soldiers walking down a main road but stopped because he heard the tramp of army boots. Soldiers in charge aren't known for being quiet, they like everyone to know who they are. Joe managed to hide in a doorway. It was very dark and the gas lit streets didn't offer much light so he was able to avoid any confrontation. The second time he saw the group of soldiers about fifty yards away hanging around a street corner. This time he just changed direction and quick marched himself away from the area, he thought he heard a shout to stop but he took his chances and kept walking.

There was not much of Dublin Joe could remember and the darkness didn't help. He had been given directions on how to find the safe house but he had nothing written down. He relied as he did on his last visit on landmarks and tried to keep certain buildings and the River Liffey in context. There were small bridges over the river which he tried to avoid but took note of where they were. He would only have to cross one of them and that would be at double speed, it was too easy to get trapped on a bridge.

He was giving up hope when he noticed a familiar figure not too far from where he was walking. The streets were all but deserted, there was no curfew but few people ventured out unless they had to.

"Dan." he said as loud as he dared at the man now just ten yards from him, "Dan Crowley are you lost as well man?" The man turned, it was indeed his travelling companion.

"Jaysus Joe, thank God it's you, do you know where we are?"

"No but since we're both here we must be close to what we're looking for." They stopped and shared their thoughts; they both noticed some landmarks which had guided them. Then Joe said confidently, "Let's walk down that side street towards the river, I think I remember that name," there weren't a lot of street signs left in Dublin and no one was replacing them but Joe had relaxed now he had found Dan. They must be close to where they wanted. They walked another five minutes taking two more turns. "There." Said Joe, "that pub on that corner, that's the one. You walk down the other side of the street but don't go in. I'll walk this side and if we feel that it's alright, we'll give the nod and head inside." They did just that and after another few minutes Joe felt confident enough to move into the pubs doorway which was unlocked. Dan followed him and they were at once confronted by two men,

"What do you want?" one of them said his voice full of menace.

"Tom McGiff gave us this address; said we'd be welcome." Was all Joe said and hoped it would suffice. The man nodded and Joe and Dan sighed with relief. He had been expecting them and knew what their orders were. For now, they could relieve the tension they had been carrying with them since they had left Westmeath many hours earlier. One of the men took them to a room beside the bar and motioned for them to sit. A few minutes later a woman put a breadboard with bread and cheese in front of them

"Tay?" was all she said. They both nodded yes. Two big mugs were served, they had their fill and then the woman took them to a room upstairs where there were two beds. She opened the door and indicated they go in which they did and sat on the beds desperate from fatigue, "You'll be woken at six and you'll have to be on your way then." With that she closed the door and Joe and Dan looked at each other just grinned, thanked their luck and lay down and were asleep within minutes. "Thanks be to God and His Holy Mother." Said Joe as his eyes closed.

They were awoken by a loud banging on their door. It was six in the morning and Joe felt he had just fell asleep. They were shown a bathroom for a quick face wash and toilet break. They were then ushered down stairs and given a mug of hot tea and a crust of bread by the lady of the establishment. One of the men from the night before joined them.

"You're going to see Ernie O'Malley. I'll tell you how to get there. Don't walk together and when you get there don't go in together. One of you wait ten minutes and watch the other's back and make sure there is no one hanging around. Understood?"

They both nodded but couldn't understand how the man knew who they were seeking, but there was only one Ernie O'Malley in Dublin. He was well protected by this group and if any visitors came from out of town that was who they wanted to see. He was one of the two top men in the IRA in the city and was head of the most wanted list of the Staters.

Joe listened as they were given instructions, he was expecting an hour's walk but was told it would only take them a few minutes to find the house. The man pointed at Joe,

"You go first, don't stop outside the address, walk past about fifty yards then turn back and go straight in the door will be open, " he turned to Dan "You wait ten minutes and follow but take the directions I gave you and do the same thing, walk past for fifty yards, then double back. Go straight in to the house and don't knock. And watch his back!" he said nodding to Joe. It was still reasonably dark outside and cold. Joe turned up his collar on his overcoat and pulled down on his cap and walked out the door giving the man a brief thank you on the way.

The instructions were more than adequate, three corner turns and he was on the street he sought and looked for number thirty three which he found. He walked past fifty yards as he was told to do then turned looking all the time for anything suspicious. He opened the garden gate of the attractive little cottage and walked straight in the front door. A tall, thick set, well dressed man was just inside with a revolver in his right hand and Joe noticed it was ready to fire. The man just said,

"Wait." They stood there in silence Joe not knowing if he should say something but decided not to. Within ten minutes Dan walked through the door just as the day was starting to brighten. The man with the gun closed the door and locked it. He motioned for them to follow him down a small flight of stairs into a type of annex to a dining room, there were three chairs and a desk covered with papers. They had just been greeted by Ernie O'Malley, commandant of the IRA 4th Eastern Division in Dublin and one of the most wanted men in Ireland. This was his fourth safe house in two months. Brave women who had been widowed by the other side wanted to help the Republican cause. His hostess Ellen O'Rahilly looked after him and had even arranged a hidden closet in the house where he could sleep. Finally, he indicated for them to sit, "And how's my old mate Tom McGiff getting on these fine days?" He asked with a bright smile.

CHAPTER 31
Custume Barracks Athlone

As 1922 headed towards a new winter and the weather became colder and wetter and the grass greener, Sean McKeon was establishing himself as a senior officer. Even though young in years, his influence in the Free State Army at its midland headquarters in Athlone was substantial. Sean's duties covered a large area through the counties of Longford, Roscommon, Westmeath and up to Sligo and Mayo. He was responsible for keeping those counties clear of IRA problems.

The railway network was a favourite target for the Irregulars as the Staters called the IRA who were keen to make the country difficult to govern and run. Railway signal stations were difficult to protect twenty-four hours a day, seven days a week. In Sean's area in the last couple of months, Streamstown, Castletowngeoghan and Horseleap signal stations on the main Dublin line had been burned down and a railway bridge at Ballnabarna blown up. The war seemed endless and tedious but each engagement confirmed for Sean that the anti Treaty forces had to be brought under control. General MacEoin met with Sean in Athlone he was under increasing pressure from the government in Dublin, they wanted more patrols, more arrests. The Home Affairs Minister Kevin O'Higgins was keen to put more fear into the remaining IRA men who refused to say die. But MacEoin was concerned and worried about the local civilian response to Dublin's crackdown.

"There will be some outcry soon from the people and probably an upsurge in rebel activity. I've just heard from O'Higgins in Dublin that some IRA prisoners will be executed by hanging sometime soon. The government wants to show it's not being soft and send a strong message. There'll be no trials. Be ready for any reprisals. As I say it will stir things up." It seemed that the government was fully intent on showing its strength. The four men would be the first of over eighty executed in the next six months.

"There's a concern about the prison in Athlone General, there's a lot of overcrowding and it won't take a lot to cause a riot. Those hangings or even rumours of them, could do it." Sean had heard reports of problems in the prison, his information was correct. Athlone prison was part of the army's Custume Barracks and was built as a regional prison to hold perhaps sixty prisoners but with the IRA roundup and no were else to send them. It now held several hundreds of prisoners causing the overcrowding that could cause unrest and uproar.

So, it happened in this prison in October 1922. As is often the case, it didn't take much to start a riot. A prison guard working his second straight shift, after twenty hours on the job, lost his temper with an arguing IRA man. He lashed out violently with his night stick causing the prisoner to collapse unconscious on a landing near a bunch of other men. The guard was lucky he wasn't killed and would have been except for three other guards who came to his aid and managed to fight their way off the landing and lock the gate.

The prisoners had been complaining about the fact that they were being treated like common criminals. They considered themselves prisoners of war and expected more respect and privileges than what they were getting.

But the government in Dublin had given strict orders not to treat them as prisoners of war. O'Higgins said they were simply criminals who ignored the laws of the country. When that order had been first read out to the prisoners the trouble started brewing. Men started meeting in larger groups than allowed and agitating for their rights and the overcrowding was a major issue, eight men to a cell that was meant to hold two or at most four. The government and the army hadn't foreseen the problems that would be created by their overzealous arrests of anyone who looked like a potential IRA foot soldier. Anyone who wouldn't sign their amnesty pledge was picked up. They had underestimated the stubbornness of their fellow Irishmen and were now paying the price. The vast camps that they were planning to open in the Curragh in Kildare to hold the IRA detainees were not yet ready. So the limited prisons of many regional towns bore the brunt of the overcrowding and the situation had reached crisis point as in Athlone.

The senior men in the prison called for volunteers for a hunger strike, often the IRA's first weapon of choice. For three days most prisoners rejected any food that was on offer but the guards just ignored them. Then the men wouldn't respect lights out orders and often kept shouting and singing till the early morning hours. When they were ordered on to the parade ground for counting and checking they meandered about and wouldn't stand still to be counted. All of which created problems for the people running the prison.

It was in this atmosphere that the truncheon attack on the prisoner took place and started what was afterwards officially referred to as a riot. Prisoners roamed the landings and wouldn't return to their cells; some broke out of the poorly secured landings and ran up and down the stairs and into the parade ground area. It was after three days of this commotion that the prison governor decided to call in reinforcements in the form of Free State Army soldiers.

They were armed with bayonets fixed to push the prisoners into their landings and then into cell which were firmly locked.

Captain Sean McKeon now found himself doing prison duties when he had hardly seen the inside of a prison. He quickly realised that brute force was the only language that the prisoners would respond to. He led a group of thirty men onto a landing and the noise was incredible, the prisoners banging their tin plates and cups on steel bars and shouting obscenities at the Staters whom they hated. On each of the two landings, soldiers and prison guards pushed in from either end and if someone didn't move when told, there was another broken head to deal with. Sean was at the head of his group and wielded his rifle butt efficiently. Men who knew who he was from the Tan War and had grown up with him swore vehemently at him and in some instances spat on him which angered him more. His use of his weapon was indiscriminate and he came down on a prisoner with a rifle butt to the stomach and nearly followed up with the sharp end. Then he realised it was Hugh Murtagh. There was no apology and no acknowledgement by either man. Sean had a job to do and his friendship with Hugh was long forgotten. Hugh knew the face and managed a burst of profanity at Sean before he crumpled under the rifle assault.

"Put him in that cell." Sean shouted to two other prisoners as he held his rifle up bayonet first, "and get in with him." The men did as they were told and the guards pushed another two men in with them, there was blood all over many of the prisoners and soldiers but Sean could see they were prevailing. The place was getting quieter and a number of men had retreated to their cells not able to fight back against the weapons the soldiers wielded. The guards followed along and locked all the prison cell doors leaving just a few prisoners who were incapable of moving to be carried down to the infirmary.

Sean looked around and spotted the prison commander talking to General MacEoin who had joined in. MacEoin had his pistol in his hand and blood on his uniform. Both landings had been taken and all prisoners locked in, the soldiers retreated and the General saw Sean and called him over.

"Good work lad, that'll show the rebels who is in charge now." He turned to the prison officer, "leave them there locked up till morning to nurse their sore heads." Sean could see the general had been drinking as he slurred his words, Sean wondered whether a skin full of whiskey makes these fights easier to have.

"Back to barracks men," Sean said to his company and the men, mostly raw recruits and youngsters put on their forced smiles and gladly got out of the prison environs. Sean paused for a moment on his way down, was that really Hugh Murtagh he nearly killed?

CHAPTER 32
Joe finds urban warfare in Dublin

It was the last week of October and Joe and Dan met with General O'Malley for nearly an hour in the suburban house where he was sheltering. They explained what Tom McGiff wanted him to know. The Drumraney Column had precious few arms and ammunition and were running out of explosives and there were no more to be easily stolen. They couldn't continue to fight without more supplies.

O'Malley listened, patiently nodding and agreeing from time to time but Joe could see he wasn't going to be able to help much. From O'Malley's attitude, the men worried that he was, despite his patriotism and energy, almost a defeated man but he couldn't let them see that. The winter was coming on and though the long dark nights offered the best chances of doing damage to the enemy the men in the field were losing patience. There were strong IRA leaders such as O'Malley and others who understood the reality they all faced. Unfortunately the leadership was scattered all over the country and communication between the field and Head Office was at best haphazard. The field commanders had to make big decisions on their own but they had no way of knowing if what they were doing was having a positive effect for the cause. In reality, they didn't know if they were winning or losing the war against the Free State Army and it was beginning to affect morale. As Joe conveyed to O'Malley,

"Tom said that IRA can't keep expecting men to leave their families or their jobs if they have one and not know what is happening in the rest of the country." Joe wasn't comfortable talking like this to a senior officer but he was only conveying Tom McGiff's message.

Ernie O'Malley knew what the score was and he was worried about it more than he could tell these two men. He put on a brave front though and said to Joe,

"Make a list of what Tom wants and I'll personally see to it that he gets as much as we can manage. We're facing difficult times everywhere lads but that's what we took on. We have to see it through." Joe could see he was under immense stress and just nodded in agreement.

Then O'Malley's expression changed, he had another task he wanted Joe and Dan to become involved in. He thought he would make use of a couple of experienced fighters while they were in the city. God knows there was never enough of them.

"We have plans in a few days to attack Wellington Barracks and let the Army know we're still here and still fighting for our cause. We'd like you to join in it'll be different to fighting in the country. Instead of trees and hedgerows to hide in we have buildings and houses, but like you, we hit and run to fight another day. What do you say?" Joe and Dan weren't sure if it was an invitation or an order but they were both up for it, anything to hurt the enemy and assist the cause.

"Of course, sir we'd want to be involved but we need to be getting out of the city after, we don't have anywhere to stay." Joe answered.

"Don't worry about that we'll get you out of Dublin and show you the way home. We have a small van that can take you part of the way. With any luck it won't be searched." O'Malley had a big grin on his face now and it was obvious to the two visitors that he wanted to carry on the fight and win. The strategy was all his but his seniority necessarily kept him out of the front line which he would have loved to join. "Go back to the place you came from and have a rest and keep out of sight and you'll get new instructions soon. You can have a couple of days off but don't become tourists. You need to listen closely to the men you are with. You're dismissed now and thank you for bringing the message from Tom and relay to him that we'll do everything we can to get him what he needs."

Joe and Dan were ushered out the front door in ten-minute intervals again, Joe first, who headed to the right when he hit the street and Dan who headed left, followed. Joe hoped they could find their way back to their lodgings which they did quickly. Joe was grateful for that he didn't enjoy the streetscape, too many windows, too many prying eyes, you didn't know who was looking at you or from where. Give me the forest and the land any time thought Joe at least there you had a better feel for your surrounds. But Joe realised it was horses for courses, he was sure some of the Dublin Brigade wouldn't like to find themselves in the forest defending themselves.

The taciturn IRA man at the lodging where they stayed was still his silent self, he gave them two meals that day but when he was asked anything he usually replied with a grunt and told them nothing. They decided to call him Smiley and they just played cards most of the day. At nine that night Smiley called them into one bedroom and gave them the outline of the planned attack, he had a sheet of paper with a plan scrawled on it.

    "Okay here's what we have. This is the barracks beside the canal and on the other side are two buildings which we have access to." Joe saw the map and followed the man's finger pointing out the landmarks they still didn't know, his name which he wouldn't divulge. "At seven am the soldiers have their morning parade, there'll be one hundred or more of them in the parade ground here and they'll be sitting ducks for our marksmen. They tell me you're pretty good shooters you two." He looked at Joe and Dan as if confirming what he had just said. Joe shrugged and replied,

"Well in the country side you don't get too many chances for a second shot there's too many places to hide." It was all he could think to say. The IRA man grunted, that would have to do.

"There'll be twenty of you going into the buildings, some on the roof. You'll be there at six thirty am just before parade time and when given the order just start shooting at the parade ground." He made it sound so simple and most plans were until you had to execute them.

"One problem," Joe said smiling, "we don't have any rifles."

"They'll be given to you and you'll be woken up early on the day and on your way. After the ambush, which won't last too long, because the Staters will start with their Lewis guns on you and you'll all be leaving quickly so you don't get trapped in the building. Someone will take your rifles and you'll walk to Macauley's Bakery in Grafton Street, you will be put in a van and taken out of the city. Don't stop until you get to the Bakery. Understood?"

Both men nodded, they had no questions now but when the shooting started, they certainly would,

"Why does General O'Malley want us in on the fight?"

"You'd have to ask him that but I'm pretty sure he wants to see what some of you country folk are made of. Also he wants you to tell your commander that there is a real war going on in Dublin as well. Plus we need all the help we can get." What Smiley didn't tell them was that Dublin was also running short of soldiers and O'Malley decided to use them while they were there. Smiley left them and they didn't see him again, such was the need for secrecy and keeping on the move when you're constantly on the run and hiding. "You'll stay here for a couple of days, we're not sure what day the attack will be but keep yourself busy learning about weapons and doing your drills." They would have two days to fill in and would have preferred to be on their way, but when you're given orders you don't question them.

On the third day, they received dreadful news about General O"Malley and were devastated. They hoped they hadn't contributed to his capture. That wasn't the case since O'Malley was probably the most wanted man in Dublin and there were many trying to find him which they eventually did. The cottage where he was staying was attacked by Free State troopers. Not wanting to make the house a battleground O'Malley fired off his revolver and ran into the back yard looking to escape via a lane there. He was too late and there were too many soldiers. He was cut down with at least four bullets entering his body. By some miracle he was not killed but taken to hospital for operations. His war was effectively over and he would remain a prisoner until the end of the next year while also escaping execution.

Joe and Dan were shattered by the news. They had been inspired by O'Malley and felt his courage and dignity during their talks. He would be a major loss to the movement. Their contact came to them that night.

"The city is in an uproar because of O'Malley's capture, he's in hospital and will be for a while. We've decided to give the city something else to think about in two days time. That's when we'll make our move. They'll know that the Republicans are still around by the time we have finished."

Joe and Dan kept themselves busy the next day pulling apart rifles and revolvers and putting them back together again and playing cards. The night before the raid on the barracks they slept poorly and as expected, were woken early the next morning with a loud knock on the door.

"It's time." Joe and Dan got their things together and met a group downstairs. It was pitch black outside and four other men were waiting for them. They didn't recognize any of them but the head man introduced himself as Tim and welcomed them to the group,

"You're well recommended boys." He said referring to General O'Malley no doubt. The officer looked at the other men, received a couple of silent nods and said, "Right let's go." With that they went into the darkness at the back of the building into a laneway and made their way single file to their destination which was fifteen minutes walk away.

Joe and Dan followed the rest of the group to some old buildings next to the Grand Canal and went inside and up the stairs to the top floor which was three flights of stairs. It looked to Joe like a disused warehouse with boxes and sacks strewn around the floor. Four of the men took a door out onto the roof and signaled for Joe to follow them and for Dan to stay inside the building with the others. It was still dark outside but the cloud was thinning out and the sun was battling to make its presence felt. The six men on the roof went to the edge of the building and one, who Joe recognized as Tim, said to Joe,

"Keep your head down and move slowly but look over that way." He handed Joe a pair of binoculars and pointed to the canal side of the building. Joe couldn't see much until his eyes became accustomed to the gloom. He could see that they were above and on the opposite side of the canal from what he was soon told was Wellington Barracks.

It had high walls around it but within was a parade ground and a number of other buildings two of which housed Republican prisoners who had been picked up by the Staters in the previous weeks. Joe gave the binoculars back to Tim and as he watched over the edge of the roof, he could see soldiers coming out of the buildings and lining up to receive the orders of the day. There were probably one hundred soldiers in the parade ground. Joe by this time had his rifle primed and noticed one of the IRA men had a Lewis Machine gun and the others were all armed. Tim had given them instructions: On his command they would all open fire on the parade ground across the canal, as would the men on the floor below. They waited about five minutes.

"Right now, fire away lads." The roof erupted with a volley of rifle fire and the Lewis gun though not accurate over long distance could certainly scatter a large number of bullets over the area very quickly. Joe joined in the firing and suddenly felt the terror and excitement of combat action again, it was as if someone had flicked a switch and he was a soldier again. They could see the soldiers on the parade ground running in all directions looking for a place to hide. The firing kept up for around fifteen minutes. Joe could see dust rising every time a bullet hit the ground and most of the firing was random as the soldiers were now out of sight as they had moved to safe cover. But a few were lying on the ground obviously wounded or dead. Joe wasn't sure if he had hit anyone as soon as one shot was fired you had to ready the next one. After about ten minutes machine gun fire was returned from the barracks and individual rifle fire as well. The soldiers had overcome their initial shock and had finally armed themselves and started firing into the building opposite from where the attack came. Joe could hear the screams of the officers pushing the young soldiers to fight back. Fire was exchanged for perhaps another five minutes when Joe heard Tim shout,

"Right lads that will do, let's get out of here." Consistent with the nature of the war they were fighting it was hit and run. They wouldn't stay to try and hold off the soldiers who would shortly storm their building otherwise it would have ended with them in a siege and all being captured or killed.

Joe found Dan on the way down and Tim gave them their instructions when they reached the ground floor,

"Leave your rifles at the door, someone will pick them up, you have been told how to get to Grafton Street and that bakery?" Joe and Dan nodded both hoping they wouldn't get lost in the maze of laneways in inner Dublin but they had been told which lanes to use, "Right we'll be going the other way, don't draw attention to yourselves and you should be alright. Good luck." With that Tim had gone and Joe and Dan followed him out the door. They could still hear rifle fire peppering the upper parts of the building from the barracks as they took the direction Tim had pointed in. It was a dark lane that offered plenty of doorways and little light. They kept to the sides constantly looking back and wondering when a lorry load of soldiers would descend on them. But Tim had given them the best getaway option. He knew what direction the soldiers would come from and sent Joe and Dan the opposite way. After they had been walking for five minutes, they started to feel safer. If you're stopped, Tim had told them, just say you're on your way to the bakery and you are both delivery men, the bakery will back up your story. Another three lanes were walked and the last led onto a main street which Joe recognized from earlier. There were still many damaged buildings which had been left in ruins. They were now obviously lost and had confused the instructions they had been given. Joe said to Dan,

"We'll walk along here for a while then we take the second left lane. That might take us to Grafton Street" It was said more in hope then anticipation and Dan was in awe of Joe's supposed sense of direction. But Joe's next words betrayed his concern. "Don't worry Dan if that's not the one we'll find it soon enough."

He touched Dan's elbow and urged him along to hurry them both up, the streets were starting to fill with people going to their factories and offices and shops which made Joe feel safer. After another ten minutes walk there it was, Grafton Street and Joe could see the bakery.

"That's the one let's get inside." Down the lane beside the bakery they found a door which opened and they went in, a young man covered in white flour challenged them,

"What d'ya want?" It was Dan this time who answered

"Ernie O'Malley said we could get a loaf of bread here." The baker looked at him for a few seconds while the message sank in and he signaled for them to follow him past the hot ovens into another room, and another wait,

"Have you come via the Barracks?" the man asked, Joe and Dan looked at each other and wondered how the news could have travelled before them, Joe answered with a nod and the bakery man said,

"Good days work it seems, stay here, someone will come and get you soon."

Joe and Dan sat on hessian bags of white flour, exhausted and grateful to be safe at least for now. It was only then that they started to process what they had been involved in that the reality of their situation sank in.

"Jesus Joe," said Dan "I hope they can get us out of this godforsaken city and back home, I'm buggered I know that." Dan's exposure to danger had been a little less than Joe's during their Flying Column activities. He was a steadfast Republican but after six months on the run his nerves were starting to fray and it was clear he didn't like Dublin. Joe understood how he felt and wanted to give him hope.

"O'Malley knows what he's doing and he wants us to get back to Tom and give him the message about the supplies, he'll deliver us home alright. I'm sure he would have organized everything for us before he was arrested, he doesn't leave much to chance."

Dan seemed less than convinced but trusted Joe enough to calm down a little,

"Joe, see if our friend inside knows what's happening. I don't want to sit here all day waiting for the Staters to pick us up."

"Okay Dan, wait here I'll see if he knows anything." Joe was gone about five minutes and came back to Dan with a smile on his face, "He says there'll be a truck leaving within an hour for deliveries for another bakery they own and we'll be on it, though not in a front seat. We'll be under some bags of flour." And so, they would be. The bakery manager would put them in the truck first and load thirty bags of flour around them and sundry other items keeping them out of sight of any cursory search. Joe told Dan the plan while they were waiting,

"We'll be dropped off on the edge of the city and then it will be shank's pony for us for a while but we might be able to hitch or catch a rail to get us back to near Athlone." Dan nodded, he couldn't wait to see the back of the city and its grime and decaying buildings. He didn't see any of the beauty that some had described to him many years earlier. Perhaps he thought, it had all been blown up by the war. As promised, the bakery manager summoned them to a loading dock, where a truck was being loaded,

"Hop in and keep out of sight and don't speak or make any noise especially when the truck's stopped. Understood?" his tone was harsh; his business was at risk if he was found helping IRA men escape. Dan and Joe did as they were told and were soon surrounded by bags of flour and loose hessian bags, enough to hide beneath at least. They set off with the truck crashing gears and bumping down the road towards the River Liffey which they soon crossed and head west towards the edge of the city. After nearly an hour and cursing the driver for hitting every bump he could, they heard the rear door open,

"This is it boys, you're on your own from here but it's a quiet area and no soldiers or coppers around, keep safe and stay out of sight as much as possible." He was pointing towards a road that would take them to the rural area just outside Dublin, "down there about half a mile you'll find the fields, head into them and keeping going west. Do you think you'll find Athlone?" he was almost making a joke but Joe nodded, they had gotten this far they weren't going to get lost now.

"Thanks," was all Joe said and Dan nodded agreement. It was now mid morning and people would be well and truly about their business but they didn't see anyone around as they made a fast walk to the fields the man had promised. They made the fields safely and Joe noticed the stone fences and bush hedges. It was the same type of area he and Sean and others had spent time amongst when they were fighting the Tans. In fact, they appeared the same all over the country. He allowed himself an inner smile as he remembered the times they had worked together to save each other's lives, it seemed a long time ago now.

Though rural Ireland had many features, it tended to be dominated by farmed fields, hedges, stone fences and expanses of green, some with crop some without to keep the sheep fed. Joe didn't like the idea of walking all day as they would more easily be spotted and arouse suspicion, he saw a wooded area not too far away and nodded to Dan,

" That's our home for the day we can start walking later when it starts to get dark." Dan nodded agreement, as long as they were headed towards home, he was happy to be moving.

They had only been walking for a couple of minutes and Joe threw Dan to the ground hitting him with a tackle that would get him in a rugby team,

"Sorry Dan but I've seen something and I didn't want to shout. Over there near the road that we just left; do you see a vehicle?" Dan lifted his head a couple of inches not wanting to become a target, he raised the peak of his cap and could see a car that looked too much like a police car for his liking. There were three uniformed men standing around it looking into the field that Joe and Dan were hiding in, "I hope to God they didn't see us otherwise they'll be coming after us." Joe said unsure if they had been spotted or if it was a routine patrol. They had no option but to stay as still as possible and hope they were out of sight from the road. Joe calculated that the woods were still about two hundred yards away from them, a long way to crawl but they might have to.

"What the hell are they doing Joe? They must have been tipped off by someone local who saw us get out of the baker's truck." It was a reasonable assumption to make, people were nervous all over the country and no one knew who they could rely on. They didn't know the area well enough to know if it was IRA friendly or not, but the presence of the police wasn't promising.

"They're still a long way off Dan let's crawl while we can and keep the long grass between us and them with any luck, they won't see us." Joe noticed one stone fence between them and the woods and two hedges which would be easier to get through, they didn't want to have to jump over a stone wall in broad daylight. "Let's head for that hedge, it'll give us better cover anyway." Joe led off on his belly, his training camp days coming back to him though he had never imagined himself having to crawl along the ground to save his life though the camp trainers insisted it would be very likely in their line of work.

They stopped every ten yards straining to hear if they had been spotted, hoping they were still okay but not prepared to put their head above the long grass. They then pushed on for another fifty yards. They reached the first hedge without incident but Joe noticed they had left a trail of flattened grass that was an obvious giveaway if the trackers got that close. At least the hedge would give enough cover to enable Joe to look back towards the road to see what was happening. They were on the far side of the hedge away from the road and Joe carefully got on his knees to get more height and see what was happening. As soon as he did, he wished he hadn't. There was now another vehicle with another two policemen so there were five of them apparently debating what direction to start searching in. If they came their way, Joe knew it wouldn't take them long to cover the distance. Joe could see a civilian talking to the policemen and luckily for Joe and Dan he seemed confused and was pointing to a field south to where they hid behind the hedge. Joe watched as closely as he could, confident he couldn't be seen behind the hedge. Finally, the five police fanned out and headed in the opposite direction away from the two fugitives.

"Thanks be to God," said Joe as much to himself as Dan, "Come on Dan more crawling, the silly buggers have been sent in the wrong direction, maybe that farmer was a Republican after all." Joe had no way of knowing but they would take advantage of the lucky break. After another hundred yards of crawling they were within fifty of the woods, Joe put his head up and the searching Garda were nowhere to be seen, "Let's go Dan, we'll make a run for those trees." Dan was already on his legs and running like a champion racehorse. Joe never knew he possessed such speed. They reached the tree line almost at the same time, Joe also finding speed in his legs he thought he had long lost. They crashed to the ground and sort out cover anxious to see if they had been spotted. There was still no sight of the five police though Joe thought he saw some movement in a distant field.

"We'll have to push into these woods as far as we can, if they come this way, they'll find our tracks and know we're up here. Can you push on lad?" Dan nodded in agreement though the expression on his face belied any joy in his chosen lifestyle. After walking another sixty minutes the woods grew denser. They had been dropped towards the south-west of Dublin as there were more hills and woods even though it meant a longer walk to head back to Westmeath. But it offered more places to hide, more likely to come across a Republican camp now than the police. They had no time to look for or admire the ancient monuments from the much earlier inhabitants of the area which Joe had heard about in his younger years at school. Maybe one day thought Joe, I'll come back and have a long walk in these mountains and enjoy the view. Finally, Dan said,

"Let's have a break Joe, I need a drink and a rest." They came across a fresh water stream coursing through the wood and both lay on their stomachs to get their fill then they ate some plain bread rolls given to them at the bakery. As he ate Dan looked at Joe with a pained expression, "How long do you think the IRA can keep up this pace Joe? I'm as loyal as any man but if we have to keep fighting like this for much longer, we'll be buggered in more ways than one."

Joe knew he was right and nodded in agreement but they were on a treadmill and someone else was in charge of the running of it. He had no idea how or when they would get off. For the time being, it was a fight for survival but not for victory, that looked further away than ever.

After a short rest they pushed on confident that they had left any danger behind, the approaching darkness would give them more protection. Athlone was more than forty miles away cross country and they would have to walk most of the way, finding any food or shelter where they could.

CHAPTER 33
Sean Handed a New Task

Captain Sean McKeon was now a senior officer of one of the largest National Army bases in Ireland based in Athlone's Custume Barracks. While his boyhood friends and Tan War comrades were doing their best to gain a Republic, Sean was building an impressive military career.

The National government's intent was to not only cut the head off the snake of the IRA but destroy its whole body. Arrests of possible IRA men were relentlessly carried out and sweeps of groups of men who were suspects continued. The prisons became more and more crowded. There had already been one riot and Sean's command had assisted the wardens. Now he was summoned to see his CO General MacEoin and was advised of a new task.

The newly police force, the Civic Guard had replaced the RIC (Royal Irish Constabulary) and its job was to maintain civil harmony and enforce the basic rules of society. Its name would later be changed to the Garda Síochána na hÉireann. Arresting thieves, keeping domestic order and all the other matters the police forces need to do. It was the Provisional Government's idea not to arm the new Guard, they did not want them compared to the RIC. The RIC had virtually been at war with the IRA and the people during the War of independence and were associated in people's minds with the hated Black and Tans and the Auxiliaries.

The IRA had treated the RIC as the enemy and since they were armed it simply escalated the violence. The thinking now was that an unarmed Civic Guard would not provoke the IRA who would let them go about their civic duty except it didn't always work out that way. It was everyday people who simply didn't want a new police force as well as a National Army ordering them about.

Consequently, the Guard lacked the necessary physical and moral force to ensure public peace and needed assistance from the Army or the Staters as the IRA preferred to call them. This was particularly the case in the rural areas where the Government feared a new Land War would erupt. The people were encouraged by the IRA in their complaints and this fueled the general lawlessness of the country side. The small land holders in many cases felt dispossessed and refused to pay rents. After all, hadn't they just fought a War of Independence? The government had a fear of the countryside again collapsing into anarchy, empowering the IRA and giving them more general support. The government wasn't going to allow that to happen.

General MacEoin spoke to Sean and delivered the government's clear message,

"The Special Infantry Corp, or SIC as it will be known, has been put in place to confirm any special laws made by the Government and to assist the Civic Guard with a show of force when necessary. There is a lot of freelancing activity out there, much of it inspired by the Irregulars but also by brigands and gangsters who are refusing to accept the new Provisional Government's right to put laws in place. You will head up a company of around fifty soldiers, many of whom will be new to you as we don't want too many of our existing men to be involved." Sean was a little puzzled,

"Why not General, they know the area and they know the people." It was the response MacEoin was expecting.

"Precisely, but we feel a new bunch of soldiers will be more accepted. We're trying to make the people in the community accept the new status quo and respect our authority." This was quite a challenge as the army was tolerated but not respected due to the constant searches for IRA members. "But this force will be specific and focused on certain issues not just the Irregulars. The SIC will be needed to back up the Guard and make sure that farmers particularly can go about their business without threat from squatters and brigands. You will be in charge even though you are locally known because we don't want outside officers coming in and riding roughshod over everything we've achieved for the past year. You will cover at least three counties, Westmeath, Roscommon and Longford and you will move around as necessary and as required with a base here in Athlone. So, I'm charging you with those two tasks, one, keep the SIC effective, tight and under control and two, earn the respect of the people you will be enforcing laws on and for."

Sean accepted the new command with mixed feelings. He was an officer and it was his job to carry out orders of his commanders but he still had unfinished business with the IRA. Particularly with the Drumraney Flying Column which still evaded him. He had heard it was now back in the area and hiding in the forests and hills and outlaw farms of Westmeath. But orders were orders, for the present the Column would have to wait.

On patrols with the new group Sean stood back from confrontation with local landholders and let the senior SIC men make their presence felt. Sean was willing to step in if more authority was needed and a local face would assist. However, for many of the land disputes there were no easy solutions and everyone involved would end up unpopular with one side or the other. IRA men had in some cases just confiscated farms from people they had suspected helped the enemy. Now that the Civic Guard and the

SIC were available, the original farmers enlisted their help to get their farms back. It was ugly work and rarely simple, it was one's word against the other with both sides appearing believable. The arguments were compounded by the rural nature of the disputes. Farmers lived their lives away from the towns and cities and developed different attitudes to authority and the rule of law. The past few years had brought a wild west element to dispute settlement and the side with the biggest gun often had the loudest voice.

But Sean took it all in and considered whatever he did as more training for the senior role he saw himself reaching in the National Army. It was also educational to watch the civic arguments from government reach into the disputes and try to make a settlement. Up to this time, it was the army insisting on its solution and that was it, but everyone realised that would eventually have to change and civil society must play a role. It would be a slow and painful process.

What was more straightforward for the SIC was the crackdown on the criminal enterprise of the poitin menace, as it was called by the SIC. Poitin or as it was later known poteen, was the illegal manufacture of sprits and liquor which would be sold direct to consumers with little restriction and no government taxes or oversight.

In one area of Longford, Sean's SIC group led a raid with the Guard on a suspect village and broke up several poitin stills. The raids weren't very popular with the local distillers one of whom recognized Sean from the Tan war days.

"Sure, and a man like yourself from a good family of republicans shouldn't be working with the Guard, you're a disgrace to the whole movement."

"And what movement would that be Shamus?" asked Sean now recognizing the man who had verballed him.

"The Republican Movement. I can remember meetings when I saw you clapping and cheering speaker after speaker and even Dev when he called on us to fight for our Republic."

Sean didn't want to get into a side argument but felt he had to set his record straight.

"That's an old argument Shamus, we all had to pick our sides and I picked mine and I know I'm on the right side." The man wouldn't be convinced by logical argument in any case but Sean made his point and he continued. "So, you think the Republic will be built on the back of illegal whisky?"

Shamus was never one to walk away from an argument and wouldn't this time irrespective of the rank of the man in front of him.

"We need to eat and sleep and feed ourselves and have a drink without the government taking everything from us, we need our dignity not just our whisky." Plenty of heads nodded in agreement from Shamus' side. But Sean knew where he stood and what his job was.

"Well you can do that but you'll have to pay taxes to do it, the government doesn't run on thin air." Shamus took the opening and riposted,

"No, it runs on hot air and needs money to pay soldiers who destroy other Irishmen's livelihoods" with that Shamus spat on the ground indicating he'd made his point and wasn't going to go further. Sean just nodded to the Guards to go ahead and confiscate the equipment and pour the liquids onto the ground, he knew the poitin trade was part of the Irregulars fund raising efforts and for that reason alone it had to be contained.

He watched as his men and the Guards who took the lead in this civic matter rounded up the equipment plus two men chosen for arrests. He then felt a tug on his sleeve and turned for his sergeant to give him an envelope which he saw was from MacEoin at Athlone barracks, he tore it open and read the brief note,

"Take your leave from SIC and return to Athlone, there's been a sighting you need to follow up."

CHAPTER 34
Arms From Dublin

It had taken Dan and Joe a number of days to make it back to the outskirts of Athlone and to the Republican owned farm that still enabled them to hide out. They were hungry and dirty and tired, all that time on the run had exhausted them and they were looking forward to someone else keeping watch for them while they rested. Joe saw Tom McGiff almost instantly and was surprised at the look of him, for a man who always took pride in his appearance Tom was looking almost scrawny, clearly the war was taking its toll on him. They had been at this now for nearly six months and the reserves of resilience were wearing down.

"Tom, good to see you man, how is it all?" Joe tried to sound more upbeat than he felt at least he had some good news for Tom from Dublin about supplies. Tom embraced Joe and Dan.

"Good to see you boys again, we hadn't heard what was going on, we have to rely on gossip and most of that is made up of course. Someone told us the Staters had picked you up, we weren't expecting so see you so soon. But we're told so many stories we don't know what to believe."

"Not that they didn't try "Joe said, "but we managed to shake them thanks to some help from some good Republicans. How are things faring here?" Joe looked around at the run-down farm which was in need of a good deal of work.

"Not good Joe, to be honest, the Staters and the Garda have been giving us hell, we barely have enough time to get back here and have a break. We go on some raids and it seems they know what we're doing and where we are going. It's not like it was in the Tan war Joe, we can't trust too many people any more. They're all in it for themselves and us Republicans can go to hell as far as many of them care." Tom was more downhearted than Joe had imagined but the group of men he surveyed did look weary and he hated to admit, almost defeated. Tom continued, "the problem is Joe we don't hear much from Headquarters, we don't know if we're winning or losing. Any papers we see are full of stories about how well the government forces are doing. You're the first new people we've seen in a week."

Joe thought Tom needed to be drawn away from the problems he was outlining. It can't be easy keeping positive when they had to live the way they did away from their families all the time. Joe proceeded to tell Tom and a few of the others what had transpired since they last saw them. Their trek to Dublin, their run ins with troops on the train then the meetings with Ernie O'Malley and his subsequent arrest. They told about the attack on the barracks in Dublin and finally how they had made their way home. Tom was impressed but disappointed about the news of O'Malley, but Joe saw his enthusiasm lift at Joe's next news,

"Can they send us anything Joe? We're running out of everything we need to be effective."
Joe smiled and looked at Dan and Tom,

"Well we can now tell you the really good news, O'Malley says he'll have the supplies you want at the old mill near Kilbeggan on the twelfth which I think is the day after tomorrow if the calendar in my head still works." The twelfth would be two weeks from when O'Malley promised the supplies for McGiff's column. Joe hoped O'Malley had been able to organise what he had promised before his arrest otherwise this Column was out of the fight.

"That's grand Joe, we can head over there tomorrow after you and Dan have had a good rest. Go on with you now, you can give me more details later, get cleaned up, have something to eat and a good sleep, we'll keep post for you." Tom embraced Joe again and pointed him towards the barn, "Sure Mrs Farrell has some good rabbit stew on the burner as always."

Joe and Dan were happy to take their leave, now that they were able to relax, the more they realised how tired they were. Joe put his arm around Dan's shoulders,

"Told you we'd make it Dan, just need to keep putting one foot after the other for as long as possible. " He smiled and Dan nodded in agreement. He was looking forward to the rest and hopefully a bed for a change instead of the forest floor for a mattress. What Joe hadn't told Dan was more news which Tom had told him separately. Four IRA men had been executed by firing squad in Kilmainham Gaol and others were planned. The government kept its promise that any IRA prisoner could be summarily executed by the State if they had been captured bearing arms. There was no more dangerous time to be in the IRA than the present.

CHAPTER 35
Kilbeggan

As Tom McGiff had warned Joe, he had found it more and more difficult to find Republican supporters they could rely on. The Civil War was six months in and the people, Tom felt, had had more than enough of the situations and the shortages and the violence. For the people, the dream of wanting a Republic was less in their thinking now. They were becoming more content with the limited option the Provisional Government offered. The Staters had made the Republican supporters life hell and they were no longer reliable.

As much as the Dublin Brigade leaders wanted to help Tom's Column, they couldn't do it without involving a number of others in the chain of supply from Dublin to Athlone and Mullingar. It was almost impossible to keep the movement of any substantial cache of arms a secret. Men had to be involved who Dublin never knew and they in turn had to rely on others. O'Malley had been adamant to Joe and Dan that he would get a supply of what he had promised to McGiff into Kilbeggan, drawing supplies for wherever he could. The day before he was captured, he went to arrange the supplies for McGiff's Column. He had to enlist and then virtually threaten the Quartermaster in Dublin who always shook his head when he was asked for anything. This time O'Malley lost his temper,

"For God's sake man how do you expect we can fight a war without guns and ammunitions and explosives in the places we need them?" The Quartermaster was sympathetic as always and continued to look at the list that O'Malley had given him and where he wanted it delivered.

"It won't be done easily Ernie, we don't have a delivery service. We just have volunteers who are constantly watching their backs for Staters and Garda. It's slow work and we need more time." But shortly after, the Quartermaster found some arms for the men in Westmeath and for the now wounded and hospitalised Ernie O'Malley's sake he would do his best to deliver them.

Now that O'Malley was out of the picture Tom McGiff knew they were in the hands of an IRA bureaucracy that was fast running out of funds and support and volunteers but they had no option but to go to Kilbeggan in any case and hope for the best.

Tom's Flying Column was always in the minds of the Athlone command of the National Army and as fate would have it, Sean McKeon was now aware of their movements due to an informer. He had told him of the Flying Column and its likely movement to Kilbeggan and the reasons for the move.

Like most informants, Harry Kelly was motivated for several different reasons. He felt insulted when as a member of the IRA Athlone Brigade, 3 Company, whose CO was Tom McGiff, that he had been found not capable of joining the Flying Column. Harry had a troublesome leg and a limp he had sustained stopping a Tan bullet in a barracks raid in early 1921. Tom had let him down as kindly as possible,

"Your leg would never hold up man, sometimes we walk for ten hours at a time and if we're lucky we'll find somewhere warm to sleep otherwise it's the forest floor with a lump of wood for a pillow.' Harry protested but Tom couldn't jeopardise the Column by bringing along someone who wasn't fit enough for the rigours of guerrilla warfare in the hills. Harry wouldn't be able to join.

Harry Kelly had aging parents and siblings and his own family who he was responsible for. His occasional talks with Colonel Lawler, an officer senior to Sean at the barracks, whom Harry had met in an Athlone pub had slowly turned him into a pro Treaty man. But in truth it was his ego and manhood that he felt had been compromised by his rejection from the Column. He believed at the time he could have contributed to the struggle and wanted to. A festering resentment for Tom McGiff grew within him over the past months and when the chance came to settle what he felt was an old score he took it.

"So where does the information come from Harry?" Sean asked the informer who had been passed along to Sean by Lawler. But he was not prepared to give any names, he knew it could get back to him and he had to cover himself.

"It's just pub talk Sean, you know the kind, someone hears a bit of gossip and talks to someone else and soon enough the whole village is in on the secret. So, I don't know exactly who told me or where I heard it but it's good information."

"And that's why you were able to pass it on to General MacEoin?" which is where Sean had heard it from.

"I wouldn't have bothered the General if I didn't think it wasn't good enough. But it wasn't the General, it was Lawler his sidekick." Sean was well aware that Lawler his immediate superior in the barracks and a close confidant of MacEoins fancied himself an Intelligence expert. He kept a stable of informants in Athlone and surrounding areas. Most of who fed him lies in the hope of getting a free Guinness when they came across him in a pub. But Sean had to admit that from time to time his information proved useful and accurate otherwise they wouldn't have been able to keep sweeping up IRA suspects in the three counties around them.

This time Lawler had passed the informer on to Sean because he had mentioned Tom McGiff and Joe Keegan whom he knew Sean keenly sought.

"So, it was recent like, the last few days and they mentioned Kilbeggan around this time of the month? Are you sure Harry? We don't like to send soldiers on wild goose chases we need good reasons to mount searches." All of which amused Harry who felt like most of his countrymen that these things were done on the slightest pretence, to keep the men busy and look as if they were in charge.

"All I can say, Sean is all I can say. That's the time and place and I hope you get that upstart McGiff, he's got it coming." Sean was aware of Kelly's motives and the hatred for McGiff but he was surprised that he would serve him up on a plate. Still it was information he needed and it was less than three days old and he was obliged to follow it up. He slipped two One Pound notes to Kelly hating himself for doing so. If the man had done the same thing in the Tan War Sean would have gladly put a bullet behind his ear and not felt a twinge of remorse.

CHAPTER 36
Kilbeggan Ambush

Tom McGiff decided to take just three men to Kilbeggan to see if the arms cache had arrived. Joe and Dan volunteered, sure the good news they bad brought back from Dublin would prove correct. They set off on foot mid-morning, Joe and Dan having recovered from their visit to Dublin. They had to visit a nearby village before they could collect anything. There was a Republican contact there, Ned Irwin a strong IRA man, who Joe had worked with before. He would have been informed from Dublin where the goods would be and he could supply a truck to take them and the goods back to their camp. But Ned had other news as well:

"There's been a report of a Staters lorry going through late last night and a bunch of soldiers on board, it might be routine but you might keep an extra eye out Tom, the buggers have been like flies around a dead carcass lately."

McGiff wasn't surprised to hear the news there was always troops on the move which is why they kept to the fields as much as possible. Taking the arms back to near Drumraney would require the use of roads which made him ask.

"What have you got to hide the load Ned?"

"We'll have a load of hay they won't be wanting to move if we're stopped, it'll hide whatever you have to hide." Ned had been in the IRA through the Tan wars and had a good reputation and like many men of his type hadn't accepted the Treaty and would hold out for his Republic. He was always relied on to make his lorry available for runs like this. Plus his group had a radio to receive messages from Dublin and elsewhere. He had been told to meet another truck near a Republican farm two miles on the south side of Kilbeggan. The meeting would be late at night to reduce the chance of any sightings.

McGiff had his plans but as usual they had to be highly vigilant. They were to meet the other truck, load Ned Irwin's lorry and get out of the area as quickly as possible it was all to be done in the dark and without much knowledge of the roads. Tom hoped Irwin could be relied on to get them out of the area safely. Like all groups like this they had to rely on spotty intelligence reports from loyal supporters but it was a fraught process. McGiff addressed his three men,

"Well we'll be relying on Ned but he's a good man and knows the area. But the usual rules apply if we're surprised by the Staters; it's every man for himself. Shoot what you can and get out if you can and head back to Drumraney, the less the Staters have for any effort the better."

Joe and Dan and the third man, Kevin nodded agreement. They were all experienced at night time work and finding their way around. Being on the run had sharpened their sense of survival. Hopefully, it would be business as usual and they'd be back to Drumraney and ready to wreak havoc with whatever Dublin had delivered.

"Right let's get underway", said McGiff. It was now nine thirty and they had a forty-minute drive to the rendezvous farm. The four men climbed into the back of the truck and covered themselves with the loose hay that Ned had prepared. Their rifles ready to be fired in case they were stopped on the way. They endured the bumpy ride with good humour and Dan remarked at that point the driver must have found every rough spot he could. It was obvious that the springs on the back of the truck weren't made for passengers lying on the bare boards!

They had been driving for about thirty minutes when all hell broke loose. The truck has just rounded a bend on the unsealed road and swerved violently to the right throwing the men in the back against each other and the side of the truck. The men strained to hear what was happening they could just hear a voice and knew it was Ned's and he was violently abusing someone.

"Why would you leave that truck there in the middle of the track you could kill someone, you blithering idiot." but Ned was just stalling for time and as a prearranged signal he thumped his fist on the window as the back of his cabin. The next voice they heard was an order and from a soldier,

"Get out of the truck and lay on the ground, where are you going anyway?" At this point Tom knew what was happening, they had been ambushed and he expected there would be more than one or two soldiers outside.

"Okay boys get ready, it's every man for himself, on my count of three make a run for it and good luck. Okay, one, two three.... GO!" The four men jumped up shedding the hay and trying to get their rifles into position. They followed Tom's lead, he was first off the truck and the road was now lit by the headlights of the Stater's truck. He could count at least eight soldiers around the vehicle but his rifle was at the ready.

"Stay where you are and drop your weapons." It was a vaguely familiar voice to Joe and Tom but they didn't have time to think about anything. Tom fired from the hip towards the lights hoping to hit them and bring some darkness. "Stop now or we open fire," came the shout, but Tom had by this time jumped down from the truck and headed for the undergrowth with a hail of bullets after him. Joe could see the soldiers taking aim and firing after Tom and he feared the three of them wouldn't get out of the truck alive. He turned to his two companions,

"Throw the rifles over the side and get rid of any pistols, don't let them catch you with them. You can make a run for it if you fancy your chances but there must be ten of them out there." Dan nodded but Kevin decided he'd take his chances, threw his rifle over the side of the truck and went into the other direction from Tom but he was cut down before he could run ten yards. Joe couldn't see Tom, maybe he'd made it out of the lit-up area but he could see three soldiers still firing in the direction he had run. Then Joe and Dan were told to put their hands up before they could jump down. They saw Ned Irwin held by two soldiers away from the truck, his face was bleeding and had obviously stopped a rifle butt at some point.

Joe could now make out more as his eyes got used to the light. There in front of him on the ground with his pistol drawn and pointed straight at Joe was Sean McKeon in full uniform the other soldiers were all aiming their rifles at Joe and Dan.

"Well this is a nice way to meet again Joe Keegan, why don't you get down from that tray and say hello." Sean was always keen to make smart arse statements and his satisfaction at finally cornering Joe Keegan was manifest in his mood on that cold night in the forest, "Sorry to upset your night drive through the woods but you see we have been expecting you for some time." Sean signaled for his men to drag Joe and Dan down and push them to the ground to be searched. Neither of them was carrying a pistol and they had rid themselves of their rifles though Sean would know they had belonged to them. Summary execution of captives was not unknown by Staters and the penalty for carrying arms against the State was death, but the charges could be trumped up anyway to suit the arresting officers.

Joe knew they had been betrayed and that for the time being at least, his war for a Republic was over and all at the hands of his onetime best friend.

For the first time he could remember Joe was lost for words. He badly wanted to answer back to Sean and put him down with some smart remark. His mood was moving between anger at being caught, anger at whoever betrayed them, and disappointment that they wouldn't be able to continue their struggle. He just shook his head knowing no words would satisfy him, he was thinking that at least Tom McGiff must have gotten away as he couldn't see him being dragged back to the truck. Tom was always a fast runner Joe remembered from whenever he had to mark him in a Hurley match. Joe had been caught too many times striking at thin air where Tom had just been standing.

Finally, after he was allowed to stand up, he could see Sean face to face and he looked him directly in the eyes. Sean held his gaze and the two former friends processed a thousand thoughts and memories of earlier days. Joe was first to speak,

"Jaysus Sean, how did it come to this?" then added shaking his head, "and how did you come to be wearing that uniform?"

Sean allowed himself another smile, perhaps more of a smirk Joe decided,

"Joe, there's no point in going over that ground again, we both know how we got here, and we always knew it would end up something like this, you just chose the wrong side." Then to his men, "Take them away. We'll talk again back in Athlone eh Joe?" Like the cat that had finally got the canary, Sean climbed into the front seat of the lorry, Joe heard him ask the driver about the fourth man and where was he? The driver just shook his head in the negative, now it was Joe's turn to smile. Tom McGiff had been able to get away and with what remained of his Flying Column he would give Sean many more headaches before they caught up with him again.

Joe and Dan were thrown into the back of the truck they had come in. Ned Irwin was made to drive the cantankerous old machine but this time with two soldiers crammed in beside him. Kevin's body was thrown in beside Joe and Dan and five State soldiers kept them company for the drive back to Athlone. Joe was surprised at their young age of perhaps eighteen or nineteen. The Government had been accepting all comers simply to boost their numbers. Many young men needed some kind of work even if it was fighting against other Irishmen. Joe's head slumped into his hands and he turned to Dan,

"Sorry friend but we didn't talk our way out of this one, did we?" Dan looked at Joe but all he could manage was a shake of his head, they both were left to wonder what was in store for them. They were now well in the hands of their enemies and didn't expect any favours.

BOOK 4

INTERNMENT

CHAPTER 37
PRISONER

The drive back to Athlone took the best part of two hours and Joe wasn't looking forward to seeing the place again. He allowed himself a brief memory of Maggie and the times he had been able to spend with her in this town. It was the only happy memory he could recover and he indulged himself and kept her face in his mind as long as he could. He wondered how she would handle the far away land she had gone to with her sister. She had been gone a while now, Australia, God he thought, it may as well be another universe.

His peace was shattered by a heavy thump from one of the Staters rifle butts,

"Out now, we're here." Here was the grey of Custume Barracks and it was around three in the morning. The place looked and felt miserable. Joe and Dan landed on their feet and Joe tried to look as unconcerned as possible holding himself upright and staring at the state soldiers daring them to come at him.

"Get that inside," one said to Joe and Dan, he was referring to the lifeless body of Kevin their compatriot. Joe and Dan carried him in the direction they were told and tried to give him some dignity in death, but it was difficult. He was a heavy man and they were tired and freezing. They were glad to leave him on a table in what looked like a mortuary.

"This way." The Staters weren't going to let them loiter, they prodded them with their rifles and went out of the mortuary and into another building where their names were taken and they were pushed into a cell with four other men in civilian clothes. More jetsam from the Republican cause thought Joe, poor buggers have run out of places to hide no doubt. The men exchanged looks and a couple of recognition nods. There was nothing to say. They would do that later when they were all left to wallow in the shame of their captivity, knowing that their war for a Republic was over, for the time being at least.

They stayed there for perhaps an hour. Joe and Dan had been given a mug of water through the bars that was all they were going to get from this lot. Joe sat on the floor lodged against a wall hoping that he might sleep but not really expecting to. He was roused by movement outside the cell, he recognized Sean all smart and shiny in his long boots and his peaked cap and uniform. Sean was talking to one of the warders and pointed at Joe,

"That one, have him put in that empty room and make sure he's manacled and guarded. I'll be there shortly." Joe watched as the two guards opened the cell door and dragged him to a small room and literally threw him in and slammed the door behind him. Joe stopped himself from smashing into the wall but stayed on the floor searching for some peace and quiet again.

No windows, a dim light in the centre of the ceiling and a table and two chairs. Joe let out a breath, his mind in turmoil. He had spent some nights in prison before when he had been detained by the Black and Tans and given a hiding for just being who he was. Now he was feeling total despair believing that what the future held for him was a lot of time in prison at the least. More if the Provisional Government was still intent on executions to prove their point to the IRA.

The door opened and Sean walked in, no smirk this time, all business and official,

"Take a seat Joe, time we had a talk."

"You'll get nothing from me and you know it, no names, no locations, no information at all so why don't you just go and leave it be and leave me in peace."

"Peace Joe? There'll be little peace for you. If it's not me talking it will be others doing more than talking to you."

"I know how the Staters work thanks Sean, I've seen the results of talks with better men than you. You're all a disgrace to your uniform and this country, you're worse than the Tans knew how to be." Joe knew that was the worst insult that the Staters could be given. They hated being compared to the Tans who were notoriously uncaring of anything Irish.

"It's not a good idea to be insulting your prison guards Joe, if you say that to anyone else you'll get a rifle butt where it will hurt most. For Christ's sake man, just settle down and hear what I've got to say." Sean took a folded sheet of paper from his uniform pocket and spread it out in front of Joe. "We like to give anyone we bring in the chance to correct their ways. If you sign this, things will go a lot easier for you and your friend." Joe looked at the paper. He knew what it was as soon as Sean took it out. The Pledge, Joe was being asked to give up everything he believed in and swear allegiance to the Provisional Irish Government and the King of England. He looked at Sean with a pitiful scorn,

"Sweet Jesus and Mary you are asking me to sign that, here, now. You must be mad. Sure, and haven't I had enough time to sign that piece of shite before now. I won't now and I never will."

Sean tried to look bemused and took the sheet of paper back,

"I thought that is what you'd say Joe but we offer it as a matter of course, to give our prisoners the option."

"What, the option of not having the tripe beat out of them for wanting a Republic? Your government doesn't even recognize our rights, you lock up Republicans and their sympathizers without a trial. You've got thousands of men in prisons now who won't sign your God forsaken pledge, and you talk about options. God Sean you've got a short memory. A few years ago, you wouldn't have signed it yourself you had too much respect for yourself, where's that all gone?" Joe was surprised at the ill feeling he felt and was expressing to Sean. It all came pouring out of him Sean was the first non-Republican he had spoken to for a long time. It felt good to make his points and feel again his strength of commitment. But Sean wasn't buying.

"Joe I've had this discussion so many times with so many people and stronger Republicans than yourself. I'm sick of explaining myself and I won't again, I know what I am and I know what I want for Ireland and it's not a Republic. Not yet, at any rate."

"Sounds like good Michael Collins talk that Sean, they've trained you well and they've broken your spirit. Sure, all those men John McCormack talked to us about like O'Connell and Parnell, when we were kids would be spinning in their graves to see the country as it is now."

But Sean had heard all this before:

"Collins was right, he was a realist, he knew we couldn't fight on and we took whatever we could. If it was up to Dev the country would be fully occupied by the British now like the North is. The real problem Joe is that men like you and Tom McGiff won't accept when you're beaten and don't know when you are. But good luck with what happens because you're going to need it. I'm here to give you one last chance, once you leave this room, I can't do any more for you. If you sign this now, things will go better for you. Do it for old time's sake Joe if nothing else"

Joe stared at Sean with venom in his eyes and shook his head,

"No." was all he said. Sean sighed and stood up looking at Joe but couldn't find any more words. He just shook his head in despair and with that Sean left the room. It would be some time before the two former comrades would see each other again.

Joe was dragged back to his cell, no food, no water, no washing, no hygiene just despair.

The next day as Joe had expected, the men who had been arrested that day and some earlier were collected. They were marched over to the prison cells of Athlone Prison or Custume Barracks as the Army called it. There were now already over nine hundred men in the prison originally built for just two hundred! The cells were such that all the men could not lie fully down to sleep or rest and the filth from inadequate sanitary systems added to many illnesses. The Army had built cages to accommodate the growing prisoner numbers further humiliating them. Such was the treatment of the Irish government of other Irish men.

Joe saw some old friends and comrades but there was none of the usual 'Up the Republic' cry and good cheer. He was now greeted by the sad stare of defeated men who were locked away from their families, their work and their parish. Men couldn't meet his gaze and looked away when asked how the fight was going in their areas. Just a shake, and a drop of the head which told him everything. Most of the prisoners came from the western and midland counties and a few further north, their back ground was rural and farming of various kinds. They missed the open air and their homes. All of them had been picked up and imprisoned without trial or any legal process and there was usually only one charge; being a member of or being associated with other members of the IRA, an outlawed body.

It was two days after being thrown into a cell with ten others that Joe was finally let out to the so-called exercise yard. There he found what he had been hoping to see since his arrival, his brother Hugh. They embraced and Joe could feel that Hugh had lost a lot of weight and his handsome face was drawn from hunger. Hugh's eyes filled with tears and he struggled for words, but finally managed,

"Joe we thought we'd lost you."

"And I you," said Joe, "Tom McGiff told us you had been lifted but we knew nothing else." Hugh took out his tobacco pouch and they shared a rolled cigarette. They swapped stories of life on the run and betrayals and sympathies for finally being caught up in the National Government net. There would be more than time enough to talk about old times. Joe discovered from Hugh that their brother James was also a prisoner in Custume Barracks, it took Joe another few hours to find James amongst the hundreds of prisoners and they reunited with Hugh. to share their stories. Joe was horrified as James told him what happened to him.

"Tom and me were working with Da in the field, when we saw a Stater lorry pull up and six soldiers jumped down led by our old friend Sean. At first I think he thought I was you Joe he looked so happy with himself. When he realised it wasn't you he grabbed me anyway and dragged me here. Probably didn't want to waste a trip from Athlone. He has to meet his numbers I suppose."

"But had the Brigade done anything, I thought many of them had gone over to the other side?" asked Joe.

"A bunch of us were always having meetings, and created what mischief we could despite the Brigade. You didn't have to do much to get swept up to get you thrown in this hellhole." Joe had been away from the family home for some months and didn't realize that so many of his friends and neighbours were being arrested. Their main crime was their age and the potential to be recruited by the Irregulars if they hadn't been already. Even some past indiscretion such as being a member of the IRA was sufficient. For now Joe at least had some company in his misery.

CHAPTER 38
Christmas 1922

Christmas of 1922 held little interest for the now thousands of IRA men and women who were in prisons and detention camps throughout the country. Athlone's Custume Barracks was no different. It was a day they had previously celebrated with a visit to their parish church for mass and a day off from work. They could rejoice as they watched the young ones receive gifts that were all too rare in their lives.

Edicts had been handed down earlier by the Bishops of Ireland using their bully pulpits to excoriate the Republicans and their propaganda on what was best for Ireland. The prisoners could not even look forward to a Christmas mass and communion. The Catholic Church in Ireland had effectively excommunicated all members of the IRA. Many of the men and women incarcerated were devastated by this action. These were people who had spent their life in thrall of the Catholic Church and had obeyed it without question.

This Christmas for Joe and Dan and hundreds of others in Athlone prison would be more of the same discomfort that many of them had endured for the past few months living on the run. Overcrowding, poor food and water and rigid discipline from their guards was all they were offered. They busied themselves with political talks and arguments even, to reinforce their Republican fire. They would repair their own clothes and many men became proficient tailors and shoe makers and tried to keep themselves busy and healthy in a system that had forsaken them. Playing cards was always favoured and chess tournaments were popular as well. Anything to pass the time and keep their mind off their miseries.

A number of men were always contemplating and planning some form of escape from the prison and find some way to outwit the guards and the system. There were committees of longer serving prisoners who listened to any plans which were often fanciful and full of wishful thinking rather than practical solutions. The idea of escape appealed to Joe and Hugh and a number of others who came from many of the areas surrounding Athlone. Drumraney was less than ten miles away, an easy walk across the fields and they would be home!

But the mood in the prison as Christmas Day neared was more somber than usual, if that was possible. The men were mourning the loss of Patrick Mulrennan a prisoner who had been shot a couple of weeks earlier, in cold blood. The killer was known to everyone, it was Colonel Tony Lawler, the swaggering second in command to General MacEoin. He simply decided to take a pot shot at the young man who was standing above the Barracks Square looking out a window. Lawler insisted he told the prisoners to move from the area but no one else heard that warning but they heard the shot that killed Mulrennan. Lawler wanted to have eight other men executed so he could prove the point of who was in control but fortunately MacEoin declined his idea. But such was the danger the men lived in. At the whim of some crazed officer, anyone could be selected and killed. Despite three official hearings in subsequent months, Lawler was never brought to account for the cold-blooded killing even though he had boasted about it in a letter to his mother.

Further atrocities would strike fear into the hearts of the toughest of the IRA men that month. News of the execution by firing squad of four prisoners at Kilmainham in Dublin filtered through to them. Again, there was no trial just summary execution by a military dictatorship which in the view of the IRA was disguised as an elected government.

Joe and his comrades absorbed the sad news of the executions. It was exacerbated when they heard that one of their most respected Republican leaders, Erskine Childers was put on trial, the outcome predictable. An enigma, Childers was born in England but in later life involved himself in Irish politics and became a passionate spokesperson for independence and a Republic. Ironically, he was convicted of being in the ownership of a small pistol, a gift to him from Michael Collins. He was executed soon after his trial.

The horror continued for the prisoners as they heard reports in early December of the execution of another four more prisoners in Mountjoy prison in Dublin. It was a simple case of retribution and revenge. The men had been in prison since June 1922 and had nothing to do with the ambush of two Dail Deputies on the streets of Dublin, one of whom died. The men were from each of the four provinces of Ireland. Someone in the Provisional Government recognized some perverse symmetry in their selection. They had after all been arrested bearing arms against the state, reason enough in some minds to have them put to death. It was a continuation of the tit for tat justification of the war. You kill one of ours and we'll kill four of yours. No trial just 'summary' justice by those who had the power.

The reports of the executions filtered into the prison and reached the ears of Dan Crowley and the Keegan brothers. News was usually through a few friendly guards who risked their lives to pass on information. Some smuggled in newspapers which of course were banned from the prisoners. Visitors brought information and more news which multiplied in intensity as it was passed from prisoner to prisoner.

"Jaysus, Hugh, what's going on in the country? Are none of us safe, isn't it enough that we've been put in prison and can't fight anymore?" Joe was exasperated and looked to Hugh for solace and answers, but he couldn't supply any.

"It's all about power Joe, they have it and they want to show us they have it and they want to make an example of anyone who doesn't agree with them." Hugh was equally exasperated but with a few more years on him perhaps he had a different perspective. He was totally frustrated and though he would never admit it to Joe, he felt defeated.

Finally, Joe heard some good news. A friendly guard had passed on that Tom McGiff's Column had raided a village in Ballinacaragy and relieved the locals of supplies they would need in their continued struggle. It wasn't a big deal but it showed the men inside that the struggle was still being carried out in the country side.

"I knew Tom would make their life difficult." Said Joe to Dan, more in hope than anything else. He was just happy to hear some news of something positive from their side of the action. Still the misery continued and the negative stories kept coming. They were totally shocked when they heard of the execution of seven Kildare IRA men in the Curragh, a prison camp in Kildare.

It was at this time Joe noticed and felt a hardening of Dan Crowley's attitude. It appeared to Joe that he was being consumed with hatred by the actions of the Government.

"Joe I can't accept any defeat, we have to keep going, we need the Republic we need the thirty two counties in one country. I won't rest until we have that in this country and we'll have to get it by whatever means possible."

"It seems so far away Dan, we got close and it was taken away from us. I don't know if we can make that happen." Joe was being honest with a man he had spent so many dangerous hours with. While he sympathized and indeed felt many of the same emotions, he now saw in Dan the difference between dedication and fanaticism. Dan had gone over to the far side of the ledger and Joe could tell from the men who Dan was spending time with that his soul had been sold to them. They were the hard men of the North who hated Protestants simply because they were Protestants. They would never forget or forgive the pogroms of the past couple of years and would never forgive the British for their imperial ways. Irish nationalism would prevail regardless of the politics of the day. Joe spoke to Hugh about it,

"Have you seen how Dan spends his time with the men from the North?" Hugh had noticed as well and had feared that Dan would take Joe into that area of ideology that offered no easy escape.

"Dan will go where he feels he has to; God knows this war has driven men to extremes and will continue to do so." Hugh and Joe didn't know what the future held but were starting to wonder if their future was in the land of their birth as much as they loved it. They would have to compromise too much to endure the status of being a British subject in their own country. But for Dan there would be no compromise. His oath to the Irish Republican Brotherhood would never be broken and men like Dan had decided they would not rest until they achieved what they had declared in 1916. Dan's passion would affect many generations of Irishmen and women which followed after him and he would make his presence felt when he had his opportunity.

CHAPTER 39
Life Changes For Sean

Sean McKeon's star continued to rise with in the National Army. His arrest finally of Joe Keegan and Dan Crowley and spoiling the handover of a cache of arms from Dublin raised his profile. He was disappointed though that Tom McGiff had slipped his net.

Soon after the arrests Sean's private life also took a positive turn. He had recently taken up with a childhood friend of both his and Joe's a girl who grew up in the same area and was known to all the families. Fianna O'Farrell was an attractive girl of nineteen years of age and had ambitions to become a teacher of primary school. In those days that path was usually taken through joining a Nun's order which did not appeal to Fianna. Still she thought, if she had the right connections, she might qualify for a Teacher's College scholarship in Dublin or even Athlone. She had done well in high school and the teachers there spoke highly of her intelligence and capacity for learning.

The childhood friendship was reawakened with a chance encounter. He had not recognized the attractive young woman who was waiting in the reception area of the barracks office. It was a few days after they had captured Joe. He had just finished a staff meeting and was going through some papers in the office when the attractive young lady approached him,

"So, it seems that your too high and mighty to speak to your old friends now you're an officer in the army?" there was a hint of cheekiness in her approach but she thought she knew Sean well enough to tease him. He looked at her and it was all of thirty seconds before recognition dawned on him, then he gave a huge smile, he was still a young man after all and being approached by a pretty girl was good for his ego.

"Fianna O'Farrell, well how long has it been? Must be four years if it's a day, the last I saw of you was in a school uniform off to class with a bunch of friends. It's grand to be seeing you again and here of all places. What are you doing here?" Sean was genuinely surprised and delighted by the turn of events, his duties over the past few years had not given him much opportunity to socialize and certainly not with pretty young ladies. Now he remembered a day long ago when Joe had teased him about Fianna asking after Sean.

"Well I don't have a top-secret clearance but I work for the Woollen Mills in town. They sent me down here to collect some papers for some new orders they been expecting from the army." Her transport driver was outside waiting in a vehicle keen to get away from the Barracks,

"That's grand and are they looking after you? Do you need some help?"

"No thank you Sean, the officer I spoke to said he'd be back in a couple of minutes with what I needed. So how are you Sean? Gosh it's been so long and we've all aged so much." She was trying to be polite, now that she had approached him, she wasn't sure how to handle the conversation. They were young adults now not kids and they both felt a little awkward. This Sean was certainly very different to the tousle haired boy of eighteen she remembered but the good looks were still there and the winning smile. Fianna continued,

"It has been a long time. I couldn't tell you were the time has gone and what with everything that has been happening in the country. It's been easy to lose touch with so many friends."

Fianna was more than aware of the social restrictions of the last four or more years herself. Many of the young men she grew up with went missing for long periods of time. She did not know where they were and she always felt in the dark about events and people. Even her friend Rose Egan had been sent away to Australia. Any question at her home about anyone was met with a dismissive response from her brothers or parents. The family during the War of Independence had kept her sheltered and was keen that a young attractive girl be kept out of sight as much as possible. Away from the prying eyes of the Black and Tans and Auxiliaries in particular who were not well regarded by decent Irish folk of any political persuasion. Fianna was only in her second week of her new office position at the Mills and this was her first visit inside the barracks. While she knew that Sean had joined the army, she had no idea she would come across him on this visit. She was desperate for information about the last few years.

"And have you seen Joe or Hugh or any of the Keegans or McCormacks lately? Lord knows I haven't seen any of the Keegans for years, except very occasionally Mrs. Keegan at Sunday mass in Athlone when she's visiting." It was a genuine enquiry. When they were kids it was not unusual for Fianna and some of her friends to join in an impromptu game of Hurling. Like any teenagers they tried to forget about what was happening around them and just tried to enjoy themselves.

Sean was nonplussed by the question. He was so immersed in his work he just assumed that everyone knew what was going on at the moment. But his viewpoint was a military one and it was his job to know as much as possible. He never considered how much was kept from the civilian population who were mainly fed propaganda by a press compliant to the National Government's edicts and politics. Fianna spoke again saving him an answer,

"I did see in the newspapers perhaps three years ago that Joe was selected to play Hurling for Westmeath for a game in Dublin. You must have been proud of him, I wish I could have seen him play, he enjoyed it so much." Sean was aware of Joe's success and it was before the Irish games were suspended by the British Army whilst hostilities were under way. Joe had hoped to go on to the all Ireland Hurling Finals. But his dream was shattered along with so many other young men who would have rather played sport than soldier.

Sean was shuffling papers, not sure what to say to Fianna, the truth? Or lie to her? But he knew any lie would come back to haunt him so he decided to just tell her the truth.

"I'm sorry Fianna, the country with the state it's in and everyone going every which way, it seems that Joe and I found ourselves on different sides. I'm sorry to tell you that Joe and Hugh and James decided to stay with the IRA and they have recently been arrested and are in prison here in Athlone." He hated having to tell her but he wanted to be honest.

Fianna was taken aback and the shock showed on her face, old friends she knew from childhood in prison and facing God knows what! Her politics were defined at that time by what was happening in her home. Her parents while open minded, had decided to support the Government but at the same time they refused to condemn the men who felt a Republic was still worth fighting for. It was having a bit each way but they realised that the hold of having a Republic was still strong with many people.

"Oh Sean, are they alright? I know it's a long time since I saw them but the Keegans were always a dear family to me." She withheld some tears she felt coming but was angered, "Damn politics. It's tearing this country apart. God knows what will become of us all." She looked at Sean and he couldn't tell if she blamed him or what she felt about him being in an army uniform but it was clear she was upset and confused by the information. "I didn't realize the Keegan boys were so strong about their feelings but of course we didn't discuss it much when we were kids. Certainly they weren't going to tell a bit of a girl like me who was more interested in school work. I suppose you boys talked about it a lot Sean. Did you?"

Sean was again at a loss to answer, how could he explain the huge rift that had occurred between the boyhood friends who many had described as thick as thieves. Again, he felt he owed it to Fianna to be upfront and tell her what had happened.

"You're right Fianna we were just kids and we didn't bother you and the other girls with our thoughts about politics. There was a lot happening and as boys coming into manhood, we felt strongly about what we should do and when. As time went on the three of us got involved with the struggle and joined the IRB and then the IRA. By the time we were nineteen we were fully fledged soldiers of the Republic and got involved as much as we could through the Athlone Brigade."

"That's why I hardly saw any of you for so long? You were off fighting the Tans and my family had me locked down in school and home and didn't tell me much about what was going on." She resented it now that her family had treated her as a child and usually kept her out of family discussions. She knew that the national split had happened after the Treaty with England. And that many had to choose either the Republican side or the Provisional Government and the Treaty for the Free State. She had been confused and felt that she hadn't enough information to make up her own mind about it. Some of her friends who weren't so confused had joined the women's Cumann na mBan. They supported the Republican cause and had paid dearly for it in some instances. Fianna cursed herself for not being more political, more aware of the troubles in her country and regretted that her family had protected her too much. Her confusion was complete.

"So why are they now in prison and not you Sean?" Now the point was being brought home, he looked at her eyes and could see the confusion, again he would tell her straight. It was an innocent question with no malice.

"After the Treaty was signed, we all had to choose sides Fianna. Joe and Hugh chose the Republican side and I chose to go with what had been decided with the Treaty and help build a new independent Ireland. It happened all over the country, people were forced to choose what side they were on. It changed everything for many people including your own family I'm sure." She had known some of that of course, but she had never wanted to admit the extent of it to herself.

"I didn't want to think about the differences Sean, I just hoped it would all go away and everyone would be on the same side again and things would get back to normal just like it did after the Treaty for a while. I thought that would be the end of it." She realised how immature she was sounding and she felt the shame of not being more political, as was expected of almost everyone in Ireland. But she was from a strong Catholic family and she took her guidance from her parents and the Bishops and the Parish Priest who thundered against the Republicans every Sunday from the pulpit. She didn't want to put her fellow countrymen into right and wrong categories like the priest did, so she chose not to think about it. Hearing the news of Joe and Hugh and others now and what they faced mortified her.

Sean could see she was shocked a felt an immediate tenderness for her. Something he hadn't expected to feel for any girl such was his commitment to his work and career. He wanted to tell her more, explain his feelings and what had happened between the friends, but not here, not now.

"We need to talk about it more Fianna and I'd like to see you again soon; I'll call on your parent's house on Saturday and see your Mam and Da and ask if it's alright." He was as surprised as Fianna was. Suddenly out of nowhere something new and unexpected had come into Sean's life. He felt elated and wondered if that was how Joe felt when he tried to explain once how he felt about the departed Maggie Egan. Fianna took a minute to collect herself. Sean had taken her by surprise, but she managed an answer,

"I'm sure my parents would like to see you again Sean, as would I." She felt herself blushing and wanted to be away. "Now I have to get back to the Woolen Mills, they'll think I've gotten lost and won't let me out on messages again." Her smile melted Sean's hard expression and he helped her collect her papers and escorted her to her waiting car.

"Till Saturday then, Fianna take care." He said as she got into the vehicle. Sean felt his life and outlook on everything had changed somehow. But didn't understand how much that was so from the few minutes he had spent with Fianna. He had locked himself so tightly into his work over the past three years. He had failed to recognize that there were different aspects of life outside the armed struggles he had become involved with. He was surprised and taken aback with this change he now felt and was looking forward to his visit to Fianna's home the following Saturday. He couldn't explain the smile on his face when one of his fellow officers cheekily asked,

"What are you so happy about?" and just responded with a broader grin.

CHAPTER 40
Republican Prisoners on the Move

Life in Athlone Barracks offered no joy or happiness for Joe and Hugh and Dan and the hundreds of others. Unrelenting misery gave them a Christmas which meant nothing and delivered less and the news of the executions from Mountjoy depressed the men further. Soldiers of the Republic and leaders like Erskine Childers, who gave an intellectual element to the meaning of their struggle, were being battered down by the state for their beliefs.

To get through the hard times, the prisoners busied themselves as best they could. There was always discussion of prison escapes and detailed planning that often got nowhere. Rumours were always circulating and it was impossible to tell real news from gossip and propaganda. One story that developed a life of its own was the possible transfer of many of the prisoners to the Curragh in Kildare. It was repeated too often to be ignored and Hugh felt it was a definite possibility.

"There's too many people here Joe, they need to do something, it's overcrowded to buggery and they can't take any more." Which is what they all felt until yet more prisoners were thrown in from time to time confounding their expectations.

Finally, there was an official announcement on January 5th, 1923: five hundred men would be transferred to Tintown A over the next four weeks. Twenty five of the Athlone men via Mountjoy and others direct. Joe and Hugh were selected to go to Mountjoy for reasons they didn't understand but they hoped it wouldn't be their permanent home. There was good news for their brother James. He was released before Christmas and allowed to return to his family home in Drumraney. No reasons were ever given which just drove the rumour mill to new heights but again Hugh thought he had an answer,

"I'm sure we're being kept over because we had rank of Quartermaster Joe. They knew you were fossicking for A Company and they had my name down as Brigade Quartermaster. The silly buggers didn't realize those positions changed with the wind. Whoever was around was often given the job. James didn't have a rank and he's bit younger so they let him go home. That's what I think at any rate." Joe could only agree he had given up trying to understand what the Staters were trying to do with the prisoners and the war generally.

"Sure, James will be able to help Da and Mammy. They must be up against it with the amount of work to be done."

"You could be sure that the Staters wouldn't be thinking of helping anyone, they're just trying to reduce numbers. They'd be only helping themselves. From what I heard they have camps filled all over the country with Republicans. It would almost take their whole army to guard them, there are about ten thousand prisoners in all I believe." Hugh's information was correct a huge number of arrests had been made since the start of hostilities. Starting in July 1922 there would eventually be over twelve thousand Republican men and two hundred women in the Government prisons and detention camps by mid 1923.

In the meantime, Dan Crowley had been working on his own escape plans without telling Joe or Hugh. He was assisted by the men from up north and had managed to get hold of a Free State soldiers' uniform which he dressed in and just walked out of Custume Barracks unchallenged! This was just as well because he also had a revolver and would have used it if he had been challenged. Dan went back to his Flying Column so he could wreak havoc as he put it and continue his war with the Free State Government. He would do so for far longer than anyone imagined becoming a Division Commander of the IRA in Northern Ireland for many years and stirring new generations to continue the fight against all odds.

In early January, once again Joe found himself on the way to Dublin. Christmas had passed without any celebration. The Catholic Church wouldn't even allow a priest to give mass because the Bishops had forbidden it. Parcels from friends and family had been stopped from time to time out of sheer bloody mindedness. Every now and then the prison authorities would relax their rule and some parcels would get in. But they had often been rifled through and who knows what taken by the guards. But worse was to follow and the men just tried to get through whatever was thrown at them. Joe and Hugh had been told officially in early January that they were being transferred to Tintown A in the Curragh. They would be among hundreds and the transport was always a problem. Trains in some cases, lorries in others, closely guarded and desperately cold due to the fact that winter had set in.

The transfer would not be straightforward for Joe and Hugh who were to be sent via Mountjoy Prison in Dublin. For the time being, Joe and Hugh were kept together having come from the same Company in Drumraney. They were able to enjoy for a short while the friendship of men they knew from home.

The first sight of Mountjoy would depress even the most ardent supporter of the Republican cause. Joe had seen it once in passing when he came to Dublin with Sean in 1917 for the funeral of Thomas Ashe who had died as a result of a hunger strike in that year. Hugh also remembered the grey walls towering over the streets as he had walked by a few years ago when he came to

Dublin with his father and later with Patrick McCormack. But prisons are totally different on the inside as any prisoner or even a visitor would attest. As soon as they were inside the main gate they were disembarked from the lorries and were pushed into a square compound, small, dark and crowded. They weren't allowed to talk and were just expected to follow orders. The repression was intolerable. No human rights, no prisoner rights, just processing of large numbers of men who were cold, hungry and bewildered as to their fate.

The walls in the courtyard were about eighteen feet high and no one could imagine escaping over them which was the reason for their size. The prison was already crowded with day to day criminals and hundreds of Dublin area-based IRA who had been imprisoned over the past nine months and in some cases longer. The food was edible but only just and you only got one meal a day anyway, the water was best avoided to minimise the risk of further disease. Piping hot tea was the preferred drop though some men were making illegal poteen in some cells which were as crowded as in Athlone and just as dirty, men were expected to keep them clean and some did but many did not.

It soon became obvious why many of the men, mostly of rank had been sent to Mountjoy. The Staters wanted to have one more go at them for interrogation. It wasn't a pleasant experience as Joe recounted later. He was taken in manacles to a small room sat on a small chair and stood over by guards and plain clothes police who didn't hesitate to use the back of their hand if they didn't like the answers they were given. They were questioned for about two hours but had little to add to their stories. How the hell would Joe know where Tom McGiff was? But the question was asked again and again and a negative response met with another backhander. Joe decided to mock the process and one answer was that he knew Tom was planning a holiday in Paris. That earned him the biggest backhander yet. Eventually they gave up, sent Joe out and brought in another man. Hugh got the same treatment as did many of their comrades until the Staters realised the futility of the exercise but they had managed to prove they were in charge which was important to them thought Joe. The prisoners returned to a daily routine such as they could manage.

Boredom set in very quickly and again men met in groups talking about escapes and politics and wondering of the whereabouts of former comrades. On their fifth day Joe was approached by a man he vaguely recognized and when he spoke, it came to him. He was one of the men from the lodging he had stayed in when he and Dan had come to take messages to General O'Malley a couple of months earlier.

"I've got someone who would like to say hello to you Joe" the man said who introduced himself as Tom. Joe was confused, he was sure he didn't know anyone in Mountjoy apart from his immediate circle of comrades,

"Come with me." Said Tom.

Joe followed Tom into the main building, one of many that made up the prison and wondered how anyone would ever find their way around the joint. Up three flights of stairs, down two long corridors, past some guards who gave them cursory looks but didn't interfere. Finally, Tom stopped outside a cell door and nodded his head in the direction for Joe to follow him inside, which he did still not knowing what to expect. He was knocked sideways by surprise when his eyes landed on Ernie O'Malley, the man he had met a couple of months ago before the raid on Wellington Barracks.

"General O'Malley!" Said Joe, his voice unable to hide his surprise, "Good to see you sir," But Joe was taken aback by the state of the robust man of good health he remembered. Though he recognized him Joe could see the man was now far from good health.

"Nice to see an old soldier again Joe how goes the fight?" it was a strange greeting but one often made between old soldiers. Joe shrugged his shoulders and dropped his arms by his side,

"Not so good, as you can see, they seem to have me at a disadvantage." O'Malley smiled at the reply,

"As they do for all of us at the moment Joe, as you can see, they have just kept me alive, because they still want to execute me but they're not feeding me too well." Joe noticed the thinning frame and it wasn't till later that he found out that O'Malley had been wounded twenty times in the firefight he had trying to escape the Staters. They had ambushed him in the house where Joe and Dan had met him. To say it was a wonder he was still alive was no understatement. He still carried three bullets in his body and he had spent many weeks in hospital and was still partly bedridden in the prison. He was assisted with his convalescence by a young prisoner. He still insisted on defying the hierarchy of the prison and demanding political prisoner of war status for all the IRA men. He was a legend among the men and not just because of his rank, they respected him greatly for the work he did for them.

"So, Joe, you had a good morning after you left me in Dublin and joined the lads for the work on Wellington Barracks." It wasn't a question, he knew how the operation had gone and was happy with it, "and you got back to Tom McGiff alright?"

"We did, but it was along walk with few close shaves." Joe couldn't help but warm to the charismatic character. He instilled confidence just by his presence and bearing even though he was carrying so many injuries. "Sadly, when we went to Kilbeggan to collect what you had sent us we got hit. Someone had betrayed the pick-up, Tom got away, one of our men was killed. Dan and I were picked up arrested by my old friend Sean McKeon."

"Yes, I had heard of him, a good man in the Tan war but sadly he lost sight of what we were all about. Now you're here and he's In Athlone with the Government planning our destruction and doing a good job of it, it seems."

Joe shook his head as if he was going to apologise for Sean but realised that wasn't expected so instead he told the General about Dan's escape from Custume Barracks. How he had walked out in a stolen uniform unchallenged. O'Malley had a good laugh at that, always glad to hear of any Republican victory no matter how small.

"So, are you here for long Joe or are you moving on?" O'Malley asked.

"We've been told we're going to Tintown but who knows when?" Joe answered, "And yourself, are you holding up well, everyone will like to know about how you're getting on."

"Tell them day by day Joe, that's all we have, that's all we're going to get until we get rid of this mob in power. But our day will come even though we can't see it now."

Joe noticed the soldier who had brought him nodding his head towards the door and said,

"It's time for the General's rest now Joe. He needs to have his rest." Joe stood up and O'Malley shook his hand vigorously,

"I'm afraid so Joe, I need my rest now more than ever, my body needs more time to recover. Thanks for coming to see me and good luck for the future. Long live the Republic!" he said smiling, "we'll get there one day. Don't lose the faith."

Joe took his leave of the great man and found his way back to Hugh and told him about the meeting with O'Malley. Hugh hadn't realised that anyone of O'Malley's importance might still be in the prison and he was thrilled by Joe's story.

The next day the men from Athlone were told they would all be shipped out for the Curragh and Tintown the following day. Could it be any worse than Mountjoy?

CHAPTER 41
Deadly Duty for Sean

Sean's first meeting with Fianna's parents went better than he had expected. He was uncomfortable with socialising and certainly unsure of how to be a suitor for a well-presented young lady like Fianna. But he survived and her parents, though not staunch Free State supporters, were pleased to see a young man of Sean's stature taken an interest in their daughter.

The couple of months since Joe had been arrested had passed quickly and Sean had not seen him again, there was nothing he could say to him anyway. Their lives had gone in very different directions and there was no commonality in their approach to the politics of the day. Of course, Sean knew that the men in Athlone prison would be eventually sent to the camps in the Curragh. But knowing that would not have helped Joe, it was just another prison to them, so Sean kept away from any further contact. Sean's personal focus had all passed to Fianna and as he had suggested, he had come 'calling'. Fianna enjoyed the attention and was pleased to be seen on the arm of a handsome young officer in Free State uniform when they walked in the town. Accept of course the few times that some Republican supporters would scream abuse at Sean from a distance causing him to break off and try and make an arrest but always to no avail. The abusers were younger and couldn't be caught. Strong but small political protests like that were often made, letting the Staters know that they didn't have the game to themselves.

There was some embarrassment for Sean and his fellow officers following the incident that saw Dan Crowley walk out of prison in a Free State troopers' uniform. Though his men weren't directly involved in overseeing prisoners at that time, it was one of his battalion men's uniforms that had been stolen. Dan would have enjoyed the subsequent formal enquiry that called up soldier after soldier and quite a few officers to find out what had happened and how. It ended with two troopers being suspected for IRA sympathies and suspended for a month without pay. The charges couldn't be totally proven and the men didn't confess. Occasionally Free State soldiers did come across former comrades from the Tan war in the prison and tried to help them out. Their loyalties would be divided and subverted by the pressure of old friendships and incidents would occur. Sean was given a dressing down even though he could not have prevented the incident.

"Captain McKeon you should have been on top of this situation, we've been made look like idiots by an IRA desperado." This was the assessment from the Brigade 2IC Lawler when Sean was called into his office the day after the hearings finished. But much worse was to come.

Lawler's expression changed to one of malevolence as he went on to let Sean know that Sean's Company had been rostered to carry out the set of executions scheduled for the following Saturday, in Custume Barracks,

"So have your men prepared, you will need eleven men, seven to do the firing and four to act as guards and move the bodies. Select them by ballot. Do you think you and they are up to it?" Lawler asked aggressively. He was a square peg in a round hole totally unsuited for Army command and he didn't particularly like young officers who might threaten his authority. Intimidation of younger officers was his way of dealing with ranks lower than his own. Sean simply replied,

"Of course, sir." Lawler then gave him three typewritten pages which outlined the procedure and what was expected of the men involved. Officers and men of the Free State army couldn't ignore the reality of the execution policy pushed from Dublin. If men were to be executed there would need to be executioners. Sean was devastated when he received the news, he knew it was always a possibility but like his brother officers, chose not to think about it. But now the worst had now happened

Sean came face to face with the reality of the policy very early on Saturday January 20th. The men he would be in charge of executing were likely to be local men, certainly all former Tan War comrades. But some newer younger men who had since joined the resistance to the Free State government would be involved. But nearly always they were young men who were to be executed were contemporaries of Sean and his soldiers all with similar backgrounds and interests, sport, farming, working and families whom they had left to fight in an ugly guerilla war. Now they were going to pay the ultimate price, they had been found guilty by a Court Martial and sentenced to death by firing squad. One of the men had only been arrested twelve days earlier and his Court Martial trial rushed through.

The men of the firing squad had been chosen the afternoon before by ballot out of one hundred men in the Company. Once you had participated you were excused from further ballots unless it became necessary to go around again. There were seven men in the firing squad and four to assist. Their officer had less choice, it was his company and he was ordered to oversee the procedure, having the rank of Captain locked Sean into the responsibility.

There would be five men executed that morning each facing the squad separately, each execution would take five minutes approximately. The men would be brought into the walled courtyard one at a time, offered a blindfold and then the officer would give the order. Ready, aim, fire!

The men of the firing squad had been primed by Colonel Lawler with a few shots of whiskey before they went into the yard. Lawler had seen troopers faint at the prospect of killing other Irishmen so cold bloodedly. The men were capable of doing what they had to but perhaps their senses were sufficiently dulled for the event by Lawler's whiskey. One soldier who was just eighteen was the exception and Sean could see the tears running down his cheeks. Sean swallowed hard trying to avoid showing his own emotions. He walked up to the soldier and though he wanted to excuse him from the mission he knew he wouldn't be able to do that,

"Steady trooper, it'll all be over in a few minutes." He lied, anything to get through the next half hour.

"Sir," was all the boy managed to say as he marched into line. Sean suspected he would aim high or low, anywhere but at the men's body. He hoped the others wouldn't do the same thing, lengthening the time of the ordeal for the victims. Sean own eyes filled with tears but he'd be damned if he would let anyone know how he felt.

"Squad line up, over here, on the double, let's get this done." Busy yourself and stop thinking, of all things, stop thinking.

It was all over in thirty minutes, the executed men did not grovel or plea for mercy. They knew what was ahead of them and they would die proudly for the Republic. They faced their executioners with dignity. They had attended Mass early in the morning and given last rites; a friendly priest had been found for the purpose and the authorities turned a blind eye.

Each of the volleys reverberated around the prison. Every prisoner knew what had happened without having to see anything. Five young Irishmen were killed to become an example to all the other rebels as to what fate may await them. It was state terror exercised at a time when few people even knew what that meant.

Sean dismissed the firing squad four other men from his company took each body and lowered them into the coffins and the prepared graves in the prison yard. A medical orderly had ensured they were indeed dead. Sean said a silent prayer selfishly thankful that he had not had to deliver a coup de grace to any of the executed men. His duty was over for the day. He made his way back to his barracks found an empty toilet block and threw his guts up.

#   #   #

He decided not to see Fianna that afternoon but sent a message that he had to stay on the base. He hated lying to her but couldn't face socializing after what he had been through that morning. He wondered if his capacity as an officer had been compromised or if he ever had that capacity in the first place. Surely this wasn't what he had signed up for, killing defenceless Irishmen because of their beliefs. The tears kept coming.

War is an ugly process and its results are measured in cold hard numbers that meant something to those in charge. For men on the ground it meant doing things like that which was ordered on that Saturday morning. His men seemed to get over the executions more quickly as they took safety in numbers and went out that afternoon and drank too many Guinness and whiskies so they would forget. Officers didn't have that luxury; they were expected to give an example, be an example and not show any emotion or what could be perceived as weakness. The day continued to weigh heavily on Sean as he struggled with how he should present himself. He kept out of everyone's way as much as possible and retired early avoiding the officers' mess completely.

Sean's confusion and emotional upset continued through that sleepless night, when the sleep came there were horrible dreams. Sean woke up a number of times in a confused rage his body soaked in sweat.

The morning finally arrived and Sean was advised by Colonel Lawler that General MacEoin wanted to see him. Sean was so upset and confused by the previous day's events and his tormented night he seriously wondered whether he should tender his resignation to the General. He took a long walk after a mug of tea for breakfast and contemplated his options and indeed his career and what he wanted to do. By the time he found the General's office he had calmed down. His sense of duty had prevailed over his many doubts and he had assured himself that military life was what he wanted. He had to accept the inevitably that it would include unpleasant and perhaps ugly elements to his duty as an officer.

For now he assumed that the incident with the escapee using one of his men's uniforms would be forgotten or he was going to get another bollicking. But the army knew it had to keep men like Sean in the fold, they would be needed to ensure proper order if this infernal Civil War ever ended.

It was to be a short meeting. General MacEoin had Sean standing to attention in his office. There was no mention of the stolen uniform. MacEoin was promoting him to Major He was just twenty-four years of age. He handed him his new pips and said:

"Congratulations Major. We're sure you won't let us down." Sean saluted and took the pips from the General,

"Thank you, Sir." Sean replied.

MacEoin dismissed him and then made his daily tour of duty of the prison and the barracks with Colonel Lawler sometimes as was his habit, with his revolver in hand. Terrifying both his own men and the prisoners.

Sean returned to his own quarters and sat on his bed with the pips in his hand. His thinking was all over the place, yesterday after the executions he had been prepared to resign and just leave the army. Now he had new responsibilities to take on. He sat dazed for some minutes until the reality of what had happened sunk in. The army needed him he decided and he needed the army.

The recruiting for the army continued. Untrained and often unschooled young men were given a uniform and a rifle and a couple of weeks basic training. Then posted somewhere, anywhere, to boost the numbers. The Government was hell bent on outnumbering the IRA and continued to arrest and imprison any republicans they could find. They would then terrify them with seemingly random executions. There was up to fifty thousand men in Free State uniforms and over ten thousand men in IRA internment camps and another five thousand in the field fighting. The country was in the ridiculous position of having a huge proportion of its potentially productive youth engaged in a futile war.

It was another two days before Sean could muster the energy and courage to face Fianna. He knew he would never be able to tell her about what his duty required of him that Saturday morning. He was surprised by the depth of feeling that he was developing for her and was confident it was returned. It had only been a short time, less than a month, but he wanted her to know how he felt and decided to push his point.

"Do you think your parents would welcome a new member of their family so soon after meeting him?" Fianna was intrigued by the question; she did feel strongly about Sean but she also still wanted to study to be a teacher. She felt she wasn't ready for the commitment he was hinting at, she would need to stall him.

"I'm sure if you are talking about what I think you are talking about, they would be delighted but they're not the ones who have to make a decision like that." She smiled as she said it and Sean didn't take it as a refusal. He had no idea how young women felt about these things and he had no experience dealing with it either. "This is happening very quickly Sean; I do feel strongly about you but I also have some plans of my own. I'd like to study to be a teacher and work with children in primary schools." This took Sean by surprise as his only understanding of teachers was that you have to be in a religious order, at least for the Catholic Church you did.

"But is that possible Fianna? Wouldn't you have to be a nun?" the look on his face made Fianna laugh.

"Not at all, the schools need teachers and the national schools don't have nuns, they have lay teachers and it's what I've always wanted to do ever since I was a little girl." She seemed so set and confident about her direction in life that Sean knew he should back away. He had taken too much for granted which was his way. His life had been so hectic for the last four years he had lost sight of what was going on in the rest of society. Certainly those people who weren't in the military.

"Of course, I understand," he said, even though he didn't, "perhaps we can talk about things a bit down the road."

"I think that would be best, let's give ourselves some time and get to know each other more. I can assure you Sean I feel very strongly about you but I don't want to rush matters just yet."

"Certainly," was all Sean said, he wasn't used to this sort of conversation and decided to finish while he was ahead. He held Fianna's hand and tried to forget the events of the last few days then he told her his good news. "I've been made a Major as of yesterday, the General has promoted me from Captain." He was beaming and could tell Fianna was proud of his promotion even if she didn't quite know what it meant.

"That's grand Sean, I'm very happy for you and my parents will want to congratulate you too. Let's tell them now." But Sean begged off and took his leave of Fianna having decided that he didn't want to face the possible future in laws, not without knowing Fianna's real feelings.

There was plenty of military work to be done and the General had plans and the next day. Sean was to take a troop to Tuam in Galway, forty miles away to retake the local Town Hall which had been requisitioned by Republicans for meetings. Now the General wanted a show of strength in the town and he wasn't expecting it to be a simple task. He needed a strong officer to show up the IRA.

CHAPTER 42
Tintown A

The introduction to Tintown for Joe and Hugh and hundreds of other irregulars transported there in January 1923 was anything but positive. Detained without a trial and transported away from his home county, Joe was despondent but determined. He would keep a positive outlook for the future. But now the detention camp of Tintown A sprawled before him. It was the second time in three years that it would become a prison for the IRA men who had fought so hard for their Republic. It had been run by the British Army from 1919 to1922, together with a large number of other camps across the country. Detained at His Majesty's pleasure, the camps were used to contain the rebels though they had not been tried or found guilty of a crime. Now it was the turn of an Irish government, who was also using the powers of detention but on a bigger scale with up to thirty camps spread around the country. Tintown would be the largest, situated on the plains of the Curragh in County Kildare.

Joe had arrived with Hugh and other men transferred from Mountjoy. They were still unsure of why they had been sent there but decided it was because the Staters wanted to question them again under duress. The hundred or so men transferred from Mountjoy on a series of lorries, arrived late afternoon and it being winter the chill winds were still blowing across the Kildare plains. Most of the men were not dressed for the cold, trench coats were often lost in other prisons or stolen by soldiers or even inmates. They were left with jackets of various kinds that they had been defending with their lives. Some had pullovers but many didn't and their shoes and socks had seen better days. Few had extra clothes to change into if anything happened to the clothes they stood up in. They would grow to rely on parcels from home or from charities if they were allowed to help.

But life was what it was and their complaints were ignored or greeted with shouts of abuse or the butt of a rifle by the guards.

The camp would eventually hold over three thousand prisoners. All in wooden huts that weren't insulated against the cold and there was precious little warmth to be found in the winter months. The food was terrible and many men relied on food parcels from their families. That is if they got through the censors without too much being stolen. But the parcels from home kept them going in many cases. The men felt they were treated worse than criminals in actual prisons and were determined to gain the status of Prisoners of War. But the Free State government was just as determined to deny them. The dispute would lead to further trouble to try and eventually force the issue.

Joe and Hugh and a number of other Westmeath men were consigned to three huts together. They were able to maintain friendships and contacts with former comrades.

"Well Joe, this looks like being our home for however long. Best we get used to it." Hugh said to Joe as they selected a wooden bed with a thin mattress and even thinner blankets, "We'll have to make sure the men are organised and make the best of what they have. There's a meeting for tomorrow with the senior IRA man here, they want to talk to five huts at a time and lay out whatever rules they have been able to make work." Hugh wasn't smiling and Joe realised the gravity of what was going on, it wasn't as bad as Custume Barracks or Mountjoy but it was no resort hotel either.

"Jaysus Hugh, we have our work cut out here. I wouldn't know where to start."

"That's why the senior officers have formed their committees, and some of them have been in other camps, the earlier ones run by the British. But a lot of them say it is worse now, our own countrymen treating us worse than the Brits." he spat the words out and couldn't hide his disgust, "this is all new to most fellows but as I said we have to make the most of it until we can figure out an alternative." Hugh tried a smile, he knew there weren't many alternatives, escape perhaps? Or full surrender by signing the Pledge and walking out then having to find a new life because old friends would never talk to you again. Escape was the one thing that was on everyone's mind, the barbed wire didn't look that difficult but they hadn't yet absorbed the tenor of the place. Then they could decide more intelligently what was possible. Hugh suddenly realised something that might lift Joe's spirits,

"You might even get a game of Hurley in Joe; I was speaking to someone earlier who said there were a number of men who wanted to start a County championship."

"That'd be grand Hugh but will the Staters trust us with Hurley sticks? I know what most of the men would want to do with them if they had one." Joe was serious but interested at the prospect of again being able to play his favourite game in some shape or form. But this time certainly not at the county level he had before he went on the run.

"Well we'll see how it pans out, but give it some thought you could contribute a lot with your experience." Hugh was keen to get Joe involved with something positive, being older he could see how Joe's spirit was challenged, "And let's not forget there is a number of younger lads who would enjoy a game, you could teach them a thing or two." Hugh could see that Joe's thinking was changing; it would give him a focus until they settled into a routine.

"Well it would be grand there's no doubt, I'll speak to some of the other players I've seen we should be able to get something happening." Now at least Joe was not thinking of how uncomfortable things were but of what he could contribute to resist the misery. Unfortunately, his first thoughts were correct. The prison authorities wouldn't allow Hurling clubs in case they were used as weapons so Hurling was off the list. Gaelic Football became the sport of choice and was supported in the camps by some chapters of the Gaelic Athletic Association when they could.

Despite the sporting activity, it didn't take long for the boredom to set in for the new arrivals at Tintown. Boredom was their worst enemy and it was up to each man to find an interest or a niche to keep himself busy. The worst thing was to not be involved with something, anything, or you just sat around looking into the distance hoping the day would end. Most men didn't succumb to complete misery and they became used to the routine and the surroundings. Joe and Hugh found men with like interest. Though Joe wasn't able to form a Hurling team, he was able to join in the Gaelic Football matches that seemed to go on every day when ever weather permitted. As there were men from nearly every county in Ireland that seemed to be the obvious selection for teams if one county was short the numbers were made up from a neighbouring county until there were enough teams to make a competition. It started with ten teams and slowly grew to fourteen, not all the prisoners were able to join in. Injuries from too much time in the field and general lack of fitness and good food took their toll but they were enthusiastic spectators. Even the guards couldn't resist sometimes cheering on their own county, much to the amusement of the players and other spectators.

Hugh was not interested in playing but he helped the men prepare for games notwithstanding they didn't have proper footwear or clothing. But they all made do with donations from home or whatever they could scrape together. Hugh used his leatherworking skills to repair any footballs and shoes that came his way and this kept him busy. Joe of course would have preferred Hurling but it couldn't be. He learned some skills he hadn't used since his school days and joined the combined Westmeath, Longford football team and played every Saturday and often during the week.

But still the days and weeks were slow and often sad for most men. They saw little relief from their prison life and the Free State army guards weren't very sympathetic to them. The end of winter 1923 was greeted with some thanks and the spring brought slightly warmer if not totally reliable weather. The open plains did nothing to stop the winds and rain if they chose to close in and the huts were still not in a proper condition to protect the inhabitants from the weather. Other pursuits such as learning the Irish language were popular but a lot of the men didn't have good education and found it a struggle. Political talks and debates also went on and were followed by vociferous arguments. Michael Collins and Eamon de Valera were favourite subjects as well as Lloyd George and Winston Churchill, tactics of the past were questioned and the ever present question of why did Michael Collins and Arthur Griffith accept the Treaty. There were never any answers. History lessons were given and lectures on health and hygiene drew attendances as did the reciting of poetry or reading from Irish classics. Concerts where rebel IRA songs were sung with enthusiasm always drew a crowd and the musicians made do as best they could with old fiddles and hornpipes. But boredom was the constant companion.

The men were always considering a way out of the place and the most logical seemed to be to tunnel from under one of the huts to the outer perimeter. Escape committees with a senior officer in charge were set up in various huts. As Spring wore on into April Joe and Hugh became part of a group chosen to build a tunnel and hopefully escape. Their hut was set up as the main entry point and a military operation was put in place. It would ensure that the enterprise was carried out with discipline. The slightest slip would see the camp authorities close the whole thing down and make life hell for those who were involved and often those who weren't. Finally, the site and route were chosen and digging started.

It would take nearly three weeks with several men utilising whatever tools they could to move dirt, usually they were screwdrivers purloined from a repair shed or spoons and forks. The work was arduous and dangerous with the constant threat of collapse onto the diggers on everyone's minds. Joe was included in the third group to go in and dig,

"I'm not looking forward to this Hugh," he confessed," tight spaces don't thrill me but I'll give it a go. If I can't do my share, they can take me off the list and let someone else in."

"You'll be fine Joe. "Hugh answered in that time-honoured tradition of giving encouragement when he had no idea of what Joe would encounter. But encouragement was what was needed plus planning.

They could only dig at night of course and they had difficulties going in the right direction what with there being no visual aids so far underground. The soil was to be brought out by the man behind the digger and deposited under the hut or brought into the hut and hidden. It would be disbursed the next day in the main yard by men just walking around and emptying their pockets or whatever they could carry soil in. The effort was helped by the more than eighty men involved and secrecy was kept. As one reported later, it was done by ensuring that any doubters knew how important silence about the project was. Any indiscretion was dealt with harshly. The tunnel they worked in was just two feet high and three feet wide at the widest point. Joe recounted later that he got used to the confined space but like everyone else he had to spend at least two hours down there before being relieved. It was a relief to get out he told Hugh, the air was foul and you sweated like a pig so the smell of yourself and other men was never pleasant.

The main officer in charge was a veteran IRA man from Cork. He had been involved in a great number of incidents in the Tan War and the current strife until he was caught near Dublin. His IRA unit was running out of options and supplies, Mountjoy looked like being home for some time but he ended up in Tintown. Perhaps it was because he had been able to disguise his true identity and pass himself off as a foot soldier. Dan Herlihy had a strong reputation as a good organiser among the men from Cork and he proved so in this enterprise. He addressed the men late at night in one of the huts and laid out the plan they had determined that only two huts would be involved in this escape attempt,

"We have a couple of tame Free Staters and I'll keep their names to myself but they'll prove useful to us. They're Cork boys and though they're in the army, they haven't forgotten where they came from. I've let Hugh Murtagh know who they are and he's the only one, we'll make the best use of them we can. But the rest is up to us, up to you men to work hard and get the tunnel done. If you don't want to be a part of it you can walk away now and no one will think the worst of you." He looked at this group of about thirty men in one hut but they all stayed still, every one of them wanted to be part of getting out of this place. "Right, seems we're all of one mind, Harry here will give you your rosters and with any luck we'll be out of here in three weeks."

It didn't seem that simple to Joe but he accepted the officer knew what he was doing and was inspired by his confidence. Joe was on duty the second night and would start digging at eleven pm. As Joe expected, it was not an easy task and he was glad when his shift was over, he would rotate every second night with other men and help out distributing soil each day. The pillaging was always on for sturdy timber pieces that were used to shore up the tunnel to make it safer. Men's beds were left with fewer planks to lie on and a few internal doors went missing to the dismay of the guards. The men said they had to burn them for fuel and left it at that.

The work was started and carried out with dedication, hard work and resolve by the chosen prisoners. Finally came the day of April 23 and the men and the tunnel were ready to go. Joe and Hugh and most other men were amazed that they were able to keep it secret for so long but they did. Unfortunately, a day before the time, Hugh came down with a bout of gastric which in the camp could often turn to Typhoid so he took to his bed and wouldn't take part in the escape.

"You go Joe and find Tom McGiff and the boys and join them, the lads will look after you once you're free." Joe was reluctant but knew Hugh wouldn't be able to handle the tunnel or the escape and agreed finally to go. "When you get to Athlone tell Mammy and Da we're thinking of them and I'll see them soon." The tears welled up in Hugh's eyes, he didn't usually succumb to sentiment but he was not well. His thoughts and his dreams through his fever had been turning him back to his childhood and home in Drumraney. He had thought that together they could make it but now Joe was on his own. Joe's plan was to join up with a Column in the Wicklow Mountains south of Dublin where there was still plenty going on. There men were fighting for their cause but he knew he had a long way to go. First, he had to get out of Tintown. Joe was number thirty five into the tunnel which was seventy feet long and tight and damp. He crawled along behind other men and had some behind him so there was nowhere to go. It was the slowest seventy feet he had ever travelled just shuffling along then waiting. Listening for any danger of capture and what was happening up ahead. Finally, his turn to emerge came, like the other men he stuck his head out of the hole like a rabbit and it was totally dark except for the sweeps of the searchlights. Once it came directly into his eyes and he was nearly blinded but the guards were too far away to see his head stick out. Then it passed, he had his orders, there was a string on the ground, grab that and follow it running in a crouch as fast as he could before the light came back. It led to a cutting in the barbed wire, he fell on his back and edged under it, two men were right on his tail urging him on. He struggled under the wire. It was totally dark as a thin fog was settling on the damp grass. He was out beyond the wire, he was free, and running like the wind hoping he didn't fall and break something but he kept going. The men behind could hardly keep up.

"Joe, where are you heading?" he heard a voice. Joe could only think of one thing and it made sense to him,

"Home." He said and again to himself, home and as he said the word the image of Maggie came to his mind and he was reminded he had more to live for than he thought. His legs took on more strength and he ran for the cover of the forest.

CHAPTER 43
Tuam Town Hall and an IRA Confrontation for Sean

Sean's months passed more quickly than Joe's and he had received a recommendation for the work his Company had carried out in Tuam. They had to clear the Town Hall of Republican sympathisers who had taken it over and threatened to take over the whole Galway town. His quick action impressed MacEoin. Sean had decided not to just come into town and take up camp. With his new rank of Major, he had to demand authority. He surprised everyone by fronting up to the Town Hall and surrounding it, not leaving those inside the opportunity to arm themselves or even consider resisting. He marched into the hall with ten armed men and confronted the Republicans some of whom were known to him.

"Who's in charge here?" He demanded, his men had their rifles at the ready and aimed at several men. It was an intimidation tactic that MacEoin would approve of, none of the men wanted to identify themselves and all sat mute. "Right then, all of you clear out then, this is Government property and you have no right to be here." He motioned to four men sitting in apparent positions of authority at a head table, "You four, stay here." He designated five of his troopers to take them aside, "the rest of you out." It was total bluff. Sean had no real intelligence as to whether the IRA had men ready to fight or not. He had heard that the local IRA was struggling to arm itself and though their cause was popular in this part of the country, the IRA men were becoming disheartened by the lack of success of their leadership.

MacEoin had wanted a show of force by the army in the important town and that's what Sean gave him.

"Power, Major, that's all the IRA understand, put the fear of God into them, they'll soon melt away." MacEoin had been fortified by more than a few whiskeys when he spoke to Sean but his reputation was solid from the many times he had confronted the Black and Tans.

So, force and power were what Sean brought to Tuam that afternoon, his men were tired and hungry and he promised them a good pub lunch as they had done well at the Town Hall. But first he had to deal with the four men he had arrested and had his men sort through the rest of the Town Hall visitors. It didn't take much for anyone to be considered an IRA member or sympathiser and they arrested another ten for good measure. They took them all back to Athlone prison the next morning. No need to front a Judge and justify the arrest, just throw them in prison and let a Court Martial deal with them when they got around to it.

He left thirty men in Tuam as a show of force and told them to hold the Town Hall and not let anyone enter, even the local council. Sean blamed them for letting the IRA have their way in the first place. The men would be relieved by the reinforced Garda in a couple of days. The army didn't want to occupy another town at this point, not in Galway anyway. An attack would be possible once the local IRA organised and got over losing a few leaders.

As he led the men back to Athlone, Sean decided the time had come to force the issue with Fianna. He had two days leave due and would take them and determined to see her the moment he could take leave of the Barracks.

He found Fianna at her home with her sister her parents were out visiting a friend which always made him more comfortable. Just as in Tuam, he decided on confrontation, when he had her on his own.

"Will you marry me Fianna?" he wasn't on one knee but his attitude had softened and it was a much a plea as a question. But Fianna didn't want to be bullied into a decision like this one and let him know it.

"So that's the way Free State officers get their way is it? Demanding a girl's hand in marriage? Had you not thought to ask nicely?" she barraged him with questions, annoyed as much as thrilled by the thought of Sean finally asking the obvious question. Her thoughts had changed over the past months and she realised she wanted him as much as he did her.

Sean was put off by her attitude, again unable to tell how young ladies should respond to such offers. His inexperience left him embarrassed and he didn't know how to answer her. But she saw his discomfort and took pity.

"If my Da and Mammy give me permission, I'd be happy to accept and be Mrs Major Sean McKeon." She smiled broadly, "But we have to wait. Not while there's a war going on, I don't want to get married with that hanging over our heads, I'm happy now being a teacher's aide and a couple of months more won't matter I'm sure. Sean took her in his arms and gave her a passionate kiss and realised that he longed for her in many ways. Unsure if his resolution would hold out for a couple of months.

Later that day they approached Fianna's parents with his request and they smiled and agreed. A date was set for July when summer would have arrived. Maybe the war would be over by then if all the news in the papers was correct. It had been reported that Mr de Valera had approached some Cabinet Members and the IRA leadership had apparently given their approval for the talks.

CHAPTER 44
Joe on the run

Seventy men had managed to escape through the newly dug tunnel that night in Tintown. They all headed off in different directions and were hopeful of making it back to the safety of their loved ones or compatriots who would take them in. But unlike the escapees from the Curragh and other prisons in the Tan War, there was less sympathy and assistance from the people for the men of the IRA who now sought help from their countrymen. Attitudes had changed over the last two years and the IRA could not depend on simply turning up in what they hoped was a sympathisers home and receive shelter. The Free State Government had also made it difficult for anyone who may have been tempted to help by arresting anyone who might have taken in escapees.

Joe's mistake on leaving the tunnel had been striking out on his own. He hadn't made any effort to link up with other men he knew would be escaping because he thought he would have Hugh with him. But Hugh's illness at the last minute left him without a partner. Still he was undaunted and the freedom he felt when he was running towards the woods near the Curragh racecourse which was close by to Tintown had kept him going and kept his spirits up.

He felt if he had gotten this far; the rest was going to be easy. But lying at rest in the woods exhausted from his running and spending the day by keeping out of sight and away from any searchers was starting to tell on him. He had a good sense of direction and geography and knew how far he would have to go. But knew he would need help and not just from the countryside but from the people he would inevitably encounter. There had been whispers of reliable Republican farmers in the area but their location was vague and only known to a few. Now he was hungry; he hadn't eaten in nearly two days and though water from streams was plentiful he needed food. You either got it by asking for it or stealing it.

Since Joe didn't want to trust anyone or put them in danger. He decided on the second option and he remembered he had passed a farmhouse on his way into these woods he would double back and try his luck. He found the house and it looked deserted as most farmhouses were in the late morning. He made his way to a rear door which was sheltered by some trees, it was unlocked as he suspected it would be and he made his way in and raided the empty kitchen. He quickly ate some bread and cheese and helped himself to some raw milk in a jug. He stuffed his pockets with more bread and feeling refreshed he decided it was time to move on.

He hadn't checked the house out fully and had missed the farmer who had been standing at the top of a small stairway with a pitchfork in his hands. Luckily, Joe took the same way out as he had coming in and tore off for some shelter. But he had been spotted and it wasn't an IRA sympathiser who had spotted him, this farmer had been inconvenienced too many times by escaping prisoners and Free State troopers who helped themselves too often to his provisions.

The farmer drove his trap three miles to the nearest police station and reported the theft. The police were aware of the escapes from Tintown and were already looking for escapees. It only took them four hours to track down Joe and arrest him in the woods nearby. They gave him a hiding for his audacity in escaping and another for his stealing.

Joe was unceremoniously taken back to Tintown and handed over to the prison guards who also welcomed him with a few body blows and plenty of insults. They then threw him into solitary confinement for two days on bread and water. Of the seventy men who escaped that night with Joe, thirty were back within days, twenty after another week and just twenty never returned. Prison rumour had it they had joined the IRA in the Wicklow Mountains.

A new rumour swept the camp at the end of April. Word had come in from visitors that the IRA had been in talks with the Provisional Government. The outcome of the talks was announced by Frank Aiken then Chief of Staff for the IRA. He had assumed the role after the death in action in early April of Liam Lynch the former holder of that position. Lynch was an ideologue and a fierce Anti-Treaty warrior. His appearance was that of a mild mannered school teacher and belied his strong emotional attachment to Republican ideals. His death was said to effectively signal the end of the Civil War. He tended to see the IRA as having a need to be martyred if necessary, to further the cause of Republicanism. He had an unmovable view on any surrender. He had held out many times not to surrender despite mounting evidence that the Republicans could not win the Civil War.

Aiken had a more practical outlook and having met with other senior officers of the IRA, just twenty days after Lynch's death they came to the conclusion that the IRA could not win the war. Furthermore, the majority of their men were in prison and they decided the fighting would have to stop.

An order to 'Cease Fire' was issued by the IRA leadership on April 30th.

The men in the camp were stunned. Joe sought out Hugh following a game of football and asked him,

"What will it mean Hugh? Did any of the senior officers here know about these talks?" Hugh as usual was slow to give much information but as a former Quartermaster of the Athlone Brigade he was high enough in rank to be included in some of the discussions by senior men in the camp,

"There had been some rumours reaching us for a couple of weeks Joe but you know how it is, who and what do you believe? There's so much rubbish doing the rounds. But now it does appear to be official, the leadership doesn't think we can win. Liam Lynch is dead and it was his beliefs that kept many of the leadership in line. Without him the thinking has changed and quickly. We're running out of money, the majority of the Republican side are in prison, some say as many as thirteen thousand. The government has forty thousand troops and more in reserve. We're outnumbered, outgunned and now the bosses think we may as well turn it in."

It was a succinct and accurate picture of the position of the IRA at that time. They had not been able to mount any major battles against the army. They had relied totally on guerrilla tactics which would only work if the population supported you as they did in the Tan War. But the people didn't support the IRA as much as what was needed, they had had enough. They just wanted a break from the fear and the fighting and the politics. By now so had the IRA leadership, the continued arrest of IRA men and potential recruits had heavily impacted the ability to carry on the war.

"Does everyone know Joe?" asked Hugh, who had heard the murmurs from the men.

"I think they do, the whispers went like wild fire, I was told by four different men in three hours so I think they all know. But what they don't know is what to think about it, they have to accept that we have been beaten and that's no easy thing to do." Both Hugh and Joe's thinking reflected the majority of the men in the camp. There was confusion, disappointment and fear of what was likely to happen next but also some hope that perhaps many could now be released if the fighting was to stop.

But the announcement of the ceasefire did not bring any immediate or dramatic change from their captors, the misery continued and, in some ways, increased. Scabies was rife in the camp with most men affected by it as well as lice, and impetigo. There were no shower facilities in parts of Tintown forcing men to walk hundreds of yards in all sorts of weather to bathe. Then a flu epidemic struck the camp affecting over two hundred men with little hospital care, though no fatalities eventuated. It seemed to the men that the Government just wanted to ignore them.

The IRA leadership in the camp was also in chaos with three different commanders taking on the role over just a few weeks. The leaders were treated harshly by the Staters and beaten when they wouldn't come forward with information. The prisoners were becoming more desperate and a number of new tunnels were started but as their command structure was not consistent, they came to nothing and were easily discovered by the guards. The prisoners believed that the 'Cease Fire' order meant the war was over and started to disobey the guards. They wanted some signal or information from the authorities that their lot would improve or they would be released. But such agitation just brought further reprisals with men being locked in their huts for days on end and casually beaten.

May went on and though the weather was warming, the mood wasn't improving. Then on May 25th, Hugh spoke to Joe about another story that had come in from outside,

"There's been an order to dump arms Joe. You know what that means they have definitely decided there's no point in going on." Joe was again confounded; he understood that 'Dump Arms' to the IRA had a special meaning. They weren't surrendering them to the other side they were simply giving up their arms and ammunition often to local churches and priests, or burying them in forests or farms. Anything but give them to the enemy.

"Jaysus Hugh, that's it then. Does Aiken know what he's doing?" he was referring to the new Chief of Staff for the IRA who had determined the need to bring fighting to an end.

"We can only hope so Joe, he's a good man and wouldn't give up without good reason. He must believe we don't have what's needed to force a victory and he's in close with Dev, so I assume he's had a lot of input into the politics of the matter. You know Dev, you couldn't have breakfast with him without it becoming a political matter." Hugh was confident in the leadership but having spent the last nine months as a prisoner all he had to go on was rumours and gossip from his comrades. He personally couldn't see any way out of the dilemma.

Joe nodded agreement, he had come across Dev himself when he had visited their area in the Tan War and he had stood guard for him and his group. He couldn't help but feel some kind of kinship with his oratory and vision for the country and agreed that Dev was indeed charismatic though he wasn't fully sure what that meant.

"Well Hugh, let's hope some good comes out of it, God knows we've had enough of living like this. Every one of us is fed up with the Staters and their attitude to us. We want it to end somehow." Joe was quietly angry he also was a party to gossip and knew that the State was still rounding up IRA suspects even after the cease fire order. He learned later that over four hundred men had been arrested in April and May including even after the "Dump Arms" order. It was difficult to have any confidence in Government announcements.

Joe's, and indeed all the prisoners' hopes, were dashed as time went along. There was no prisoner release from the Free State Government after the cease fire and dump arms order to the IRA men in the field. Then as if to press home their advantage in July the Government passed a new law, the Public Safety Act. This gave them further power and simply turned the Free State Government into a virtual military dictatorship. The round ups of IRA suspects continued and no release date was given to the prisoners in the vast prison camps which now held over twelve thousand IRA prisoners. There were national elections in August and Sinn Fein the party that supported the IRA's direction was successful in some areas but the government of William Cosgrave and Kevin O'Higgins was returned. The Sinn Fein members elected to the Dail would not take their place because they had to take an oath to the King of England their party policy determined they would not do that. It seemed like a hollow victory to the men in the camps.

The Republicans kept to their promise and their stance of non-entry to the Dail and their attitude to the Civil War itself was described later: *"The real struggle was for the mind and soul of once proud nation, and now, in the end of it all, they were asked to pledge allegiance to a foreign king and acknowledge the right of the former enemy to keep troops in Ireland. These symbols of domination contrasted so violently with the inspiring vision of a free and independent Ireland that they were utterly unacceptable."*

The months dragged on for the prisoners with no release in sight and then in October 1923 the decision was made by the prisoners to do what many had been promoting for some time. The IRA had one last weapon to utilise and with it the prisoners were determined to use it to force the Government's hand.

CHAPTER 45
Sean and Fianna Marry

As sometimes happens with young people, the passion of their romance overcame Sean and Fianna and their marriage date was moved forward to late May to try to avoid embarrassing questions from friends and family. Fianna was with child as the priest put it privately but the circumstances did not have any negative effect on Sean. Perhaps because he was male and his family more liberal-minded, he couldn't understand what all the fuss was about. It was Catholic Ireland in the 1920's and society took a dim view of some situations that young people found themselves in during the troubled times. Fianna would have the support of her fiancé and they would hold their heads high and weather the storm of gossip if it came. Her mother had a meltdown but got over it quickly when her husband pointed out that one of her sisters had found herself in the same position a number of years earlier.

Sean and Fianna had the traditional church wedding in May and it was attended by many including Sean's CO General MacEoin and a number of other fellow officers. The reception was held in Sean's Bar in Athlone, no relation to the groom, but it had the reputation of the oldest pub in the world. It was a tight fit for the guests although being the oldest pub it was certainly not the biggest pub.

General MacEoin had organised a number of Troopers to stand guard in the street outside and a few more were stationed nearby in case any of the local republican lads decided to make any trouble. But the day passed without incident. Before Sean took his leave for a few days of honeymoon, the General took him aside. He wanted to briefly discuss a troubling situation for the army and perhaps the government.

"You may have heard whispers about some unrest in the higher ranks, I just wanted to assure you that nothing will come of it." He looked at Sean expecting an answer and Sean scrubbed his foot on the floor, he had indeed heard whispers and was involved in some himself. Being Ireland, it was difficult not to be drawn into a political discussion and this one was potentially explosive but Sean had not taken any side as yet.

"Yes General, I've heard things, it's hard not to; men come to you with ideas and gossip and you have to listen to them but I don't let it affect my judgement." He hoped it was the right answer, he knew MacEoin was in the politics of it all up to his ears but Sean preferred to keep out of it for the present.

"Yes, well that's the right approach my boy, as I say nothing will come of it but let me know if you become concerned about anything you hear." His comment was laden with irony and meaning. He was anxious that the disquiet didn't move to lower officer ranks and become a different problem. He needed to know how the lower officer ranks felt and he relied on Sean to keep him aware of any potential problems.

MacEoin's concerns were to be realised in the next year in a series of incidents that would seriously threaten the stability of the government and the country. As the Civil War wound down it transpired that the Free State Army Officer Corp was separating into three ideological groups. The Irish Republican Army Organisation led by Liam Tobin were "Old IRA" officers who had been strong leaders in the Tan War. They were considered to be waverers and still sympathetic to the Republican cause. Their loyalties were with the Free State Government but if matters went bad for the Government it was felt that this group of officers would find solace and perhaps link up with the IRA. A second group coalesced around the newly reformed Irish Republican

Brotherhood whose influence had dropped significantly after the death of Michael Collins. A third faction was the traditional Army Chain of Command which was harbouring a distrust the other factions.

It all created tensions at the top of the Officer Corp and also for the government who relied on the Army to keep the peace and keep them in power. General MacEoin was feeling the strain and saw only too clearly the dangers inherent in the tensions these three groups created.

The Government had also decided it needed to demobilise much of the Free State Army which had grown too large for the country to afford. This decision was causing dissension as many men could see their careers and security disappearing. As Sean understood it, the tension was also increasing because in the second half of 1923 the government couldn't decide what to do with the thousands of interned prisoners whose number was still growing. The army was still rounding up IRA suspects, despite there being an official cease fire in place. The camps were simmering with discontent the prisoners knew they were being held illegally without any charges. Internment was purely at the whim of the government which was too scared to let them out en masse in case the Civil War started all over again. What the government didn't comprehend was that the men just wanted to get out and go home. The passion was still there but the wherewithal to fight was not.

Sean wondered about his old friends in these times and spoke about it to his new wife,

"You know that Joe and Hugh and a number of others we know are in Tintown and have been for a number of months?" Sean was curious as to whether Fianna talked about such matters with her family and friends and what the mood was in the community towards the prisoners.

    "I had heard Sean and my own thinking is that they have paid a heavy enough price for their different point of view. My Da and Mammy think the same and so do many of their friends. The IRA has called a cease fire and has dumped arms but the men are still kept in detention. A lot of people don't understand why." Fianna was sincere and somewhat saddened by the plight of young men whom she had grown up around and thought Sean should know her feelings. As an army officer's wife now her political instincts had been heightened. He was taken aback somewhat, not really expecting her to have an opinion he simply nodded without commenting further. He would play the thoughts back to the General who should be aware of what non military people were thinking.

For now, they were off on their honeymoon and the train to Dublin enabled them to spend a few days on their own without any cares. Later that year they would be parents and life would take on a whole new meaning. Sean was looking to the event with more enthusiasm than he realised he had for fatherhood. There was still tension throughout the country even though the IRA had effectively capitulated and Sean still had a role to play in containing that tension.

CHAPTER 46
Hunger Strike

It started in Mountjoy Jail on October 10th 1923 when four hundred and sixty two prisoners began their hunger strike. Within days it had spread to all other prisons and camps in the country and around seven thousand prisoners had joined what many felt was their last weapon because their plight had been ignored by the Government. The cease fire and the dump arms ordered by the IRA's government in exile had been swept aside and it was like they never happened. They weren't even officially acknowledged by the Irish Government.

A hunger strike was not believed by all to be the best way to proceed but desperation had won over the doubters. Having so many prisoners on a hunger strike meant that not all taking place could go the distance and so it proved to be. But most of those who took part restricted themselves to water only for at least ten days. Others went on for fourteen or twenty days, many reaching the end of October before succumbing to some nourishment. It was said by all of those who participated that they had never realised the challenge involved.

Joe and Hugh and many in their hut in Tintown lasted for twenty one days. The men wandered listless and alone in their thoughts for much of the time. They tried to keep themselves busy with camp pursuits, anything to keep their mind off their hunger.

Joe remembered the time he visited Dublin with Sean when they were just seventeen to attend the funeral of Thomas Ashe. He died not because of his hunger strike but because the prison authorities had force fed him causing damage to his system. In the event they made a martyr of him for all Republicans. Thomas Ashe came to Joe in his dreams, encouraging him and praying with him. It was obviously Joe's mind wandering off looking for solutions to his dilemma and Ashe offered one by consoling him.

Hugh and Joe were joined by twenty other men in their hut and the listlessness after five days hit them all. They weren't strong or over nourished in the first place having lived on prison rations and bad food for so many months. Hugh spoke to Joe about his feelings,

"The idea is that the Government will weaken and let us all out of prison, you know that don't you?" Joe just looked at his older step brother,

"Yes, I heard it but I don't believe it. O'Higgins and Cosgrave aren't going hungry. They probably haven't even seen the inside of a prison." This wasn't correct as Cosgrave had been imprisoned after the 1916 Easter Rising. But Joe wasn't in any mood to be hospitable about the leaders of the government.

"They'll see us all in hell before they do anything to help." But it was all they had the prisoners believed. It was the only way to put pressure on a recalcitrant government that still, months after a cease fire, arrested IRA men and kept the prisons full. There were those who chose to sign The Pledge which had been watered down by the Government. They would risk the wrath of their comrades outside, but Joe considered that was their problem, he wouldn't even contemplate it.

But the thought they were making the government uncomfortable gave most of the men some motivation to try and last as long as possible. But it was a terrible struggle and affected prisoners in serious medical ways, as later studies reported about other Hunger Strikes:

"In many ways, the bodies of prisoners generated knowledge as they decayed. Attending physicians learnt to recognise characteristic symptoms such as decreasing heart rate and physical wasting, even if the precise nature of the physiological processes of starvation remained unclear. They saw the bodies of hunger strikers rapidly decay during the first week of fasting, arousing fears of imminent death. Indeed, the speed of this initial decline had previously encouraged prison doctors to force-feed. The hunger strikers' bodies were quickly exhausting the fat reserves held in the adipose tissue. Once these had depleted, their bodies set to work consuming the glycogen stores, a secondary energy store located in the liver and muscles. Ammonia was produced at this stage, creating a distinctive smell. However, this ammonia was then excreted with keto acids to spare sodium loss and decrease the speed of weight loss. Physical decay began to slow. Doctors also saw other physical symptoms at this early stage including a loss of heart mass and the development of bradycardia, a resting heart rate of less than sixty beats per minute. It was this slow pulse that had encouraged doctors to force-feed just days into a hunger strike and pay close attention to the heart rate of prisoners"

One's conscious thoughts were also affected:

"Outsiders spoke of our 'pangs of hunger'. Nobody would ever believe that there are none. There is revulsion at death, a wild longing to live, but no physical call for food. That ceased on the second day. Now tastes and smells are pleasant to think of, but mean nothing. If the mind took the fast as quietly as the body does, the whole thing would seem like a joke, there would be so little suffering in it. If our friends outside would not believe this. But it is true and they never will."

Every man reacted differently, physically and mentally. The prisoners later spoke of the pride that they felt in having conquered physical hunger using will power and mental determination. But one element of the strike that no one contemplated was the disruption to the daily routine of the prisoners. Mealtimes, though the food itself was always paltry, punctuated the day and gave a social involvement to their incarceration. Few had realised that having the day broken with such rituals as meal times was very important and only noticed that importance when it wasn't there. They kept on with the hunger strike with melancholic results.

After twenty one days, Joe had had enough, he couldn't see or hear any change from the authorities and he started to doubt that the prisoners were being effective in changing government attitudes. He, Hugh and others had taken to their beds due to physical weakness without any real support from medical staff apart from what their own comrades offered. Now they called it off. Joe and Hugh took their first lot of soup and a small amount of bread on the evening of that day as did many of the other men. Recovering was a challenge as the body had to get used to being nourished all over again.

The calling off spread like a virus but was helped by some senior men who could see that it was having a negative effect on morale and not achieving its goals.

"We should call it off except for those we think can hold out but it won't be many." It was the prisoner commander speaking to Hugh and worried about what it was all doing to morale.

"They'll know when they've had enough," said Hugh, "They're human and they're bodies will tell them when."

"It's not their bodies I'm worried about", the commander answered, "It's the ones who want to be martyrs. They can make it hard for everyone."

It was true and perhaps a little unkind but the reality was that some men, certainly very few, had the ability to become martyrs for the cause. Not much would stop them continuing once they set their mind to it. Denis Barry died after a thirty four day hunger strike in the Newbridge Camp and Andy Sullivan died after thirty nine days in Mountjoy. The prison authorities wouldn't intervene as they were under orders to stay away from the starving prisoners and ignore them as much as possible. The prison medics such as they were, would only come if summoned. The Hunger Strikes took on an identity all of their own; many prisoners felt they should partake but felt despair when it got too much for them. Many like Joe and Hugh felt they had nothing to show for their sacrifices.

Joe and Hugh later discussed that the hunger strike had been the hardest thing they had undertaken.

"Jesus Joe I never knew what it would be like to be that hungry. For the first few days I would have eaten the leg off a chair but after a few days I didn't seem to miss the food at all. I guess my mind just goes into a blank. I was certainly confused about a lot of things; hallucinations I think they call them." Joe agreed,

"Yes, I got the same way, trying to keep busy but after a few more days, you have no energy to do anything. It all becomes a blur. God knows if it did any good Hugh but we had to do something. The government just seems to want to forget about us." Joe didn't mention his dreams of Thomas Ashe. He had dismissed them as hallucinations as Hugh had called them. The important thing now was to somehow support the men who continued the strike and see how they could help them.

Despite the government's dismissing of the hunger strike and their propaganda against it in the press, it clearly had an effect on them. The Ministers were deeply worried that too many deaths would make for more civil unrest. Already funerals were becoming major events with mile long processions and endless Requiem Masses for the deceased. The government offered prisoners who came off the strike early release. This was mostly refused in honour of all the fighting men who were still forced to eke out their war in prisons and internment camps. Finally, the government arrived at a policy of sorts in mid November. There would be no mass release of prisoners from the camps but it was decided to stagger their releases over several months. This was to be the end result for thirteen thousand men and some two hundred women who had been held in some cases for up to two years, without charge or trial. Officially it would begin at Christmas 1923 though for some the incarceration would last until July 1924. Like many other policies of the government, it was porous. Hundreds of men were released starting soon after the announcement by Minister O'Higgins in mid November. Then they still struggled to release thousands of prisoners with their ill thought out dribs and drabs policy over the following months.

After Christmas 1923, and through the rest of winter, Joe and Hugh, who had both been officers when arrested, would watch as men simply disappeared. Numbers in the camp dropped over December, January, February and March. No official advice, generally men were just tapped on the shoulder and told to gather their belongings, usually in groups of ten to fifteen. The brothers consoled themselves with the thought that at least men were getting out of the hellhole that was internment.

Joe and Hugh weren't released till early April 1924. Possibly because they had been Quartermasters in their respective units the Army decided to keep officers longer than the men. They were hoping that by keeping the officers back it would be too difficult to organise further rebellion. Little did they realise that most of the men and the officers had had enough, they accepted the loss and just wanted a normal life. In April, after nearly eighteen months in Tintown and Athlone prison, Joe and Hugh were dropped at a railway station and given a train pass for Athlone from Kildare, and told to be on their way.

They were going out into a new society of which they had little recognition or knowledge of. It would bring huge personal challenges for them as it would for all released prisoners.

CHAPTER 47
Home

Athlone was not a city that welcomed former IRA internees who had just been released from prison. It was an army garrison town and held the Midlands Division led by Brigadier General Sean MacEoin. Of course it was home to Joe and Hugh's former comrade Sean McKeon and it already had problems with so many army men being demobbed and now unemployed.

Arriving by train Joe and Hugh, and a few others who had been released with them, didn't delay too long in Athlone. They had little money anyway to spend and were anxious to get back to their home farms and greet their families, many of whom didn't know they had been released. Some news just didn't travel fast and there were precious few ways to contact family except by post and they would beat that by several days. Four men, including Joe and Hugh, Ned Irwin and Alex Carolan set off on foot from Athlone station for Drumraney which was about ten miles away.

They were no more than a mile out of town when they encountered their first problem. A truckload of Staters was heading back to town and as was their habit, stopped to see what these four men might be up to. Hugh quickly identified there could be trouble.

"Leave the talking to me, "said Hugh, "no point in getting into an argument now, they're just looking to be a pest, they know very well we're on our way home."

"So, Paddy where are you off to?" asked the officer who was no more than their own age but seemed full of himself. "Had enough of the fighting, have you?" he thought this was a joke and looked at the six other men who were with him waiting for a response. Some laughed, some just ignored him. Hugh had to bite his tongue, he didn't like being called Paddy, the Tans had done it continuously in the past and it didn't behove an Irishman to refer to another Irishman in that condescending way. Hugh pulled out his release paper and motioned for the three with him to do the same.

"Going home Colonel, after a nice break down south, here's our papers from the government." He had purposely increased the rank of the Lieutenant to annoy him and pay back the Paddy barb. He held the papers of the four men out for the officer to inspect them, he knew it wasn't going to be a pleasant encounter. He glanced at his comrades, winking to convey his suspicions and not wanting them to bite back.

"So, they've let you all out to wreak havoc on the countryside again have they Paddy? Think you can just come back home and forget about it all? You Republicans have another thing coming." The Lieutenant's expression, somewhere between a sneer and a smirk conveyed how he felt about the returning Irregulars.

"No Colonel we haven't all been let out as you say, just dribs and drabs as the Government has said, we were allowed to go just two days ago, A nice present don't you think. We're heading to our homes now and not wanting any trouble. Sure, we've had enough of that for the past two years." Hugh was the model of civility and the other men held their tongues.

"Don't be calling me Colonel, can't you understand army ranks?" he was getting more edgy, looking for any excuse to unleash some violence on the men. Hugh replied quietly:

"No sir, never had the training in uniforms, we didn't have the luxury." Hugh adjusted his cap to cover his eyes further knowing it would annoy the officer. By this time three of his troopers had gotten down from the truck and were starting to handle their rifles in a menacing way, for no good reason. Just at that time a motor car in army colours pulled up behind the truck and voice called out,

"What's going on Lieutenant?" The young officer went a bit white and turned to salute the voice in the car.

"Just checking these men sir, making sure they're not causing any problems."

"Come over here son," the voice in the car said and Hugh and the other could see it was a very senior officer with braid and badges showing a high rank. He was angry and didn't need this nonsense to make him worse. His voice was sharp, "I think you would have heard the briefing at the barracks that there would be a number of Irregulars coming our way and going to their homes, it's obvious these men are some of them. We agreed with the men in the Curragh and Dublin that we would let them proceed so as not to create any incidents."

"Sir" said the younger officer. The senior officer spoke again sharply,

"I suggest you do just that without delay."

"Sir" said the Lieutenant again, saluted smartly and moved away from the car and got back into the front of the truck.

"Could we have our papers back please Colonel?" said Hugh holding his hand out. "We'll need them to prove who we are and that we've been released. We can't go on without them." The Lieutenant threw them back at Hugh and they landed on the ground.

"Thank you, sir." Hugh said as he collected the papers knowing the exaggerated politeness would annoy him more than anything else.

"On your way then and don't be causing any problems or we'll get you inside again." The Lieutenant made another salute to the officer's car and they drove away. The officer's car was quick to follow and as it passed Joe noticed another officer in the back seat with the General who he was now sure was MacEoin. It was a brief glimpse and the officer didn't look his way but Joe was sure he recognised the face of Sean McKeon. He nudged Hugh but the moment had passed and so had the staff car. Hugh apparently didn't see what Joe had, and he said,

"So, Joe, Generals do have some use after all it seems." Hugh grinned more broadly this time glad the confrontation was over and that it had finished without further incident.

"They must do more than just issue orders, I'm glad he came along."

"You know it was General MacEoin don't you?" Joe said to Hugh and the other two men.

"I expect it was, I don't think there are too many generals riding around this part of the countryside." Hugh answered, "Did you see who was in the back seat?" Joe's head shot up at this, so Hugh had seen!

"Our old friend Sean, seems you recognised him but he didn't recognise us."

"More likely didn't want to see us I'd say." Said Hugh, "he looked rather smart in his crisp uniform don't you think?" Hugh was joking and teasing Joe. Joe was lost for words for a moment and turned to Ned Irwin, who had been sent to Tintown as well after his time in Athlone after being picked up at the same time as Joe and Dan Crowley.

"You used to know Sean McKeon Ned, he lived not far from your farm?" Ned nodded and agreed,

"He was a good fella when we knew him but he had a change of heart about his politics. No doubt about that." but he didn't want to discuss it any further. Hugh broke the mood,

"Come on we've got more miles to walk and those clouds are looking as though they want to bring us some rain."

The three other men nodded their agreement, they didn't have much to carry, no suitcases just old clothes rolled up and slung around their shoulders with a belt. They wouldn't be bringing much home to their families after so long away from them.

As the army staff car drove away the officer in the back seat did manage a brief glance at the men and at first, he didn't make any recognition. Just more vagabonds on the road and more trouble likely to deal with in the future. He wondered how the army was going to handle the returning Irregulars but was impressed as always by the General's handling of the young Lieutenant, no need to make trouble, it will find you if it has a mind to.

They were some way along the road to the barracks before the recognition came to him, of course, Joe Keegan and Hugh Murtagh! He had seen their names in the report that had come from the Curragh three days earlier. A warning that released Irregulars would be coming their way over the next few weeks and months. The dribs and drabs prisoner release program was continuing and the local forces had to deal with it as best they could.

The Keegan family farm was a small white washed stucco cement two story house. There were three bedrooms and a kitchen come eating area. This doubled as a room the whole family would use for lounging around in or prayers or whatever. The house wasn't far off the road which was just a track rutted by horse and carts over many years. Joe and Hugh had bid good day to their travelling companions who were going off to their own farms and families. They stood outside on the track as if wondering what to do. Hugh finally spoke,

" Well we've come this far; we won't be delaying it any longer."

There was apprehension because they hadn't been able to warn the family they were heading home and they weren't sure how their Da would greet them. He hadn't exactly forbidden them their rebel activities. But once the Treaty had been announced he had been happy enough to accept it and settle down to a normal life again. He wasn't totally pro Treaty and his neutral position had been the cause of many heated discussions in the home. Joe and Hugh went off to meetings with anti-Treaty Republicans and got involved in the politics again and more fighting.

"Just let it go!" Peter Keegan had said to his sons, "no good will come of it. Just get on with your work and let the politicians handle it."

"We have to take our side Da, we have to let them know that the Treaty doesn't give the country what we fought for. It's a rotten compromise and it doesn't work." Both brothers had argued back and the discussion had been echoed in many homes around the country with little resolution.

General MacEoin and Sean McKeon made the argument moot by arresting over one hundred and twenty IRA men and sympathisers within Westmeath before the IRA forces could get organised in their bailiwick. Joe hadn't realised that the arrested men in many cases would be locked away for the next fifteen months. Joe and Hugh were missed in the early sweeps and managed to keep their freedom for a while longer than some.

The two brothers presented themselves to their family by simply knocking on the front door and any concerns they had just fell away. Both parents were in tears and their younger siblings mobbed them with hugs; the elder boys James and Thomas shook their hands till they were likely to fall off. It took some minutes for the excitement to die down and gradually the reality of being home sank in and they quietly enjoyed the goodwill and warmth of their family.

Everyone had lots of questions and a number of crossed conversations took place. Joe and Hugh asked James about how he fared after being let out of Custume Barracks in December 1922.

"Well it was no circus; we were all starving when some of us were released and we heard you and many others were going to the Curragh. I came home here and Mammy and Da put me back together again and for the past year we sent you and Hugh what we could but as you know there hasn't been a lot." James was being honest, there was now a family of eight children before Joe and Hugh arrived back home. They could see the strain on Peter and Mary's faces, they had aged many years in the time they had been away. Joe spoke wanting them to know how much they had appreciated the parcels.

"We appreciated what we got, we knew there wouldn't be much with the lot you had to feed here but whatever we got was welcomed and helped to keep us going. Sometimes the guards took the pickings out before we got to them. They found your cakes a treat Mammy." He smiled widely at Mary who reddened a little but he gave her another hug and more tears came to her eyes. At many stages of his imprisonment Joe had dreamt of this moment and his own eyes now filled with tears.

Then Mary excused herself and headed for the kitchen. They would all share that night in a good Irish stew she said. Whatever potatoes and vegetables they could muster and somehow there would be some meat to go into the mix. Mary had become adept at making small portions seem larger and managed to feed the whole family when rations went short.

They said the rosary before dinner and the young ones tucked into their meals. The fire was raging even though it was summer. The house was warmer than Joe and Hugh could ever remember and they felt as content as they had for the past two years. The young ones went off to bed soon after and Hugh, Joe, James, Thomas, Patrick and Teresa sat around with their Da and Mammy and shared some rolled cigarettes from Hugh's tobacco pouch. They drank tea and talked into the night about the Curragh and Custume Barracks and life on the run. But they managed to avoid any arguments about politics which was not a simple exercise in an Irish family gathering, but Mary had been insistent.

Before they went to sleep for the night, James and Thomas took Joe and Hugh aside,

"It's been very tough for Da and Mammy; the weather, the crops, the amount of work, the young ones needing school and all, but they're tough and they deliver somehow or other." But they could see James was genuinely concerned and he went on, "Pat and I have been trying to find work everywhere but there isn't much to be had. We have walked into Athlone time and again but there's nothing there either. The Woollen Mill isn't taking anyone on and the whole area has slowed down. The biggest industry was the army but now they have been letting men go."

This didn't come as a surprise to Joe and Hugh. They had heard the army had swelled to almost fifty thousand men in the last year and it wasn't possible to sustain those numbers for such a small country. They had started to demobilise creating major problems for the country, up to thirty thousand soldiers were to be demobbed. With up to twelve thousand Irregulars also being released over a period of the same months it meant a huge number of men would be looking for work that just wasn't available.

Joe and Hugh looked at each other. The last thing they wanted was to be an extra burden on their family. But they had nowhere else to go and had badly wanted to come home to see their family. They would talk about it extensively over the next few days but for the time being they would do whatever they could to take some of the load off Peter and Mary and try to work out their future plans.

CHAPTER 48
An Army Mutiny?

The winter of 1923/24 was coming to an end and Sean McKeon was enjoying his role of father and husband. His wife Fianna had safely delivered a baby boy just prior to Christmas and life had changed considerably for them both. It was also rumoured another promotion, this time to Colonel was a distinct possibility. With the demobilisations under way the army was undergoing major changes and a reshuffle of the officer ranks was inevitable. The need for the army to reduce its numbers had created ructions and factions within the hierarchy of the army. Many former officers of the IRA had joined the Free State army after the Treaty negotiations as much as anything to support Michael Collin's position. They had created a cabal within the officer ranks that wasn't trusted by the government. Others sided with Irish Republican Brotherhood which was still a secret society and created tensions by demanding loyalty to it over the government.

Most of this was going on in Dublin but officers like Sean in other parts of the country couldn't just ignore it. He had been approached by both sides of the dispute. The hard core of officers still loyal and bound by their oaths of office were nervous about what the IRA faction would do. He spoke to his wife of his concerns.

"God knows where this is going Fianna, I'm not even supposed to be aware of some of the intrigue but it appears to be everywhere. The old IRA men feel they have a grievance as it is most of their men that are being demobilised. They feel as though they are being neutralised which of course they are." Fianna couldn't see the dilemma; her position was straightforward.

"Your loyalty is to the government and the army, any move away from that means mutiny and God knows what the outcome of that would be. You know what General MacEoin feels about it, talk to him. But you must be aware that you must be loyal to your government."

"Of course you are right. I don't know what I was thinking." To his surprise, her political acumen had grown quite rapidly and she had a clear view of the situation. His head had been turned briefly by some younger officers who were facing demobilisation and they didn't like the prospect. Sean wasn't in that position. His expertise was respected and needed by the army and the government. But Sean's feelings were complicated by another matter and that was the attitude shown by his leaders, General MacEoin and Colonel Lawler. He had long lost respect for Lawler for the way he had treated the IRA prisoners and had killed one in a ridiculous and indefensible act of authority the previous year. The General also wasn't beyond pulling out his revolver and holding it to the head of any argumentative prisoner even if just to frighten the Christ out of him. Sean had expected more from senior officers but certainly much more from the General, who had let Lawler have his way and gave him too much authority when it was obvious he couldn't handle it.

MacEoin had also taken to drinking too much and Dublin seemed to care less. He was out of sight and out of mind. His part of the country was relatively quiet in the Civil War apart from the active columns in the west and northwest of the county, but matters seemed well in hand.

There was little Sean could do about MacEoin's drinking and maybe it wasn't any of his business, he was his commanding officer and that was all there was to it. But the gossip and talk about a major change in the senior officer's ranks intrigued Sean.

He decided to swallow his pride and approach the General to get a better feel of what was going on and what might happen.

"General, this business in Dublin between the Ministers and senior officers, what do you make of it?" He was pretty sure of MacEoin's response but needed to be reassured. The General as usual, was adamant.

"Storm in a teacup I'd say. The fact is the government must prevail or we go back into another and worse Civil War. This time the IRA would have more weapons from the army side. It can't be allowed. That's all there is to it". He looked at Sean directly, "there is no likely compromise, the Brotherhood and the old IRA have to be stared down. Eoin O'Duffy has been made Inspector General of the Army and he will make his decisions for the good of the country. He has consulted widely and he's an intelligent man and capable." Sean nodded in agreement, His dilemma hadn't been fully solved but any remaining questions would be answered by subsequent events in Dublin in the coming week.

A number of days after Sean's talk with the General, Inspector General Eoin O'Duffy had the Devlin pub in Dublin surrounded and arrested a number of serving Army officers who were having a secret meeting. Minister of Defense Mulcahy saw the writing on the wall and resigned. He was criticised for tolerating the IRB interference and also for letting the old IRA develop power in the army.

The government stepped in and made the major changes necessary to retain control. The IRB was banned, new senior officers in Dublin took control and MacEoin was confirmed as General Office Commanding, Western Command. Secret societies would no longer be tolerated within the army ranks. The events were portrayed as an Army Mutiny by the media and had made the government look vulnerable at a critical time.

The whole thing had blown over before the end of March and Sean had been relieved of having to make a career threatening decision. He himself had also secretly been in favour of not demobilising so many troops but he had wisely decided not to share that thought with anyone.

He would focus again on his army career and enjoy the promotion if it came his way. Life ahead looked promising since the Civil War ended, hostilities had, apart from some roving columns in the south been eliminated.

CHAPTER 49
1924 The Year of Change and Decision

Well into his first month of freedom back in Drumraney, Joe was enjoying the hard work of the farm. He was toiling from first light till after dark and had immersed himself in the problems of agriculture, carpentry, building and clearing the scrub. He just wanted to fill his mind with anything but bad memories of his internment. If possible he would block out all politics until he had a better sense of where the country was heading. Sadly, apart from a few games of field Hurley with his friends, he wasn't able to go back to where he had left with the game. He had hoped for an All Ireland championship with Westmeath but that was as far off as ever, now there were other priorities.

He finally allowed himself memories that he had kept out in the last months of his confinement. But being back near Athlone made it easier to think of Maggie Egan, the girl who had left Ireland for Australia, and whom he now couldn't stop thinking about. The thoughts of their last encounter were dear to him. How she had looked at him and how he felt, new feelings he had never experienced before in his life. Joe, a fighting IRA man, who had terrified the RIC and the Tans, turned to mush when he remembered that look in her eyes.

After six weeks, he had made a decision, he would go into Athlone. He knew where the Egans lived and he would try and find Maggie's brothers John or Ned and get an address from them to send a letter to Maggie in Australia. He told Peter he needed the day off and where he was going the next Sunday after mass. Peter hadn't heard of Joe's feelings about Maggie and was a little surprised but Hugh was able to fill in the gaps for him after Joe had left on his long walk.

It was necessary for Joe to be careful; the roads were still patrolled by the army and he was determined not to come across the Staters who had given them grief when they first arrived from the Curragh. There were also a number of demobbed soldiers around and it wouldn't take much for a brawl to erupt between them and any former Irregulars they encountered. So, Joe was extra careful, fighting and trouble weren't on his mind; he was focused on finding the Egan boys. He knew the address was in Irishtown within Athlone and was sure even after a couple of years of being able to find the house, which he did. What he hadn't done was work out what he would do when he had found the house so he sat on a bench in a nearby park and pondered his next move. But after an hour there was no sign of the two Egan brothers.

"Bugger it," he said to himself, "what are you afraid of you big ninny? Just go and knock on the door." So he did. It was answered by Maggie's mother.

"Mrs Egan?" he asked, starting to feel fear for the first time in a while, he would have preferred a night time raid on an RIC barracks than this.

"Yes" the lady answered politely. Joe grasped for words trying not to look as concerned as he felt. He had been hoping one of the lads would have answered the door which would have made matters simpler.

"I'm Joe Keegan, I've um, been away for a while but before I went, I had the pleasure of meeting your daughter Maggie and I know she doesn't live here anymore but I was keen to be in touch with her." Mrs Egan expression was quizzical but she was politeness itself. Joe remembered his first meeting with Maggie's mother but wondered if she did. She soon put him out of his misery.

"I thought you looked familiar Joe. You came here once to see Maggie before she went away didn't you? Why don't you come in." They went into a small front room which was lightly furnished and Joe couldn't help but notice what looked like bullet holes on the outside walls of the house so he indicated them as much as anything to make a conversation.

"Seems you had some other visitors at one time, not welcome I'll wager."

"Yes," she said looking at the damage, "The Tans in 1920, very scary, bullets going everywhere." She seemed unfussed by the incident now but Joe knew it would have been terrifying for a family unable to defend themselves. What she hadn't said was that the battle with the Tans had raged for about three hours with a huge amount of gunfire terrifying the unarmed residents.

"Now", she said as she sat on her lounge "tell me about Maggie."

Joe was taken aback not expecting to be challenged so directly, there wasn't a lot to tell. He had met the young lady and was smitten by her and couldn't stop thinking about her. Now he wanted to be in touch with her to see if she felt the same way or even remembered him. Joe's felt his face redden and his mouth went dry, he swallowed once or twice and hoped it didn't show.

"It's very embarrassing Mrs Egan I can't really explain it," he played with the cap in his hands and could feel himself going redder in the face, finally he said it, "I just can't stop thinking about her!" Mrs Egan went quiet and could see the young man was embarrassed but she was sympathetic.

"That's very nice of you Joe, Maggie could affect young men that way." She said with a slight smile, then she paused, "Well you know we sent her and her sister Rose to Australia. We felt we didn't have any choice; we had an offer from an aunt of her fathers to take them in for the duration of the troubles and we felt it best if they went. But it's so far and takes so long for the mail. We miss them terribly but we know they're safe. The incident with the Tans made up our mind, this town was no place for young ladies to grow up and be safe in."

"I'd like to write to her," Joe blurted out wishing he could find a hole to hide in, but he realised he needed to elaborate, "we only met for a short time but I still think about her a lot. She's the only lass I have thought about."

Mrs Egan went quite for a minute or two again obviously thinking about what Joe had said and pondering the ins and outs of it. But she knew she had to confront this unexpected situation.

"Well they have been gone now eighteen months and we were hoping they would be sent back. But it seems they had a falling out with my husband's Aunt who wanted to treat them like slaves apparently when they got to Sydney. My husband's Aunt and her husband apparently owned six terrace houses near the city, which they let out. They expected Maggie and Rose to keep them clean and work seven days a week for a roof over their own heads. But Maggie and Rose had other ideas. Maggie was too stubborn to be treated that way and she wanted to look after Rose who was younger and more frightened of the lady. She was supposed to pay their fares and send them back to us when we asked and when the fighting had stopped. But she wouldn't."

"So, what happened then?" asked Joe his concern growing.

"Well they're both very industrious and they decided to go their own way. They left the lady's employ and found new lodgings helped by an Irish lady, Mrs Murphy, who befriended them and got them settled." It was clear that Mrs Egan had been distressed by the run of events her young daughters faced so far away and she had been unable to help them. It had been a source of great concern for her and her husband but she now seemed a little brighter. Joe had to ask:

"Are they okay now, have they settled in?" he didn't know what else to say. Mrs Egan could see Joe's concern was real even though she hadn't thought of him before this day, but he was certainly genuine.

"Yes, we hear from them regularly and they have found work in a department store in Sydney called Mark Foys not far from where the have found lodgings with Mrs Murphy. They're trying to save as much as they can to come home but it's very difficult for them. Of course we're saving as well to help them, but...." she shrugged and that said it all. Money was very short.

"Now tell me young man, about yourself and what you have been up to."

Joe was taken aback. He knew the Mrs Egan had the right to ask the question. He had avoided polite company since he had been home as much as anything because he didn't trust himself after having spent so much time talking rough and tough with other prisoners. Also he didn't know what to say to the lady but now he had to come clean.

"Mrs Egan you know as well as I that there is a lot of strong opinions in this country, and the last year or two have shown those as much as anything could." He was referring to the Civil War but didn't want to mention that but he also wasn't going to apologise for his stance and beliefs. "We young men had to take sides as many others did as well, and after the Tan war and the Treaty we were forced to declare ourselves. I have been a member of the local IRA in Westmeath since I was sixteen and so have my brothers. Many were rounded up by General MacEoin who had been our commanding officer in the IRA, in July and August 1922, he knew who and where we all were. The arrested men were locked away in Athlone Barracks for five months without a trial and then sent to the Curragh for another year or more. I had been able to join Tom McGiff's Flying Column and I wasn't arrested till November. We were just released a couple of months back. So, I am a Republican through and through and have paid for the privilege and I won't apologise for it. But it hasn't been an easy time and I don't know what the future holds except to say it doesn't look too good. The only positive thing that I had in the last two years was the memory of your daughter and how I felt about her even though we didn't see a lot of each other." Joe surprised himself with his eloquence and now felt a stronger feeling, he felt tears welling up inside and wasn't sure how to cope or if Mrs Egan would let him down easily. But he wanted to finish, "We know we've been beaten and that the people want no more fighting and they have accepted the Treaty and we have to as well, so we have to make the best of our lot and get on with it."

"I understand Joe, this country has been torn apart and often there's no right or wrong and we all have had to take sides. Hopefully the country can heal itself now that the worst has been done. But I think it's going to take many years." She got up from her chair and went to a sideboard and took out some papers and returned to sit down.

"Thanks for coming to see me Joe, I can't see any harm in you being in touch with Maggie. This is her address in Sydney, in a suburb called Glebe. If you write to her, remember she is facing many troubles herself. They have been saving to buy a ticket home but it is very difficult. I'm sure she would love to hear from you, you are a sincere young man and you have shown that by coming here today. We would have no concern with you being in touch with her." Joe almost did cry but it was something he hadn't done since a boy when he stopped a hurling stick with his shins in a fast game. He swallowed a few times before he spoke.

"Thank you, Mrs Egan, you have made me a happy man. I'll let you know if she replies." With that, he took his leave and walked down the street smiling to himself all the way. For her part Mrs Egan couldn't see the harm, after all her daughter was twelve thousand miles away. This young man, though he was dedicated to his cause and seemed very sincere he had created a good impression with her. But he was never likely to see her daughter unless she could make it back to Ireland. She would enjoy receiving a letter from someone from her home county.

Joe contemplated how he would get some writing paper and then buy a stamp to send the letter on its way. Everything was in short supply and Joe's money was even scarcer and his handwriting needed to improve considerably. But he had accomplished what he had set out to do even though he would have preferred to speak to one of the brothers than Mrs Egan. She was a nice lady he decided and she wasn't too judgemental about him and his story.

#   #

Joe and Hugh had been to a meeting with the local IRA a week earlier and though the IRA wasn't active as an army anymore, it was still active as an organisation. And it still wanted to have a hold over its members. There was always the latent hope that if things changed, they could still achieve their ambitions of a

Republic. The IRA hadn't been made illegal yet but they were gradually being driven underground from the constant interference by the Garda and the Army. Men like Hugh, Joe, James, Patrick and Thomas still felt an affiliation with the IRA. After all, it had been a big part of their lives for the past six or so years and they had served time in prison for its ideals.

But the country's economy was to say the least, stagnant. There was no economic growth and very little work particularly in rural areas, there was no Roaring Twenties in rural Ireland. The brothers knew they couldn't rely on their parent's farm for too long as it didn't have the capacity to sustain them all. God knows they all worked very hard but that didn't make the ducks or hens or turkeys lay eggs faster or get the crops out of the ground any quicker. There was always a struggle to get enough for the family to get by.

Hugh and Joe were always looking for work to bring in extra money and apart from some piece work that didn't pay too well there wasn't a lot about. Some people were prepared to support ex IRA men but not enough. Throughout the country there were also thousands of demobbed soldiers competing with thousands of recently released prisoners, all looking for work. This caused resentment and made the ex prisoners feel unwanted by society. The running sore for the IRA men was that it was a badly kept secret that ex army men were to be given preference over all others. That's if and when any jobs were made available. Some tried to hide it behind weasel words but everyone knew it was an unofficial government policy. It was reinforced by the prejudices of the employers who often resented the problems the IRA had caused during the Civil War.

So, the question of emigrating always came up whenever the brothers discussed their future.

"Would you go to the States Joe" Hugh asked the day after the IRA meeting "or God forbid, England?" Hugh had been thinking a lot about their situation and what their options were. Joe kept his counsel for the present. He had thought about moving of course but it was always pushed to the back of his mind. There was too much else to consider and they had to help their family but they felt ultimately they were more of a burden than a help to their parents.

"We'll have to think about." Joe answered, "from what we hear there's thousands of men going there whether the IRA likes it or not." The political reality was that the present government was in power and Sinn Fein was as dormant and defeated as the IRA. But the IRA wouldn't entertain the idea of their men leaving the country. The meeting they had attended had heard a warning from the Chief of Staff Frank Aiken saying that anyone who wanted to migrate had to have IRA approval. The likely outcome was that it wouldn't be given. The IRA didn't want to lose the bulk of what had been their fighting force to the 'Wild Geese' phenomenon. That was the name given to many thousands who had also left the country in the 1790s and again in the 1840s after losing their independence struggles at those times.

To a large extent, the IRA had won this independence struggle but the victory was seen as hollow by many of the men. The goal had been an IRA victory and a thirty two county Republic of Ireland. What they got was a half-baked Dominion status with the English still clutching at their throats and the six Northern Ireland counties in the firm grip of the Protestants.

Joe and Hugh had been out of Tintown for three months now and summer was at its height but the sun didn't bring much cheer. They couldn't find much work around Drumraney and Athlone offered even less opportunity. The cards were stacked against them. In fact, Joe had come to the firm conclusion that leaving Ireland was their best option. Hugh was thinking along the same lines and Joe knew some of their friends, Ned Irwin among them wanted to make the move as well. Finally, Joe decided to make the case: "We'll just have to ignore the IRA orders Hugh; they can't find us work and we can't find any. We can't go on like this." Hugh was conflicted, his loyalty to his mother was extremely important to him. He respected his step father Peter enormously. But at one time there was just him and Mary even though he was very young when she married Peter. But Mary had a toughness about her which was evident in what she dealt with everyday. After some time he answered Joe,

"It's a big step Joe. Are we up to it? A new beginning without family."

"That's what we've been doing for the least two years Hugh, we had no family in Tintown and we survived." Joe said.

"Yes but we knew they were always close, if we go away we may never see them again."

Joe knew that but couldn't let that decide their fate.

"It's not fair to Da and Mammy or the young ones if we stay Hugh. There's not enough food for everyone and I'll be buggered if I'll stay and see my sisters starve because I took the food out of their mouth." Joe was more emotional than Hugh had ever seen him. They both loved their family and didn't want to be a burden any longer. "We can go to England, there's more chance of getting some work there. I don't care what we do but we won't be a burden here and we can make enough money for a boat trip."

Joe hadn't yet told Hugh that he wanted to go to Australia because that's where Maggie was. He didn't want to go to the States and

Australia would be easier to migrate to. The Americans had started to introduce quotas with extra requirements but Australia was part of the British Empire. The formalities of changes to the passport rules and regulations had not yet taken place. Ireland was still being treated by the English mandarins as a recalcitrant child. This thinking made it easy for the Irish to continue to flow into England. The Irish were still considered to be British subjects for passport purposes, entry into Australia would not be a problem. The irony wasn't lost on Joe, he didn't want to be a British subject in Ireland but he would have to be in Australia!

Joe had to tell Hugh that for him it would be Australia. But Hugh was free to go to the States if he chose.

"I've spoken to you about a lass I met here before we were arrested. I've since been to see her mother and I've written to her." Joe said, Hugh's eyebrows shot up he never had imagined Joe as a romantic letter writer and was genuinely surprised.

"Has she answered? "Hugh asked.

"Not yet," Joe mumbled, "but I think she will. The thing is Hugh she's in Australia, in Sydney and steamers from London go there every four weeks. When we have enough for a fare that's where I want to go. I'm hoping you'll join me; I've spoken to Ned Irwin and he prefers it to the States as well. He has some friends there already." Hugh was surprised at Joe's news about Maggie he hadn't known his feelings were so strong. Their main concern was to stop being a burden to their family. They needed to get work and sadly that meant getting out of Ireland.

"Joe, I didn't know you were that sweet on the lass and I'll not stand in your way. If you want to go to Australia then I'm with you." Hugh hugged Joe, smiled widely and said, "you'll not get rid of me that easily my boy." They both felt elated, they had finally made a decision about their future

One other consideration for the brothers was that they never trusted the Government not to come after them again. There had been stories of men picked up because of their specific activities during the Civil War. No amnesty had been issued for acts committed during the Civil War and wouldn't be till the end of that year. In the meantime, many IRA men felt exposed to the whims of a revengeful administration.

Now Joe and Hugh had to tell their Da and Mammy and the rest of the family of their decision. Before they did, they spoke to James, Thomas and Patrick but they hadn't wanted to join their journey for their own reasons. Going so far away in those times for people of limited means didn't offer a way back home, even though it was physically possible it was in most cases unlikely. The break would in all likelihood be permanent and it was happening to many families. All who went believed they would be the exception and they would strike it rich and somehow manage to see everyone again.

It was five days after the IRA meeting when they had been told not to emigrate that Joe and Hugh met with their parents. They had made their decision. After a meal of oatmeal, cabbage, turnips and potato stew, they sat at the dinner table and Mary had put the young ones to bed. James, Thomas and Patrick knew what was coming so they wandered outside for a smoke. Peter and Mary had a pretty good idea of what was coming when Hugh asked them to stay at the table.

"We have to tell you that we have decided, Joe and I, to move out, first to England and then to Australia." It was all Hugh said, he had wanted to make it quick and simple.

Mary and Peter realised the challenges the young men faced and knew of their frustration of not being able to contribute more to the family circumstances. Mary was the first to speak:

"I've been offering all my Rosaries for you for so long and spoke to Father Slattery and we had many a mass said for you while you were down south." Mary didn't like to use the word prison and never did, "You'll always have a home here but we know that it's been hard for you both and you're proud just like your father. You need to find your own way now, you have our blessing."

"She wiped away the tears that now flowed down her cheeks and she took Peter's hand. He was not a man who spoke much and like many of his generation shied away from sentimental occasions but he was moved to speak now:

"You have been through a lot lads nearly two years locked away and coming home to no work. God knows life is always a struggle but now in this country it seems we have made it impossible for young people and so many are leaving. We talk down at the village and everyone knows a family who has lost someone to emigration. It is worse further west but it seems it's the same everywhere." Peter by now was clearly distressed and swallowed many times to avoid showing tears. "We know you are doing this for the family as well as for yourselves. We wish it didn't have to be but we understand." Finally, he wiped his eyes no longer able to hide the intensity of the moment. Joe and Hugh reached out at the same time and each took a hand of Mary and Peter. Hugh spoke first, his own tears now flowing,

"We can't thank you enough Da, especially me, taking me in as a young one when you and Mammy were married. I've had two daddies and been very lucky with both of them."

Joe wanted to add his thoughts and decided at the last moment to tell them of his writing to Maggie and his hopes of meeting her again in faraway Australia.

"I never knew I would want to see a lass so much but it pushes me on, just the thought of seeing her again." Joe's mother smiled, she knew Joe had a kind heart and hoped he found this girl in the new country. She had known because Hugh had told her of Joe's pining for Maggie and she was now glad he had spoken of it with his parents.

The four of them sat there in silence taking in the moment, until Hugh finally spoke,

"We think we'll go in a couple of weeks time and get the train to Dublin and the ferry to England. We know some lads in London who will help get us work and we have saved a bit of money and want to leave some with you." Hugh was being spare with his words; they had only made up their minds to go recently. Whenever they got any work at all he and Joe would store some of the money away and not waste it on Guinness. He looked at Joe who nodded subtly and Hugh took five shillings out of his pocket and put it on the table, "We hope this will make a better Christmas for you and the young ones this year." That left them enough for a train to Dublin and a ferry to Holyhead in Wales then a train to London. The rest they would trust to luck and hard work.

It was then Mary's turn to surprise. She went to a nearby drawer and took out a small package and gave it to Joe.

"You'll need these when you're travelling." Joe opened the small purse and there were the Rosary Beads he had given his mother when he came home for a brief visit before he was captured.

"Thanks mammy, I had forgotten about them all this time." Mary nodded knowingly she didn't want her sons to lose their faith.

Joe and Hugh excused themselves from the table they were emotionally spent and needed to get outside and break the mood before it became any more sombre. Mary and Peter hugged them both and Peter said,

"God bless you lads, we will miss you."

Joe and Hugh joined their brothers outside and they all hugged and shook hands,

"We'll tell the young ones in the morning." said Joe rolling a cigarette from James' tobacco pouch. He was happy now they had made a decision and happier still that they had told their parents. Hugh was in his late twenties and Joe in his mid-twenties. They had lost so much time because of wars and prisons and they couldn't expect their family to feed them forever.

The brothers talked for hours about the IRA, the war with the Tans and the politics of the Civil War. They talked of heir imprisonment, the harshness of prison life but also the camaraderie, the friends they had lost and the friends they had made. They worried about where the country was now and what would happen in the future. Joe then spoke of his friend Dan Crowley who he knew would never give up on the country or the Republic.

"People like Dan Crowley can hold a grudge forever and he'll fight on despite the law of the day. I hope he doesn't damage the country in the process." It was a faint hope. Men like Dan would keep the Republican ideal and an Ireland of thirty two counties aflame for the next seven decades. They would bring new fears and terror to every one of those decades. They didn't know whether to admire him or feel sorry for him. But they accepted that it would no longer continue to be their fight. So many questions and so few answers, so much had happened in their young lives. They sat in silence eventually having exhausted their thoughts, then Hugh spoke, wiping away a final tear,

> "Now it is time to move on. We all have a life to get on with."

CHAPTER 50
IRELAND QUO VADIS

"The saddest thing about betrayal is that it never comes from your enemies."

The few weeks before their departure passed quickly for Joe and Hugh. They had to organise their movements albeit in some secrecy as they didn't want the IRA to know what they were doing. It tended to be a moot point as so many men were doing the same thing. There was little the IRA could do about it except utter threats and retribution for the act. But the brothers persisted they had made up their minds and they would no longer be a burden on their family.

The day to leave finally arrived and Joe and Hugh made their tear-filled goodbyes. It was best to make them quick otherwise the agony just lingered on. The young ones didn't quite understand that they would never see their older brothers again. For the others it was excruciating and for Mammy and Da a day best forgotten. The tears continued to flow as the brothers walked off the farm.

Today they wouldn't have to walk to Athlone as they were able to take a horse and cart ride with a neighbour, Ned Irwin had arranged for them all to go together. The journey took a couple of hours without incident. Joe was still reflecting on the irony that in Australia he would still be part of the British Empire it seemed that there could be no escape from that. They arrived at Athlone station with an hour to spare before the train's scheduled departure time. The three men stood around the platform which was starting to crowd. They smoked and talked and managed a cup of tea and their Mam had slipped some bread into their packs for the train trip.

Suddenly there was a commotion outside the station and they wandered over to see what the fuss was about. An army car had pulled in and General MacEoin had emerged and four soldiers from another tender joined him, his regular personal body guard no doubt thought Joe.

Then from the car, another officer emerged and Joe stood stock still. It was Sean McKeon. It was the first time Joe had seen him up close since his arrest and confinement in Athlone Barracks some eighteen months ago. Sean was resplendent in a brand-new uniform with boots and leggings well polished. His cap sat at what seemed a slight angle on his head. Joe could see in the car and there was a woman with a baby in arms just a few months old he recognised her as Fianna O'Farrell and smiled to himself. Sean fussed over the two of them before he left the vehicle, it was clear they weren't going with him. Then MacEoin took Sean aside and gave him what must have been final instructions, so the General wasn't going with him either. They talked for a couple of minutes then the General left in the car with Sean's wife and baby.

Two of the soldiers lined up beside Sean to escort him to the station platform. Joe still stood on the spot staring. Against his better judgement he felt his emotions were getting the better of him and anger was rising in his throat. Hugh noticed what was happening and saw Joe's face redden. He tried to take him aside,

"Joe, over here, Ned and I need to talk to you." But Joe wasn't listening he started to walk towards Sean. One of the soldiers noticed and stood in front of him with his rifle poised ready to land the butt where it would do most harm. Sean looked up when he heard the movement, then smiled,

"Joe, Joe Keegan, is that you?" it was what it was, he was greeting an old friend, "I heard you were back in the area, how are things with your family?" he was still smiling but Joe's face was crimson, he didn't realise he could be this angry.

"You know bloody well how things are with my family and every other family in this God forsaken county." Joe paused to take a breath and collect his thoughts. He hadn't expected this encounter and was extremely angry at the fact that Sean was treating it like a fun encounter. Joe continued but found he couldn't be civil to the man,

"Don't you look the part in your fancy uniform, spit and polish, body guards, pips on your shoulders, peaked cap. What are you now a General?" Joe scoffed, "or does the army have too many of those nowadays?"

Sean could see the situation deteriorating. Joe clearly didn't see the meeting in the same light as he did, he hoped he could mollify him,

"No need to be like that Joe, we've been through a lot together can't we shake hands on it and forget the past, we could be friends again" he started to put out his hand to take Joes,

"Don't try to shake my hand, I'd sooner shake hands with the devil, if you put it out, I'll spit on it." Joe was trying not to shake with anger, "so why would I want to be your friend for God's sake? You who crossed over to the Treatyites to feather your own nest, joined up with that other traitor MacEoin. Had us all arrested and you know very well we spent nearly two years in prison. Months in that hell hole here you have the hide to call a Barracks in Athlone and then sixteen months in that lice ridden camp in Tintown." Joe was just warming up, "Yes Sean, me, Hugh and Ned here and ten thousand other men around the country. Men who had taken a loyal oath to the Brotherhood and knew what that meant. They didn't spit it out the minute it suited them and turn tail like you and MacEoin and your lot. You took the easy way out, saw where the power was and signed up to it. Do you remember the oath Sean, the actual words when we were, what eighteen?" Joe was standing just two feet from Sean who himself was now reddening with anger, the two soldiers waiting on the nod from Sean to bring this loudmouth under control.

"*We solemnly swear allegiance to the Irish Republic.* Those were the words Sean; do you remember them? I'd say not, you chose to forget them because it suited you. Couldn't stand the fighting anymore Sean? Didn't want to sleep rough anymore? And I heard you were in charge of a firing squad in '22 that killed a couple of our boys in cold blood in your damn prison. Had you forgotten the oath by then Sean?" Hugh had moved closer to Joe to grab him if he made a move towards Sean but it wasn't necessary. Sean had his own bodyguard and Joe wasn't that stupid to risk his life now, but Sean wanted to speak also.

"We had this conversation nearly two years ago Joe and you didn't see my side then and you can't see it now. Look around you what do you see, a country at peace making its own way in the world, no more fighting and killing. We are independent and one day we will be a Republic, if we all stay and work for it. But I hear you're running out Joe, can't stay and fight anymore." He didn't mean to insult his boyhood friend but he was as angry as Joe, after all who was betraying who in this war? Who was guilty of treason?

Joe's fist balled up it was the closest he had come to smashing into Sean such was his hatred at those words.

"You wouldn't know Sean, you and your fancy uniform, you don't understand what you and the army and your precious

Provisional Government have done to the country. We should have all stayed together and fought the English none of us wanted to be killing other Irishmen. But you and Collins and Cosgrave and O'Higgins and the rest of them forced us into it. Yes, I'm leaving because I don't want to stay and watch my country become a vassal of the English again and I want to be able to feed myself and my family, I can't do that anymore." Tears of anger welled in Joe's eyes but he realised too that the argument would get nowhere. He had said what he had to, what he needed to, what he truly believed in his heart. Joe knew if he moved towards Sean, he would end up in prison again and his life would be ruined, finally a tear of anger ran down his cheek.

Sean stepped back slightly astonished at the depth Joe's emotion. He adjusted his cap and gloves, no words he could say would change Joe's thinking. He swallowed his anger and said,

"God go with you Joe I hope you find peace where you're going. I don't think you'll find it in Ireland."

Joe unclenched his fists and turned to join Hugh, the train had just pulled into the platform but he continued,

"I hope you enjoy your Treaty Sean, your British Empire and your oath to the King of England, it's what you deserve." With that Joe turned and walked towards the third-class carriage, Sean walked towards his First-Class carriage with his body guard. Then Joe stopped, turned and took one last look at Sean. He shouted as he thrust his fist into the air, "Long live the Republic!"

About The Author:

Phillip Kerrigan Phillip Kerrigan is of Irish descent and lives in Sydney, Australia. His former careers were as an senior executive with a cosmetics company, an accountant and an Apple computer Reseller and then a Consultant to small and medium businesses in the personal computer field.

Phillip wrote this novel to pay tribute to his father and his family and the many Irish families who suffered during this period. It is not an accurate story of his father's involvement as there aren't enough details known of that. But it is a story of a time that challenged the people of Ireland as they fought to free themselves from hundreds of years of colonialism.

Their descendants are all around the world in many countries and have contributed to the politics of those countries with their love of freedom and self expression. Phillip would like to acknowledge and thank many people in Ireland, Australia and Canada who contributed to his research.

This is his fourth novel the first being about the depletion of the world's supply of oil, the second about nuclear weapons and their dangers in the Cold War, see "The Russian Major" on Amazon.

He has also recently published on Amazon "Where There's a Will" a story of a bogus inheritance and a US based insurance fraud on a grand scale.

Thank you for reading my novel. Please leave a review of "Treaty or Treason" on the Amazon site.

Other Books By This Author:

The Russian Major: A Major in the Strategic Rocket Forces of the USSR sits at the control panel of a ballistic missile on the planes outside Novosibirsk. There has been a State of Emergency declared. He waits. The missile has the power to destroy an area the size of Manhattan. Its launch will be ordered by Central Command in Moscow, or somewhere, the Major does not know where. All he waits on is a specific set of instructions he has utilised a thousand times before. Then the system starts to send mixed signals..............

Where there's a Will A windfall inheritance from the USA becomes a nightmare for Australian Freddy Tycehurst pitting him against Wall St lawyers, suspect bankers and the FBI.

The story of Freddy's struggle is interwoven with the story of how the bogus inheritance was created after a major insurance fraud in the USA twenty years earlier.

Both available on Amazon as ebooks.